MARIAH MUNDI

Also by G. P. Taylor

Praise for *Shadowmancer*

'The biggest event in children's fiction since Harry Potter.' *The Times*

'The adventure unfolds at a vivid and breathless pace.' *Observer*

'*Shadowmancer* is flying off the bookshelves as if a wizard had incanted a charm on it.' *Herald*

'A magical tale of vicars and witches.' *Daily Telegraph*

'A compelling and dark-edged fantasy . . . highly recommended.' *Independent*

Praise for *Wormwood*

'*Wormwood* is breathtaking in scope . . . an extraordinary achievement told by a master storyteller. The book is, quite simply, marvellous.' *Guardian*

Praise for *Tersias*

'It is, in a word, brilliant. Colourful, dramatic, relentless, accessible to children – and more frightening for their parents.' *Scotsman*

'The plot hurtles along carrying the reader from one cliffhanger to the next.' *Daily Telegraph*

G. P. Taylor

Mariah Mundi

THE MIDAS BOX

faber and faber

First published in 2007
by Faber and Faber Limited
3 Queen Square London WC1N 3AU

Typeset by Faber and Faber Limited
Printed in England by Mackays of Chatham plc, Chatham, Kent

The right of G. P. Taylor to be identified as author
of this book has been asserted in accordance with Section 77
of the Copyright, Designs and Patents Act, 1988

A CIP record for this book
is available from the British Library

ISBN 9780–571–22650–4

2 4 6 8 10 9 7 5 3

To Suzy and all the team at Faber – without your help and support none of this would have been possible – you are the people who turn my dreams into a reality

MARIAH MUNDI

[1]

Mariah Mundi

MARIAH Mundi stepped into the long thin railway carriage and for several moments blinked his eyes in the bright light. Swirls of steam and the sound of the stoking engine rattled the neat wooden floor of the corridor that appeared to run the length of the train. It was ghostly empty, as had been the platform where he had waited patiently for the last train to take him to the coast. He had watched the old beast arrive. Out of the dark and stormy night it had juddered along the track and under the large canopy of glass and halted abruptly at platform five. A heavy engine drew six dark and grubby coaches covered in dirt and mildew, so that it looked like an old leviathan rising from the depths of darkness. The guard had jumped from the mail van and shouted out the destinations and connections in his gruff voice. A large moustache curled from his top lip to under his chin, and a long pipe arched from his scaly chops. Mariah had watched as the man had wiped the grease from his hands upon the oily black waistcoat that held in his bulging belly. With every shallow breath that the man gulped, its buttons looked as if they were on the verge of popping as they heaved and strained.

3

Now as Mariah stood in the glare of the carriage he hesitated, unsure as to what he should do. The coach was much brighter than he had thought. A narrow gas lamp lit the drab walls and window blinds, billowing gusts of hot air that rolled across the ceiling of the coach and out of the open door. He looked again at the painted sign on the glass pane: *First Class*. He read the words on the ticket and matched the carriage to the number that had been scrawled in thick black ink by the hand of the old fat ticket collector at Kings Cross. Coach number one, compartment three, seat number two. First Class. Cautiously he counted the seats and looked at the silver numbered tags that marked each place.

In his own seat sat a tall man with a muscular frame, wearing the uniform of an army officer and with a thick scar across his right cheek. Mariah studied him as he took the seat opposite, holding out his ticket as if at any moment he would be challenged and the ticket would be snatched fom him, condemning him to the wooden benches of Third Class, just short of the mail van.

He had set off to travel north from London early that morning. In his hand he had clutched a ticket, presented the day before by Jecomiah Bilton, headmaster of Chiswick Colonial School, which had been his home for seven years. Mariah's parents had travelled to Sudan and had never returned. They had paid in advance and so, even on their death two years before, Mariah had been allowed to stay until he had reached his fifteenth birthday. That day had come and gone, along with a further six months of grace and clearing the refectory tables and washing the floors. Now he had been despatched with a Third Class ticket, a first-class suit and a writ of worthiness signed by the gentle Professor Bilton. In his pocket he also had a letter of introduction and a neatly ironed five-pound note given to him by his father on the day Mariah had waved his parents goodbye from Southampton docks.

It was as he had stood by the ticket office on the Euston Road, his train ticket in his hand, that he had noticed an agitated gentleman strutting along the recently laid pavement in a new silk top hat, examining his fob watch and looking up and down the street, closely scrutinising every horse carriage that drew close by. The man had cast him a quick glance and then looked away as several carriages drew up at the station and left their passengers on the cold stone pavement surrounded by their hastily thrown-down cases. The man had inspected from a distance the names on the cases as he had pretended to swagger the wide avenue in the cold December dawn.

Mariah had been fascinated, drawn in by the way in which the man twitched his head from side to side. Once, he had taken his long black cane and prodded a thickly lacquered trunk that had been bundled off an old landau and left unattended for several minutes before a petulant old porter dragged it on to his barrow and whisked it away. He watched the man and then the man watched him. The station clocked chimed the seventh hour. The gentleman looked up and then pulled a narrow pair of spectacles and a thin piece of paper from his pocket. He perched the glasses on the end of his nose and peered at the tiny writing that was scrawled on the bright white paper.

Then, when a tall dark carriage pulled up quickly before him, the man flushed with panic. He spun on his heels and dropped his gaze to the ground, marching towards Mariah as if he were the only person to be greeted in the world.

'My dear friend,' the man had said in the voice of one who had not long resided upon these shores. 'I beg of you a favour for which you will be highly commended. Here is a travel voucher, First Class, for any destination you choose.' He handed Mariah the thin piece of paper emblazoned with the crest of the Great North Eastern Railway. 'Take it as a gift, but I ask you one thing, tell no one you have seen me and . . . look after these.'

The man handed Mariah a crisp pack of Panjandrum playing cards, still boxed and sealed with candle wax. On both sides was the face of the Joker, cross-eyed and holding his wand as if to cast a spell.

'When you reach your destination send me a postcard to Claridges Hotel. Mark it for me, Perfidious Albion, and I will make arrangements for the cards to be collected. Tell no one.'

Mariah didn't speak but silently nodded as the gentleman dashed off into the crowd, not to return. Two men stepped from the black carriage and scurried into the throng. It was as if they sought to follow the gentleman but had not seen in which direction he had gone. The boy had exchanged the voucher and acquired for himself a First Class ticket for the journey. As the train had ambled to the north, he had sat in state, looking from the window of the carriage at fresh fields that sprawled out before him. They soaked up the cold sun, and as the dark of the winter's afternoon had fallen he had looked upon the bright stars as they peeked from the high heavens.

Nine hours later, he exchanged trains and boarded the branch line to the coast. Now he sat in the warm carriage nearing the end of his journey, the crisp note and writ of achievement still folded neatly in his pocket.

'Please, sir,' Mariah said quietly as he held out his ticket towards the man sitting opposite him in the carriage. 'I believe that is *my* seat.'

'Seat? You believe it is *your* seat?' the man said, raising a furrowed brow and squinting at the boy. 'I believe this seat belongs to whoever owns this railway and that we only rent this space until we find our destination.'

'But my ticket says . . .'

'Your ticket says that you should sit quietly and not disturb your elders or your betters,' the man replied gruffly as he took a penny dreadful from his pocket. He opened the creased pages and buried his head deep within as he grumbled to himself. 'And another thing, boy. If I choose seat number two, it is because I like to see neither what is beyond the window nor what is in the passageway. It is a quiet seat, where I will not be disturbed and where I can rest. Now if you don't mind, save your complaints for the ticket collector and keep quiet.'

Mariah sat quietly, holding his ticket in expectation of its early examination. The man buried himself in the dreadful, chuckling when he turned the pages again and again as he read the adventures of Fiery Jack over and over.

There was a long jerk as the train stretched and then contracted again as the engine pulled the carriages into motion. Mariah lurched forward but the man didn't move, holding fast to the paper that he held before his face. As the train pulled from the platform and moaned along the track, gathering speed, the lamp dimmed and the sound of steam hissed from beneath them.

Outside, the lights of almshouses flashed like phantoms in the dark. Faster, called the rails as the wheels clanked and churned and the great leviathan raced on into the night.

The door to the compartment opened suddenly. A perfunctory man in long black coat and a funeral tie wrapped around the neck of a crisp white shirt peered in.

'Compartment number three?' he asked mechanically.

Mariah nodded. The officer shrugged his shoulders as he read on, not bothering to take his face from the columns of black ink and cartoons that filled each page.

'A dark chilly night for us to be abroad,' the man said, hoping to bring a spark of conversation and smiling at Mariah. 'Do you travel far?' he said to the boy as he rummaged in the carpetbag that he held nervously close to himself.

'The end of the line,' Mariah said. He fumbled with the ticket in his fingers and looked at the small leather bag by his feet.

'If I am not mistaken, you're a Colonial boy,' the man said, nodding his head and taking his seat next to the soldier.

'That I am. Do you know the place, sir?' he asked expectantly.

'Well, very well. Had a suit like that myself once. The five-pound suit, given for good behaviour and never to repay a penny.' He laughed as he leant forward and felt the collar of the boy's coat. 'Finer cloth than I ever had. Sent into the world to make the best of all they taught me, and now . . . I am a man of leisure, forty-one years of age and taking a winter's rest by the sea. Tasting the waters, with a prescription to bathe in the Oceanus Germanicus every morning, rain or shine. Good for the constitution. They say the water is remarkably warm, even in winter.' The man took in a deep breath as if he inhaled the fresh sea air; he then paused and looked about the carriage, talking as if he didn't want to be overheard. 'Travel from London this morning? Seven-twenty from Kings Cross?'

'That . . . I did. I never thought it would take so long or that I would come so far,' Mariah replied as the thought of Perfidious Albion flashed through his mind. He slipped his hand into his coat pocket and fingered the deck of cards that he had pressed deep within, not wanting to give their presence away.

'Strange,' said the man. 'I should have travelled that train myself, but my companion didn't wait for me. I waited the half hour and caught the next train. Travelling alone can be so tiresome.' He tried to peer over the top of the penny dreadful and see the face of its reader. 'Do you travel together?' the man asked, attempting to engage the army officer in polite conversation.

'Alone,' the officer said monotonously, hoping it would bring an end to the questioning.

'Far?' the man asked, looking behind the paper and smiling smugly as he rubbed his hands in and out of each other.

'From the ends of the earth, by sea and sail and hackney cab and now by rail,' the officer replied, reading the words from the

8

hoarding above Mariah's head. 'And all in the day . . . If you would excuse me, my eyes tell me that they desire to sleep as within the hour we will all be thrown from this place to the cold street.' He slumped into his place and threw his feet across the carriage.

'Very good, very good,' the other man muttered, and he gestured for Mariah to be silent, shaking his head in agreement with himself as he rubbed his hands faster and faster in time to the clunking of the carriage over the chilled iron rails.

Together they sat in silence for the next nine miles. Mariah held his arms across his chest, holding himself against the thick piled seat as the man stared at him and they listened to the soldier's heavy snoring. The long journey north had numbed his mind. He wanted to join the soldier in slumber, but some inner thought or deep fear kept his eyes from closing, not trusting the man to be alone with him in sleep.

Clutching the large carpetbag upon his knees, the man looked back at Mariah and smiled a sheepish smile through his thin blue lips. 'You know a lot about me and I nothing of you,' he said as he fiddled with the strap of the bag, rubbing the leather through his fingers. 'Do you work at the end of the line, or are you there to take the waters?'

Mariah hesitated. It was as if the coach had filled with a thin mist that glazed his sight. He snuggled back into the deep pile of the seat as the carriage rattled back and forth along the shaking track. 'I go to the Prince Regent,' he said slowly, hoping never to have to say another word.

'Well, well, well, bless my soul. If that isn't a coincidence beyond all coincidences. I too shall be a guest in that fine place. The Tower Suite, a reservation for one until Lady Day. They say you can see the castle and the harbour and on a clear day the windmills of Holland . . . And you, in what capacity will you be gainfully employed?' He spoke quickly, not giving time for

9

Mariah to reply. 'Perhaps you will be my butler. Now that would be a fine thing, meeting like this in a *First Class* carriage and you being a servant.' The man stopped and looked at the ticket that Mariah held nervously in his fingers. 'You do have a ticket for this compartment, don't you? It wouldn't be good order for a Colonial boy to be thrown on the platform of the next station for riding without the proper papers.' There was a hint of scorn in his voice; the pleasant tone in which he had passed the time of day had suddenly gone. The man leant forward and snatched the ticket from Mariah's hand. 'Aha,' he said as he closely examined the writing on the ticket. 'You appear to be in order. First-class suit and First Class ticket, things certainly have changed since my time at the Colonial School, certainly have changed.' He sat back into the seat and cast a glance to the soldier sleeping next to him.

'Men! Men!' the army officer shouted as he twitched like a sleeping dog that dreamed to itself, his feet kicking out with every spasm of the vision that played with his mind. 'Line of fire, line of fire!' he screamed, and he woke from his dream with a sudden start, picking the penny dreadful from where it had fallen to the floor of the carriage. He gave a deep yawn and shook his head, rubbing his face in his hands and chomping his lips as if the taste of something awful filled his mouth. 'Not used to the English weather,' he said to the man next to him, who had leant away from him and now clutched the carpetbag even tighter. 'Haven't had a decent sleep since the Sudan, can't sleep on the ship, too hot by day and too cold by night. No place better than a carriage to rock you like a baby, though.'

'Sudan?' Mariah said without thinking. 'My parents were in the Sudan.'

'I take it they are not there now?' the bagman asked before the officer could speak.

'Lost – missing – dead,' he said slowly, the words coming in the order of events that had broken his heart two years before. Mariah stared through his piercing blue eyes at the leather bag thrown into the luggage rack above the soldier's head; he read the words etched in black on the tan hide: *Captain Jack Charity*. 'It was in the uprising, a mission post. My father was a doctor and my mother a nurse,' he blurted out. 'At first we heard they had been taken prisoner,' he said hopefully. 'But later, Professor Bilton told me that news had come that they were . . .' Mariah couldn't get the words from his mouth. They stuck like dry bread on a hot day.

'On your own, boy?' the soldier said as he edged the man away with a sharp dig of his elbow.

'Now that I have graduated from the Colonial . . .'

'Family?'

'Not one left,' he said as he looked to the floor.

'A hard life, but still, worse things happen at sea,' the army officer said as he leant back in his seat and opened the penny dreadful, immersing himself in the reverie, every now and then chuckling yet again at tale of Fiery Jack.

'A story like my own,' the bagman said as he took a packet of thick toffee from the carpetbag and offered a piece to Mariah, handing him the crumpled sack of brown paper filled to the brim with matted lumps of sticky goo. Mariah quickly filled his mouth. 'Whatever your circumstances, let it be known that despite your present station in life, by virtue of our being both old boys of the Colonial School we are practically brothers. Isambard Black – here is my card.' He held out an empty hand; then, with a twist of his wrist, a neat gold-edged calling card sprung out of fresh air to the tips of his fingers 'Take it,' he said with a smile. 'If you are ever in London and need gainful occupation then call upon me. You never know, the coast may not suit you and the London smog may be a place to hide.' He chuckled to himself, twisting his hands again, and brought forth an old Panjandrum playing card.

Mariah gasped, his mouth bubbling with frothing toffee.

'I have a friend at Claridges, he could help. In fact I was supposed to travel with him today but he never came.' The man held out the card to Mariah. 'The fool, the Joker without jest, behind his smile is great tragedy and malice, never one to be trusted.'

Mariah couldn't speak, Albion's command to tell no one echoing in his mind. He swallowed hard as the Joker with its telltale cribbed edge and brightly coloured mantle flashed before him, spinning in the man's hand as he made it bob back and forth and then twist on his fingertip in some elaborate conjuring trick. It disappeared suddenly, vanishing from view.

'Gone,' said the man as he reached towards Mariah, who pressed himself harder against the seat, one hand firmly in his pocket clutching the pack of cards that Albion had entrusted to him. 'And now . . .' He reached into the top pocket of Mariah's new suit and pulled forth the card as if it had been there all the time. 'Aha!' he exclaimed. 'The card dances about my new friend.'

'Party tricks,' muttered the Captain from behind the rustling paper. 'Next you'll be littering the carriage with rabbit droppings and pigeon feathers from all the beasts hidden in your dangerous undergarments.'

'Such a trick would be too crass. I am a magician – part-time, of course, but sleight of hand that fools the eye is my passion. I travel the world collecting the most audacious illusions that I can find and using them to bring mirth to those I meet.'

Mariah sat wide-eyed, twizzling strands of his thick, dark, curly hair in his fingers as Isambard Black balanced the Joker on the tip of his finger once more – and then in a puff of smoke that blew from the palm of his hand, it vanished, never to be seen again.

'Where does it go when it disappears?' Mariah asked.

'That I cannot tell you. I am bound by oath never to divulge the secret of the Order of Magicians. It would be on pain of death to give such vital knowledge to the uninitiated.'

'You can buy those tricks on any street corner where you're going, boy,' the Captain said without even raising his head from his paper.

'There is one illusion that cannot be bought,' the man said quietly to Mariah, hoping to be ignored by the soldier. 'A magic tin box that turns anything placed within it to the finest gold. That would quench all of my desires; it would surpass any sleight of hand or scurrilous palm. If I could have the Midas Box, I would be a happy man. '

'You could turn anything to gold?' Mariah asked.

'Anything, and everything,' the man replied. Just then the train's whistle blew as it was consumed by a tunnel, disappearing into the blackness.

[2]

The Curse of the Prince Regent

MARIAH peered through the side-slat of the heavy blinds that were firmly pulled over the carriage window to keep out the night. Squinting into the blackness he could see the twinkling of lights from a thousand windows as the train slowed over the high viaduct that took the track into the heart of the town at the end of the line. Below him were the roofs of fine houses that snaked along the contours of the railway leading the train to the sea. It was as if there was an enquiring face at every window as the train slowed, steam billowing from the engine, brakes squealing as it panted to a halt.

Neither Captain Charity nor Isambard Black had spoken another word since the train had left the tunnel many miles before. Mariah too had sat in silence, trying to avoid the grinning face of Mister Black as Captain Charity had slept again, this time silently, the penny dreadful folded over his face to keep out the light from the gas lamp that hissed above his head.

The carriage shook violently as it came to an abrupt stop, the engine clanging against the iron buffers that marked the end of the track. Mariah was catapulted forward, tumbling head-first into the lap of the Captain and waking him awkwardly from his deep and mournful sleep.

'Never!' he shouted as he grabbed Mariah by the arms, picking him up and throwing him sideways to land heavily upon Mister Black. 'Never in a million years will you take me!'

'It was the . . .' Mariah protested as Black struggled beneath him, compressed by the carpet bag, Mariah's foot pushed against his chin and squashing his head against the back of the seat.

Black attempted to spit the boy's boot from his mouth, but then the train rolled back from the buffers and Mariah was thrown to the floor of the carriage. As Black jumped to his feet he dropped his cherished bag upon the boy and fell backwards into the Captain's lap.

'I'm not here to be used as a hobby horse,' Charity barked as he pushed Black from him, giving him a sharp jab in the back with his tightly clenched fist. 'Once more and I will pull the ears from the side of your head and . . . and make you eat them, one by one.'

Black fell forward, tripping over Mariah and landing face-forward in the seat, spilling the contents of his coat pocket to the floor.

'I have never been so treated in all my life by such a ruffian as you,' Black complained bitterly as he tried to free himself from the convulsion he was now placed in. 'If this is the North, then I shall find myself on the first train back to the city. Man-handled, uncosseted, battered and –'

'END OF THE LINE!' screamed a voice in the passageway outside the compartment. The guard walked the long corridor, tapping on every window and reminding the occupants of the terminus. 'CARRIAGES AND OMNIBUS AWAITING ALL!'

'At least I will get a civilised journey to the Prince Regent,' Black exclaimed as he picked up several silver coins and the chain of his broken fob watch from the carriage floor. Mariah stared up at him as Black scowled angrily. 'Move, boy. You stop me in my quest. Help me, come on. Out of the way and pick up the things I've dropped. Move, move,' Black chuntered angrily as Captain Charity took his tan bag from the rack and pushed past them both, sliding the stiff door.

'It's time you went,' Charity said as he pulled Black from the compartment and into the corridor by the collar of his coat. 'The boy has helped you enough, he's not your servant yet and his job won't start till the morning so leave him be.'

Black lurched into the corridor, fob chain and coins in hand. 'My bag!' he yelled in protest as he was dropped unceremoniously. Charity leant in, grabbed the old carpetbag that pressed Mariah to the floor and threw it at Isambard Black, who put his hand to his head to protect himself from the blow.

'I'll have you arrested, taken from the train in irons and transported to Australia, never to see the light of day,' Black grumbled loudly as he grabbed the bag and scurried off backwards like a fat rat edging its way along a sewer. 'Never, never have I known anything like it,' he said as he quickly pushed through the door and on to the cold night platform.

Mariah lay motionless on the floor as the Captain stared down at him, his immense frame filling the door and casting a dark shadow across the boy's face.

'What shall we do with you?' he bellowed. Then a hand plunged from the darkness, grabbed Mariah by the collar and lifted him to his feet. 'We never did get introduced. I'm Captain Jack Charity. Too tired to talk and that imbecile would have driven me mad with his chivvying, so come on. Who are you?'

'Mundi . . . Mariah Mundi,' he said sheepishly as he cleared his throat and shook the mop of thick curly hair that sprouted over every inch of his head like the coat of a Newfoundland hound.

'Well, Mariah Mundi, you have reached the end of the line and from what I can remember you have an appointment at the Prince Regent.' Charity laughed as he rubbed the side of his sharp nose. 'Not a place I'd like to stay, so watch yourself. Better seen in daylight and too many tales of devilish doings for my liking. There's rumour that a madman walks the streets, taking the children and leaving no trace. Never be alone in the old town, especially after dark.' Charity rummaged in his pocket. 'If they give you a day off, come and see me. Just look from the Regent to the harbour and on the quayside you'll see my place.' Charity beamed proudly as he handed Mariah a gold-edged calling card. 'The Golden Kipper, the finest place to eat on God's earth. I have a chef who can cook the most luxurious fish that man has ever eaten, and if you get yourself along there's one waiting for you. I bet you'll never be able to eat it.' Charity held out his large hand as if to seal all he had said in a soldier's bet.

Mariah grabbed his hand, squeezing it firmly. This, he had been told by his father, was the way to show you meant what you said.

'Done,' said Charity as he stepped back into the compartment, pulled up the blind, opened the window and leant out. 'Careful what you do with my trunk,' he shrieked down the platform to the luggage van. 'Break a single thing and you'll end up the same, mark my words.' He looked at Mariah, who cowered back into the seat. 'Doesn't do to be nice to everyone,' he said with a slight, lopsided grin. 'Got to keep them on their toes. Now boy, pick up your things and off you go. I'll see you to the street and point you the right way.'

Mariah didn't reply, his eye captivated by a small trinket that dangled from the seat where Isambard Black had fallen. He reached out, nimbly picked it from the snagged fabric and held it to the carriage lamp. There, dangling on a small thread of fine chain, was a golden skull the size of a honeybee. Two green

17

jewelled eyes stared at him, twinkling in the light. Its jaw dangled open, set on the tiniest hinges he had ever seen, a full set of intricate diamond-tipped teeth sparkling like drops of morning dew.

Mariah held out the skull to Charity. 'Not mine,' the Captain said as he looked at the object. 'Could belong to the madman, dropped from his pocket when he fell over.' He laughed. 'Give it to him when you see him at the Prince Regent, I can trust you with that, especially if you're coming to dine with me.'

'What is it?' Mariah asked as he twisted the piece in his fingers, allowing the light to shine upon its fine jewelled eyes.

'Never seen the likes of it before. Once saw an earring of a skull, but that had been shrunken by pigmy head-hunters and it certainly didn't have jewels for eyes. Best you keep it safe. Doubtless if it belongs to Black, he'll be squealing for it by the morning.'

Charity turned and stepped from the carriage, holding his tan bag on his shoulder like a shepherd with a lamb. Mariah clumsily lifted his own bag as he followed on, balancing all he had on his head as he swaggered along the corridor to the platform door.

The cold night air cut sharp against his skin, taking away his breath. The smell of the sea nuzzled his throat as if he was being wrapped in a blanket of seaweed. The flagstone platform glistened with a sheen of frost-like grit that crunched underfoot with every step he took. Charity marched on, protected from the sea gale by the station canopy that rattled, glass upon steel, high above their heads. Whistlers of night breeze pushed sand around their feet in thick swirls. A row of small shops stretched out in a long parade, each lit by its own gas lamp and, even on this winter's night, bustling with the business of the late hour as, inside, brown paper and string wrapped objects of every kind.

By the iron gate stood a tall thin ticket collector, a pair of the neatest spectacles perched on the end of his hooked nose and held in place by a thick strap that circled the back of his head. His hand was held out as if he were a fine waxwork or shop mannequin dressed in pinstripe trousers and a thin overcoat with tattered elbows.

Charity belaboured the porter who dragged his sea chest along the platform as quickly as his stunted legs would carry him, trying to keep pace with the Captain's stride. 'Quickly, man,' Charity harassed him. 'I've been away for seven years and I want to see how this town has changed. My eyes eagerly await the delight that is before me and your poor provision of limbs holds me from that enchantment,' he snapped at the porter, who tried in vain to run faster. Dragging the case behind him, he was red-faced and wheezing as they headed past the row of shops to the gate.

'Tickets, please,' said the collector through his nose, his lips never moving, as if he had trained his nostrils to speak.

Charity pressed by, ignoring the man and signalling for Mariah to walk on. 'Too busy to pass the time of day with you, Postill,' he bellowed at the ticket collector. 'Stood there on the day I left and there when I return. Didn't have a ticket then and don't have one today. In the service of the Queen and if the Queen doesn't need a ticket neither do I.'

Postill grunted through his nose, which quivered and twitched with each syllable of discontent as Charity marched into the dark night. High above, the station clock chimed midnight. Charity looked towards the town he hadn't seen for so long. Tall railings surrounded the station like the bars of a prison stopping all from escaping to distant shores. Beyond, a row of houses soon petered out into the fields of the North Way, which gently sloped down to the pleasure ground of Northstead and the deep cut that bit through the cliff to the open sea. All was as it was before. The paint had flaked from the high windows of the boarding house that clung to the corner of the white, decorated square glowing in the moonlight. The hackney stand bristled with fine black carriages and tired drivers as the horses chomped in oiled leather nose bags, hoping the night would soon be over.

'There she blows,' Charity shouted, pointing to a carriage etched with a silver outline and carrying the name of the Prince Regent emblazoned upon the door. 'Hey, you,' he shouted like a seafront drunk to the cabby, who had perched himself, rug-wrapped and double-coated, upon the driving plate above the cab. 'I have a guest for the Prince Regent. Stand and be made ready.'

Charity pushed Mariah forth and into the station yard. The cabby looked down, unwilling to offer even the slightest hand of friendship as Mariah scurried like a worried lamb across the gravel under the harsh moon, his back beaten by the strong wind gusting from the sea.

'He is a Colonial boy, sent to work. Treat him well or you'll have me to deal with,' Charity hollered as he humped his sea chest into the back of the cab, tipped the porter with a penny piece and patted him heavily on the back, knocking him to the floor.

Mariah held fast to his travelling bag and looked up at the driver, who grimaced down with cold grey eyes. A thick brow cut across his forehead like a field hedge of gorse underneath a heavy wool hat pulled down over his ears.

'Get on the back. You're late. Already got a guest and have to wait for the servants, not a good start to your life at the Prince Regent,' the cabby muttered as he flashed his wand above the horses' heads, dangling it like a menacing summer fly, and ushered them on with a tug of the reins.

Mariah jumped to the back of the coach, grabbing the cold

brass rail as the carriage pulled into the cobbled street and turned sharply right.

'How long to the hotel?' Mariah heard Isambard Black's voice muffle impatiently through the leather hood.

'A couple of streets and then to the cliff top, sir,' came the bored reply as the cab made its way slowly through the empty streets, past shuttered inns and coffee shops. It turned past a sandstone church with rain-cut carvings running through each stone, then left towards the cliff top. The sound of the roaring sea grew louder and louder and the salt spray billowed up from the beach far below, churned by the violent tide.

'Not a night to be out,' the driver shouted. The horses brayed like donkeys against the wind. 'Get yourself down and under the oilskin. As soon as we turn the corner the gale will be upon us.'

For Mariah it was too late. The sudden gusts blew harshly against the carriage, bringing a damp dusting of sea and sand that lashed against his face, filling his eyes and nose with coarse grit plucked from the Oceanus Germanicus. Rain blasted against the carriage like stair rods that cut the air and smashed against the ground, surrounding the horses' hooves as if they danced in boiling lead.

'Quickly, man, I'm drowning in here,' Black said, tormented by the stinging rain that broke into the front of the carriage, dowsing him in cold strands.

'Only go as fast as the horses will take you,' the coachman muttered under his breath, and he cracked the whip to persuade the chargers to go against the storm. 'You, boy. You hailing well?' he shouted.

Mariah cowered against the gale as he gripped to the carriage straps and balanced himself on the back box. He had pulled the oilskin over his head and curled up his legs as he was bounced and jolted from side to side with every turn of the hackney wheels.

'Fine,' he said as another turn in the cobbled street threw him sideways.

'Not much further. Once you can smell the sea, the Regent isn't far away,' the driver shouted, his voice fading into the whining of the wind that howled and moaned in and out of the dark alleyways running between the houses. 'There she blows.' Mariah peeped from the side of the oilskin as cold drips like salt tears trickled down his back. He gasped – there before him stood the finest, most gracious building he had ever seen. The rain slowed to a trickle as the immense building shielded them from all but the finest drizzle that blew overhead, swirling like a rainbowed mist in the gaslight.

The hackney stopped, the horses slipping on the stone slabs that had been laid to form a long courtyard in front of the Prince Regent. Mariah slipped from the carriage, clutching his leather bag and pulling up his collar against the wind and chill of the night. His eyes were dragged upwards, on and on, almost to the pinnacle of the sky, searching out the high towers that perched on every corner of the building.

Glowing in the darkness like the gateway to some strange magic kingdom was a golden sign lit by bright limelight. Above the large doorway its letters were a yard in height and shone brighter than anything he had ever seen before, dazzling his eyes as he tried to read the words: PRINCE REGENT.

As Mariah stood in the drizzle Isambard Black stepped from the hackney, pulled a floppy felt hat from his pocket and squeezed it upon his head, tugging the brim over his eyes. He glanced at Mariah and grinned, his smoke-yellowed teeth illuminated by the phosphorescent glow of the limelight. 'Be seeing you again,' he said slowly, and he began to walk the twenty paces to the steps of the Prince Regent. 'This is for guests. I'm sure you will find your way in somewhere. If not, there is always a park shelter.'

Black disappeared behind a large marble column that towered like the trunk of a giant tree. Mariah looked up: there in the domed vault of the entranceway, topping every column, was a tight growth of marble palm branches, dripping with gold leaf and pomegranates. Staring back at him was the face of a blue monkey, teeth bared and snarling, clutching on to the pillar as if for life itself.

'You'll be in the staff quarters, up there,' said the cabby as he slammed the door to the carriage and pointed to the heights of a tower above them.

Mariah looked up, his eyes straining to see the pinnacle that touched the black, rain-filled sky above their heads. 'I've never –' He stopped in amazement.

'They all say that when I drop them off, every one. The biggest pile of bricks in the known world,' the man said as he steadied Mariah with a gentle hand on his shoulder. 'Just think of the view, almost in heaven. Twelve floors, three hundred and sixty-five rooms and four towers, one year old on Christmas Day and still standing.' He spoke as if in awe of what stood before him. 'Wait till you see it from the other side – makes a man know where he stands in the universe.'

'Can you see the windmills of Holland?' Mariah asked as the drizzle wet his face.

'Some say you can, though I have never dared to go up that high. But watch the storms rolling in to the land. A thousand white horses chasing the ships as they run for harbour and then in an instant it'll be flat like a millpond. Don't let looks fool you, lad. All that glitters isn't gold. Keep your wits sharp and watch out for Mister Luger. Been a lot of dying around here lately – some say it's a curse from what was here before, the curse of the Prince Regent.'

Mariah turned, but the man was gone, nowhere to be seen. The horses stood stock still, braving the rain as the door swung on the empty carriage. In the side of the wall below the high tower a door opened suddenly, slamming against bright red bricks. 'You, boy!' shouted a girl's voice louder than the rain and wind. 'Stand there and you'll die of cold. Get yourself in.'

Mariah turned as behind him the hackney lurched away with the crack of a whip and the clatter of hooves on wet stone flags. He jumped to the pavement, startled by the carriage. The girl laughed, a bright smile gleaming across her face as her voice echoed from the terrace of large houses that lined the cliff-top square.

'Colonial boy!' she shouted again. 'Told you were coming. Get in, you've work to do . . .'

[3]

The Steam Elevator

THE door slammed behind Mariah and he was now alone. Whoever had called him from the dark doorway had gone. He stood dripping wet in a long corridor tiled with the darkest, greenest tiles he could have imagined. They stretched on into the distant shadow of the vast tunnel that seemed to stretch for miles ahead. A gas lamp was posted by the door, like a sentinel of light in a dark chamber. Mariah stood for several moments and listened, hoping to hear nothing and know he was truly alone. He shook the rain from his coat and folded it over his arm, pulling the long flaps from his wet shirt and allowing them to flop over his trousers. Professor Bilton would never have allowed this, he thought to himself as he walked slowly along the passageway towards the ever-darkening gloom ahead of him.

'Colonial boy . . .' The sharp voice came again from somewhere behind, rolling along the passage like a storm wave crashing to the beach. 'Colonial boy!' It came again, sharper than before and etched in anger. 'This way, can't you see?'

Mariah turned and saw the girl standing by the door. To her right was the outline of an entrance that had been hidden from view when he had stepped into the tunnel.

'It's this way,' she said scornfully. 'Never trust a boy when there's work to be done.' Her voice altered, sweetening until it became soft and warm. She had bushy dark hair that was pulled tightly back and tied in a strict knot at the back of her head. 'I've been sent for you – we're working together.' She stopped and looked Mariah up and down. 'First job, fresh out of Colonial School?'

At first Mariah couldn't reply. He felt as if he was on public display and was being meticulously inspected by the girl. Her eyes searched every crease of his white shirt and focused upon the blue school tie that was tightly wrapped around his neck. She raised a long dark eyebrow in disdain at what she saw and a wry smile crept into the side of her mouth.

'Do you get paid for wearing that outfit?' she asked in a broad Irish accent. 'Looks like you've stolen the pants from an old man.'

'It's a first-class suit. I earned it at the Colonial and don't have to pay it back. It's mine to keep,' Mariah replied softly as he looked to the green tiles beneath his feet, not wanting to look at her eye to eye.

'Well, you'll get the pick of what you want here; the wardrobes are full of things to wear. One day a prince, the next a pauper. Look at me – today I was a housemaid.' She smoothed the creases in the white pinny that covered her long black dress with its tidy cuffs and ruffled collar. 'We'll get you started in the morning and you'll be ready for tomorrow night – better be quick, a steam elevator never waits . . .'

The girl turned and vanished through the narrow doorway that would have been invisible if Mariah had not seen the girl disappear before him. He quickly followed, turning sideways between two narrow walls of green tiles that opened out into a large room. The girl stood waiting at a tall metal gate covered in shiny brass rivets that held the pieces together. Behind the gate was a deep shaft that sank into the depths below. From high above Mariah heard the sound of laughter and distant music echoing down the shaft.

There was a sudden, quick hissing of steam and the whirring of a large flywheel. The gate rattled as the sound got louder and louder, shuddering the floor beneath his feet.

'Don't worry. It's only this loud here because we are next to the engine. When you get upstairs you can't feel a thing.'

A bright light appeared in the shaft, coming closer, and billows of steam oozed from the blackness, filling the room like a thick London smog.

'Only a minute and it'll be here,' the girl said loudly above the sound of the steam generator that rattled and clanked even louder. 'It was built by Mister Luger – he's an inventor, owns the Prince Regent, designed it with his own hand.'

'I've never seen an elevator before,' Mariah said nervously as swathes of thick steam swelled about his feet like a rising tide.

'There're many things I had never seen before until I came here. Now I don't even turn an eye and just get on with it,' she said as the elevator chugged from the bottom of the deep shaft, winched by a steel wire the thickness of a man's arm that vanished upwards in the darkness of the shaft, pushed by a steel piston that powered it higher.

'Is it . . . Is it safe?' he asked as the sound got even louder and the shaking more intense.

'Safe, no. Fast, yes.' The girl peered down the shaft to the approaching elevator as the light grew brighter, illuminating the grease-covered walls. 'Work or lodging? – what is it to be first?'

'Lodgings?' asked Mariah as the elevator ground to a sudden and noisy halt before them. The girl turned the brass handle and slid the metal gate open. She stepped into the elevator and beckoned Mariah to follow.

'Thirteenth floor,' she said out loud as she pressed the button. 'That's where you're living. Nothing special but you can call it home.'

'What will I do here?' Mariah asked as the girl slid the door shut and pressed the button again.

'Work in the theatre, general dogsbody . . . That's until you learn the ropes and then like me you'll walk the boards. Best job in the place. Lucky you came when you did. Felix had the job until he went . . . *missing*,' she said, gripping the brass rail that was heavily bolted to the wall of the elevator as if she knew what was to come.

'Lucky Felix,' Mariah muttered. The lift was thrust up the shaft and the open wall sped by at speed, too quickly for him to count the floors. His ears popped as the steam elevator pushed them higher. 'What happens when we stop?'

There was a ping of the bell as the lift hit the thirteenth floor as if it had crashed into a stone mountain. Mariah was lifted from his feet and into the air, his head banging on the wooden roof as he let go of his bag, then he smashed against the floor. The girl never moved, braced against the wall of the elevator, her foot hooked beneath a discreet handle in the corner. He stared at the polished black shoes with silver buckles that peeped like two mice from underneath her Bible-black dress.

'Should have warned you,' she said as she turned a key in the wall that appeared to shut off the surging steam spewing from the roof. 'But I had to see the look on your face . . . priceless.'

'Glad you think it so amusing,' Mariah said as he got to his feet, picked up his bag and jacket and brushed the dirt from his damp shirt. 'So that was a steam elevator.'

'Not only that, but the fastest in Europe. Mister Luger told me and he should know, he built every one of them,' she said as she pulled back the metal gate and stepped from the elevator into a small corridor with three narrow wooden doors that formed a semicircle before the lift gate.

'Lodgings?' Mariah asked.

The girl pointed to the doors. 'Mine, yours and the stairs. That one belonged to Felix – but I mustn't go in, that's what Mister Luger said.'

Mariah looked at the first door. There was a tiny scrap of paper that had the smallest handwriting etched in black ink. 'Sacha,' he said, reading the inscription from the paper. 'Is that you?'

'My short name. You're English so you could never say what I'm really called, so you call me Sacha – do you have a name yourself?' she asked without drawing a single breath.

'Mariah –' he said, unable to finish what he would say as she quickly interrupted.

'Never tell your last name. I don't want to know it and if I did, I would know you too well. Who's to say you'll be here in the morning? After all, you may run off and hide like Felix. Here three weeks, then goes off without telling anyone. So keep your name for yourself, Mariah will do for me and for old Bizmillah . . . You take over Felix's job, so you're his assistant.' Sacha spurted out the words as if they were lines that she had learnt well. 'There isn't a lock so hide your things well. We clean them ourselves and get fresh sheets on the first Sunday. We eat where we work, and Mister Luger wants to see you first thing in the morning.'

'What will I do for Bizmillah?' Mariah asked as he pushed open the door and stepped into the darkened room.

'A magician's apprentice,' she said excitedly. 'Cleaning his illusions, polishing his boots and allowing him to cut you in half in the Sunday matinee. Better than scrubbing floors and doing dishes, but then again you did come from London in a *first-class* suit.' Sacha laughed at him as she took a Lucifer from her pocket and lit the mantle of the gas lamp that hung over the small fireplace. She saw Mariah look at the empty grate. 'You'll never be cold, not in this tower,' she said as she brightened the room with a turn of her nimble fingers. 'We have water heating, the finest in Europe –'

'Mister Luger says,' Mariah broke in, finishing her sentence.

'It's true,' she protested. 'Gurgles like a great dragon. Hot as Hades, winter and summer. Everything runs from steam, everything. The cooking, washing and even the harmonium in the theatre. There's nothing better and thank the saints you're not the one stoking the boiler.' Sacha laughed.

Mariah looked about the room. It had a fusty smell like an old church he had once visited with his mother. He had gone for the funeral of a great aunt and was squashed in the pew next to an old stone font, as far to the front a man dressed like a pantomime dame had sprinkled water over her ebony sarcophagus. It had smelt of musty unopened books and damp old ladies who pressed against him with a heady odour of burnt toast. Yet even that gave the room a feeling of being known and familiar.

The chamber had a small bed with clean but tatty blankets folded back beneath two duck pillows whose feathers puffed with every movement. By the side was a small cupboard that looked out of sorts next to the fireplace. A fine wax candle was pressed neatly in an old brass holder by the bed, with two matches and a striking pad lying in the wax gutter.

Mariah could hear the howling of the wind that blew round the high turret of the tower. Above his head there was the cracking of the flag that festooned the tower. It carried the banner of an unknown land, trailing out more as a signal to the blowing of the gale than as reverence to the tattered state. The grey slate tiles creaked and moaned in the sea gale that beat against the side of the Prince Regent, as if it battered some ancient cliff. The windows rattled in their frames, shaking the sashes, cords and weights that hung like dead men's toes behind the thick green damask curtains.

'You can take a look,' Sacha said as she saw him gaze at the chink in the curtains. 'You'll not see much on a night like this, just black of night and a few lights from the harbour.' She stopped and thought for a moment. 'But you'll see the lighthouse. Keeps me awake. Sends its beam out to sea time and again, never stops.' Sacha seemed pleased by the thought, as if it was a reassuring presence in her life.

'Can you see the windmills?' he asked as he slumped on to the bed.

'Never once. I was told that when I came here. I looked and looked but all I looked upon was the sea . . . and the castle.' Sacha closed the door to the room quietly as if she wanted to speak to him privately. For a brief moment he glimpsed a look of discontent upon her face.

'Do you like it here?' he asked as she stared at the gas lamp and gently turned the knob to dim the light.

'These are for you,' she said, as if she hadn't heard what he had asked, and she picked a suit of clothes from the door back. 'Hope they fit. We wear black in the theatre so we cannot be seen as the scenes change. Bizmillah will give you something to wear when he cuts you in two – you're the same size as Felix and his never got too . . . bloodstained.' She laughed.

'So I am to be cut in half every Sunday matinee?' Mariah asked as he poured himself a small glass of water from the bedside jug.

'Every Sunday, three o'clock. Cut in half for all to see. That's after he has plunged five long daggers deep within you *and* put your head in an iron mask. All for a silver shilling and six pence in the balcony.'

'Every Sunday?' Mariah asked, unsure as to why this day would be so special. 'Why the Sunday matinee?'

31

'Monica won't work Sunday,' Sacha said as if Mariah should already understand. 'She spends the time with Mister Luger, he says.'

'So only young boys should be cut in half on Sundays – is that why Felix escaped?'

Sacha was silent. She laid the black coat upon the bed and stroked the sleeve dreamily. 'The truth is, Mariah, no one knows what happened to him. The night before he went missing I had heard him arguing with Bizmillah. He shouted at him that he would tell Mister Luger what had happened, Bizmillah said that whatever went on he would take a pound of flesh from Felix as payment for his lies. Then he was gone. I came to the room the next morning and his bed was unruffled and not slept in. This suit of clothes hung behind the door and everything was as it was. There's . . . there's a rumour in the town that a Kraken has been taking the boys. Catching them when they've been out on their own.' Sacha stopped and looked away.

'You must go on,' Mariah said as he reached to her and jabbed her arm.

Sacha looked back and forth from window to door and thought of running from the room. She grasped the bedpost, twisting the wood in the palm of her hand. 'How do I know you haven't been sent to catch me out?'

'I've never met you before, never even heard of this place until Professor Bilton gave me a note saying I was being transferred.' Mariah rummaged in his pocket for his writ of worthiness. 'See this, it'll tell you who I am and why I'm here. I don't come to catch you out,' he said as he handed her the folded vellum tied with a single red ribbon.

She held it in her hand unopened and looked at him. 'Promise me one thing, Mariah. Whatever you hear tonight gets forgotten by the morning.'

32

Mariah nodded, hands in pockets, fingers secretly crossed. 'Promise . . .'

'When Felix vanished, he told me he had found something. It was more of a secret than something precious, but he wouldn't tell me what it was or where he had discovered it. I asked him again and again, but the more I spoke to him the more silent he became. The only thing he said was that the secret was hidden in the Prince Regent, somewhere people would never think to look but see every day,' she said quickly as she caught her breath. 'The night he vanished I heard something at the door of my room. I lay in bed as the door opened slowly, it creaked an inch or two. It was thick black with no light. Whatever it was had come by the stair and turned off the gas lamp by the elevator. Not a single drop of light was to be seen.' Sacha spoke slowly now, looking about her, keeping her voice to a whisper for fear of being overheard. 'I pulled the covers over my head. I didn't want to see it, whatever it was. I thought if I didn't look it would go away and find someone else to torment . . .' She gasped for breath, her hands feeling the ruffles of her collar, pulling them from her reddening skin. 'I couldn't move. I wanted to scream, but no one would have heard me. Whoever . . . whatever it was, came into my room and looked at me, I could feel their breath panting against the bedclothes over my head. Then slowly and carefully they walked back to the door. Whatever it was, I could smell it . . . It was like old mothballs and gin mixed together. I had to look, so I took a peek – I couldn't help, it I had to see – and . . . there was nothing. I heard the door pull shut, but not a trace. There was a clang as the door to the steam lift shut and a whizzing of the engine and the next morning Felix was gone.'

'Do you think it was him who came into your room?' Mariah asked as he gulped the lump from his throat and shivered as if a cold hand touched the back of his neck.

33

'Why should he? I have nothing to steal but a few old post-cards from Ireland, that and a trinket or two.'

'Did he leave anything for you, a note, a gift?'

'Nothing. When Mister Luger searched his room they found nothing, even the mantelpiece had been dusted and the grate cleaned. All that belonged to Felix had gone except this stage suit,' she said as she brushed the sleeve. 'That had been put on the hanger and placed behind the closet against the wall.'

'What about his family?' Mariah asked nervously as he twizzled a long strand of his curly mop.

'No one, he spoke of no one. Mister Luger only takes orphans, boys from the Colonial School and the workhouse,' she said as she saw Mariah look at her with enquiring eyes. 'Did you know Felix? He must only be a year older than you.'

'Felix? No, can't say I did . . . There were so many of us, one of many really,' Mariah replied. 'Worked here long?' he asked, hoping to change the conversation.

'My father got me the job here. I'm the eldest of nine children and there's no room at the inn.' She laughed at her own joke. 'My mother keeps the Kent Arms in Paradise, it's a bar by the harbour – we get Saturday afternoon to ourselves, so I'll take you. My father's a coastguard. In the morning you'll see the castle. Look to the street below and that's Paradise.'

'So you lived in Paradise?' he laughed.

'But some parts of Paradise are so full, now I have to live here.' Sacha lost her smile as a distant church clock struck midnight, its shrill chimes carried by the wind. 'Best be leaving you,' she said as she opened the door. 'There's no lock, but since Felix disappeared, I've taken to blocking the handle with a chair. Haven't slept for so long . . . I'm glad you're here, I'll sleep tonight,' she said tearfully as she turned to go, shutting the thin wooden door firmly to keep out the night.

Mariah crept to the window and opened the thick curtains. He looked out to sea. The room appeared to be at the very top of the hotel, hidden in the very top of the tower. It was as if it was as high as the clouds that swirled about the round turret and rattled the glass panes. Through the rain-streaked windows he could make out the square shapes of the bathing machines on the narrow strip between the Prince Regent and the sea two hundred feet below. The scene was clearly lit by the gas lamps from three hundred windows and several cones of limelight that illuminated the hotel so it could be seen from far out at sea.

Far below, the lighthouse poked like a thin white finger through the rolling waves breaking over the pier, drenching the fishing boats that clung to the harbour wall. Wave after wave crashed from the darkness, briefly phosphorescent in the glow of the light, then plunged black-dark into the night storm.

Mariah turned the element of the lamp until the mantle glowed with the strength of a firefly, barely lighting the palm of his hand. Then he sat on the bed, wrapping himself in the wool blankets as he listened to the storm beating against the windows and crashing against the beach below.

It was then he heard the sound. It was neither storm, nor sea. The gentle tap, tap, tap of fingernails on the broad water pipe that ran across the wall of the room, and with it the faraway sound of voices in sombre conversation.

[4]

Galvanised Bathing Machine

MORNING came quickly. The storm had ebbed into a gentle, December breeze that chased mountainous white clouds across the sky. Mariah had been woken by the scream of the seagulls that lodged on the roof and squawked and prattled well before the rising of the sun. He had dressed quickly in the black shirt and suit left for him by Sacha. They fitted well, as if tailored just for him. In the dirty brown wardrobe he had found a dainty pair of black pointed boots with neat ankle straps and a silver buckle – they too had fit perfectly, and as he paced the room he was entertained by a gentle leather squeak from his right foot. In the minutes he waited for Sacha he stared from the window of his room, captivated by all that was before him.

To the north he could see the castle with its bombarded keep, high walls and a garrison house that proudly flew a Jack from a stubby flagpole on its grey slate roof. Mariah had looked for Paradise and traced the street with his eye, following his finger across the windowpane as he drew its length from the castle to the sea. Far below, in the calm that followed the storm, was the harbour. Every inch of water was crammed with small boats that even in the first light of dawn jostled to flee out to sea. On the slipway a large brig stood half built, its ribs and keel open to the elements like the carcass of a dead whale being stripped of its meat. It crawled with men, who in the distance looked like small black lice.

Mariah had never expected it to be such a beautiful sight. The crisp blue morning sky was edged in gold thread from the rising of a southern sun that skipped across the horizon, shedding its light below the high clouds. It was the first time he had seen a dawn such as this. Even from his tiny room in the Colonial School he had only ever witnessed the drab rising of a foggy orb that would, with its feeble arm, scatter the smog by late afternoon and allow its return as it quickly set to the west. For him, the sky and the sun had been a mere backdrop to his life, of no importance but to provide him with light for his steps. Now they commanded time and attention as they stretched out before him to the distant horizon of the German Ocean.

Mariah tidied the room. He felt as if it were not yet his, that the presence of Felix was still close. Trying to imagine what his predecessor had looked like, he set about searching the room for a slight trace, a mere thread or particle of dust that would give some clue as to the disappearance of the boy and why others had vanished before him. He had looked everywhere for something to tell him that the boy had been there. But it was as if every memory, trace and thought of Felix had been totally eradicated by a meticulous hand that desired not to leave anything behind. He felt as if whoever had done this had been purposeful in their plan and, in his confusion could not decide if Felix had been the perpetrator or victim of some elaborate plot.

In the minutes that followed, Mariah allowed himself to think that which until then he had kept from his mind. He remembered the penny dreadful that had been smeared over Captain Charity as he slept. The black ink cartoon of Fiery

Jack, snatching children from their beds and dragging them across the rooftops of London to be devoured in his lair, filled his head. He again checked the window, feeling the securing bolt to see if it had been tampered with. He looked outside to the small balcony that encircled the tower and wondered if Felix had escaped that way, on to the roof and down to the street. Or had he been carried sleeping by Fiery Jack, the demon creature that plagued the city with his sulphurous breath and spring heels, across the rooftops to another world?

Mariah folded his first-class suit with great care and placed it in the wardrobe. It was then that he remembered the playing cards wedged deeply in his pocket, kept away from prying eyes. Slowly and carefully he dipped his hand into the pocket and, before bringing the cards and the jewelled skull to the light, looked over his shoulder to see whether he was being watched. Mariah stared at the Fool, dressed in his clown's guise with chequered shirt, ruff collar and painted face. He studiously examined the stiff wax seal that held tight to the flap, squeezing the box lid securely shut. With another glance he looked behind him, sure that he was being watched. Then he quickly took the cards and the skull and hid them under the bed, wedging them between the mattress and the oak boards, hoping they would never be discovered.

As he got from his knees there was a knock at the door. From the rattling of the handle and the stamping of feet outside, he knew it was Sacha. 'Mariah,' she whispered as she pulled on the handle. 'If we go now I can show you something before you see Mister Luger. You have to see it . . .'

Mariah opened the door and stood back to allow her in. Sacha didn't move, but looked him up and down, not speaking.

'Cat got your tongue?' he said as he tired of her staring.

'You look just like him,' she said, surprised at his appearance. 'Same hair, same eyes. You could be brothers.'

He ignored what she said, uncomfortable in his new clothes and feeling as if Felix was closer than before, that he had never left the room but just changed into dust and now stared down from the thick cobwebs that hung in the corners of the room. 'What do we have to see?' he asked, reminding Sacha of her excitement.

'Something special. Mister Luger said he'll see you in an hour. Monica's been causing trouble and Bizmillah wants her cast out of the Music Hall. They're all in his office. You can hear the shouting, she's screaming and . . .' she said quickly, her voice excited as her hands danced her words. 'That's it!' she shouted as she remembered what she wanted to say. 'I found a galvanised bathing machine, it's incredible. Arrived last night from Luger's workshop, the only one in Europe and destined to cure all of life's ills –'

'Mister Luger says,' Mariah echoed.

'Precisely. And it's in the hotel, I found it this morning. Quickly, we'll have to go by the stairs.'

Sacha took him by the hand and dragged him through the narrow door and into a thin spiral staircase that twisted down and down, lit only by narrow slit windows that looked out across the sea. Mariah could hear the steam elevator pounding away as the expanding piston thrust the carriage up the shaft, pulled at the same time by the whirring winch that coiled the thick steel cable around and around.

Mariah followed as Sacha ran faster, skipping the steps as she ran. Every now and then she would whirl herself around the blind corners, grabbing the brass rail and throwing out her feet, vanishing from sight then reappearing as Mariah chased after her. The sound of their chasing rumbled on ahead, drowned only by the vibration of the steam elevator as it went up and down, shivering the shaft and gargling steam from the many vents that criss-crossed the wall.

Every so often Mariah passed a small landing, each with a narrow wooden door marked with the number of the floor. He counted the landings as they spiralled down, his feet tripping in his pointy boots and his curls blowing in the strong draught that blew from the depths of the shaft.

'Much further?' he shouted as Sacha ran even faster, vanishing in the patchwork of light and dark.

'Another five floors and then we'll find it,' she gasped as she ran, stumbling over her frock-tails.

Mariah counted the landings again as they ran by, each door neatly labelled, showing that they now dashed below the level of the ground. He become aware that the lower they descended, the hotter the shaft became. The handrail was warm to his touch and the sound of hissing steam filled the staircase.

'Don't worry,' Sacha cried out above the noise of the steam engine. 'Two more landings and then we'll take the next door and all will be well.'

Mariah had lost all track of time. In his heart he felt a growing ache that he would be too late to see Mister Luger, and that this unseen master of everything would pack him on the first train to London without him even sampling the blessing of being cut in half by the Great Bizmillah at the Sunday matinee.

'It's here,' she shouted, out of breath and relieved to have found the door. 'This way for the experience of a lifetime . . .'

Mariah followed her through the door and into a long corridor. He suddenly realised that they were not below ground: the hotel was built on the side of a high cliff and one part of the Prince Regent was built against the rock face. The corridor was lined with large windows that ran its length, and was carpeted in fine green wool inlaid with golden crowns. Mariah saw the narrow beach that was covered by the full tide and the peculiar bathing huts that looked like miniature houses strapped to the back of old horse carts and wheeled out into the sea. A hoard of shabbily dressed urchins, barefoot and ragged, searched the strand for the washing of jetsam brought in by the storm.

Sacha beckoned him to follow as she led on, confident that he would now know the way back to see Mister Luger. 'Not far,' she said as the sound of the steam engine died away in the distance. 'Just at the end is the spa – drink the water and you'll turn green and die . . . But people pay good money to swallow the stuff, though it smells of Mahoney's and devils belching. You should see the look on their faces after they've been made to drink a gallon.' Sacha grimaced, opening her mouth and sticking out her tongue.

She stopped at a double door crafted from the finest dark wood and etched with carvings of holly leaves. 'This is it,' she said. She looked both ways along the passage, then stepped quickly inside as if she didn't want to be seen.

Once inside, Mariah stood in an incredible water garden. A large swimming pool stretched out before him lit with blue gas lamps that shimmered a rainbow upon the purple water. It looked like a huge cavern made of blue tile; white mosaics covered the walls and large parlour palms shot forth their long green branches. Around the pool were several wicker sofas with curiously shaped backs, humped at one end like a camel. Immediately the heat sweated his face, and his heavy black suit felt out of place.

'Not far,' Sacha said as she went on her way through the spa, looking for a gathering of tall tropical plants that protected a small doorway in the tiled wall. 'In here,' she whispered, and she slipped under the branches of a minute tree laden with yellow fruit, with a large oriental bat dangling by its thin claws from one of the branches. It slept in the morning sunlight that streamed through the high windows that formed the glass floor of the terrace above.

41

'What is this place?' Mariah asked, wide-eyed in amazement.

'People come here to swim, take the waters and sit under Mister Luger's health lamp. It's powered by electricity – after a week they turn brown. Some of them look as if they are boiled lobsters, *and* they pay,' she said incredulously. 'But if you want to be amazed, wait until you see this.' Sacha's eyes lit up with excitement as she pushed open the door and dragged him into a large room clad in fresh pine planks and smelling of a freshly cut forest. 'Look!'

Mariah stared at a large brass dome fitted to what looked like an enamel bath. Over the bath was a wooden hood like an upturned boat, with a tidy circular hole padded with red leather. From the dome, three large pipes came out; one went into the roof and the others bit into the bath like a giant spider's fangs. On the side of the bath was a brass indicator with a large green lever which at that moment pointed to the word *Resting*.

'Steam-powered,' Sacha said proudly as she stroked the soft wood. 'This really does become a wonder – one flick of the handle and it's filled with steam, two flicks and gallons of freezing salt waves are pumped from the sea and sprayed inside. Three flicks and hot water bubbles all around. Mister Luger says it invigorates the soul and cleanses the mind, the only one in Europe.' Sacha looked at the handle and smiled. 'It's a Galvanised Bathing Machine . . . I overheard Mister Luger saying that the water was mixed with a secret ingredient that gave it curative properties. He said he would pump it from under the streets and mix it with the seawater, called it *Kuck* . . . I wasn't sure what he meant, but it sounded as if it would be good,' she said, her eyebrows raised as if she too desired to try the wonder tub. 'Every bath costs an extra pound on the bill so people wouldn't pay if it weren't worth it. Shall we see it work?' she asked audaciously'

'I wouldn't do it, Sacha. What if we are found here? I have to go, got to see Mister Luger – he'll want to see me, it's my first morning.'

'So, Mariah *is* a coward. I knew it when I saw you last night. Just like Felix, I thought to myself, all talk and nothing in his britches. No one will know, Mariah. We are the only ones here.' Sacha fumbled with the starting handle. 'Get in – there's a swimming robe in the back room, get changed and get in. It'll be the best thing you've ever done.'

Mariah was torn between pleasing her and running away. He looked at the Galvanised Bathing Machine where it sat on the tiled floor, dead . . . 'You can do what you like, Sacha, but I'm not getting into that thing – I want to see it working first.'

'If *that's* what you want then *that's* what you'll get,' she said quickly as she slipped the handle from *Resting* to *Active*.

The large brass bubble made a sudden gulp, then began to gurgle and simmer, quietly shaking the floor and trembling the bath as it sucked in *Kuck* from a huge vat far below. Through the leather-clad hole it belched a breath of salty steam that rose into the air like a circular cloud. Mariah looked on, glancing to the door, knowing it was the only means of escape.

'What if somebody comes?' Mariah asked anxiously as the Bathing Machine gurgled and even more salty, sulphurous breaths rose, one after the other, faster and faster. The room began to stink like a sewer as thick brown steam gurgled and gurgled.

There was a sudden loud shudder that shook the whole room as the brass bubble belched violently and rumbled several times. More and more steam began to billow from the top of the bath.

'Ready?' Sacha shouted as she flicked the switch once and stood back from the machine.

A large guzzling of bright white steam blew through the

pipes and into the bath like the smokestack of a steam train in full speed. It gave a deep, loud roar as it rushed into the air, hitting the ceiling and blasting across the room.

Sacha panicked and hit the switch again. This time the Galvanised Bathing Machine trembled violently as the spider pipes rattled and twisted. Then with a sudden and desperate moan it began to spew forth a torrent of bright green salt water that sprayed the inside of the bath, filling it to the brim and spurting from the leather neck-hole and showering into the room.

'Stop it!' shouted Mariah as he leapt out of the way of a violent charge of spray that missed him by inches. 'It'll drown us!'

Sacha hit the handle again. The seawater ebbed back, sucked down the sluice with the force of a spring tide, glugging and globbing as it quickly disappeared down the automatic plughole.

'Don't!' cried Mariah hopelessly as he saw her move the handle again and heard the blasting of the hot water pipe as it rattled its welcome to the world. 'No!'

His scream came too late. A torrent of boiling hot water filled the machine like a swirling vortex. The Galvanised Bathing Machine shook upon its clawed metal feet, shuddering and shooping, nearly knocking Sacha to the floor as she gripped the handle, vainly attempting to stop whatever would happen next.

'Run!' Mariah shouted as he scarpered to the door, leaving Sacha hanging on to the machine as the stinking vapour darkened the room. 'Let it go and get out!' he hollered above the sound of the steam. Mariah turned and saw Sacha being pulled back and forth by the intense vibrations of the machine that appeared to have risen from the dead and developed a life of its own, intent on destruction.

'Mariah!' Sacha screamed as the handle began to glow with the conducted heat from the steam bubble. 'I'm stuck!'

He saw that she was fastened to the handle by the sleeve of her coat. Mariah ran to her, avoiding the frothing of the machine and holding his breath against the growing pungency of the stench as bubbles of dirty brown lather oozed from the leather neck-hole. Quickly he grabbed her sleeve, tearing material from the cuff as he pulled her free. 'Now run,' he said as he dragged her to the door, not attempting to stop the Bathing Machine and leaving it to rumble on discontentedly. 'If we get caught now that'll be the end of us both, Mister Luger would see to that.'

'He'd understand,' Sacha pleaded as she skidded through a large puddle of *Kuck* that had been spat from the machine and now covered the tile floor in large pools.

'He'd kill us, feed us to the seagulls at least – sack us if we were lucky,' Mariah moaned as he pulled her through the tiny door and into the shade of the tropical palms, quietly closing the door behind him and looking out across the spa from the cover of the undergrowth.

Quickly and quietly they crawled through the palms that lined the side of the spa, keeping to the shadows in the hope that they would not be discovered. Within the minute they had reached the large wooden doors that opened out on to the long corridor leading back to the staircase. Mariah panted, regretting he had ever said yes to her requests to come and see the Galvanised Bathing Machine. He looked at her, his lips thin and eyes tight, hoping she would see his irritation. Sacha smiled back with her bright eyes, a wicked smile breaking the side of her mouth.

'Was it fun?' she asked in her brogue.

Mariah was about to reply when the door swung slowly open. A thin white hand clawed across the wood and a head covered in long greasy hair peered into the room. In two paces a man stepped into the spa dressed in a long white bathrobe

45

that trailed along the floor. He walked cautiously across the tiles, his bare feet squeaking with each step as he inspected every inch of the wall as if he looked for something hidden.

Together they watched as he stopped, looked around and waited, then turned away. Mariah and Sacha cowered deeper into the undergrowth, not wanting to be discovered and hoping that the man would not hear the sound of the Galvanised Bathing Machine groaning in the bathroom beyond the door.

It was then that Mariah saw his face. '*Isambard Black!*' he gasped under his breath, the sound escaping his lips like a short squeal.

Black jerked his head as he heard the sound. Then he dived to a chaise longue by the side of the pool and sprawled upon it as if he had been there for some time. As he did so, he slyly slipped the white towel from the back of the sofa and put it over his head. He began to grunt like a pig, as if feigning sleep.

Mariah seized the moment, grabbing Sacha by the arm and dragging her from the cover of the palms. He pulled the door open and pushed her through into the passage. He looked back; Isambard Black snatched the towel from his face and sat bolt upright as the door to the spa swung shut.

'Quickly,' Mariah pleaded. 'We mustn't be caught . . .'

Together they set off at a pace towards the staircase, running along the crown-encrusted carpet as fast as they could. Mariah knew that Black would be close behind; they had to reach the stairway before they were discovered. It was then that a dark thought flashed into his wits. Mariah knew there was something more to Black than taking the waters; he had seen it in his eyes on the train and now in the spa.

They raced to the door, Sacha grabbing the handle and diving into the darkness of the stairwell. Mariah carefully and slowly allowed the door to almost close, keeping a finger's breadth open through which to peek into the long passageway.

Isambard Black peered out of the spa door. He looked back and forth to see who had escaped, his eyes devouring all that he saw as his withered lips twisted into a foul grin.

[5]

The Importunate Otto Luger

OTTO Luger sat like a smouldering old crow in his large office, clad in gold leaf, on the ground floor of the Prince Regent. In his hand he rolled an old quill pen as he attempted to perch his monocular spectacle in his left eye. The gold-rimmed glass was held precariously in place by a sagging wrinkle, squashing his eye so that it resembled the deep fold of a bull elephant's skin. His breath seethed in and out through his fine white teeth, which were tipped in several obvious places with gold caps. The whiskers of his thick and unnaturally black moustache twitched angrily as he began to roll the bald tip of the once elegant writing tool inside his nostril.

'It's not that bad, Mister Luger,' the Great Bizmillah said as he stepped back towards the door, trying to escape before Luger exploded in front of him. 'Whatever you want, is what you will get . . . She *can* stay, but all I ask is that you don't allow her to throw knives at the audience again. They were only laughing, when she fell over they thought it was part of the act, that's why they laughed.'

'No one laughs at Monica,' Luger screamed as he got to his feet. 'Not even the guests. If they laughed, then they deserved it. Monica is an *artiste*, a creative genius. Believe me, Bizmillah, the name of Monica Momzer will be known throughout the world. Understand?'

'Indeed, Mister Luger, we all understand and I will do everything in my power to –' Bizmillah stopped speaking as he saw the look on Luger's face.

'I'm glad you see it my way, because that is the only way there is around here,' he said in his sharp Texan drawl. 'I came here penniless and everything you see belongs to me. Monica stays in the act or you don't stay in the hotel, understand?' Luger raised one eyebrow and his monocle fell to the desk. 'If Monica's happy, then I'm happy, and if I'm happy that means you get paid. Understand?'

Bizmillah didn't reply. He bowed his head and looked to the floor as his hand rummaged for the door handle behind him. Several beads of sweat trickled across the top of his bald head and down among the tufts of hair that spiralled over his fine, pointed ears.

'One more thing,' Luger said as he again sat at his desk. 'The boys . . . Any questions being asked as to why they keep disappearing?'

'Not that I've heard, Mister Luger, not that I've . . .' He thought for a moment, his mouth poised as if he had been suddenly silenced. 'There . . . there is one problem,' Bizmillah went on, stumbling for his words.

'Speak, man.' Luger motioned with his hand as he waggled his thick moustache from side to side.

'Professor Bilton at the Colonial School said this would be the last boy. He asked where they had all gone, five in a year, and I told him we had lost them and he thought that *rather* clumsy. He said for the price we gave him, he couldn't give us any more and Mariah Mundi would be the last.'

'Mariah Mundi?' Luger said as he looked up at the enor-

49

mous castle-shaped clock that hung above the door, its axe-head pendulum swinging menacingly back and forth as it ticked the seconds with every sharp swipe. 'I was supposed to see the boy an hour ago. The last one . . . Mariah Mundi . . . Understand?' Luger seemed confused; his hand ruffled the papers on the desk as if he looked for something important, something lost in the depths of his memory that he tried to find in the reality of the cluttered world before him. 'That's it,' he exclaimed as he grabbed a piece of paper. 'She wrote it here, a note for me . . . from Monica. She wants to cut him in half . . . in the matinee on Sunday. Said you do it every week and now it's her turn and I had to ask you.' Luger stopped and looked at Bizmillah as he joggled the tiny scrap of paper before him like a small fan. 'It will be fine, won't it? I don't want to upset Monica, do I?'

Bizmillah ruffled in his green silk China suit, grabbing the billowing cuffs and wrapping them around his wrists anxiously. He clenched his teeth together, attempting to hold back the words that sat uncontrollably on his wan tongue. 'Fine.' He grimaced as the rage subsided enough for him to open his eyes and stare at Luger once more. 'Whatever Mister Luger requires.'

'So glad, so glad,' Luger said softly as he again looked at the swinging of the pendulum, lost in its motion, dreamily watching the axe go back and forth. As the hands came together at the pinnacle of the castle keep it gently struck the midday.

It was then that the front of the clock burst open and a fan-fare of tiny figures leapt on fine silver rods with a blast of little trumpets. They appeared to dance about the parapets and along the fine etched castellation that surrounded the clock. There was a whooshing of steam as the chorus began to blast a reveille of miniature notes that shrilled loudly across the room with great brio, rattling the wine glass that balanced precariously on Luger's desk. A gaggle of horses and armoured knights leapt from a small door, suspended upon long fanned arms, and galloped in tune to the music as the clock chimed twelve long and doleful strikes.

Luger sat charmed as Bizmillah cowered, fearing what was to come. Over his head the pendulum suddenly dropped to the floor, the axe swinging close to the wooden boards, and he leapt out of the way. High above, the clock took on a life of its own as the castle keep was filled with minute figures that danced and swirled with every bugle note. Luger looked on, bewitched and enchanted by the spectacle that took place upon the high wall of his office, shining in gold leaf and powered by his steam generator. With the final stroke of midday, the tower door opened and a small, jewel-encrusted executioner slid out on a small brass stand to be met by a silver-plated king who buckled at the knee, bent towards him and met the axe across the back of his head.

'Such a sight, such a sight, Bizmillah, and you missed it,' Luger said excitedly. 'Too busy looking at the dirt on your shoes. Come back tomorrow and sit here – you can sit at my desk and you can watch it again. Better still, come back at midnight and you will see something even more spectacular.'

'The boy, Mariah Mundi?' Bizmillah asked, hoping to remind him of who should be waiting outside the office and urgently desiring a reason to escape what appeared to be even more grotesque and insane ramblings.

'Why should I want to see him?' Luger asked as he waited for an encore from the gold clock.

'You invited him. Every boy sees you on his first day – a tradition, all part of the process. You see him and then you send him to me in the theatre,' Bizmillah said, reminding Luger of all that had gone before.

'Yes, yes,' Luger replied still distracted and far away. 'Send him in. And remember, Monica will cut the boy in half at the Sunday matinee.'

Bizmillah turned to the door, taking hold of the brass handle as he glanced upwards at the golden clock that hung high above him. It had been a strange journey that he had taken to this place, he thought. He remembered first stepping from the boat-train at Dover two years before, mumbling his intentions in broken English as he was questioned by the guard. He had amused him with card tricks and sleight of hand, twisting a living frog from his fingers and allowing it to spring upon the man, landing on his shoulder. From there he had gone to London, where he had spent a year in a small theatre, standing before the limelight and casting doves from his open hand to a crowd of sleepers huddled before him, escaping the cold.

One night all that had changed. Otto Luger had stepped into the darkness dressed like a fine London gentleman, a fat cigar bloating from his lip, fine silk gloves and a long black cane in his hand. He had sat by the door of the small theatre and laughed loudly, carousing with the singers, laughing at the jester and standing in awe, clapping frantically in appreciation of every single dove that Bizmillah had squeezed from the sleeve of his tail coat. Later, Mister Luger had forced him to sit at his table and offered him something that he could never refuse.

'I like a man like you,' Luger said as he sipped a bottle of fine brandy, clutching it by the neck with his thick hands. 'I have always been fascinated with magic, but something that takes you beyond picking a pigeon from your coat sleeve or twisting a card from the back of your hand.' He stared into Bizmillah's eyes, holding his gaze. 'I searched for something for many years, something that made me leave Texas and come to this cold, foggy and grubby city. I knew it was here and it cost me a fortune to find it.'

'I too search for something,' Bizmillah said as he flicked a card into the air and watched it vanish, the trick unseen by Luger who swigged on the bottle. 'A pack of cards so daring, so amazing that to touch them would be all I could ever desire. In the right hands the cards know your very heart and like a beautiful stage filled with the finest artistes, play out your life in the dancing pictures.'

'Dancing pictures, you say?' Luger muttered through a mouthful of brandy that dribbled down his chin as he spoke. 'Pretty ladies or ugly men?'

'Whatever is in your life will come from the cards. They are not marked or tapered and have no trickery of any kind. It is as if they have a will of their own and an understanding of the human heart. There were once two such decks and now there is only one.'

'And who has these all-dancing, all-seeing knights, knaves and queens?' Luger asked.

'They vanished many years ago, taken from Vienna. They have travelled across Europe and now they are somewhere in London. In every city I hear stories that they have been seen, that some great deception has been performed, and every time I am a month, a week or a day behind. Once, in Paris, I even knew the man who had found them. I went to his apartment and discovered he was dead and the cards were nowhere to be found.'

'How much would I have to pay to get my hands on them?'

'Priceless, totally priceless. The only way to get them would be to steal them,' Bizmillah whispered as he looked over Luger's shoulder and around the room to see if they were being overheard.

'Then that's what we'll do, my friend. Nothing should keep a man from his desires, and if we have to steal them, so be it.' Luger slapped Bizmillah heartily on the back, grabbed him by the hand and squeezed it in a crushing handshake. 'I have two men, detectives, Grimm and Grendel. They found something for me and I'm sure they could accommodate a little investigation into your poker deck.'

'Poker?' Bizmillah exclaimed as a look of disgust crossed his face. 'Nothing so crude as that, they are the Panjandrum. The finest deck ever crafted, life breathed into them by their creator.'

'Whatever,' Luger replied as he sucked on the bottle. 'One thing, Mister Bizmillah. I own a hotel, newly built and the grandest in Europe. Come and work for me and I will find your Mister Panjandrum and get you his cards. All I ask is that you help me . . .'

Now that seemed such a long time ago. Luger had never kept his promise and all talk of the Panjandrum had faded into a never-mentioned place. Every night of the week, Bizmillah had entertained the guests of the Prince Regent with an ever-decreasing supply of magical doves and disappearing frogs.

Luger had taken to inventing all manner of strange steam-powered devices to bring health to his clients. Deep in the depths of the hotel, where maids and porters would fear to walk alone, he had spent many days and nights in his laboratory, the sound of his pounding iron reverberating through the lift shaft to the very pinnacle of the hotel.

'So you'll send in the boy?' Luger said as Bizmillah stepped from the room. 'I have things to do, so don't let him keep me waiting.'

Bizmillah smiled his submissive smile, rubbing his servile hands in complete humility. 'Very well, Mister Luger, whatever you say.'

Mariah was seated on the chair outside the office in his new black suit, his feet pained by his new boots that pinched his toes into a sharp point. He had sat and watched the passing of every guest, looking for Isambard Black. He had taken the time to go to the long oak desk and, taking a halfpenny from his pocket, had bought a picture postcard of the Prince Regent. Then he had taken a short stubby charcoal pencil from his pocket and scrawled the words *Perfidious Albion – Claridges Hotel – London* as neatly as he could before placing the card in his inside pocket. He was waiting to be seen by Mister Luger at any moment.

That moment had come and gone several times as Mariah had paced the floor outside the room and looked out of the window to the busy marketplace that by day sprang up outside the hotel. He had watched the coming and going of several fine carriages, dropping their elegant guests who were swarmed upon by wasp-like porters in blue suits and yellow braid. They gathered up the suitcases and breezed in and out of the hotel through its grand, oversized revolving door that hissed like a snake as it went around.

Mariah had watched as fine gentlemen walked the wide sweeping staircase to the gaming room on the first floor, their ladies banished to look at views of the endless sea from the glass-topped veranda. No one paid notice to him as he sat waiting patiently, hoping that the muffled conversation inside would soon be over and he would be admitted to Mister Luger's sanctuary.

'Mariah Mundi,' Bizmillah said as he stepped from the door, breaking his dream. Mariah sat upright and stared at the man. He was aghast at his China suit with its green embossed dragons and thick gold thread. Bizmillah the Great looked as if he was Italian. His sun-warmed skin and dark hair spiralled in eccentric wisps around his ears and to his shoulders. 'Mister Luger will see you now, and later I will teach you how to be a magician . . .'

Mariah smiled, stood up, turned and walked into the room.

Luger sat at his cluttered desk pretending to write on a piece of paper, his pen going over the same three words. He never spoke; Mariah waited and waited, watching him trace the words again and again. From where he was standing, he couldn't make out what was being written and rewritten, but Luger made him wait until the last morsel of ink had dried from the tip of his old quill pen.

'Sit!' he shouted, his eyes fixed on the piece of paper as he read the words to himself. 'I am a busy man and not one to be kept waiting. I said first thing this morning and now it's after midday. What's your excuse?'

'I was outside,' Mariah said quietly. 'It must have been . . .'.

Luger shook his head and looked at the clock and then at Mariah. He pulled a large gold fob watch from his waistcoat pocket and held it to his ear as if he checked to see if it was still working. He raised both his sprouting, grey eyebrows, a look of puzzlement crossing his face. 'Waiting for me?' he asked unsure of himself. 'Outside?'

Mariah nodded and bit his lip, trying to keep a straight face and swallow the giggle that welled up inside him. 'Sacha said that you were busy, so I waited.'

'Waited!' shouted Luger as he got from his seat. 'Do you know what happens to the man who waits?' Mariah was silent. 'Nothing – that's what happens, nothing. Life charges by and they wake up one morning and their life is over, that's what happens if you wait.'

'Sorry,' Mariah said softly as Luger began to pace about the room looking to the floor and pummelling his fist into his hand. 'I won't wait again.'

'Time waits for no one. Already the morning has gone, soon it will be the afternoon and that will die and become the evening and you know what comes then don't you?' hc spoke frantically not giving a chance for Mariah to speak. 'The *night*

. . . dark and cold and miserable. Filthy thick, black night. And I lay a wager that you expect to sleep?'

Mariah nodded hopefully.

'And you know what happens when people sleep? They DIE – that's what happens. I've seen it a thousand times, old men get into bed, close their eyes and then they are gone. One snort and all the life vanishes. So what's the answer, boy?'

Mariah stared back vaguely, mumbling under his breath, not knowing what to say as Luger waved his arms erratically, clutching the fob watch in his hand, the chain flailing about his head.

'DON'T SLEEP! I haven't slept in years, never go to bed, and all I allow myself is to close my eyes for five minutes in the hour, whenever I am indoors, whatever the place, as soon as the quarter of the hour comes I sit and close my eyes to the world for five minutes.' Luger panted as he calmed down, his outburst ebbing away as he sheepishly walked back to his desk and sat in the worn leather chair. He looked Mariah up and down and then pulled a piece of vellum paper from a brown folder that lay on the top of his desk. 'Says you're a Colonial boy? Know Professor Bilton well, do you?'

'Very well,' Mariah replied as he fiddled with the button on his jacket sleeve.

'You are the last in a long line of boys from that school and I have heard there will be no more. All the others have . . . *run away*, gone without a by your leave. Will you do the same, young Mister Mundi?'

'No, I –'

'It would be a shame to lose someone as bright as you.' The clock struck the quarter past noon. Luger looked up and then at his fob watch, setting a small gold lever upon the side, and then sat back in the leather chair, closing his eyes.

Instantly, Luger began to snore, his broad chest heaving

under his fine gold waistcoat, his head tilted back against the chair as thick black spikes of hair stuck out from his upturned nostrils.

Mariah hesitated, unsure if he should wait or disappear from the room whilst Luger slept soundly. He looked at the desk; there in the middle, by a brass smotherer, was the crisp piece of paper that Luger had scrawled upon. He edged closer, trying to make out the words, intrigued as to what the owner of such a fine place should want to write again and again. He counted the seconds with the ticking of the golden clock, whose clicks and whirring marked the slow passing of time. Luger slept on, his tongue sticking from the side of his mouth like a dozing cow in a summer meadow. Mariah could wait no longer. He reached out and turned the paper towards him as Luger slobbered and snored. It was then that he read the words – *The Midas Box* – scrawled in thick black ink.

There was a sudden and shrill clanging as the bell in the fob watch rattled in Luger's hand. He leapt from the chair, dropping the watch and grabbing the front of the desk with both hands as if to steady himself for some great surprise. He looked about the room and then fixed his glare on Mariah.

'Yes?' he asked madly, as if he had never seen the boy before. 'Do you want something?'

[6]

Anamorphosis

A N hour later, Otto Luger released Mariah. His fob
watch had jangled in his pocket to remind him it was time
to sleep again, and Mariah was despatched with a quick grunt
and told to make his way to see his master, Bizmillah the Great.
In his hand Mariah clutched a guide to the Prince Regent, a
fine brochure etched in silver and giving him a plan to every
floor. It was like an exquisite little book, marked in several different colours, showing him where he was allowed to go and
what places were just for guests. Luger had warned him severe-
ly about breaking the purple code, which was the colour of the
rooms for guests only. 'Instantly,' Luger had said as he
twitched his nose to hold the monocular in his eye, 'instantly
you will be thrown from the building with your chattels behind
you if you break the purple code.'

As Mariah walked along the fine corridor which led from the
grand office to the theatre, the words rattled through his head.
He came to a pair of tall oak doors and saw hanging by the side
a small sign painted in gold lettering with the words *Theatre
Closed* . . . He flicked through the pages of the brochure, his
eyes searching for the colour purple. Near the back of the small

59

booklet he found a page with a drawing of the swimming pool and the room that contained the Galvanised Bathing Machine. He looked at the hand-painted edges of the page and saw that they were distinctly coloured in finest purple. Beside the page was a drawing of an attendant's jacket with an introductory note: *Here in the spa you will be attended by our finest staff, who can always be identified by their type of dress – gold-braided jackets edged in a purple stripe. We are always on hand for your every need . . . Try the Galvanised Bathing Machine, the only one in Europe, guaranteed to invigorate the most enervated of bodies . . .*

Mariah took in a sharp breath. He had been but one night in the Prince Regent and if Luger found out what had happened to the bathing machine, he knew he would be on the train to London with his first-class suit and a Third Class ticket and nowhere to go and no one to help him. He looked at his drab black suit with its patched elbows and double-sewn lapels. Suddenly it felt as if it belonged to someone else, who now wanted it back. It began to itch the back of his neck, rubbing against the skin like a colony of fire ants creeping around the collar. He shook himself as if to rid his spine from the cold tingle that shuddered up and down like an icicle hand.

Mariah looked up. Towering above him on a dividing wall that held the two sides of the passageway together was a gigantic portrait of a medieval prince sat on the back of a large white horse. It stared down at him, the eyes of the face following his every step. He stopped and walked backwards. The eyes followed him. Mariah took a quick step to the side; the eyes followed him again. Everywhere he walked it was as if the painting looked at him, its stare gaze burning into his head. He stopped . . . The passageway was empty. A little further away he could hear the rattle and hiss of the steam lift. Back towards Luger's office was a pair of carved oak doors that shuddered gently with the vibration of the steam generator many floors below. Mariah wondered if someone would walk this way – he thought he would wait and see if the picture followed them as it had sought after him.

There was a small alcove recessed in the oak panelling that clad the wall of the dark passageway to head height. Set on a tall wooden stand was an aspidistra in a brass pot, its long green leaves darting from the black earth like a dragon's teeth. Mariah looked to the painting, convinced that some force moved the eyes and that he was being watched. It was then that he realised that the face of the prince was that of Luger, his crooked smile staring from behind the thick black-dyed moustache.

Mariah checked the floor plan, hoping there would be no purple lining to the page or colour of any kind other than his meagre black. Tracing his hand along the corridor in the book he came to the margin – it was empty. Suddenly the oak doors rattled as if about to be thrown open.

Darting quickly, Mariah hid behind the large plant, out of sight of the picture with its prying eyes. The aspidistra shaded him from the light of the gas chandelier, which even in the brightness of the day was in full glow. It glistened and shimmered from the high ceiling as it dangled from an ornamental ceiling rose of sprites and elves wrapped in garlands of moribund ivy. The distant thud of feet upon the tiled floor echoed along the corridor. One tapped, the other clattered, as two people walked hurriedly towards him, a babble of chatter following on behind their heels.

'They can't stay here, they'll have to go on the first ship next week.' The woman's voice spoke in time with the tap, tap, tap of her high heels against the cold tile floor. 'That last one nearly got away. If I hadn't seen what he was doing, he'd have been long gone and the Peelers would have been in on us. Bizmillah's a blind old bat. You're going to have to do something about that man – what does he have on you, Otto, that you keep him on, anyway?' She crowed relentlessly as the man walked on silently at her side, his heavy feet tapping against the floor with a metal plate in the heel of each shoe scraping as he paced on. 'Let him go back to wherever he's from and entertain some old lady on a station platform in Transaldovia. You want this to be the finest show in Europe, don't you? Get rid of the guy.' The woman spoke without taking breath.

'He knows too much, Monica,' the man's voice replied as it blew out a huge breath of cigar smoke. 'It's better to keep him here where we can see him than to let him go around the world looking for those stupid cards.'

'Yeah, just like your stupid box. I remember when I believed in you, Otto. Now I just think you're a fool. Who'd believe anyone would look for a box that would turn anything it touches to gold? Tell that to the girls in the Bronx and they'd have you in Mister Putnam's mental institution.'

'It's not just any old box, Monica, it's the Midas Box, and it really exists . . .'

'Then show me – let me see it for myself and then I'll believe.' She groaned angrily as she slipped and stumbled to the floor. 'Just look at you,' she said as she glared at the painting of the prince regally staring at her from its golden frame. 'Every picture in the place has your face on it, everywhere I go there's your gawping face . . .'

'It's my hotel, I can do what I want,' he replied as he kept on walking, letting her struggle to her feet like a drunken cat skating on thin ice. 'Come on, Monica,' he drawled impatiently as he pounded on along the corridor past Mariah's hiding place. 'There's been a problem with the Galvanised Bathing Machine. Someone has been messing with the controls, *someone* who shouldn't even be down there.'

Mariah listened from behind the aspidistra, knowing that

what had gone on with Sacha had been discovered. Peering from his dark hide in the shadows, he saw Monica grumbling to herself as she clattered on behind Mister Luger, and it was as if he had discovered a new-found creature never before seen by human eyes. More cat-like than human, Monica was from an unknown world.

Clattering on a pair of the finest patent leather high heels was the thinnest, most elegant thing his eye had ever fallen upon. Every inch of her was covered and festooned in black and green ostrich feathers that reached to the floor like two giant wings trailing behind her. Her hands were embalmed in long silk gloves that glistened to her fingertips with innumerable silver and green snake-eyed jewels. The tip of every finger was pierced by a long red fingernail that jagged out through the glove like a claw. Upon her head was a crown of bright peacock feathers tied in a silver band that twisted around her fine, shimmering white hair.

Monica stopped, turned and looked at the aspidistra. For the briefest moment Mariah thought she had seen him as he stood deathly still in the blackness of the deep alcove, trying to keep himself hidden behind the oak plant stand. He dared to peek out, realising that she was preening her bright red lipstick and powdering her ghostly white cheeks in the shine of the brass plant pot. He wanted to reach out and touch her, to see if she were real or if a haunting stood before him. She puffed her face in a blizzard of white powder that fell like a gust of winter snow. From her tiny snakeskin bag she took a bottle of deep brown perfume and pressed the squirter, firing a sudden breath of dank musk on to her long, thin, translucent neck.

Mariah held his breath as the thick perfume filled the air around him and clung to his skin. Monica smiled and raised an eyebrow, as if pleased with what she saw, and turned and strutted off like a broody hen chasing the cockerel.

'Hey, wait for me,' she crowed as she sped after Mister Luger. 'I wanna be there when you sort out Bizmillah. *This* time Otto, give him what for.'

'Get in the steam elevator, Monica,' Luger replied coldly as the thundering came closer from the elevator shaft and the hissing of steam filled the passageway. 'First we sort out the sabotage and then we sort out Bizmillah. He's already agreed for you to do the Saw Trick. Hey,' he said as if he'd almost forgotten the morning, 'I found you a new kid. Kind of gawky-looking, with crazy piercing eyes and swirly curly hair, but he's a Colonial boy – not a care in the world or a relative to know if he ever went missing.' Luger laughed menacingly as he slid the door to the lift and pressed the button. There was a sudden whooshing as the steam piston sucked the elevator far below.

Mariah slumped to the floor behind the plant stand, his heart pounding in his chest from being so close to the most incredible creature he had ever seen. He closed his eyes to stop the vision from disappearing, but like any ghost it slowly faded. He tried and tried to bring back the memory of the feathers and her face but all he could see were the thin gloved hands and jewelled fingers that quickly disappeared in the mist of his remembrance.

Slowly he looked around the edge of the alcove and into the long hallway. The painting of the prince with Luger's face stared down, the eyes following Mariah's every movement as he got to his feet, his hands touching the oak panelling. He could hear the distant panting of the steam elevator as it waited patiently like a sleeping leviathan far below. Mariah stepped cautiously into the passageway and followed the way of Luger and Monica. He stopped by the lift and looked into the cavernous, black depths. Wisps of sulphurous smoke swirled in the gaslight and the sun's rays that broke in through the row of coloured glass panes running as a cornice the length of the passage.

Without thinking he pressed the button to call the elevator. A jarring of metal and a spurt of steam billowed up the shaft as the steam piston began to expand, forcing the cage higher. Mariah smiled to himself, hoping he had bought himself a fraction of time and that Mister Luger was still many floors below and not in the summoned elevator.

Quickly he rushed back to his hiding place and listened for the steam elevator to arrive. There was a clatter as the cage stopped at the floor. Mariah waited; there was no familiar sound of the gate sliding along its metal runner. He looked out; the passageway was empty. In ten paces he was at the gate. Mariah unhooked the latch and slid the gate open, forcing it back as far as it would go and then, taking the chain that hung loosely inside the cage, hooked it back. He knew that the elevator wouldn't move until the gate was shut. Luger and Monica would have to use the stairs – all three hundred and sixty-six.

Mariah then took the folded silver-edged brochure from his pocket and looked at the ground floor plan. He held it before him and turned it so that the map pointed in the way he faced. At the end of the passageway was a double door with large golden handles: the theatre . . . He looked up once more to the painting of the prince to see if the eyes were staring directly down upon him.

It was then that he saw something that he thought must be from his imagination. The horse on which Luger rode so proudly had a strange fetlock that had suddenly doubled in thickness and now resembled a long thin hand pointing back towards the aspidistra. Mariah stepped back, wondering why he had not seen this before. By anamorphosis it changed back into the front leg of the horse, just above the black hoof.

He looked to the aspidistra, wondering if it were just by some coincidence that the strange hand pointed directly towards it. Mariah looked at the plan and for the first time noticed a small golden lion painted in the margin just where the plant stood on its fine wooden stand.

Taking a step forward he looked up again, and as he moved nearer to the painting he saw the fetlock change back into a hand – it could only be seen from that angle and from no other place in the corridor. Mariah wondered if it had been seen by anyone before and why it should be there. If Mister Luger had commissioned the picture, then surely *he* would know about the hand, hidden in such a way. He ran the several paces to the huge aspidistra and turned and looked to the painting. All he could see was Luger staring down from the horse, clutching the reins as the beast rose up on its hind legs as if to leap from the ground. Around his shoulders was an ermine cloak that flowed out over the horse, blown by a winter wind. On his belt was a long fine sword with a jewelled hilt glinting brightly in the falling sun that cast deep shadows across the canvas to a distant castle set upon high cliffs.

Mariah checked the monstrous plant and stared into the brass pot. He saw red lip-paint smudged upon the mirrored surface where, unbeknown to him, Monica had kissed her own reflection. The heavy scent of her perfume clung to the aspidistra and traces of white powder tipped the leaves. It was as if she were still there, those dark, burning eyes staring at him in the darkness. He thought to himself and for a brief moment closed his eyes, hoping to remember what she was like, trying to drag back a memory of her.

He was heaved from his dreaming by the sound of the elevator bell being rung far below. It clanged harshly, growing from a faint echo to a loud buzzing that vibrated through the shaft and into the passageway. Above the cage door a small glass panel suddenly slipped from the wall and waved back and forth; on it was painted the word *Door*. The cage rattled as it tried vainly to close itself and answer the call of the bell and the frantic finger that pressed in desperation.

Mariah realised that someone wanted to call the elevator to a floor far below. He looked at the alcove one last time, his eyes trying to pierce the darkness and see if there was anything hidden in the deep recess. Nowhere could he see the lion's head that was shown in the silver book; all he could see was the plant sitting majestically on its stand and enclosed on three sides by the bright oak panelling. It was then, as the frenzied bell-pushing grew louder and more ill-tempered, that he saw a glint of silver in the shade of the pot. It glistened in the lamplight, hiding from the world under the brass vessel that sat on four clawed feet.

Mariah attempted to lift the pot, using both hands to raise it from the oak stand. But some hidden thing gripped it in place; it was as if the claws dug themselves furtively into the wood, holding fast to the secret beneath. He pressed the tip of his hand underneath, tantalisingly close, and touched the cold metal of what was hidden. With his little finger he slipped the object into view, scraping it slowly towards him and into the light.

Mariah saw before him the golden head of a grand key, engraved with the letters CCCLXVI. He looked both ways as he checked the oak doors and then the lift. He glanced up at the painting of the prince. Luger stared down at him, the eyes following his every movement. In an instant he grabbed the key and slid it into his right boot, checking to see if anything else had been placed beneath the dragon teeth of the plant. There was no reason to steal the key, he thought to himself as he turned to walk towards the theatre doors, yet he knew within himself that this was something he had to do – to show Sacha and then find the door which the key would fit.

Mariah fooled himself that Monica had left the key for him, knowing that he was in the darkness of the alcove, and that her kiss had been a present of welcome to a new friend. As he walked stealthily by the elevator he could hear Luger shouting at Monica far below, his words rising higher like his anger. Mariah unhooked the chain and the door sprang shut, almost trapping his hand as the metal gate snapped from wall to wall. The shaft rattled as the elevator was suddenly sucked into the depths in a gush of hot steam.

The Great Bizmillah

THE Prince Regent was like a fine ocean-going vessel. Every corridor was etched in gold leaf, every door was made of the finest oak and the whole building was pervaded by the gentle hum and rumble of the steam engine deep in the basement. On a full tide, when the waves lapped viciously around its foundations, the Prince Regent looked like a man-o'-war in full sail and set for sea, a brick dreadnought, billowing steam from its fine chimneys by the high towers.

Deep within its cavernous belly, and far above the line of the highest tide, was the theatre. Mariah pushed open the doors and stepped inside. It was pitch black, but for a simmering limelight shining upon the painted stage-boards that raked away into the darkness. There was not a sound, nor a person in sight. In front of the high proscenium arch were row upon row of bright red velvet seats, edged in cold iron cladding and burnished with gold. Before the stage was a deep pit that, in the shadows, he could see was filled with an array of musical instruments of every kind.

He took the liberty to sit upon the end seat on the row furthest away from the stage. As his sight grew used to the darkness, Mariah felt into his boot and plucked the key from where it snuggled next to his ankle. In the half-light he looked at the key, holding it close in case someone were to find him and he might have to hide it quickly if. He ran his fingers along the warmed edge and felt raised lettering with his fingertips. 'What have I done?' he said, louder than a whisper. A sudden flush of guilt swept across his face. The key trembled in his hand. He thought of running back and placing the key beneath the plant stand and leaving it for whoever had placed it there. He knew he would risk being caught and he knew that whoever had hidden the key would soon discover it had vanished.

It was then that he had a sudden thought that wouldn't leave him. He looked at the sleeve of his coat and felt the wide black cuff, twice sewn and once turned. It was as if Felix spoke to him, telling him what to do – as if in some way he now repeated an action that had gone on before and had never been completed. 'Felix . . .' he said out loud as the thought came to him. 'It was Felix – but why?' Without thinking he took the key and slid it into the thin gap between the cuff and the sleeve, pushing it deep into the fabric.

All thought of returning the key quickly went from his mind. In his heart he knew that it would bring him misfortune, and yet its possession suddenly became utterly important and deeply exciting.

He smiled to himself and patted his jacket, knowing the key was in a safe place. Mariah somehow knew that the coat had been used before for this very purpose and that the key had rested there until its discovery by another. With every breath he took, Mariah began to have the strangest feelings. He sat gazing at the phosphorescent light shining upon the stage, casting long fingers of thin black upon the high walls. Lazily he looked up to the highest point of the theatre, where a thousand tiny sparkles dimly lit the roof like a night sky.

'He was supposed to be here an hour ago.' A voice echoed around the theatre and the sound of heavy rumbling thundered across the stage. 'How can I teach someone if they are not here?' Bizmillah asked as he pushed a long trunk from the darkness of the wings and into the limelight.

'Delayed,' said Sacha as she followed on, carrying a large saw and two square silver knives the size of double-dinner plates. 'Mister Luger could have sent him somewhere, he could be along presently,' she chirped hopefully as she scampered behind him.

'But I am to cut him in half,' Bizmillah moaned as he set up the box in the centre of the stage. 'How can I do that if he isn't here?' He looked about him as if he had forgotten something. 'Doubtless *she* will take over and this will become her trick. Would be a fine thing if *she* made a mistake and we ended up with two halves of the same boy.' He grinned menacingly as he combed his thick bushy eyebrows with his spindly fingers. 'Blood on her hands . . . and she would be away from this place for good. Can't escape the gallows when you have three hundred and sixty-five witnesses to murder in a full house,' he said to himself in a whisper, his words seeping like frost through the cold air.

'Sorry, Mister Bizmillah,' Mariah shouted as he leapt from the velvet seat and ran down the steps towards the stage. 'Mister Luger had much to say and insisted on sleeping whilst I waited . . .'

'Typical, typical,' Bizmillah moaned as the boy ran towards him. 'I don't want you to become a last-minute boy. Young Felix had that as a very bad habit and look what happened to him,' Bizmillah said boldly.

'What did happen to him?' Sacha asked as she set the saw and the knives on the boards of the stage.

Bizmillah coughed nervously, suddenly losing his willing-

71

ness to speak. 'Ran away,' he muttered. 'They all run away, never can stay the distance, never last more than a few weeks. I think *she* eats them . . .' He glared at Mariah. 'Now you are here, I can show you what you have to do. It is quite simple. I provide the *magic* and you provide your lovely bones – for me to cut in half.'

The magician signalled to Sacha to get ready as he opened the lid to the box. She ran into the wings and brought back a chair on which she quickly stood and stepped into the box. At one end was a hole cut for her neck and at the other end two smaller holes for her feet. Sacha lay down as if she had done this a thousand times before. She turned and smiled at Mariah, who by now had walked up the small flight of steps at the side of the stage. He looked anxiously on as Bizmillah closed the lid with great ceremony and locked the top with a large golden key that appeared in his hand as if it had been plucked from the air.

'Now the lock,' Bizmillah said as he turned the key and then made it vanish into thin air. 'Ladies and gentlemen,' he said, as if he were before a full house. 'I, the Great Bizmillah, bring you something so magical that you have never seen the likes of it before. Tonight I will cut in half this young girl and restore her to full health. I demand one thing – SILENCE.'

Mariah stepped back, unsure what was to come. He looked at Sacha, trying to catch her attention, as a smile played peacefully upon her face.

Bizmillah took the two knives and, one by one, thrust them into the top of the box as if to cut Sacha in two. She screamed and writhed, her face contorted, her feet kicking and shuddering and then suddenly stilling. Her head flopped to one side, eyes closed as if she were dead.

'See!' Bizmillah shouted. 'DEATH! And now to prove to you that she is truly cut in two I will saw through the box for all to see.'

He grabbed the saw and began frantically to cut the box in half. Mariah couldn't contain himself any longer. He ran to Sacha, who, hearing his footsteps across the stage opened one eye and winked at him. 'It's a trick, Mariah – I'm not dead . . .'

'Help me, boy,' Bizmillah called to him as he finished sawing the box in two. 'I need you to turn the box and all shall see that the Great Bizmillah has worked his wonderful magic yet again.'

Together they turned the two halves of the box so that all could see that Sacha had been cut in half. From one end her head flopped from the hole. From the other her feet stuck out, her shiny black shoes and white stockings for all to see.

'Now,' he shouted, 'I will bring her back to life!' With that he blew upon his hand. Sparkles of silver dust shot from his fingertips and purple and blue flames danced like fireflies across his palm, then exploded in a bright white light, engulfing the box in a shimmering cold flame.

Sacha moaned and wailed as if in great agony. She tilted back her head and looked to Mariah, then she looked to her side and saw the box with the feet next to her head.

'Are you alive?' Bizmillah asked. It was obvious to the entire world that Sacha was very much alive and in great pain. He didn't wait for her reply as she continued to moan. 'Then waggle your feet.'

Mariah gawped as her feet moved from side to side then up and down.

'See – even though she has been cut in half, by the power of the Great Bizmillah she has power over her feet.' Bizmillah took the box and spun it on its little castors; Sacha's feet were still moving, separated from her body. 'A wonder of magic, the human frame cut apart and yet through the tendrils of the imagination she has control over her body.'

Mariah stood back amazed at what he saw, unsure if this was magic or some kind of dark sorcery that held her apart. Bizmillah noticed the look of surprise upon his face and gave a gentle laugh as he pulled on the strands of his long moustache.

'NOW,' he said in the loudest voice he could gather, 'the magic of the ages will take the girl and by spiritual forces knit every piece of flesh together again.' He nodded to Mariah to turn the other box towards him, then he moved the two halves together and pressed them firmly shut. Bizmillah began to pull on a long red cloth that slipped from his sleeve and covered the two boxes with what soon became an ever-growing mound of red fabric. He fumbled beneath the cloth, his hands slipping the two flat knives from their place and throwing them to the floor. 'It is time,' he said, and he threw two white doves high into the air as they magically appeared from inside his jacket. 'The girl will be joined together.' One of the birds flew high into the air, circling around his head, whilst the other fell to the stage, twitching and unable to open its wings.

Bizmillah magicked the key into his hand, then he plunged it into the lock, released the catch and set Sacha free. She leapt to her feet, jumping to the ground and giving a majestic bow. Mariah began to applaud, enthralled by what he had seen and taken in by the power of the moment, unsure if he had been part of some miracle or magical spectacle.

'Your first lesson in magic,' Bizmillah boasted as he stepped forward and took Sacha by the hand to join her in the encore bow that she gave to the empty theatre. 'Tonight it will be your turn – do you think you can do as well as Sacha?'

'But what if my guts won't join together again or I cannot tell my feet what to do when they are set so close to my head?'

Sacha laughed. 'It's a trick – false feet that move mechanically. Look . . .'

She took his hand and lifted up the lid of the box. There before him a complex mass of wires and springs filled the bottom of the trunk. By their side was a pair of imitation feet, dressed in an identical pair of shoes and socks to those she was wearing. Next to them was a large cogwheel and coiled spring.

'Clockwork,' she said as she wound the key and pushed the feet through the two holes. 'See this – this is the catch that the Great Bizmillah presses when he brings you back to life. Watch the feet dance.' Sacha pressed the switch and the spring whirred into life, pushing the feet up and down, jangling the shoes on the end of the narrow wooden ankles. 'Who would know the difference?' she said as she reached into the box and pulled out a black pair of boots. 'Look, we have these to match your boots. All you have to do is get in the box and as you do, push the feet through the hole.'

'That's not what bothers me,' Mariah said as Bizmillah busied himself, picking up the stunned dove from the floor and trying to shake life back into it. 'What happens about being cut in half?'

Sacha smiled. 'As soon as he puts the lid on the box lift up your feet and curl them against your chest. When the knives go down you are already out of the way. When he slices through with the saw, there's nothing there to cut in half. At the end of the trick you come back to life . . . Don't forget to pull back the feet. Felix once left them sticking out of the box and everyone started to laugh.'

'Apart from me,' Bizmillah growled as he attempted to revive the dove by pressing upon its chest and breathing in its beak. 'I don't like to be made a fool of. I am the star and you the puppet – never forget that and we will be the best of friends.'

'I'll never,' Mariah replied. 'What else do I do?'

'Sweep, clean, polish and feed,' Bizmillah said as he put the dead dove back into his top pocket like a folded handkersniff. 'You are in charge of the doves –'

'And the snakes,' Sacha interrupted quickly.

'And the snakes,' echoed Bizmillah. 'You also clean everything I use. Clean but don't touch, especially the frontier pistol. It was given to me by Mister Luger and only *I* can fire it.'

'Very well,' Mariah said as he looked to Sacha, hoping she would take him away. 'What now?'

'Desperate to go from my company?' Bizmillah asked as he combed his eyebrows with his fingernails. 'Sacha can take you to the cellars and show you what to do. There is a place for everything and for everything a place. Set the traps and the drops and make ready for the performance. Tonight is your big night. There is nothing like the roar of the crowd to fill the heart with passion. It is more potent than any sorcery I know.'

Together they pushed the sawing box into the store at the side of the stage. Sacha motioned for Mariah not to say a word, placing her finger against her lips as she kept an eye on Bizmillah who paced the stage, gesturing to himself as if he addressed a large crowd. She dragged Mariah by the sleeve and down a long flight of stairs lit by faint gas lamps on every landing.

Mariah could smell the sea as they descended ever deeper. It was a strange red-brick staircase that went one way then another without a fulcrum or any visible means of it being supported. Fingers of brine hung down from the ceiling like icicles that shuddered with the rumbling of the steam engine. He wanted to speak, but every time he opened his mouth or made even the slightest sound, Sacha gestured for him to be silent. It was only when they had gone down several levels and the walls began to drip with long drops of foul salt water that she stopped and turned to him.

'We are beneath the sea,' Sacha said. There was damp green algae around her feet, cladding the step like a slippery glove. She turned to face a dark, stained door with rat-gnawed edges. 'This is where we keep all his tricks. Sometimes the tide seeps its way down there and you can hear the water flooding the passageway,' she said, pointing to a dark passageway that led off into the blackness.

'You can go down further?' Mariah asked, not believing that there would be anything below where they now stood.

'Three more floors,' she said proudly, as if it were a great achievement of hers to have such a fine building. 'Mister Luger has his laboratory down there, although I've only been once and then wasn't allowed in. You can only get there at low tide. Down the steps, along the passage then up the other side above the height of the sea. I nearly got trapped.'

'What's inside?' Mariah asked, intrigued that anyone could have a workshop so deep underground.

'It's where he makes his inventions, that's all I know.' Sacha slowly turned the key in the lock. 'This belongs to Bizmillah. No one comes here. If he wants anything he will send you. Keeps a lot of his stuff in his room, but he'll never let you see it.' She stepped inside and lit the gas lamp that sent a shaft of light spinning around the room.

There in the deep cellar was a jumble of boxes, masks, old discarded conjuring tricks and costumes of princes and pharaohs. In the corner sat a stringed doll with a shiny porcelain face that stared blindly with its bulging eyes at Mariah. It had ruby-painted cheeks that shone in the gaslight and thin purple lips that scowled at him as if he shouldn't be there. He shuddered at the look, feeling that the doll knew who he was, that beneath the fine china skin were flesh and blood, cold blood that was pumped by a lifeless heart.

Mariah followed Sacha into the room and purposefully turned his back to the doll, making no mention of it. Sacha babbled on, explaining everything in the cellar, pointing to the various items and explaining their use in *Bizmillah's Magical Extravaganza*.

For some reason Mariah couldn't concentrate on her words.

They went over and around him like fresh mist. All he could feel was the stare of the porcelain doll chilling the back of his neck and making every hair stand on end, as if a grave-walker had crossed his path. As she spoke he was convinced that he could hear someone taking laboured breaths behind him. Each one punctuated by a single wheeze and gentle cough.

It was then that a large looking-glass caught his eye. It hung majestically in its dark wooden frame on the wall before him, dangling from two rusting chains. He glanced quickly, more out of curiosity than to see his own reflection, and gasped: the doll had gone . . . He could clearly see there was nothing where the manikin had been. It was as if, when his back was turned, the plaything had got to its feet and walked from the room.

Sacha still babbled, not realising that her listener had left her world. Mariah dare not turn for fear of what he would see. He knew that the staring face of the porcelain doll had welcomed him when he walked into the cellar. It had sat scowling by the door with its red cheeks. But now as he looked in the mirror he saw that the wooden chair on which it had sat so sadly was empty – the doll *was* gone . . .

'And another thing,' Sacha said energetically as she brogued about this and that in a matter-of-fact way. 'Let me introduce you to –' She turned and swept her hand in a long gesture, then looked puzzled. 'She's gone . . . I'm sure she was here a moment ago. Did you see?'

'A porcelain doll?' asked Mariah anxiously as he edged his way slowly to the door, the whispering of the tide lapping against the stones in the faraway passage.

'I'm sure she was here . . . Sat right there as we came in.' Sacha pointed to the empty chair. 'Someone must have moved her.'

'Or she moved herself?' Mariah asked warily as he looked around the room for the doll.

'Impossible,' Sacha shouted, and she went to a tall cabinet that stood like an upturned coffin behind the door. 'Once I found her in here. Funny, the same thing happened then too. It was the first time I brought Felix into the cellar . . .'

Mariah didn't want to see what was in the upturned chest. He looked to the floor and kicked a piece of driftwood across the stone slabs. He heard Sacha pull open the two wooden doors that creaked on the salt-rusted hinges.

'Told you, must've been seeing things,' Sacha said as if she had made a great discovery. 'Meet Old Skratty – she's from Iceland. Bizmillah bought her from a wreck sale, all that was left from a four-masted ship that had gone down on Mascus Rocks. They found her bobbing in the sea, smiling . . . All the crew were dead. Some of them gnawed with small teeth.' Mariah looked up warily and greeted by the thin china smile of Old Scratty, dressed in her black velvet dress and green silk slippers, hanging limply by a long cord from a metal peg.

[8]

Similia Similibus Curantor

THE great black curtain fell across the stage as Bizmillah took his final bow. From the shadowy wings, Mariah peeped out of the thin slit that was secretly cut into the panel at the left of the stage. The immense gas chandelier that hung from the gold, domed ceiling burst suddenly into light. For the first time he could see that he had played his part to a full house.

Staggering from the theatre there came a multitude of finely dressed men and women who had looked on in awe as Mariah had been successfully cut in half and then reunited with the rest of his body. The only blemish to the evening was that Mariah had over-coiled the spring to the mechanical legs, and when it had been time for Bizmillah to flick the switch the legs had burst furiously into life. As he had asked Mariah to move his feet – the audience fully believing the poor boy had been severed in the trunk – the artificial legs had beat back and forth so quickly that the box had been violently shaken and Mariah looked as if he would be beaten about the head as his faux feet twisted and kicked beside him.

Bizmillah, being the Great Magician, had quickly seized the moment and in his finest Transoldovian accent had told the audience that the boy had fallen under the influence of his sorcery and when rejoined would feel nothing. He had even gone so far as to call a fat old man from the bemused spectators to come and inspect the boy to see if he had any visible wounds. This the man had done with immense enthusiasm, roughly squeezing Mariah around the middle and exclaiming to the world that he didn't leak. The old man obviously did . . . Mariah had clamped his nostrils as the smell of the vile mixture of cheap wine, mothballs and aged dampness had made him gulp. Once the inspection had been completed, Mariah was hailed a hero by a standing ovation which lasted for several minutes, turning his face redder and redder as the embarrassment crept from his neck into his cheeks and finally engorged his ears. Bizmillah pushed him from the stage into the darkness of the wings, throwing from his hand a dove that circled high above their heads and then exploded into a shower of silver petals which floated gently upon the crowd.

Now, Mariah watched as the theatre slowly emptied, the audience trudging to the open doors and the long passageway that would take them back into the Prince Regent.

'It's not over,' Sacha said as she pushed him gently in the back to gain his attention. 'Bizmillah leaves everything to us. There's no time to stand dreaming.'

Mariah was about to reply when he saw a man by himself in the back row of the small side balcony that overlooked the stage. He was wearing evening dress with a silver bow tie, and constantly brushed back his long hair with his hand as he looked around. It was as if he was looking for someone or something, waiting for the theatre to empty. Mariah squinted through thin narrow slit, unable to get a clear view of his face. Suddenly all became very clear as the man got to his feet, walked slowly to the edge of the balcony and looked down into the stalls, casting his eyes over every, empty seat.

81

'Isambard Black,' Mariah said as he instinctively ducked back into the darkness.

'Who?' asked Sacha as she quickly caught a white rat that scurried about her feet.

'The man from the spa pool – he was on the train from London – said he was staying here till March,' Mariah whispered as Sacha took the rat and loaded it back into the barrel of the small cannon from which it would be fired.

'Let me see.' She pushed Mariah to one side, peering through the narrow slit.

Isambard Black climbed from the balcony, past the vine-clad columns and into the stalls below. Sacha now watched eagerly as he searched every seat, checking underneath each one with his hand whilst he looked about him as if he did not want to be discovered.

'He's searching the theatre,' Sacha said, too loud for a whisper, her sharp voice echoing from the stage.

Black stopped what he was doing and hid behind a seat. For several moments he was out of sight. Slowly and carefully he peeped from his hiding place, looking around for whoever had spoken. Sacha looked on as he gawped about him, not realising that the voice had come from behind the stage. Black again began to search every seat, slowly and meticulously searching underneath each one as he made his way along the empty row.

'You watch,' she said quietly in Mariah's ear. 'I'm going to ask what he's up to . . .'

Before Mariah could reply, Sacha was gone. Slowly Mariah got to his feet. He peered out of the secret place and watched Isambard Black checking every row of seats.

The huge chandelier grew dimmer by the second, as if it were starved of the gas that gave it light. Far to the right came a sudden flash that caught his eye – a door jumped open and before anyone could notice quickly closed again. Black searched on, his head down, a sullen grimace upon his face as he slid his hand underneath each seat.

Then Mariah saw Sacha, sneaking quietly along the row getting closer and closer to Isambard Black, who was unaware of her presence.

'Lost something?' she said in a loud voice that startled Black, causing him to twist around in surprise and then fall backwards to the floor.

'I . . . I . . .' Black said, unable to think of what excuse he could make.

'I can help you look if you want,' Sacha said cheerfully, as if this sort of thing happened every day. 'What are we looking for?'

'A . . . cufflink,' he said without thinking. 'Great sentimental value, belonged to my brother, actually . . .'

Isambard Black got to his feet and looked at Sacha. She smiled benignly, then took hold of his sleeve and pulled the cuff of his shirt. 'Like this one?' she asked as she grabbed the gold link that tightly squeezed the cuff of his crisp, starched shirt.

'No, quite different,' Black said plainly as he stepped back from the girl, unsure of how she had managed to find him. 'What business is it of yours what it is like?' he said, his voice changing as he screwed up his face.

'Just want to be helpful, Mister Black,' Sacha said innocently. 'I work here and often find many things the guests leave behind. I know how painful it can be to lose something of value and not find it again.'

'Yes, painful,' Black replied as he took two paces back and looked her up and down. 'You work here, did you say?' he asked as he rummaged in his pocket. 'Well, if you work here then perhaps you would keep a lookout for what I search for?' Black held out his white-gloved hand. 'These were once a pair, but coming to the Prince Regent I am unable to find the other. I know my brother will be most disappointed should I have lost it.' Black held out a small golden skull. Two green jewelled eyes stared at her, twinkling in the light from the vast chandelier. Its jaw dangled open, set on the tiniest hinges she had ever seen.

'What is it?' Sacha asked, enthralled by its beauty.

Black saw the look on her face. 'You admire that which is well made and you have a good eye. Find the other and there will be a five-pound note, crisp and new, for you to spend on whatever you want,' he said. He took the skull and dangled it before her eyes.

Mariah saw the skull, the match for the one hidden beneath his bed. Charity had been right: it did belong to Isambard Black.

'A lot of money for the ransom of a cufflink,' Sacha said as she prodded the jewelled eyes and flicked the hinged jaw with her finger.

'A special pair, the only one of its kind, never to be made again – and more than that, they were my brother's favourites.'

'Must be special, your brother,' Sacha said as she sat on the seat and looked up at the domed ceiling.

Isambard Black said nothing. He turned and slumped into a seat four places from Sacha and looked up.

'What do you see?' he asked quietly as the dim flickering of the enormous crystal lamp danced off the golden dome.

'A night sky, angels dancing . . .' Sacha replied.

'That's a good thing,' Black said as he pulled a handkerchief from his pocket and dipped the crisp white corner into his eye. 'I came here to rest and yet I haven't yet found any peace in this place,' he said melancholically.

'My mother said that peace and contentment is found on the inside and not the out. Just going somewhere different won't change your heart,' Sacha replied.

'Then she is a wise woman,' he said curtly. He got to his feet, folded the handkerchief back into his pocket and brushed several flecks of shining dust from his coat sleeves. 'Now remember, five pounds. I am in room three-six-five.' He stopped and looked at her quizzically. 'How did you know my name?'

'You're a guest, here until March – Mister Luger told all the staff.'

'Are you sure it was Luger who told you who I was?'

'Who else?' Sacha asked with her best, innocent smile.

'Is she bothering you?' came the sharp voice of Bizmillah from the doorway behind them. 'You've work to do and talking with guests isn't part of that, Sacha.' He spoke sternly as he ambled towards them, gripping his black cane with its silver tip. 'I will see the gentleman out of the theatre. They can be very dangerous places late at night and we wouldn't want an accident to befall you, would we?' Bizmillah gestured with a quick nod for Sacha to go as he turned to escort Isambard Black to the door.

'She was only –' Black sprung to her defence.

'And now that *only* is finished and she will return to her work,' Bizmillah said slowly as he walked him to the door. 'Get Mariah to feed the doves before he turns in and load the cannon . . . and polish the swords. Then you can finish for the night,' he barked as he walked away, pulling Black by the sleeve.

Mariah slid from behind the curtain as Bizmillah and Isambard Black left the theatre. He jumped from the stage and ran across the back of every row of seats, jumping like a gazelle until he reached Sacha.

'Quickly,' he said anxiously, as if he had something of great urgency to share with her. 'We have to go back to the tower, to my room, I have something you *must* see.'

'But Bizmillah said –' Sacha protested.

'We'll come back later and do it then, he never said *when* we had to do the work. Those pigeons can't fly, they've eaten so much, and we've cleaned and cleaned all day . . . Please?'

'*Then*, we come back?' she insisted as she looked at the clock that ticked away under the balcony. 'One hour – promise?'

The steam elevator rattled to the top floor of the hotel. In the far corner from where they stood was a discarded umbrella with a white bone handle cut into the shape of a swan's head. It had been tightly wrapped; the fastening strap twisted around the shiny black material several times, and then was secured in a small knot.

'Always wanted one of those,' Mariah said as he picked the umbrella from the corner of the cage and began to pluck at the tight knot. 'My father had one just the same, took it out even when it wasn't raining.'

The elevator rattled violently as it began to slow down. Mariah gripped the brass handrail that circled the cage, and with every inch that the steam ram pushed them they jerked and shook. Then the shaft became filled with gushing steam that filled the cage, making it difficult for Mariah to see where Sacha was standing.

'I don't think it's going to make it. They turn off the steam and let the boiler cool. I was once stuck for hours.' Sacha's words faded as the elevator shuddered to a complete halt, the gas lantern dimming to a soft glow that could hardly fill the carriage. 'Open the gate, Mariah. We could have made the top floor.'

Mariah hung the umbrella over his arm and slid the heavy gate to one side. The steam elevator had stopped a floor below the tower. He looked into the long corridor, then turned to Sacha as he pointed to the door. 'Three . . . six . . . five . . .' he said quietly. 'Isambard Black.'

Mariah stepped from the lift and listened at the door. There was no sound: all was quiet. In the centre of the door was a brass plate that could be slid from one side to the other.

'Out,' Mariah said softly as he read the sign. 'It says he's out.'

The sound of footsteps clattered from the stairway by the side of the elevator.

'Hide,' Sacha murmured, as she pulled open a small cupboard door at the far side of the elevator and jumped inside. 'Quickly, inside.'

Mariah squashed himself into the cupboard that appeared to be filled with old teapots and empty bed-bottles with their cork stoppers.

'Careful,' Sacha said as he pressed her against the far wall, pulling the door until only a chink of light cast a shadow down the side of his face.

The door to the stairs opened. Bizmillah walked on to the dark landing, cane in hand, his tailcoat blustering in the furious draught that followed him like a dragon's breath. He stopped outside the room opposite the elevator and looked down the corridor, unaware that he was being watched from the maid's cupboard.

Taking a key from his pocket, he placed it in the lock and, looking over his shoulder one more time, turned the key and vanished quickly into the darkened room, closing the door and locking it behind him.

'Bizmillah went into Isambard Black's room,' Mariah said as another set of footsteps pounded the floorboards of the stairway above their heads. Sacha slithered to the floor of the cupboard to see out into the passageway. The doorway to the corridor opened again.

Isambard Black looked back and forth as he toyed with the cufflink on his left sleeve. He appeared bedraggled, as if tattered by a savage wind, his long locks forlorn, his dress and manner dishabille. In his hand he gripped his silk top hat, the top crumpled and torn, fine strands of silk hanging down. Mariah watched from their secret place as Black rubbed a streak of mud from his face. He fumbled clumsily in his pockets, dropping his hat to the floor and turning to watch it roll towards the maid's cupboard.

'If this is life . . .' Black cursed as he bowed to pick his hat from the floor. 'First my umbrella is missing and now my hat,' he said out loud, as if he wanted to be overheard. Black picked the dishevelled top hat from the floor, took the key from his pocket and opened the door to his room. A chink of amber light from the wick of the gas lamp flooded into the darkened corridor, illuminating the crowned pattern on the deep runner that went the length of the passageway, edged by dark wood. Isambard Black looked back and forth, checking the passageway, then stepped into the room. Before closing the door he peered out again, staring over his long nose like an angry corvid, making sure he had not been followed.

'He'll find Bizmillah in his room,' Sacha whispered closely in words just above a sighing breath.

'We can listen at the door,' Mariah said as he grappled with the large umbrella that he now knew belonged to Isambard Black. 'He'll have found him by now. If he thought Bizmillah was an intruder it wouldn't be so quiet. This is a gathering that has been prepared for. When I saw him on the train I knew there was somewhat more to the man.' Mariah dropped his voice quieter than a bird's breath, so that Sacha had to follow the shape of his lips to see what he said. 'In my room I have the other cufflink. He dropped it in the train – that's where I found it. And there's something else, something far different and quite amazing,' Mariah panted, knowing she could be trusted with his secret. 'It was given to me by a man on Kings Cross station, said I should keep it safe then tell him where I was and he would come for it.' Mariah paused and looked through the narrow crack in the door, listening intently for the slightest sound. He looked at Sacha in the half-light. 'And something else, something that I know Felix once touched – I found a key.'

'Key? What kind of key?' Sacha asked as she pushed open the door and got to her feet, then edged her way towards Black's room. She left him no time to reply as she pressed her ear against the door, gesturing for him to be quiet.

Inside she could hear the muffled voices of a conversation. Sacha pointed to the door of the stairs and opened her eyes wide to signal for Mariah to make clear for their escape. Bizmillah and Isambard Black talked quickly, sparring with their words in a language that Sacha could not understand.

'What are they saying?' Mariah asked as he pushed on the door to the stairwell.

There was a sudden thump inside the room and the sound of heavy footsteps making towards the door, knowing that they had been overheard.

'Quickly, man!' shouted Bizmillah. 'Unlock the door – someone is outside.'

At the same time footsteps came from the stairwell.

'Twice in one day,' Monica complained, her words tapping out faster than the heels of her stilettos. 'Fix that elevator, Otto, it's killing my feet.'

Sacha looked at Mariah, her face lined in panic as the door handle began to rattle while Black fumbled on the inside with the key.

'The elevator,' Mariah seethed through his teeth as the door to the stairwell slammed with a gusting breeze.

Sacha jumped from the door to the open gate, quickly followed by Mariah. He slammed the gate of the carriage, hoping that there would be one small gust of steam to take them up a floor.

'DOWN!' screamed Sacha, pressing the buttons one after the other, frantically banging each one as Isambard Black finally opened the door to his room.

There was a loud hiss and a sudden grunt as the steam elevator guzzled in anger at being woken from its sleep. It juddered and groaned as a feeble pressure rose in its pipes. Suddenly and without warning the carriage dropped several feet in the splitting of a second. For that brief moment they took off from the floor and floated like dandelion seeds, then were crashed into the deck of the carriage as the steam elevator stopped dead . . .

Mariah looked at Sacha as she rolled on the floor. 'Do you think we got away?' he asked. He got up, brushing the dirt from his trousers and leaving the girl to scramble to her feet.

'Open the door,' she said quickly. 'They'll have heard the lift and will be down the stairs after us – we have to get out.'

Mariah grabbed the door and slid the gate quickly to one side. This was not the hotel, it was somewhere far different. On the wall opposite was a large clock the size of a man; a long golden second hand swirled around its circular wooden face . . . backwards.

[9]

Antithetical Accumulations

IN two steps Mariah had left the elevator *and* Sacha behind him. The clicking of the huge clock and the swirl of the second hand had drawn him out and into the long, brightly lit corridor. Sacha followed quickly, picking the umbrella from the floor and slamming it into the track of the gate so that it couldn't close. She looked for the staircase that she knew should be on the right hand side of the shaft. To her surprise, all she could see was a wall covered from floor to ceiling in flock wallpaper decorated with large red swans with piercing black eyes. Several dark oak doors were spaced evenly along the far wall, each one edged with a polished brass surround. They had neither handles nor locks, just circular brass plates with a small jagged slit.

'We'll have to get from here and back to the tower,' Sacha said urgently as she pulled and pulled on his coat sleeve. Mariah was transfixed by the whooshing of the clock as its large golden hands spun round and round, one forward, the other back.

'Where are we?' Mariah asked as he stared at the small gold numerals that edged the clock face.

'I've never been on this level. I thought I'd seen the entire hotel, but . . .' She looked surprised, her eyes staring at the row of silver-spanned crystal lamps that dangled from the ceiling and lit the passage. 'They shine without gas, they're so bright . . .' Sacha covered her eyes from the brilliance of the light that shone from every crystal as if it were on fire. 'We can't stay, Mariah. If Bizmillah comes down the stairs they'll know we're here.'

Mariah didn't reply. He stood before the wooden face, watching the hands spinning faster and faster. With every tick of the seconds and every quickly passing hour, Mariah fought the urge to reach out towards the spinning blades and plunge his hand deep within the winding hole and stop the movement there and then. The hour blade flashed brightly in the dazzling light of the chandeliers, flickering bright gold glimmers against his eyes. The second hand spun like a whip, its tip bending back with the furious speed at which it went about the face.

Mariah began to slowly reach towards the flashing blades, pushing his fingertips closer and closer.

'No!' screamed Sacha. 'It'll cut you through!'

Mariah broke free from his staring at the clock, the whirring of the hands blurring his eyes. 'What?' he murmured, not knowing what he was about to do or what had been said.

'Bizmillah, Isambard Black – they'll have heard us get in the elevator, we have to get out,' Sacha said as she pulled on his sleeve again to drag him away. 'Quickly, Mariah.' She left him standing by the clock as she searched the corridor for a doorway to take them to the tower. 'It must be here somewhere . . .'

Mariah followed, his mind numbed by the whirring of the clock and the thump, thump, thump of every second that seemed to vibrate though him, shaking the muscle from the bone until he felt like his whole body was a mass of dripping marmalade.

'Find a door out of here,' Sacha cried as she ran to the end of the corridor, pushing against the doors. None of them opened.

Mariah felt drawn back to the clock as if he had to stand before it and feel the ticking beat deeply within him. The spinning hands mesmerised his mind with a fascinating wonder. 'Yeah,' he said as he stumbled off in a daze, unsure how to plant his feet upon the rich pile carpet. In the distance he could see the brass-edged frame of a window, partly covered with thick velvet curtains printed with gawping swans. 'There's nothing here, nothing,' Mariah muttered, still mesmerised by the clock as Sacha ran back and forth looking for a way out.

'There has to be. We have to get out!' Sacha squawked as she pushed past him, running to the window and pulling back the curtain.

There before them was a brass-framed window that had no glass. Where each pane should have been fixed was a black painted square wedged with fresh putty that smelt of night oil and seaweed. Sacha tapped a panel with the tips of her ghostly white fingers. It clunked with the dull thud of thick metal. Without speaking she took hold of the brass handle at the side of the frame and pulled it creakily towards her. There was a hiss of escaping air as if she had opened the lid of a jar of boiled jam. The smell of the sea was sucked up into the passageway as shreds of sea mist fell about their feet.

'It's not a window, it's a tunnel,' Sacha said as she pulled the frame towards her. 'Look!'

Mariah rubbed his eyes, trying to rid his mind of the ticking of the clock. He stared into the blackness of the hole that seemed to go on forever.

'That's a way out,' Sacha said as she panted out of breath. 'But as long as we can get out we should see what's here.'

'What about Bizmillah?' Mariah asked, suddenly remembering who they had escaped from.

'Don't you see?' she said. 'The only way to this floor is by the elevator. We are here by mistake. If the steam pump hadn't failed it would have taken us back to the theatre, but we're here. This *is* the hotel. We are between floors, a secret level, and this leads to the sea. You can smell it.'

'Then how do *they* get here?' he asked.

'They can stop the elevator or come through the tunnel. Bizmillah and Isambard Black won't know of this place. It belongs to Mister Luger.'

'How do you know that?' Mariah asked.

'It's obvious,' she said in her finest brogue. 'The sign of the swan – they're everywhere. Luger has a ring with the same crest, I saw it in the theatre when he came to watch Monica cut me in half. He sat on the front row and lit a cigar and there it was, the size of a sovereign, wedged on his fat finger.'

'Why a secret floor?' Mariah asked.

'Why not? He built the hotel, he can do what he likes. Now I know where he comes to. He often disappears for hours and no one can find him. I bet you he comes here. Look at that,' Sacha said, pointing to the door behind Mariah. 'That one has some letters upon it – do you think it says Luger in Latin? CCCLXVI.'

'I've seen them on the clock – they're not letters, they're numbers, Roman numbers . . . numerals,' Mariah said quickly. 'The key that I found, under the aspidistra in the corridor by the lift. I was walking to the theatre and there it was, by the picture of Luger on the horse. So I took it and hid it.' Mariah fumbled in the sleeve of his coat and pulled out the key. 'The letters match.'

'Try it, Mariah,' Sacha insisted as she snatched the key impatiently from his hand and looked at the numerals on the fob plate. 'We can see inside.'

'No, Sacha, it's not for us to go looking in other people's rooms,' Mariah protested.

94

'Then why did you take it? Gonna give it in, were you?'

'Maybe,' he said diffidently. 'Maybe I would.'

'Maybe you were gonna look for the room by yourself and sneak in and see what there was to take,' she said quickly as she looked for the matching lock. 'Now you've found it by chance. So come on, let's sneak a peek. That's all we'll do and then we'll put the key back where you found it, that's all.'

'I'm not going in. It's too much trouble. Luger already knows about the Galvanised Bathing Machine. I heard him talking this morning. If he finds out we've been here, then . . . then I'm finished.'

'We're already finished. Better be hanged for a sheep than a lamb, and you never know, it might just be another way out and back to the tower.' Sacha looked at the door, searching for the keyhole. 'Leave the window open so we can get out if we need to. Somewhere on this door is the lock, but I just can't see it.'

'It's not in the door, it's here,' Mariah said as he pointed to the thick brass plate that surrounded the door like a tight border. There, just above the wooden floor, was a small keyhole set into the brass. 'You do it, Sacha. I'll wait here and look out for Luger.'

For a moment Sacha looked at him and smiled. She saw the worry on his face and knew he didn't want to be there.

'Think of it as a game,' she said as she bent down and put the key in the lock. 'What can they do to us? If we get the sack then I'll find you another job, they're four a penny in these parts.'

'I keep thinking of Felix – it's as if he's still here, trying to tell us something. When I found the key I just knew that he had touched it before me. It was as if the key told me.'

'Talking keys? Whatever next, Mariah?' Sacha said as she turned the key in the lock and pushed against the door.

A strong smell of cigar smoke seeped from the room like a thick fog as the door slowly opened. It was much heavier than Sacha thought it would be. Mariah held the door open as Sacha got to her hands and knees and crawled into the dark room. He looked at the side of the door. It was then he noticed that it was made of solid metal and that a slice of wood had been stuck to it with a hessian seal running around the outer edge.

From the brightness of the hallway he could see into the far corners of the room, where long black shadows were cast by the light that flooded in. The room was cluttered with furniture. Two high-backed leather chairs were pushed together by a large brick fireplace with a smouldering glow in the hearth. Between them was a narrow table embossed with patches of red leather. In the centre of the table was a gigantic glass bowl filled with musty grey ash. Hanging from the lip of the bowl was the smouldering stub of a fat cigar wrapped in a gold band. Over the fireplace was the stuffed head of a tiger that sneered at Mariah, its tongue hanging from the side of its cavernous mouth, a bullet hole between the eyes. In the far corner was yet another door, which had brass bolts top and bottom.

Sacha edged further into the room, getting to her feet and making ready to run. She felt as if she was being watched, that someone stood very near looking at everything she did. Turning to the side she saw a tall case, a sarcophagus cut into a shape resembling a standing man. It was encrusted with gold leaf and a face was painted upon it in blue and red with deep green eyes edged in gold. A crown decorated its head, cut in lines within the wood. It stared at her with a sullen smile formed by its glowing red lips.

'Look, Mariah,' Sacha said as she stepped away from the coffin so that he could see. 'What is it?'

Mariah didn't want to step into the room. Something told him that it was forbidden, that crossing the threshold would bring tribulation upon him. He leant in cautiously, holding on to the doorframe by his fingertips. Sacha pointed to the sarcophagus. 'Looks like a coffin,' Mariah said as he leant in further. 'Some kind of tomb. I saw a drawing like that in the *London Gazette*. One had been stolen from the British Museum. They thought it was filled with gold.'

'Shall we open it? We could be rich,' Sacha said, already stepping forward and running her hand around the edge of the coffin, looking for a gap to prise open with her fingers.

'There could be someone inside.' Mariah coughed as the thought of opening the coffin made him step back into the passageway. He looked back and forth, peeking into the shaft of the tunnel and then towards the lift. 'Don't do it, Sacha, it's for dead people. Come on, let's go. We've seen enough. We can come back later.' Mariah edged backwards, away from the box, the tiger staring down at him.

'Just one look,' Sacha insisted as she pulled against the lid, trying to slide her hand into the narrow gap she had found as she squeezed her fingers deeper. 'It must open.'

'Leave it, Sacha. I read they had a curse, if you open the coffin –' he protested.

Mariah spoke too late. Sacha had slipped her hand within the sarcophagus and pulled against the lid. It held for a second and then suddenly gave way with a gentle sigh and the smell of dried figs. She slowly opened the lid as a cloud of thick dust fell about her feet and then billowed up into the air, swirling around her as if she was being engulfed in a swarm of black flies. Mariah hid behind the door, not wanting to look, the dirt-black dust spilling like sand across the polished wooden floor.

'I can see . . . I can see a . . .' Sacha said breathlessly as she stepped back from the coffin. The lid fell from its hinges and dropped heavily to the floor. It clattered against the side of the room, spilling a rack of bright military swords from the wall.

Mariah quickly looked up as the dust settled. Sacha was blackened from head to foot. She stood deathly still, hand over her mouth, staring into the darkness.

'What is it?' Mariah asked, seeing the dread in her face and not wanting or daring to look behind the door for fear of what he would see.

'FELIX!' she said slowly, her mouth stumbling to make any sound as the spit dried in her throat. 'It's . . . FELIX.' Sacha stuttered her words. 'He's . . . dead.' Through the slowly clearing dust, Sacha stared into the face of her friend. Felix stared back through open, waxen eyes, giving her a cere glare, his skin pulled tight across his lifeless face.

Sacha held back her scream, pushing her hand deep within her mouth to fight against the cry. She stepped back, pushing Mariah from the door, leaving behind the darkness and stepping into the light. Stumbling from the room, she fell to the floor and curled herself tightly like a bristling spiny hedge-pig. Her hands covered her face to keep out the light and the countenance of Felix that burnt into her mind's eye.

'No,' she sobbed, holding up her hand as if to brush away the contours of his face that hovered above her like a haunting spectre.

Mariah hesitated, then slowly peered around the door and into the room. The sarcophagus lay open, its painted lid upon the floor. Several sharp swords were scattered about, crisscrossed in superstition, a sign that some old wives would say heralded the coming of a stranger. In the glow from the hearth he could make out the features of the boy who stared blindly at him, a waxen tear cupped in his eye. Tight swaddling bandages were wrapped securely around him.

Felix had been bound from the tip of his feet to the nape of his neck. The dark brown creosote rags pulled his arms to his side so tightly that they appeared as two long lumps beneath the cold linen. His skin had faded; it had a cold translucence that shimmered in the meagre light. Mariah stepped towards the boy to see more. He gulped back a cough as the dust fell about him. It was as if the body had been covered in a fine, dry-ing lime that now glinted across the wooden floor in small desert-like mounds.

Outside, in the brightly lit corridor, Sacha sobbed, mourn-ing her friend, the sight of his deathly white skin and cold red lips filling her mind. In anger, she pulled at her hair and banged her tight fists against the floor. Inside the room, Mariah stepped closer to the body. He looked at its face, knowing something was not right.

It was then that he reached out and touched Felix's skin, and felt its soft warm smoothness. With a fingernail he scraped the skin, peeling from it a long curl of fine pale wax. He took a far-thing coin from his pocket and pulled it along Felix's bright red bottom lip. A furrow of red wax oozed against the side of the coin. Whatever Felix was, he wasn't dead.

'A waxwork, a double!' Mariah exclaimed as he wiped the wax against his finger. 'It's not Felix but a wax doll, a manikin . . .'

Sacha didn't hear. She had pushed herself against the wall, pulling the collar of her jacket around her head and pressing her face into the carpet to keep out the light.

'Sacha, it's not him,' Mariah insisted as he examined the wax manikin, pulling out a strand of neatly combed hair from its head. 'Listen to me – it's not him, it's a waxwork.'

For a moment she stopped sobbing and looked up in disbe-lief. She got to her feet and stumbled towards Mariah in the light from the corridor that flooded the dim room. 'What do you mean?' she asked as she took hold of the doorframe and slowly edged her way closer.

'It's not him,' Mariah insisted. He dragged Sacha into the room and pushed her towards the resemblance of Felix.

The manikin stared at them through its sorrowful blue glass eyes that looked as though they welled up with crystal tears. 'But it looks like Felix,' she said. She stepped warily towards the figure, reaching out with a worried hand to touch the life-less skin. 'He's warm,' she exclaimed as her fingers smoothed themselves against the soft wax. 'Who did this?'

'Luger, who else?' Mariah snapped back as he looked about the room. 'Maybe that's why Felix went missing. I don't think he's run away at all. I bet you he's still here . . . somewhere.' As he spoke he looked to the door by the hearth. It had a solid brass handle that was so polished that it reflected the whole room in an upturned universe. To one side was a key, set into a brass ring within the door. Moved by something within him, Mariah strode across the room, leaving Sacha staring at the waxwork. 'Can't have them coming in,' he said, about to turn the key, not daring to look to see what was beyond the door. Mariah stopped and listened. Coming through the dark oak panel was the gentle whirring of a steam wheel.

'What is it?' Sacha asked as she saw Mariah listening intent-ly to the sound that whispered beyond the door. 'Take a look — it could be another way out.'

Mariah slid the two brass bolts and twisted the handle at the same time as he turned the key. It gave a sudden and forceful clunk as it jumped home. He slowly and carefully opened the door to a hair's breadth and with one eye peered into the other room. There was total and absolute blackness, not a single ounce of light; all was pitch bar the narrow chink that cut into the darkness like a silver blade. He sniffed the air; the smell of the sea greeted his lips and he breathed in the salt. Far away he could hear the lapping of echoing water. In the darkness to his right he could hear the humming of the steam wheel. It was then that a barb of light pierced the pitch black. It reflected like a sharp spiked arrow from wall to wall as it jumped back and forth as if carried by an unsteady hand. The sound of scraping wet steps sludged from far away — pace by pace, footsteps were coming towards them.

Mariah closed the door, just as it was snatched from his fingers by a sudden draught that slammed it firmly shut. The sound thundered through the darkened room and along the passageway, deeper and deeper, to the depths of the lapping waters.

'They're coming!' he shouted as he turned to Sacha. 'To the tunnel!' Mariah screamed as he ran across the room, knocking from the small table a tall plaster statue that smashed to the floor.

[10]

Quare Impedit

SEVERAL lingering moments later, the shining brass handle turned slowly and the oak door was pushed open. A thin black-gloved hand with long fingers and bright red finger-nails that stuck through the dark silk curled itself slowly around the handle. A feather from a black boa dropped to the floor. It was blown lightly across the wooden tiles until it rested in the faraway corner in the strands of a large spider's web.

The door opened reluctantly, creaking on its hinges as a bur-nished, black-pointed shoe pushed against it. From the dark-ness, a thin face peered out, the bright eyes circled in thick dark kohl. Flakes of shiny pallid powder fell like minute snow flecks of silky dust as the woman scratched her chin.

'Quietly,' Luger said as he hid in the darkened room. 'They could still be there. I heard him shout as he slammed the door.'

'Why am I before you?' his companion asked in a whisper as a sharp hand pushed her forward.

'To see what I cannot,' he said curtly. 'A good thief would never hit a woman who disturbed him.'

Monica rustled like a large turkey. She walked slowly into

the room, pulling the feather dress around her shoulders and shuddering as she looked about her.

'They've gone,' she said calmly. She flopped into the chair by the fire and squeezed the shoes from her feet one by one, then wrinkled her bulbous toes. 'Who do you think they were?'

Luger didn't speak. With his hand firmly gripping the hilt of his cane he stared at the sarcophagus, the monocular spectacle quivering in his eye socket. He paced the room, back and forth, looking at the floor and then to the decorated ceiling, scoping out all that had gone on and filling the gaps with morsels from his imagination. Stopping by the sarcophagus, he bent down and picked up a handful of black dust and let it dribble through his fingers.

'We have been meddled with,' he said coldly, watching the small black particles fall to the floor. 'Could it be –?' Luger stopped speaking, not wanting to say the word.

'In the hotel – here?' Monica said nervously, sitting up for a moment then sliding back into the chair. 'That'd be too close for any kind of comfort.' She drawled dozily by the lingering flames that broke suddenly from the hearth like the breath of a sleeping dragon.

'He could be here, searching for *it* too. Maybe someone told him it was here?'

'Maybe you're dreaming,' Monica moaned as she rubbed her feet together, watching them slowly turn from pallid white as the fire warmed her bones.

'Then who did this?' Luger asked quickly as he flung the last pieces of sand at the wall, crackling it against the wood panelling. 'This didn't just happen. Someone broke into my private suite and opened the box and found the manikin. What were they looking for? The Easter bunny?'

'Did they find your magic box?' she laughed as she idly toyed with the pieces of the broken statue that were strewn across the floor beside her.

'I wouldn't leave it here. Not here – it has to be kept in the dark, locked away . . . far away,' Luger mumbled as he walked from the room and into the corridor. To his right the window that led to the tunnel was tightly shut and covered by the swan curtains that draped down to the floor. The monocle dropped from his eye as he twitched his moustache from side to side. He reached out and checked the brass handle. 'They didn't go this way,' he said as he turned and leant into the room to see Monica stretched out like a long sleeping cat over the arm of the chair. 'Comfortable?' he asked cantankerously as he looked along the passageway to the steam elevator.

Monica snored in reply, snuggled in a nest of black feathers that ruffed around her neck and blew back and forth with every deep breath.

'Do it myself . . .' Luger chuntered as he strode along the passageway to the door of the steam elevator. The hands of the clock whirred beside him, flashing and glinting in the bright lights of the corridor. In the gate to the elevator was the black umbrella, wedged in the track to stop the door from closing. 'Hey, Monica,' he shouted as he pulled the umbrella from the track and closely examined each fold of the shiny black fabric. 'He left something behind, one of them fancy rain shields, and look, it even has his initials on the handle.' Luger traced his fat finger around the neat lettering. '*P . . . A . . .*' he said slowly. 'At least we know who we are looking for, Monica. Check the guest ledger for a P.A. and if there's one in the hotel then he's the man.'

Monica stumbled from the room, shielding her eyes from the bright lights that glared down from high above her head. 'How do you know it's his?' she asked in a drawl as she juddered on the thin heels of her shoes. 'There are a thousand of those things left all over the place. He could have picked up any one of them and brought it up here. Stick it in the cellar with everything else that gets left behind.'

'I still think it's his *and* he had come for the box. I know it, Monica.' Luger pulled the dyed hair of his moustache. 'He knows it's here. Mister Grimm said the man had followed it across Europe and wouldn't stop until he got it back.'

'Then let him have it. It's just a tin box.'

'It's the Midas Box, Monica. There's nothing like it in the whole world. Soon I can sell this place and just sit and make money, time and time again. As much gold as you could ever dream of having.'

'All I want is my name in lights – gold comes well down the wish list. If you'd ever gotten on that stage you'd know that. It's not the money that does it for me. It's seeing their faces, knowing you've had them in the palm of your hand. That you cast a spell on their hearts that'll never be broken. That's magic, and not the stuff Bizmillah turns out. He's just a cheap trick, just like your umbrella.' Monica leant back against the wall and put her silk-gloved hand towards the blades of the clock. 'This is what I want to do,' she said as she pushed her hand towards the blades. 'Watch this, Otto. Do you think Bizmillah could do this?'

Monica reached out her gloved hand towards the second blade that flashed by like a steel whip. She held up her palm, waiting expectantly for the blade to crash through the silk covered skin. There was a sudden snap as the blade cut through the bone, slicing the skin straight through. Monica giggled as she waited for it to come again and again, each time slicing through the palm. Luger covered his face with his hands, not wanting to see what obliteration went on before him.

'NNNNNO!' he screamed, frozen to the floor and unable to move.

'Look, Otto – clean through and no blood.' Monica was thrilled by the spinning blade that passed through her hand again and again as if she were but a phantasm.

Luger peeked through his fingers, then dropped his hands limply and gawped at what he saw. 'How?' he asked quietly as his eyes bulged from his face, unsure if this was a dream.

'Magic.' Monica giggled as she moved her palm in and out of the speeding hands of the clock. 'You spend so much time away from me that you don't know what I can do.'

'Where did you . . .?'

'That'd be telling, Otto.' She pulled a cigar from his top pocket. 'And just to prove this was no illusion, watch this.' Monica thrust the cigar into the path of the blade, which quickly shredded the tobacco into a thousand tiny strands of Cuban Partagas as it spun around the clock face. 'See, no trick, Otto. Try putting that back together again.'

'But your hand, it never damaged your hand.' Luger dribbled as he looked at the gloved and perfectly formed hand.

'That's what I want to do – real magic. Just like your tin box. Lead to gold, cutting people in half. It's all the same to me.'

'It was a trick, a sleight of hand, something that old conjurer taught you to do between shows. No one could do that if it wasn't a trick.'

Monica grabbed his hand and thrust it towards the spinning blades that droned about the clock face. 'Then you do it, Otto. Get your hand and put it in the blade of the clock and we'll see if it's a trick.'

Caught in her glare, Luger strained to pull his hand back. 'No, Monica,' he said as he struggled to free himself from her tight grip. 'I believe you. It wasn't a trick it was . . . magic.'

'That's right, Otto,' she repeated slowly, 'it *was* magic and the sooner you get rid of that old duffer and let it be my show, the better.'

'I've told you before, Monica. He has to stay around here — there is a reason.'

'Then tell me the reason. What does he have on you that he can do what he wants?'

'He's . . .' Luger tried to think of what to say, not knowing really why Bizmillah was the highlight of the Prince Regent. 'He's . . . unusual.'

'Unusual? So is a one-legged monkey, but we don't have one of them top of the bill.'

Luger strained to think. Somewhere in his near past there was a gap in his memory, a brief moment in time that had been lifted from him and taken away. He could sense back to just before the moment started and then all was gone. He could remember everything up to that time and then it blurred and fudged as if a gate had been closed upon the memory.

'I know why,' he muttered as he walked away from her to the far end of the corridor, his mind trying to understand what he had just seen. 'But I just can't remember.'

'Well,' said Monica as she followed on behind him, balancing on her the tips of her bare feet. 'If you ask me, it could have been Bizmillah who was in here. If anyone wants your magic box, then why not a magician? It could be him, he could be the man that Mister Grimm told you about.'

Luger considered for a moment. His mind was being split in two by the thought of Bizmillah being the one who would take the Midas Box from him. 'I never thought, Monica. He could have followed me to London and then I gave him the job here. I could have brought my enemy right into my castle . . .' He held on to his moustache with both hands, biting his bottom lip and staring at her like a huge walrus with an umbrella curled over his arm. He thought to himself again, shaking his head as if to rid his mind of the thought of Bizmillah doing anything against him. 'I know the man,' he muttered. 'He has been a companion, here a long time, never a day off. He found you, brought you here . . .'

'He could just be being patient, waiting his time for you to make one slip and then he'll find your little magic box and disappear into the night.' Monica tapped him on the shoulder as he stared at the wall. 'Listen, buddy. You tell me about this box every day and yet you never let me see it. How do I know it's real?'

'Believe me, Monica, it's real and it's in the hotel.'

'Baloney, Ott. It's in your head and until I see it I'll never believe.' Monica thought for a moment as she scratched the back of his neck with a long fingernail. 'Take me to it,' she said sweetly. 'I'll close my eyes, wear a blindfold, anything, but I wanna see it.'

Luger scratched his face, then plucked a long, wiry grey hair from his nostrils as he thought of what to say. 'Sunday,' he replied quickly. 'I'll show you Sunday, but look at this.' He grovelled in his pocket. Carefully and slowly he pulled out a tiny golden moth, its thin antennae sticking from its head like two tiny golden wands, its wings outstretched as if caught in flight. 'This was the first thing I ever transformed. Found it in my office fluttering about the lamp. I picked it from the air and put it in the box. When I opened the lid it was pure gold.'

Monica snatched it from his hand, plucking the stems from its head and holding them to the light. 'Looks like you made it, Otto. You could've bought this from any trinket shop, but you want to tell me it was *transformed*?'

'It flew, was a real moth with brown wings, drawn to crisp itself within the flame. I put it in the Midas Box and it came out gold. That's not all. I have this,' he said eagerly as he dived his hand into his pocket and pulled out a rolled strand of gold, tapered at each end and wrinkled in several places. 'A worm,' he said proudly as he held it in the palm of his hand. 'A glorious worm, picked from the mud of Saint Sepulchre Street. I put it in the box as a writing creature and then with the close of the lid it was stiffened by molecules of finest gold as if it were in the grip of King Midas himself.'

'Then where is the rest of the gold? If I had such a magical box I would sweat over it every minute of every day until I had enough, if you can *ever* have enough,' Monica said as she slobbered each word.

'That is the problem,' he said as he put the worm back in his pocket. He turned to walk into the room and stared at the sarcophagus. 'There is only one minute in every day when this can be achieved. The rest of the hours it sits there, useless. I was convinced that if I could speed up the clock it would increase the time, give me a minute every hour to do the transformations, but so far nothing has worked.'

'So you get one chance every day, one measly opportunity?' Monica sniggered.

'There is always the possibility that one day I will break the secret of what makes the trans-golding of matter. Then, Monica, then . . .'

'You'll be very old and I'll be back in a walk-up in the Bronx and working for Putnam's Sanatorium,' she mocked as she pretended to sweep the floor around him. 'So what about the kid? When will he be ready for shipment?'

Luger gasped with pride as he looked at the waxen image of the boy. 'The best one yet. The finest image I have created, a new process with the finest quality wax. The dust keeps them from drying out, but there is always the chance that they will break during shipment.' He brushed dust from the neat black jacket and examined the manikin's face, his eyes clearly seeing the gouge on the lips.

'So where do they go, Otto?' Monica asked as she stepped in the black dust about her feet.

'That no one must know, not even you, not yet. My wax-works are the finest in Europe and their destination is a deeply guarded secret.' Luger brushed Felix's hair and, taking a cigar lighter from his jacket pocket, quickly rasped the flint and brushed the burning wick across the waxen lips. With his thumb he smoothed the mark from sight, then, with the edge of a sharp fingernail, pushed the lip back into shape. 'There,' he said quietly as if to himself. 'All better.'

'What about doing one for me?' Monica asked. 'I would make a pretty good model . . .'

'Beg that the day never comes. For there is more to these images than meets your eye and their cost is greater than life itself,' Luger said as he propped the lid to the sarcophagus against the wall and picked up the swords, returning them to the rack.

'It would be nice to see myself. It's not the same thing, just looking in a mirror.' She said as she looked over her shoulder as if to see herself from behind. 'I always want to get the view of someone else. What do you see when you look at me, Otto?'

'Something finer than a waxwork and yet from another world. If only you would allow me to see your hands. Always in those gloves, always covered in silk and diamonds.'

'The best way,' she said as she curled her arms around her-self as if to hide her gloved hands from view. 'Not the best thing I have. Don't like looking at them myself, never have been one for hands.' Monica shuddered as if deeply chilled, and ruf-fled in the feathers from head to toe. 'They were burnt as a child, scalded by my mother, and every time I see them I remember her face and hear her cries.'

'Then I shall find you the finest gloves in the world, inlaid with gold and silver, gossamer and beautiful, to be a beau to your face,' Luger said, and he took her by the hand, half listen-ing, his eyes searching the room as if he had mislaid something very precious. The memory of Monica's arrival came to his mind and played as a waking dream.

Luger had stood on the steps of the Prince Regent as her carriage had trundled slowly across the cobbles and picked its way through the myriad of market stalls that littered the square perched, like the hotel, on the cliff top. The driver had doffed his cap as he saw Luger on the steps in his black tailcoat and gold waistcoat. The carriage had halted abruptly at the bottom of the marble steps, its narrow oak wheels sinking into the rutted mud, and in the cold sea fret that swirled about its wheels she had stepped into his life.

As the first light of the morning crept across the hills deep to the south she picked her way through the mud and up the steps, where she held out a gloved hand. Bizmillah had grovelled in the street, pulling the heavy trunk from the back of the cab and tipping the driver with a silver coin.

'Found her, Mister Luger,' he had shouted as he dragged the case behind him. 'The greatest assistant for the greatest magician. Miss Monica will be *truly* pleasing.'

Luger had held her long, gaunt fingers as she tiptoed up the steps like a living ghost, through the revolving door and into the Prince Regent.

'Otto Luger,' Monica said, breaking the dream and bringing him back to the room. 'Eyes that were so far away and not looking at me.'

'It's not right, it's not right,' Luger said as he dropped her hand and began to pace the room, still searching for something that had been left behind. 'I have to know how they got in here . . . I need to know. Only I had the key. Only I could stop the elevator.' He looked to Monica for an answer. 'There are only two people in the whole world know of this place, you and I – who told them?'

'Whoever it was is long gone, Otto. They've just had a good

look around and messed up a few things. Why worry? Change the locks and throw away the keys. Call in Mister Grimm – maybe he can find him for you. Just look for a man who has lost his umbrella.'

'Grimm?' Luger echoed. He held his chest and rummaged in the pocket of his waistcoat, and pulled out a curled visiting card with gold edging. 'He could find him and put an end to all this, and when they are captured, they will make the finest waxen image ever . . . I'll go tonight. Mister Grimm is staying at the Three Mariners Inn – I shall meet him there and have done with this trouble once and for all.'

[11]

Grimm's Law

INSIDE the tunnel, Mariah clung to the brass handle of the faux window, hoping that Otto Luger would believe it to be seized shut and leave some other way. He had eavesdropped all that had been said, trying to make out the muffled words and piecing together, phrase by phrase, Monica's curdling and luscious accent. Sacha had gone on, deep into the dark tunnel, further and further away from him, with the promise that she would return. She had crept cat-like down the rungs of the cold iron ladder that plunged to the depths of the hotel and the water below. Then stealthily she had pulled hand over hand the three hundred treads back to Otto Luger's secret penthouse entrance, but he had not heard her return. Just two feet below him, she was unseen in the dark as she reached out and tapped his foot. Mariah looked down, hoping to see something in the crushing blackness. She tapped his foot again, pulling on his bootlace as if to tell him to follow.

Hand over hand and foot over foot he followed her down. Far below, the sound of the sea beat against cold stone steps, filling the tunnel with spouts of thick spray. For ten minutes they never spoke as together they slowly descended through the darkness. The weight of the pitch blackness pressed against Mariah, taking the breath from his lungs. He could feel his legs begin to shake and quiver as he now staggered down the cold metal rungs of the iron ladder. Flakes of thick rust cut into his hand and fell from each thinning tread, clattering against the sides of the now sea-damp walls. He stopped and touched the wall with the palm of his hand. It ran with cold dank water that dripped and dribbled through each crack and mortar line of the intricate brickwork that he now traced with his fingers. Finally Sacha stopped and stepped on to a landing. She took the Lucifers from her pocket and struck a long match that suddenly burst into a bright flame, dazzling Mariah as he grabbed the ladder.

'This way, I know how we can get to the beach,' she whispered as he struggled to wipe the bright flash from his eyes, shielding his face from the piercing light.

Mariah followed, the light from the matchstick flickering over the criss-crossed brick of the tunnel's curved roof. The floor ran like a sea stream, covered with bladderwrack and sea lettuce. The walls were coated in strands of green algae that grew from the floor like house-ivy picking its path higher and higher. Sacha struck another match and held it in her cupped hand, the shadow of her fingers glimmering against the walls. They walked on, Mariah slipping on the wet stone as he tried to pick his way by stepping from one sand isle to another. With each step the black dark followed on behind, and what had been given the warming hand of light for the briefest of moments was plunged back into night. Sacha walked on as Mariah struggled to keep pace. She hopped back and forth, sure-footed on the small mounds of sand that littered the tunnel floor like tiny islands.

'Nearly there,' she said as she lit another match, the hiss of the fading Lucifer fizzing in a pool of water at her feet. 'I was here once before, got lost down here with Felix. Never thought it would lead to the ladder. I got this far and turned back.' Sacha pointed to a large gouge in the damp brick. 'See – Felix scratched his initial into the wall. Just along here and then we will be out of this place.'

Mariah didn't reply. He kept his gaze fixed to the ground as he tried to see his way in Sacha's shadow. Every now and then he would look behind, prompted by the hackles that stood like an old guard dog's on the back of his neck, shivering his spine as if to say that someone or something was about to grab him in the blackness that always lurked at the edge of the light.

Sacha stopped and turned to him, lighting his face with yet another match. She smiled as she held the flame between her fingers. 'Did they try to follow?' she asked as the water dripped from the roof into the tunnel.

'I heard what they said,' Mariah replied quickly. 'It's a wax-work of Felix, nothing more. They think it was Bizmillah who was in the room. Luger is going to see a man called Grimm – he's staying at the Three Mariners Inn. He wants to see him tonight.'

'Then we haven't long,' Sacha said as she turned and set off quickly. 'If we follow Luger then we'll see what he's up to.'

'But Bizmillah expects us to clean the illusions,' Mariah protested.

'No, Mariah, he expects *you* to clean the illusions and me to have them ready for tomorrow.' She paused, taking in a deep breath as she filled her lungs with the cold damp air. 'Tonight I am going to find Mister Luger and see who he is going to meet. The last thing Felix said was that the answer could be found with Mister Luger. Now that we've found the secret level and the waxwork, I know that Felix was telling the truth.'

'So where is the Three Mariners?' Mariah asked as he tried to warm his hand on the match that Sacha nipped in her fingers.

'By the harbour, in a back street.' She scrunched up her nose as if it was not a place to be. 'I know it well. If we go this way we can get past Luger's workshop and on to the beach.' Sacha threw the match to the floor, momentarily plunging them into complete darkness. With one hand she struck more matches against the box as she led Mariah back and forth through narrow alleyways and long cavernous tunnels that echoed with the hiss of the steam generator and the bubble of the sea's waves. She stopped by a tall black door that looked as if it had been painted on the brick of the tunnel; next to it was a long flight of steps that went down into the murk. An oil lamp hung by the handle against the wall and flickered its scanty light. Sacha threw the match away and checked the box in the lamplight.

'Six left,' she said as she counted the Lucifers one by one. 'There's usually a lamp lit for when he comes down here to work – we'll be all right and then we'll be on the beach.'

'How do we get out?' Mariah asked as he instinctively pulled against the door of Luger's workshop.

'No,' whispered Sacha as she pulled his hand from the door and dragged him away. 'He always locks it and I would never dare go inside. You don't know what he's been doing.'

'Could be where he makes the manikins,' Mariah replied. He tried to look in through the keyhole. 'If Luger made the waxwork of Felix he could do it in there.'

Mariah fought against her wishes for him to follow. He held firmly on to the handle and, bowing his head, peered through the large empty keyhole. From his narrow gaze he could see to the far side of a large room that was lit by the flames of a glowing fire somewhere out of his sight. His eyes flicked from one thing to another, taking in what he could and allowing his imagination to lead him on. Behind the locked door was a world of pipes and ropes that seemed to go from floor to ceiling, stacked one upon another in neat, tidy rows, strapped to the wall as in the hold of a sailing ship. At the far side was an old sofa of hard brown leather, a rip gashed across its front as if it had been cut with a sabre. There, sitting snuggled in the dumpled red silk pillows, was a large doll with a pot face, rosy-red cheeks and a sombre smile. It stared at the door as if it knew it was being spied upon. It looked directly at the eye beyond the door and smiled softly at Mariah.

'Old Scratty,' Mariah mouthed. He looked to Sacha, who stamped her feet against the cold stone. 'The doll's here – what's it doing in Luger's workshop?'

'Don't be pulling my leg, boy.' Sacha hit him across the shoulder with the back of her hand. 'Scratty's locked in Bizmillah's cupboard and of that there's no doubt. I saw her myself before I closed the door, as did you.'

'She's here, Sacha, and she's laughing at us.' He looked again through the keyhole and there was Old Scratty dressed in her black velvet dress and green silk slippers. 'See for yourself.'

Sacha looked in at the porcelain doll that by now had sullenly closed one eye as if in a long and drawn-out wink to tease the girl. 'Bedad, I do believe . . .' Sacha stopped and looked away. 'Someone must have put her in there – she can't be doing it herself. With every time I see her, she looks more and more like Miss Monica. Funny thing is, she arrived on the same day Scratty did.'

Sacha spoke to herself as Mariah walked down the steps away from the door. He stood on deep wet sand that had been freshly washed by the winter tide pounding through the grille cut into the bottom of a tall wooden door. Above his head he could hear the whirring and grinding of the steam generator. It was as if the hotel sighed and coughed like a gigantic beached whale stuck upon the rocks. Coming from far away, the shrill notes of a distant piano seemed to echo through the vaults cut into the high ceiling of the tunnel. Sacha looked up as she put her hand on Mariah's shoulder.

'I can hear it,' she said, as if to reassure him that he was not on the verge of madness. 'It's from the Salon. The holes in the roof are the vents to the Steam Room where they keep the generator. If you stand near them you can hear sounds from all over the Prince Regent. Sometimes at night you can even hear the guests snoring in their rooms.'

'It's like it's alive . . . as if the building were not just bricks but a living creature,' Mariah said as he stepped towards the doorway. The Prince Regent sighed and moaned above him.

Sacha slipped the bolts to the door and pulled the latch as if she had done this a thousand times before. As they left the fading light that guarded the entrance to the cellars of the hotel, they were quickly consumed by the still, moonless night.

They walked together across the sand, surrounded by swirls of sea mist that came and went as they paced each yard. There were moments when the Prince Regent would loom above them and then as if conjured away it would disappear from view in a shawl of mist that hid it from their eyes. The sound of the harbour fleeted across the breeze just above the sound of small waves breaking across the beach at the edge of the low tide. Mariah looked back at the trail of soaked footprints they had left behind in the wet sand. He hesitated for a moment and turned to see the hotel vanish once more. Sacha didn't speak as she bent her head against the night and pulled up the collar of her smock, wrapping herself in her arms.

'We should go back,' Mariah said as she walked ahead of him.

'Not until we find out what Luger is doing at the Three Mariners.'

'What if he finds us?' Mariah asked, seeking an excuse.

'In this fog at nearly midnight?' she scoffed as she kicked a stone across the sand. 'He'll be drunk like any man and not bothered if Old Nick came to visit him.'

'But what of the Kraken? You said –'

'The Kraken won't be out tonight, the tide is too far out to sea. It can only change into a man when the water covers the drowning post in the harbour. Then it can come from the sea and take the children back for a feast.'

'Drowning post?' Mariah asked as he thought out loud.

'If you get caught thieving at Christmas, you get the chance to be tied to the drowning post. If you live for two tides on Saint Stephen's Day then they'll set you free.' Sacha picked up a piece of driftwood and threw it into the mist. 'Saw it done one year. The man lasted the first tide and when we came back in the morning the post was empty and the man gone. That's when they said the Kraken was awake.'

'Do you believe in the Kraken?' he asked, hoping she would say it was all from the imagination and nothing so terrible could ever come from the sea.

'Yes,' she said plainly. She looked about herself and gave a visible shiver as the clock from the old church chimed midnight across the town.

They walked on across the beach, coming to higher, drier sand where the sea seldom washed. It was piled against the harbour wall and led them to a row of tar-painted wooden shacks with boarded fronts and gaudy signs. Mariah read each one as they walked by, wondering what delicacies and fancies could be bought for the old penny that he rolled in his pocket. On past the huts they crossed a cobbled road that came down from the town to the harbour. It turned sharply left, deep carriage ruts cut into the stones and a fine scattering of sand covering the surface. At the end of the arcade was a bright red letterbox stuck to the side of a kipper shed. Mariah burrowed into his pocket and pulled out his crumpled card, and without saying a word he plunged it into the postbox. He closed his eyes and wished it well for its journey, hoping it would find Perfidious

Albion and bring him to the Prince Regent. Sacha had gone on ahead along the harbour side.

There, all the buildings that fronted the street were covered in nets and ropes that hung like cobwebs from the hoists as they gathered dew in the night air. Every roof was slowly becoming outlined with a ridge of silver as the first tongues of frost kissed the dark buildings.

Sacha looked back and forth. A sudden swirl of thick, icy mist rolled around her for a brief moment and she vanished from sight. Mariah chattered with the cold that ran its icy fingers across his forehead and then down his spine. Sacha appeared then disappeared; she was only an arm's length from him as the fog filled the street and then, before he had time to reach out for her, she quickly vanished in a sudden spiral. He turned again, the mist clearing and the night sky opening up above them.

He looked up from the road to a gigantic sign that spread itself across the white-painted walls of the building in front of them. Above his head a burnished board appeared to throw out all the reflected light of the night. It shone as if with eager anticipation, that it would be seen far out to sea and by every mariner looking for a port of rest.

Mariah read the words: *The Golden Kipper.*

'Captain Charity,' he said to himself as he remembered the conversation on the train, the invitation for a dinner and the biggest fish he could ever dream of eating.

'You've heard of him, then?' Sacha asked as she stood in the long alleyway that ran from the foreshore into the labyrinth of tunnel-like streets clustered against the castle hill.

'Met him on the train from London. He gave me a card and an invitation for dinner, then set me on the carriage to the Prince Regent. He was there when I met Isambard Black. I could see they hated each other from the first sight. I thought Charity was going to throw the man from the train.'

'Would be a thing he would do. I've heard a lot about this man but have never seen him. Went to fight for the Queen and left this place behind – an adventurer, my father called him.'

Mariah looked through the large plate-glass windows of the building. Inside were row upon row of polished tables, each holding a small candle and posy of fine flowers. Upon the front door was a garland of holly leaves and mistletoe, gorged with red and white berries. From it hung a small golden fish and a man made of wire and a spurting whale. He took them in his fingers and traced his hand around each shape, looking at Sacha in the hope that she would explain each one to him.

'It's Jonah,' she whispered. 'Wouldn't do what he was told so got eaten up and taken to the place he should have been and was spit out on the beach. The fish is a prize – in its mouth was a golden coin: spend it and another would come in its place time and again. Its providence would never run out.'

'The Golden Kipper,' Mariah said, as if he had surprised himself in working out why the place had such a name.

'I could never eat here, though,' Sacha went on, ignoring what he had just said. 'Far too fine a place for a scivvy. They say the fish'll melt in your mouth.'

'I have a calling card for this place. Eat with me. I'm sure he'll let us both come. Tomorrow's Saturday – we can come here for tea.' Mariah spoke excitedly as he looked at the large bowls of exotic fruits that filled the window, tempting him to come inside. There was also a fine looking-glass with a golden frame that hung down so that you could see yourself as you looked in. He took hold of the door handle, hoping that the door would not be locked.

'Leave it, Mariah,' Sacha said softly as she pulled his arm from the door. 'It'll be fastened shut. Your man would never leave it open.'

A sudden swirl of icy mist filled the street. From the harbour could be heard the bumping of the wooden fishing boats that were crammed together on the slack tide. Mariah looked up and shuddered, for in that quick second he saw the outline of someone standing behind him in the mist. Long strands of dank wet hair were matted across his face and through this mass a pair of bright red eyes stared at his reflection.

'Seen a ghost?' Sacha asked as she saw the look of fear on Mariah's face.

'In the mirror,' he mumbled, not daring to turn around or make a sound above a whisper. 'It was in the mirror.'

Sacha looked and then peered out into the street. 'There's nothing there, nothing at all.'

'I saw it, Sacha. Like it had just come from the sea. It was in the fog.'

'Well,' she said slowly, 'it's gone now. Mirrors is not the place to be looking in the dead of night. They make you see things that aren't there and tell you to believe them.'

'It wasn't in my head or in my heart. It stood behind us and you never saw it?'

'Not a thing. I was looking in the mirror the same as you and never saw a thing.' Sacha stepped back towards the alleyway that was filled with the velvety black of night. 'It's this way to the Three Mariners and no other. If we stick to walking by the wall we'll not be lost. To the end, then right and along the Bolts to Tuthill and we'll be there.'

'But –' Mariah whispered, not wanting to leave the open sky of the harbour side.

'It's only darkness, Mariah. There's nothing in the night that there isn't in the day. Just because we can't see doesn't make it fearful.' Sacha scolded him for his concern as she walked into the warren of passages that went underneath the stacked houses covering the hillside.

To Mariah, there was something in what she said that sounded like his mother. He had buried the memories of her deep within the grave of his heart. She was a bare-bone recollection stripped of any true likeness, a meagre ghost of a thought of what she once was. Yet the girl's words had set his mind to a night when, as a child, gripped by a fever, his mother had cradled him in her arms and spoke love to his heart.

'*Faithfulness will be your shield, so you will not fear the terror of the night, nor the arrow of the day, nor plague that walks in the darkness. A thousand may fall at your side, but no evil shall ever come near you . . .*'

Mariah began to follow on. He slipped from shadow to shadow and then into the utter darkness of the passageway, saying to himself his mother's words again and again.

[12]

The Three Mariners

WITH his every step, the echo of the footfall sounded out against the cold damp walls of the narrow alleyway that ran from the seafront into the depths of the town. The groans and whispers of sleepers spilled from houses that were cut into the hillside and cluttered one upon the other like a stack of precarious cards. Every now and then a door had been left open, and the glow of the fire came from the room within to light the passageway. The distant figure of the girl strode ahead of him, never looking back, as if she danced from doorway to doorway. Mariah gulped his breath and tried to look ahead and behind at the same time, convinced that the red-eyed creature that he had seen in the mirror now followed him in the darkness.

He stopped by an open doorway and stared in. There, in the faint light of the fading fire, he could see the tiny front room of the cottage with its drab painted walls and tattered curtains that clung to the damp window glass. A ladder went up through a small hole in the ceiling to a room above, whilst by the fire slept a woman, wrapped in rags and clutching a small child. To her side a small black pot steamed and smoked and filled the room with the fragrance of boiling tea. As Mariah stood and watched, the boot-clad feet of another sleeping figure rolled from side to side beneath a short knitted blanket. Unseen by the sleepers, a fat brown rat sat upon its curled tail by the fire and rustled its whiskers without a care. Mariah rolled the penny in his pocket and then, stepping across the threshold, placed it silently upon the arm of a broken rocking chair.

The man snored and bellowed as he gripped tightly to the unthreading twine of his meagre blanket, unaware that he was being watched by boy and rat. Looking into the shadows, Mariah saw that far away from the fire and nestled by the long wall were a row of sleeping children, covered in old woollen coats and snuggled together to keep out the cold. By the man was a beer pot, tobacco bag and leather snuff pouch, all carefully placed upon a small oak stool that stood on a copy of the latest penny dreadful.

He thought for a moment as he stared at the beer and tobacco and then looked at the man who snored on, sucking back a slither of dribble from his stubbled cheek. Mariah picked the penny from the rocking chair and stepped further into the room. By his feet a sleeping boy scratched his milk-white bare arm. Quietly, Mariah stooped down and placed the warmed coin carefully in the boy's hand, curling up his fingers into a loose fist. He smiled as he picked his way from the cottage, knowing that he would never see the look on the lad's face and hoping that the lush wouldn't steal it from his son and drink the penny away.

'Can you do that for them all?' Sacha asked. She chided him quietly, having watched silently from the doorway. 'I can take you to a thousand houses just the same. Do you have a penny for everyone?'

Mariah shrugged his shoulders as he stepped into the street, pulling the door behind him. 'Didn't do it for that,' he muttered. Sacha followed on behind as he stepped out his pace in the dark alleyway. 'Thought of the lad waking up and finding a penny in his hand. Looks as though his father took what he wanted and they got nothing. Why do they leave the doors open for all the world to see their misery?'

'For the Kraken,' she said softly. 'They believe that if the Kraken comes it will take one of them and leave a jug of gold pieces in their place.'

'They let their children be taken for money?' he panted.

'They would let them go for less. If the Kraken were to give a quart of gin they would queue the length of the pier to give them away. Come easily, go easily, and after all they can always have another.'

'What madness possesses them?' he asked, his voice sharpened by anger.

'Life, Mariah. Cold, hard . . . and piled room on room to the castle gate. Be thankful it's them and not you and don't give it a second thought.' Sacha spoke brusquely as she trotted behind him in the shadow of a dim gas lamp on the corner.

They said no more as together they ran through the narrow streets, past the Customs House with its barred windows and narrow door, along Tuthill and into Quay Street. They saw no one and heard only the sounds of a cawing gull and their footsteps upon the broken cobbles. Sacha led him down several stone steps that trickled with the running of the open cess-stream that seeped through the alleyways to the harbour. Mariah still looked behind him, sure that somewhere far in the distance the red eyes of the Kraken searched for him. The thoughts of his heart churned inside him as he remembered the boy who clutched at the penny coin.

Soon they waited on the corner of a wide street. Mariah could hear the turning of the water as it lapped against the side of the wooden cobbles and staithes of the pier. In the black night he could make out the large frame of the warehouse that stood on the quayside. A thin rope dangled like a gallows from a thick wooden spar that stuck out from between the eaves. Between two buildings a narrow slipway came up from the water's edge; the outline of a broken-backed fishing boat was visible against the dark patchwork of crumbling brick and stone. To one side was a tall yellow-stone house, much older than any other. It had a large wooden door nailed with black square-headed bolts. By the door was a small sandstone figure of a man enclosed in a metal cage that pinned him to the wall. He held his head in his hands, clutching a miniature metal crown placed upon his carved head.

Sacha looked about her, unsure as to the way they should take. She hesitated, then gestured for Mariah to follow as the sound of a horse carriage clattered towards them. They stepped into the deep darkness of a narrow alleyway that was more like a gash in the stone-fronted building. Stinking of sewage and seawater like a deep crevasse, it led back towards the town. They looked out as the carriage turned into the street and then stopped by the alleyway that led to the Three Mariners Inn. Suddenly its door opened and Luger stepped to the ground. He looked about him as he waved to the driver with his long silver-tipped cane, thrusting it in the air like a magician's wand casting a terrible spell.

'Did you know he would be here?' Mariah whispered through a cupped hand.

'Only one way he can come – he'd never walk, scared of getting dirt on his shoes. This is the only place a carriage can turn. Thought if we made quick time we'd be here before him.' She spoke quietly as Luger disappeared into the shadows. 'He goes to the inn and all we have to do is wait and then follow on.'

'He'll see us,' Mariah said as Sacha vanished deeper into the crevasse.

'I'll take you to within a foot of the man and he'll never know you were there. It'll be as if you were but a ghost, listening to the whispering from over his shoulder.'

Quickly he lost sight of any trace of her as she vanished into the blackness of the narrow alley. He stumbled on blindly, sure he was walking on a living carpet of rats and discarded fish heads. The ground seemed to move beneath his feet, squirming around his ankles and over the top of his boots.

Suddenly a hand grabbed the cuff of his sleeve and pulled him sharply into an even darker portal cut into the side wall of the long building. Mariah gasped as he was jerked down two stone steps. He stumbled, only to be picked up before he fell as Sacha pushed him against the dank brick wall, holding him there until he regained his breath.

'Say nothing,' she said, and she struck a Lucifer that burst into light.

Mariah looked down a long flight of steps that fell away into the night, each one casting a shadow upon the next as they disappeared from view. Stacked by the wall and blocking the alley to the height of a giant man was a hoard of empty wooden beer barrels. They were pressed one upon the other and scattered about them were discarded green bottles that glinted in the match light.

'It's the cellar,' Sacha said as she stepped on to the first stone. 'Always left open, a great place to hide and an even better place to listen,' she said softly. 'From here on we cannot speak. Not a word let slip from your lips, just open your ears and take everything in.'

Mariah didn't reply as he chased her down the steps in the fading light that gave out completely as they stood before the cellar door. Sacha slipped the catch and with one hand opened the door, then stepped inside. The light of a small oil burner lit the corner of the room, and the sudden sound of raised voices filled the void that stank and billowed out yeast and stale beer.

Above their heads, many footsteps banged against the thin boards; in several places a narrow metal grate allowed the light of the inn and the spilt beer to flood into the cellar.

Everywhere was covered in drops of crypt-dew and beer froth. Each beam of the cellar roof was decked with jewelled strands of glistening cobwebs that shuddered with the footsteps above. Falling through the grate came billows of floor dust, scraped back and forth by the sweeping of a stiff bristle besom. It beat against the floor, pushing back and forth the mounds of sawdust which soaked up the dribbled beer and fell through the metal bars and into the cellar.

Sacha looked up, her face cast in the shaft of light from the grate above, flecks of wood shavings falling upon her. She edged this way and that, looking for Otto Luger as she peered into the room above, her head almost touching the oak beams. Mariah hid himself behind two stacked beer barrels and listened to the cackle of voices that in muffled tones filled the cellar as if he listened to utterances from another, unseen world. A fat spider clawed its way from wall pillar to floor post, spinning a yarned web as it let go and wafted in the rushing of air sucked down through the grate. Mariah watched as it lowered its fat body on the thinnest of silver threads and hung before his eyes like the dangling rod of a chime clock.

Sacha snapped out her hand, grasping the spider between her thumb and finger, and in an instant she crushed its frail body of all life. She smiled at Mariah as she wiped her thumb and the remains of the arachnid across his jacket. Then she looked up again, squinting through the metal bars to see if she could find Otto Luger and whoever he was going to meet.

Above, the door to the Three Mariners opened and all was suddenly still. The voices of the drunken fishermen hushed themselves and the hubbub of the barman clanking filled tankards upon the counter ceased in an instant. The familiar

129

click of Luger's steel-capped boots and the thud of his silver-tipped cane picked their way across the floor above them. It was as if they could see him taking every step as he walked slowly from the door, stopped, turned about and then made his way to the far corner of the room. Then came the scraping of the chair as it was pulled from the table and the rustle of his thick coat being slid from his shoulders and dropping to the chair back.

Slowly the noise started again, as if each man in turn recognised his new companion or some secret signal had been given that it was safe to talk in front of this strange gentleman. Sacha edged herself to the other side of the cellar and, propping herself against a dusty barrel, looked up into the room. Mariah slid to her side and peered over her shoulder. He could see Luger's polished boots and crisp, hemmed trousers. There was a man with him, hunched over the table cradling a warmed pot of beer and sucking the froth from its top as if it were ice cream.

Luger was brought a drink without asking, the barman stumbling through the inn as Sacha and Mariah traced his steps above them. They listened intently; Luger said nothing. It was as if he were waiting for his companion to finish slurping the froth from his drink so that there would be no distraction to what he had to say.

The cellar door suddenly rattled as the stiff catch stuck in the saddle. In the half-light, Sacha gestured for Mariah to hide. The latch rattled again as someone pulled at the door from the outside and then in frustration kicked the wood and banged a sharp fist against the panel.

Mariah slid quickly to the floor, pulling Sacha close to him as they squeezed themselves into the narrowest of gaps between the damp cellar wall and the stack of barrels that were piled next to them. He put his hand across her mouth and buried his face into the back of her smock to dampen the sound of his breathing. They were trapped. The door began to open.

It scoured the stone doorstep, splintering shards of wood as it was pushed and kicked free.

'Bodkins!' shouted the man as he finally managed to push the door to its full width and step into the cellar. 'One more barrel and they should be done for the night,' he said to himself, not knowing he was being spied upon. The man stooped under the low roof as he checked each keg, trying to read the fading chalk marks in the dim light. 'This'll be the one,' he said to himself as he tapped the side of a small fat firkin barrel. Quickly he picked it up like a pot-bellied pig, pulling it to his chest. 'Up ya come and off ya go. Soon be gone and they'll want some more . . .'

The man staggered under the weight of the slopping barrel, grappling to keep upright and climb the stone steps to the dark alleyway. Mariah let his hand slip from Sacha's face as he gasped for breath, beads of sweat dripping across his cheeks. He listened as the man lurched and tottered away from the cellar, leaving the door wide open. Mariah snooped from his hiding place behind the barrels and in the dim light saw the open door. Sacha looked up at him, her face cut in two by a long black shadow.

'We don't have long . . .' She got to her feet and whispered head to head. 'It's old Mathias, drinks more than he sells and he'll soon be back.'

At the table above them, Otto Luger watched as his companion finally finished supping the creamy white froth from the top of the glass. The man took a folded handkersniff from his pocket and wiped his mouth.

'More work?' he asked Luger, looking at the tiny bubbles that blistered in his beer. 'I've been waiting in this town for a week and hoping you would be coming to see me. What is it I can do for you?'

'I have had some trouble, Mister Grimm. Someone messing

with my possessions, and I want you . . . to find out who,' Luger said as he sipped the balloon goblet and sniffed the liqueur, then took a fat cigar from his pocket and lit it from the table candle.

'Just what I'm here for. Want something finding, ask Mister Grimm and Mister Grendel. The finest detectives.' The man stirred his beer with short fat nicotine-stained fingers.

'Aah, Mister Grendel . . . And where's he tonight?' Luger asked as he sipped from the glass and puffed the cigar.

'Too much . . . too much life . . .' Grimm sucked the last drips of froth from the tip of his finger and gave a long sigh. 'He has embarked on a habit that even I cannot pursue. By this time of night he is slumbering and in a world of his imaginings,' Grimm mumbled. 'Caught it from a trip to China. It is a malevolence that has pursued him like a deathly hound ever since.' Grimm spoke as if he cared not for the condition of his friend. He put the glass mug to his fat lips and gulped the beer until the last drops trickled over his chin. 'More?' he asked Luger in a voice loud enough to be heard by Mathias.

'Not a habit that will affect the way in which he works, Mister Grimm?'

'Contrary . . . Mister Grendel is helped by his dreaming linctus. It gives him notions that can only be found when liberated from the human condition. In fact, it was such a chimera that helped us track down your little box –'

'That ain't to be spoken of in such a place as this,' Luger snapped, unaware that ears in the dark cellar could hear his harsh voice. 'I paid you well for what you did and it should be kept in the past. Listen,' he said as he quickly looked back and forth around the crowd of wind-ruddied faces, 'I have had a *visitor* to my private suite. Much was left in disarray and I need you and Grendel to find out who it was, understand?'

'Investigation is our business, Mister Luger. We will attend the scene of the crime at eight in the forenoon. Leave every-thing as it is and we will soon have the scoundrel in our grasp.' Mister Grimm paused as Mathias placed yet another pot of beer before him. 'When we find the villain, what would you like to happen to him?' Grimm asked slowly.

'To disappear – without trace – as if he never existed,' Luger whispered as Grimm whisked his fingers in the froth of the beer pot.

'Very well. Then I shall wake Mister Grendel and tell him of the details. He will set about his dreaming and find the sus-pect.'

'Good,' snapped Luger as he picked up his coat and cane and stepped from the table. 'No trace . . .'

'There is *one* thing before you leave me for the night,' Grimm bleated as he stained Luger's jacket with his grubby wet fingers. 'A slight embarrassment has come upon me. In my waiting I have drank more than my wallet would allow and I was wondering . . .?'

'It'll be settled . . . and with one more for the road to keep the cold from your back and the Kraken from your neck,' Luger said quickly as he nodded to Mathias to bring more beer. 'On the Prince Regent,' he shouted as he took the cigar from his mouth and threw it to the floor, kicking it into the grate. He watched it fall between the iron bars and into the darkened cel-lar below. 'I wait eagerly for your assistance, Mister Grimm, eagerly . . .'

Mariah watched from his hiding place as the fat cigar stub fell like a smouldering comet. It landed, sparking upon the flat-tened top of a stacked barrel, and burnt in the gloom as if it were a distant hearth fire of glowing turf.

From the alleyway came the sudden sound of the crisp steps of someone approaching. They picked their way through the darkness as if they walked in the bright of day, grunting and snorting as they crunched upon the discarded fish-heads and broken glass. Mariah ducked behind the barrel, pulling his hand away from the smouldering stub that he was about to take hold of. Sacha squashed in by his side, holding her breath as she listened in the shadow. Above their heads the sound of Luger's steel-tipped horse-boots thudded across the thin wooden floor and the door to the inn slammed shut as he stepped into the street. In the stark blackness of the crevasse-like passage, the sound of the scraping got closer to the open door, lit by the paltry glow of the small lamp that shone feebly.

From his hiding place, Mariah listened intently as if his senses had been sharpened. Each and every step was crisp and quick to his ear. As the sound approached he was certain he could make out the scouring of steel against the damp brick.

'Ast ʔú . . . ast ʔú . . .' The voice chuntered and chirped as if an old maid stood in the doorway, and its muffled grumbling filled the cellar.

Quickly realising that the voice that spoke from the cellar door was not Mathias, Sacha moved closer to the side of the barrel stack, hoping to get a short glimpse of who it was that now stalked them. She peered warily from where she hid, keeping herself to the deepest darkness of the shadow and squinting out through the meagre gap between two barrels and a crate of stinking brown bottles.

'Koma methmig . . . ¢ú lykta af svínsleur . . . ' The follower squawked in a high-pitched voice like an old sea parrot.

It was then that Sacha saw the man for the first time. He stood in the half-light of the cellar, crossed with the shadows from the floor grates above and outlined in the amber lamplight. He was wrapped in a long wax coat with black leather straps across his chest. Upon his feet he wore old sea boots that dug deep into his skin as if he had grown from them without taking them from his feet. His hair was wrapped about his face and pulled tightly to one side in long thick strands. He reached out a large gnarled hand as if to catch the falling dust that shimmered down through the fragmented beams of golden lamplight. The fingers shook with a gentle tremor and Sacha could see that each was tipped with a long black nail.

The man turned his face and looked towards her, his eyes caught by the smouldering cigar that smoked briskly as it charred the beer barrel. He was stooping and bobbing his skull as if his spindly neck could not bear the weight of his bulbous head.

She held her breath, hoping not to be seen, and froze to the wall, unable to move as the two staring red eyes darted this way and that, taking in all they saw.

In three steps the man had crossed the floor, stealthily tip-toeing through the barrels and crates until he reached the smouldering stub. He plucked it from the wood and sniffed the sulphurous, smoking tip. He flinched as the embers bit at his nose, singeing the thick hair that stuck out from each nostril. The man chirped like a seabird with a fish stuck in his gullet as he carefully held the cigar to his lips and tasted its skin with his long snake-like tongue. In an instant the cigar was gone, snapped from the air in one bite. Sacha heard him moan in deep appreciation as if he had just feasted on a morsel of the finest food. Turning quickly as though he was called by an unheard voice, the man picked his way from the cellar and was gone into the night.

'Who was it?' Mariah asked as the footsteps ran into the street.

'The Kraken – it was the Kraken . . .' Sacha said shakily.

Hedonic Calculus

FROM somewhere deep in the night, as if heard through the heart, came a distant scream. It hung like a momentary crack of thunder as it echoed in and out of the dark passage-ways, along the quayside and in through the open door of the Three Mariners Inn. For a moment it brought a stilled hush that froze each voice. Then as quickly as it came, it vanished into the stillness of the night. There was no time for anyone to speak as with one intent the inn was quickly emptied of men and women, all spilling into the narrow alley to listen again in the hope that they could hear from which direction the call of deep and utter distress had come. None had to travel far; there in the small open square, bounded by four dark alleyways that led into the labyrinth of houses, was a huddled figure. It lay slumped to the ground and in the swirling mist looked as if it were but a mound of crumpled rags.

From the narrow alley Mariah and Sacha peered out of the gloom at the crowd that encircled the body like a rough-hewn fence of shabby coats and tattered trousers. A dim lamplight shone mistily upon their backs and balding heads, some draped with sea berets, others wrapped in rags to keep out the night cold. They all muttered as one as they stared at the cadaver that lay stretched out across the cobbles and marked by the lashes of death that pierced its neck and forehead.

'Get Talla,' one said, prodding the corpse with the split end of his walking stick as he rubbed the bristles of his chin. 'Need to get the copper, can't have him left here like this . . . Not right . . . Second in a month and not a mile between 'em.'

'Deal with it ourselves, can't have the law down here. Bottom End is the Bottom End and the law has no place here, never has and never will,' said Mathias sternly as he pushed his way to the front of the crowd. 'Put him in the sea – no one'll know. They'll say the rocks did that to him.'

'It's not what to *do* with him that bothers me. Been too many dead in these streets and we can't be blaming it on the Kraken, not this time.' The man prodded the body once more for any signs of life.

'I'll find the culprit,' said the small stubby man that Mariah had seen scurrying back and forth at the back of the crowd. 'I am a detective, *private* of course and from London. You can trust me not tell the police – they always get in the way and my enquiries are very . . . *different*.' Mister Grimm pushed himself to the front of the crowd, holding his top hat close to him and wrapping his arms around it to protect the soft black silk. 'Let me see . . .'

Grimm stood before the body. He carefully examined the neat broad scratches across its forehead and the three deep wounds to its neck. Its face had frozen in a strong grimace, half smiling as if in a quiet snigger of disapproval. From his coat pocket Grimm took a silver case, quickly unslipped the golden lock and felt inside the velvet bag that lay inside. From within he brought out a pair of fine gold spectacles, fitted with bright blue lenses that looked as if they had been cut from a single piece of precious stone. He carefully fitted them across the bridge of his nose and, pushing Mathias from the body, inspected the corpse.

'Don't know if we want an outsider doing this,' Mathias said suspiciously as he wiped his hands upon his apron.

'It's either I or the police. Which do you prefer?'

There was no reply as the crowd huddled closer together, those on the outside pressing in for fear that the perpetrator of this hideous crime would pick them from the edge of the herd and drag them into the night.

'He was the one with Luger, I recognise the voice,' Mariah whispered as he stepped from the alley and beckoned for Sacha to follow. 'We have to see what he's doing.'

Before she could protest, Mariah had taken her by the hand and pulled her into the street. Looking around, he saw that the fine black carriage had vanished, its thin tracks cutting through the drifting sand that had blown across the cobbles.

'Luger got away . . . at the same time as the Kraken,' Sacha said as she looked to the warehouse by the quayside.

'Just before the scream,' Mariah answered quickly, his mind racing as to what had happened in the street and what kind of creature had made its way to the cellar. 'Could be Luger,' he said thinking out loud. 'I heard a story once from Africa of a man who could turn himself into a lion and hunt people.'

'Luger – the Kraken?' Sacha asked quietly in disbelief.

They stepped further into the street and slinked closer to the crowd gathered outside the Inn. 'Could be so,' Mariah said quietly. 'Left the inn and was transformed to go hunting – that's why so many have disappeared from the Prince Regent.'

'Luger ate them?' she said sarcastically.

'And turned what was left into wax . . .'

Mariah edged through the crowd until he was close to Grimm. The narrow street chilled with a fresh breeze that blustered in off the sea; it carried with it a multitude of crystal sand that hissed as it blew across the cobbles. Grimm hunched over the bundle of rags that was the man; thin, blue, dead hands stuck out from the ample cloak in which the body was wrapped.

'We should take him inside,' Grimm said as he prodded the wound on the neck with what looked like a long red pencil. 'I need more light if I am to make a proper examination,' he chuntered as he looked up at Mariah. 'Take his wrists and drag him to the door. It's as if an animal has bitten him to death.'

'He goes nowhere,' said Mathias as he pushed the boy away and stood between him and the body. 'You're the detective. Tell us who did this and we can have done with the body. I'm not having a corpse taken to the inn. That's a place for the living, not the dead.'

'Having eaten there I could not tell the difference,' Grimm replied quietly under his breath as he adjusted his spectacles and stared at the cobbled street. 'Whoever did this had one bare foot . . . The other was booted with an old sea boot.' He looked to the floor as his spectacles followed a trail of footprints that to the naked eye were invisible. Mister Grimm stooped to the sand-covered stones and peered at a shadowy outline set against the open drain that ran the length of the alley. 'It's as if his foot were webbed, just like a large seabird's . . . A pelican or albatross. The boot is well worn, as if he had an impediment. We may not be looking . . .' He stopped short of speaking the words that his mind rapidly mulled over. Grimm pulled up the spaniel collar of his coat; he took his spectacles and placed them safely back in the velvet bag, sealing them in the case. 'Couldn't possibly be,' he murmured. 'Quite impossible.'

'I know what you're thinking, Mister Grimm,' Mathias said as softly as he could for fear of being overheard. 'Best not be said around here. There's already too much superstition and it does a man no good at all to think such things on a dark night. Black thoughts are best for bright days, and then by the sunset you've forgotten all their bitter memories . . . and you can at least sleep.' The crowd muttered behind him as if they were somehow aware of the quiet words that were being spoken. 'Best if we say nothing and we leave it be. Don't think it would be a good thing for you to look any further, Mister Grimm.' Mathias pulled back the ragged cloak that had covered the man's face. 'Beggar,' he said. 'Won't be missed and no one to mourn him.' He nodded to a man nearby, lamenting the strange death with a raised eyebrow. 'Get the cart. You know what's to be done. All for a free drink. Come inside and let me warm your hearts and give you pleasure . . .'

'Pleasure – that would be a fine thing,' murmured Grimm. 'And only to be measured by its purity, productiveness and propinquity. One thing your gin provides, Mathias *is* pleasure – pleasure that is intense, certain and of inestimable duration, and brings the greatest happiness to the greatest number.'

Sacha stepped back into the shadows as Mathias walked through the door of the inn, followed by the crowd and Mister Grimm. The body lay in the street, arms outstretched, face covered. Mariah stepped towards her as the sound of the cart-wheels came across the stones.

'Back already,' she said as the moon broke through the clouds and momentarily outshone the gas lamp. 'What will they do with him?'

'None of your concern, lass,' said a sudden voice, and a strong hand grabbed her by the arm and pulled her away from Mariah. 'Should be tucked up at that fancy hotel of yours. Saw the American drinking in the inn, dressed like a lord and half as drunk.' The man spoke in her accent. 'I'm not having my daughter spending the night out in the streets – you'll be coming home with me.'

Sacha had not seen her father standing in the shadows of the inn, nor had she known how long he had been watching as she had been stood with the crowd, trying to peek at the body. He stank of gin; his face was smudged with snuff. She tried to smile as he held on to her arm, more to steady himself than to control her future.

'We were just going back. Came with a message for Mister Luger but when we got here he had gone,' she said, thinking as fast as she could and knowing her tongue to be quicker than his soaked wits.

'So this is your fancy boy, is it, Sacha?' the man asked as he squinted at Mariah. 'This is young Felix, all the way from London with his fancy manners?'

'No, Father. Felix has gone away. This is Mariah.' She knew what she said didn't matter. He never listened, never took notice – scaled eyes and gin-blocked ears.

'All the same,' he slurred. 'Best you be walking your father home to Paradise. The old lass will be locking me out and chivvying me for drinking at the Mariners. Fancy that, have a pub meself and drink somewhere else. Like having a dog and barking yourself.'

'I said I'd be straight back. Have to get the things ready for Bizmillah.' Sacha pulled against him as he gripped her arm.

'It's a steep hill with many steps and not a moon or lamp to guide my feet. You're coming with me and not another word'll be said.' Her father spoke sternly through his teeth as he twisted her arm tightly and stared at Mariah. 'Family matter, boy. Not for you to say a word. Not if you know what's good for her.'

Two men pushing a handcart turned into the alley. Sacha looked at Mariah, trying to smile. 'I'll see the old lad home. I'll be back in the morning. The door by the steps is always open. Go now, go,' she said briskly as she waved him away. 'Back you go, Mariah. Back you go to the Prince Regent.'

'Ay, back to your soft beds and feather pillows, never to know a day's work with your lardy-da . . . Pogmahone, boy. Pogmahone,' he growled, the spit rattling his voice like the onset of a death-cough.

Sacha took her father and turned him to the night and the darkened alleyway that led to Paradise. He swayed as he walked, reaching out to the wall to steady his way. Mariah looked on, wondering what he would now do alone. He kept an eye on the men who pulled the body from the cold damp ground and tumbled it into the barrow. From its pockets jangled seven gold coins that fell to the floor and clattered across the cobbles. Quickly the men plunged upon them, leaving the crumpled beggar heaped in the cart, buried in his own coat. They scrambled to pick each one from the dirt and, seeing Mariah, tossed the first one to him as if to bribe his silence.

Mariah caught the coin with one hand as the staggering footsteps of Sacha's father faded into the distance along with his carousing. He stepped back and leant against the doorpost to the inn, a warm draught blowing against the back of his neck. The smell of cheap beer and smoke billowed from the crack in the door that sent a chink of light into the alley, cutting through the darkness like a sharp blade. He rolled the coin in his hand and in the gloom tried to read the vague inscription, worn by a million hands. The smudged face on the coin had a strong brow and flowing locks that when new would have bubbled about its shoulders. Around the edge was a cluster of marks that he couldn't understand: they were thin and dark, stretching to the outer rim of the twice-clipped coin.

Without hesitation, he slipped the coin into his pocket and looked on as the men folded the coat about the corpse and pushed the cart towards the door of the inn.

'Keep an eye on the cart, boy and another coin'll come your way,' the man said as he rubbed a golden penny against the dark bristle of his chin. He smiled at Mariah, a grin filled with blackened teeth that looked as if they had been carved from skinned potato. 'He shouldn't be any trouble. If he moves, give us a shout.'

The men pushed past Mariah and through the doors of the inn. He stood still, surrounded by the light of the gas lamp that hung above the peeling paint of the inn door. He didn't want to move from its glow, for an echoing inner thought made clear he was only safe if he kept himself in the light. For several minutes he waited for the men to return, hoping he could follow the funeral cart and walk with them through the alleyways until he could find the main street that ran from the harbour to the grand squares and fine parades of the town. All was quiet as he listened for the singing of Sacha's father as she led him to Paradise. Somehow he knew that they were already there, locked behind a strong wooden door in the light of a cheerful fire and surrounded by her family. Mariah knew she would wake as the brightness of dawn broke from the south. The sun would rise and cast long bright fingers in the dark places, filling them with amber light as she made her way to the Prince Regent through bustling streets of fishermen and herring lasses. There would be no dark shadows and unknown sounds of the dark night to chill her soul. All would be consumed by the normality of life that banished the darkness and night-fears.

He waited and waited, hoping that soon the funeral men would leave their drinking and return to the task of taking the stiffening body on the journey to its uncertain future. In the dark of the street he saw the open cart pushed against the wall, and it was as if his eyes compelled him to look further and peek at the features of the corpse. A momentary battle took place in his mind as he fought against the desire to lift the old black coat and stare into the cadaver's eyes. Mariah knew that he would have to step from the protection of the light and stand alone in the darkness next to the corpse.

Alone, his mind whirring as to what to do, he tried to listen to the hushed conversation that crept stealthily through the door of the inn. He picked the occasional slurred phrase from the air: talk of the Kraken and sea creatures, murderous villains and the walking dead. Mister Grimm kept the conversation stoked like a raging open fire. He filled the short silences with grunts of concern, adding to the pot any story he could pick from his imagination and how *he* had been responsible for wondrous feats of detection. All listened intently in the presence of a great master.

Mariah relaxed in his anxiety, the fears of the night fading with the hubble-bubble of the half-gleaned, eavesdropped conversation. Grimm spoke ever louder of his toil and trouble, louder than the rest, in a fine Oxford accent. As Mariah clung to the cold stone step, the cackling chatter held a joy that broke the fear of darkness. He shrugged his shoulders, shaking from him a dark creature of fear that sat on his back, whispering in his ear. The night chilled colder as the sky opened and cleared of cloud. High above, the blackness was spiked with a million sparkles of crisp, flickering lights that shone brightly in the firmament. Steam slowly lifted from the handcart as his nocturnal companion quickly cooled in the frosting air. Mariah stepped from the lamplight to look up into the sky as a single grit-speck burst against it and sped like a firebrand from west to east. The shot star died before it had lived two heartbeats, yet in that time had travelled further than Mariah would ever know.

On the hilltop the clock pressed to the church tower chimed a single semi-breve. In the still night it sounded loud and bright as it chased the call of seagulls out to sea.

'One o'clock,' Mariah said out loud, knowing his companion in the cart would not offer a reply. A nagging thought persisted, whispering to him again and again. He stepped back into the light and slipped his cold fingers into the door crack, pulling it slowly open until he could see inside.

The inn was bright, filled with pipe smoke that hung in long blue strands. Grimm sat with his back to the door, a funeral man at each side as Mathias filled their glasses yet again. The old candles had been replaced and oil lamps burnt bright; a full scuttle of sea coal had been thrown on the fireback. They were set for the night as they drank the cup of conspiracy. Mariah's heart sank, knowing they would be there until first light, and he left outside guarding the corpse. He looked at the cart and then to the brightening street that was now etched in the silver moonlight.

Quickly he strode from the steps and set off from the inn, burying his hands in his deep pockets and casting a last sharp look behind. His pace slowed as he reached the corner by the alley that had led them to the cellar. Mariah tried to remember what his mother had said to him. He could see her in his mind, looking, smiling, but the words had gone. Before him were the sand tracks of the carriage that had taken Luger back to the Prince Regent. He set himself to follow, walking in the centre of the narrowing road that led by the side of the harbour. He scurried past the crumbling old sandstone houses, by stacks of twisted crab-pots and houses strewn with hanging nets. He never looked back, always keeping his eyes to the fading carriage tracks that crossed sand and cobbles, leaving a teasing glimpse of where it had travelled. His pace increased, keeping time with his deepening concern as, from close by, came the first patter of steps that kept pace with his. At first he thought they were but an echo of his own. Footfall on footfall, they sounded sharply from building to building. Then, as he again looked back, he saw him.

Following behind and keeping himself to the shadows was a man. Mariah could see the trailing wisps of his long coat dragging against the shadows and stirring swirls of sand. He could make out the hunched shape that hid its face under a thick sea cap. Mariah argued, mind against soul, that this was an innocent meeting, that they were fellow travellers making their way towards the bright streets. Just a coincidence, Mariah thought, a reveller on his way to a stacked garret, a fisherman fresh from sea. But in several paces he failed in this reverie. His wits twisted the thoughts, telling him not to stop, telling him not to welcome his new companion, telling him to run, that the follower was the Kraken.

The twisting gut and gnarled throat came quickly upon Mariah. The tip of his nose burnt as he tightened his lips to hold back the growing sense of hopelessness that magnified with each step. His mind flashed to the face of the cart-bound corpse with its slashed forehead and deep-cut neck, and with every other step Mariah turned his head to glance at his nocturnal stalker.

A swirl of seabirds took flight from their resting place on the sharp-sloped rooftops above the quayside. Mariah looked up: the sky was filled with their cawing and moaning as they circled about the moon. He turned again and the man still followed, slowing his pace as he jumped in and out of the long moon-shadows and with rat-like pace skirted the gutters.

With sudden compulsion Mariah burst into a trot, then a canter, his feet pounding against the mounds of sand blown by the wind. He cast a glance back – the man had begun to gallop, his uneven gait throwing his body from side to side, keeping twenty paces behind. Ahead, the bright sign of the Golden Kipper lit the street. Mariah thought of Jack Charity as he ran headlong towards the harbour. Again he cast a glance back, and saw that the Kraken was failing to keep up and was falling further behind. It slowed in its canter, half hobbling as the its feet scoured against the sanded cobbles. Mariah pressed on, running faster as his antagonist disappeared back into the shadow, giving up the chase.

To his right he saw a flight of long steps that led to the Customs House. He darted through the narrow yard and by the doorway of an old silversmith's shop with its boarded window and broken sign. With long strides he danced the steps three at a time, smiling to himself, knowing the street to the Prince Regent was two corners away. He sighed heavily and happily as he rubbed streaks of water from his face. He shook the fear from him and looked up at the bright night sky and hopeful moon. Then Mariah slowed to a walk, rolling the coin in his pocket, feeling the smoothness with his fingertips.

A hand grabbed him by the collar and threw him to the floor. It had fired from the darkness, hidden by the emptiness of an open doorway. Mariah rolled on the damp stone as he twisted to get to his feet. The blow came again, hitting his chest with such force that it knocked him from his feet and down a flight of steps. He looked up at the cloaked figure that hobbled towards him, its wide red eyes glowing in the shadows, its sea-wet coat dripping as it trailed across the cobbled steps.

'NO!' shouted Mariah as the creature took out a handful of golden pennies and scattered them like wedding grass upon him. It grimaced as it scraped its bootless foot across the stone. Mariah could see the webbed toes and gnarled stubs that gripped the earth like bird claws. It stood before him like an ancient mariner in a bedraggled and barnacled bilge coat that frocked to the floor. Upon each wrist was the broken band of an iron manacle that wrapped itself tightly to its faded hide, and around that a thin silver bangle etched in straw figures. From inside its coat it took a triple-bladed dagger. It grunted and coughed, spluttering seawater from its mouth as it stepped towards Mariah. Its eyes searched him out as they darted back and forth.

'More trouble, boy?' came a calm voice from behind the Kraken. The creature half turned as the staff crashed across its back. It fell towards Mariah, tripping over his feet and stumbling down the long steps. Jack Charity followed on, hitting the creature again and again as golden coins spilled from the pocket of its long coat and clinked on the steps towards the sea. 'Away with you!' he shouted as the Kraken turned and looked at him, shielding its head from yet another blow of his staff. 'Back to the sea, your ship awaits you!' Charity shouted as he held out his staff towards the sea beast.

The Kraken brushed the hair from its face and looked at Mariah and then stared at Charity, nodding to him as if it understood his raging. It turned, hobbling the final steps as it disappeared into the darkness and the labyrinth of passages that ran to the harbour.

'Not a place I would have expected to find you, Mariah Mundi . . .'

[14]

The Golden Kipper

JACK Charity gripped the long charred handle of the frying pan and was engulfed in a vast cloud of steam that sizzled from the crisping fishes that curled and crackled in the pan. It wafted like a gigantic billowing white cloud that mushroomed from the hotplate to the ceiling above, taking with it the delicious fragrance of hot sliced monkfish. Mariah sat at the end of a long table, neatly decked with upturned drinking glasses and silver cutlery, all set on the finest, whitest linen. Behind him was a tall glass window that looked out over the harbour, the crammed fishing boats bobbing back and forth, and the lighthouse that spun its beam out to the blackened sea. A large brass and wood telescope stood majestically upon an oak tripod.

From the gold-leaf chair with its velvet padding, he stared at Charity as he sweated over the large black range that filled the entire wall of the open kitchen. On the walls was a collection of curios, framed by the bright white cornice that ran around the high ceiling and the polished skirting boards that edged the shining wooden floor. He had never seen anything so meticulously clean. Whilst Charity rushed back and forth, Mariah eyed the strange creatures that hung from the walls with their dead staring faces and dull lifeless eyes. Some he recognised, others he had no idea what they were or how they had got there. He knew the bison and the moose from drawings in the *London Chronicle*. Once a Bison had visited the school, dragged from a crate by a young man with a tasselled suede jacket and pointed boots with triangular heels.

It was the large crocodile that caught his attention. The beast lay by the wall near to the door, like an upturned canoe, several feet in length, its tail purposefully curled so it could fit the room. As the fat sizzled in the pan and Charity muttered and chuntered while stirring a large vat of thick green mashed peas, Mariah eyed it enthusiastically. He began by counting every scale that jutted from its thick skin and then added to those to the number of teeth that stuck from its locked jaws. The beast was so preserved that it gave Mariah a shy grin as it stared back through large brown eyes the size of teacups. Without thinking, Mariah smiled back, captivated by the creature's apparent understanding, even though he knew the beast to be the product of a proficient taxidermist.

Jack Charity untied the pleated blue apron from around his waist and rubbed it across his brow. He picked a large oval plate from the counter and, using the apron to protect his fingers, carried it across the room towards Mariah.

'Bet you've never seen the likes of this, boy?' he asked excitedly as if it were his latest invention. 'Fish extraordinaire . . . from the deepest depths of the sea to your plate, and as fresh as the wind.'

Mariah stared at a mountainous concoction of crisp golden slices of fish, surrounded by a ring of bright green mashed peas pierced by slices of deep-fried potato. The aroma leapt across the room like thieves' fingers, gripping him by the throat and causing him to swallow deeply as his stomach raged and gulped with joyous anticipation. Gone were the thoughts of the night, the Kraken and even of Sacha. The plate filled his imagination and his half-starved gut with all the thoughts that his mind could muster, as the swirling steam from the hot fish spiralled higher and higher.

'Let's be thankful,' Charity said, and he closed his eyes momentarily and spoke silently to himself. 'Takes a life to bring this to us, never forget that.'

Mariah clutched the knife and fork in his fingertips and looked to Charity as if to be told when he could eat. The man smiled back, raising an eyebrow and winking his eye as if it were the start to a race. In the dim light of the tallow lamp Mariah ate and ate, never lifting his eyes from the dish. All that spoke of his deep contentment was the occasional grunt of glee as a morsel or fragment of delicious proportions burst upon his tongue and slithered through his body.

'Bread and tea . . .' Charity said as he returned to the table with a tray laden with a hot loaf of brown bread that shimmered on a silver plate in its own heat. 'Nearly there?' he asked Mariah, who gulped and nodded at the same time, knowing that his belly was practically full to the brim, yet wanting to eat more and more. 'Then I better craft something for a sweet tooth,' Charity said. He left the table and walked the forty feet to the open kitchen at the end of the restaurant.

Mariah guzzled on, swamping the bread in his mouth with a gluttonous swallow of hot tea. He looked at the crocodile and smiled; the creature smiled back and slowly and meaningfully winked one eye. Without pausing it did the same with the other, then, as if it too had just feasted on the same meal, closed its eyes and appeared to sleep.

A sudden sense of dread filled Mariah from head to foot. It turned his full stomach several times as he saw a short spasm of mist flit from the crocodile's nostrils and disappear into the air.

At the far end of the restaurant Captain Charity worked on, unaware that the stuffed crocodile was now alive, and not only did it have a sullen grin but winked and snorted.

'Captain Charity,' Mariah whispered, not wanting to wake the creature from its slumber. 'I need to tell you something, urgently.' He kept his gaze fixed upon the crocodile as he picked his feet from the floor and propped them as high as he could on the opposite chair.

'First we eat Pricky Pudding and then you can tell me all about the Kraken and Otto Luger,' Charity said as the sound of cracked eggs and fork-whisking echoed around the room. 'Plenty of time to sort out the world before dawn. I'll have you back at the Prince Regent before they even know you're gone.' He took a hot sponge from the oven and covered it with the golden liquid that he poured from the bowl. 'Three long minutes and then you'll be bathed in ecstasy,' Charity shouted. The crocodile opened one eye as if it followed the words from one end of the room to the other, then it stared at Mariah.

'Is the bison from the Americas?' Mariah asked feebly as he got to his feet and hopped from the chair to the long window ledge that ran across the bay of the room.

'You know well,' Charity shouted quickly as he disappeared below the counter, only to reappear seconds later clutching a silver bowl and large whisk. 'Brought it back myself many years ago. Liked it from the first time I saw it.'

'Was it hard to shoot?' Mariah asked. He was standing now on the window ledge, wondering if he could run the length of the restaurant from table to table before the crocodile could snap him from the air.

'Don't really know,' Charity replied as he tipped the Pricky Pudding on to another large plate and covered it with steaming custard. 'Bought it from a man at Dock 31 in New York, just before I sailed home. Never would want to kill something as beautiful as that. Everything you see I have picked up here and there. They are objects of art, things of fancy, keepsakes of my travels.'

'Crocodiles?' Mariah whispered, his voice tremoring, hoping the creature would stay where it lay.

'I wondered how long it would be before Cuba caught your attention.' Charity spoke with a glint of mirth in his voice as he carried the pudding from the kitchen to the table and presented it to Mariah like a great scalding prize. '*As the mournful crocodile with sorrow snares relenting passengers* . . . Didn't take her long to snare you, did it, Mariah?'

'It's real?' he asked loudly, stepping from the window as Charity beckoned him to sit back at the table.

'Real, friendly . . . and full of fish. An old girl, caught her myself.' Charity picked a leftover tail of monkfish and threw it to the beast. 'Getting too big to keep her here and yet whenever I take her for a walk, she always makes for where I found her.'

'Africa?' asked Mariah hesitantly.

'The sands outside the Prince Regent,' Charity replied. 'Found her on the beach a week after that place opened, just a tiny thing no bigger than your hand. Kept her in the cellar ever since. Floods with the tide and she's good for eating any . . . leftovers.' He laughed the words to himself. 'We were burgled once. Two villains got into the cellar by the old coal hatch. They say you could hear the screams on Castle Hill. Never did find much and for some reason the police didn't want to investigate the scene of the crime . . . Not like any crocodile I've seen before,' he went on. 'She has the legs of a lizard and only one webbed foot. More of a dragon than a crocodillo.'

Mariah didn't reply as he looked from Charity to the sleeping Cuba and back again.

'Have some Pricky Pudding,' Charity said as he doled out two large scoops of thick sponge, encrusted with wild brambles and syrup, and covered in yellow custard. 'Just the thing for an early breakfast.'

Mariah looked to the large golden clock that hung above the door. Its hands clung to the face to herald the next hour of the night. A spinning second hand flew quickly between each mark, dragging the minute closer to the hour. With infinite precision it gave out a melancholy chime that jangled and jarred about the room. Cuba snapped at the air, sprung to life by the two bitter notes. She chewed an empty breath, a year's worth of teeth snapping tightly shut as her large eyes gazed about her.

'Hates sudden moves and loud noises . . . Never could train her to ignore them. Not best to be near her at midnight.' Charity laughed as he took the spare spoon, dipped it into the centre of the pudding and filled his mouth to overflowing.

'On the steps,' Mariah asked quickly, 'the creature – what was it?'

'That, Mariah, we will never really know. A Kraken, a Croque-mitaine to frighten children . . . There are many things in this world that are beyond our understanding,' he said as he chewed the pudding and wiped a dribble of thick custard from his chin. 'One thing is certain – it wanted you.'

'What of the money?' Mariah asked as he felt the coin in his pocket.

'Some say the Kraken comes from a sunken ship filled with Icelandic gold. A Viking treasure, stolen from the grave of a king. That he carries the money to give as a gift for the death he leaves behind.' Charity got up from the table and pulled the thick red velvet curtain across the large pane of glass. 'Some things are best said in private,' he said softly as he paused and looked about the room.

'There was a man killed by the Three Mariners, a cut across the head and three wounds in his neck, just like the Kraken's knife.' Mariah thrust out his hand into the air. 'If you hadn't been there it would have . . .' He stopped and thought for a moment as for the first time he looked directly at Captain Charity. 'Why were you there?' he asked. 'How did you know?'

'Questions, questions. I have a great many for you. Here you are, hardly more than a day in the town and already being rescued from murder. What of that man on the train, what became of him? Tell me, what of Otto Luger and Bizmillah, how do they treat you?'

'You were following me, Captain,' Mariah insisted as he placed the spoon and fork neatly side by side on his plate and folded the large white napkin.

'When will you realise that it was a coincidence?' Charity snapped.

'You *were* following me.'

'So, what if I was? And a good job to boot. That thing would have had you in pieces. If you stand under the window of the Golden Kipper talking to your lady friend, then a man like me *will* be intrigued.' Charity smiled and held out his hand. 'Came along in friendship, remembered you from the train and wanted to make sure you were all right. I warned you then and I'll warn you now. There are events taking place that you will never understand and you are caught in the middle of them, Colonial boy in your five-pound suit and shiny shoes.'

Charity put his hand on Mariah's shoulder and stared him eye to eye. In that brief moment, Mariah could see every line of the man's battle-worn face. He wondered what sights that piercing blue gaze had looked upon before, what wonders, marvels and misery they had beheld. There was no awkwardness in their looking, no embarrassment in the stare or unease in the glance. The boy looked to the man and in some hidden, half-thought way, saw his own future.

'Were you really in the Sudan?' Mariah asked.

'In the rebellion, fought for two years.'

'Did you ever . . .?' Mariah asked, unable to finish his question.

'Your parents?' Charity replied, as if he knew the question before it was spoken. He went on quickly. 'I thought of them when we met on the train. Never give up hope – search for truth until you find the answer.'

'I would go there tomorrow,' Mariah said as he gritted his teeth. 'Search every inch of the land and look for them. If I could have just one bone or knuckle to say it was them, a fingernail to remove the doubt, then . . . I would have the answer.' Mariah paused as he nervously twirled a long strand of hair around his finger. 'Somehow, a scrap of paper telling me they were gone couldn't end their lives. The Professor made me tell the school they were dead, had me repeat the word again and again as if it mattered. But they're not dead, not in my mind, no matter what people say.'

Charity listened, his eyes glistening with the flames from the lamp. They reminded him of a small village with a circle of burning huts that brightly glowed against the black Sudan sky. In his mind he stood there again, the hot flames taking away the chill of the desert night. Seven black scorpions scurried from the burning brush, waltzing back and forth as they darted about his feet, down a rocky slope and into the dry riverbed.

'Sometimes things happen in war,' he said dreamily, 'things we never mean to do. Often so cruel that our minds find them hard to remember and our silence is looked upon as grim, heroic modesty, when all in all we hate ourselves for what we have done.' Charity looked at the few remains that lay scattered about the plate. 'Filled and ready for the night,' he said, and a sudden change came to his voice as if the world gripped him again. 'Time to have you back to the Prince Regent. Cuba needs a walk on the beach.'

Charity stood and clicked his fingers to snap the dragon from its sleep. Cuba lifted herself to her feet, all but one of its long legs tipped with a clawed foot. She slinked quickly in and out of the tables and sat by the door, her tail twitching excitedly as she waited for her master. Mariah wiped the remains of the day from his face and followed at a distance as Captain Charity donned a heavy overcoat and from its pocket took a long leather strap that he slipped around the beast's neck.

'The locals get frightened if she's not on the lead. Only reason they tolerate Cuba is that they believe she keeps the Kraken away. It was an old fisherman gave her the name, said it was that of an angel that kept guard over children as they slept, and she's looked after this place whilst I've been away.' Charity tugged the lead and the crocodile shuddered, rising on her back feet and scratting the door. 'Must be a rat somewhere. Loves the chase and you never hear a single squeak when she crunches them in her mouth.' He laughed, wrinkling the lines upon his face etched by many hours of warm smiles.

From the door of the Golden Kipper Mariah could see the outline of the Prince Regent drawn against the fragmenting mist by the full moon. He stepped ahead of the crocodile and its keeper as the beast pulled against the leash and sniffed the salt air.

'Still can smell a rat,' Charity said as he locked the front door and pulled up the collar of his coat. 'Mist bad again,' he whispered. 'Ever since they built the Regent, the sea's got warmer and the mists last longer.'

They crossed the cobbled street, down the slipway and on to the sand. Cuba sprang back and forth like a young puppy, snapping at the air as she gulped breaths through her leathery nostrils. Charity quickly slipped the leash from her neck and watched her sprint across the sand and into the darkness. Mariah followed on close by as he looked for the creature.

'Don't worry lad,' he said merrily. 'Old Cuba will be chasing sea hawks. You're far too big a mouthful for her tonight, even though you are stuffed with the best fish and potato.'

Mariah reached into his pocket and pulled out the calling card he had been given by Charity on the train.

'For my feast,' he said as he tried to hand it to him.

'Not needed,' Charity replied quickly. 'If I take the card I may never see you again. This way I know you'll be back for a free meal – whenever you need one, of course.' Charity held Mariah's arm as they walked on. 'Tell me one thing – Isambard Black, the man from the train, what became of him?'

Mariah paused, not knowing if in speaking he would say something out of turn. He looked to the houses and shops that littered the foreshore. Far to his right were three new bathing machines with candy-striped hoods, half-doors and ladders that led to the sea. 'Saw him a couple of times,' Mariah said, not wanting to speak too openly. 'Bizmillah keeps us busy. Him and Bizmillah keep company. Last night they were together in a room speaking and that.'

'And what of the hotel? Do you get further than the place of your work?' Charity asked quietly as he guided Mariah across the sands towards the Prince Regent.

'Seen as much as I need. Sacha knows it better than anyone. Took me all round the place. From the highest towers into the dark depths. Can be hot as hell down there. Dark and steamy and smells of fish.'

There was a cry of gulls far across the strand by the water's edge. The steady beat of Cuba's feet sounded across the soft sand, telling of her coming. Like an obedient dog she sat at Charity's feet, her long reptilian tail curled about her, its tip giving away the tiniest hint of excitement. In her mouth she gently held a fat squawking herring-gull, its bright white feathers pressed against her dark skin. She blinked constantly, growling to herself as she moaned and wailed, several drops of tear-water slowly trickling from each eye.

'Let it be, Cuba,' Charity scolded the crocodile. 'Not for you.' The crocodile obediently opened her mouth and the frightened bird leapt from the jaws of death and took flight. Mariah clapped his hands at the spectacle and Cuba danced on her back legs, swirling the sand beneath her with her long tail as the seabird circled and called out overhead.

'So warm for such a winter's night,' Mariah said innocently as he picked a piece of driftwood from the sand and threw it far away for the crocodillo to chase.

'Touch the sand and feel the warmth underfoot,' Charity said as he scooped a handful of steaming grains from the beach. 'The sea is as hot as bath water and the sand no better.' He tipped the sand into Mariah's palm. 'Do one thing for me, Mariah. Find me the reason for this and I think you will have the answer to all that you search for.' As Charity spoke, the mountainous dark shadow of the Prince Regent towered above them.

[15]

Reductio ad Absurdum

MARIAH had always thought that the longer he slept, the longer he would live. So much so that he had even contemplated the idea that if he were to sleep ad infinitum then he would be able to live forever. It was a notion that had often kept him going when the world with all its problems had grown too much. He would keep a diary listing the hours he slept and the hours waking, always hoping to have an excess balance, an abundance of time when his eyelids were firmly shut and he was oblivious to the outside world. Since the apparent death of his parents, Mariah had tried to sleep even more. In the Chiswick Colonial School he would find a place far away from the others, often by the refectory fire, to close his eyes to the world. Lunchtime and the long free hour following tea and before vespers were his favourite times to sneak away and try to sleep. More often than not he would close his eyes and just listen to the world, thinking those inner thoughts and living an interior life known only to him. Mariah imagined that by thinking hard enough he could change the course of life. In his dreams he would see his mother, talk to her, know her again. They would fill each second with unending chatter like two turtle-doves, always in the same place. They would be on a bridge by a river, staring at each other's reflection in the changing waters. There was no sun, just a radiant light that edged its way around the high grey clouds that blanketed the sky.

In every dream he had never looked at her face to face. It was only her shimmering reflection that he had seen, often broken by the wisps of breeze that blew through the tall oaks and cedars that surrounded them. He would then slip deeper away from his dream, knowing that soon he would wake, but holding fast to the hope that he would see her again.

Waking was always the same. The bitterness of rousing would snatch the glory of her life and allow the memory of shouting out that she was dead to come to his mind. Sleep was, for Mariah a great comforter. Kindling to life cheated him of all that he held dear.

As he left Charity on the beach and climbed the long steps that ran the height of the cliff by the Prince Regent he thought of sleep. He knew that somewhere ahead there would be a door, and that far behind Charity and Cuba would wait until he was out of sight and safe within the red brick walls of the hotel. Mariah gripped the cold iron railing as he dragged himself foot over foot, higher and higher, beads of sweat glistening on his forehead. A quartet of tall black gas lamps lighted the treads of the steep stone staircase. Their amber light flickered in the thinning swirls of mist that followed his every step. Set in the thick brick wall was a dark wooden door, clearly marked in bright white paint with the word *Deliveries*.

Mariah turned to the sea and looked far below. There was Charity, waiting and watching from the shore as Cuba scratched in the sand and swished her tail back and forth, relentlessly chewing the driftwood that he had thrown for her. With one hand he pulled on the brass door handle as he waved to his watcher. The door pulled open easily, squeaking on one hinge and dragging itself across the chipped brickwork of the threshold.

He looked back momentarily, a noise from the top of the steps catching his ear. There, by the tiny parade of shops, the Italian café and gentlemen's hairdresser, was the lamplighter. He looked to Mariah and nodded as he hooked the gas handle under the wick and turned off the hissing supply.

'Two-thirty,' he moaned with a gargling voice of chewed tobacco, feeling he had to explain his presence to Mariah. 'Light 'em up then snuff 'em out, bit like life really. All off at two-thirty . . . Night shift?' he asked Mariah as he fumbled in the pocket of his tattered wax coat for another wad of black masticate. 'Never see daylight, dusk to dawn, dusk to dawn,' he moaned mournfully through his long bushy beard, not caring if he got a reply but thankful he had seen another living soul.

Mariah smiled to him as he stepped inside the doorway of the Prince Regent, pulling the wooden door firmly shut, waiting as the steps of the lamplighter clattered down each stone tread. He listened as the man made his way to each lamp, leaving darkness behind as he snuffed out the quartet one by one.

Inside the Prince Regent he was greeted by the sound of the steam elevator and the smell of sulphur and goose grease. It was as if the walls of the delivery room had been coated with a thin covering of brown slime, painted upon the whitewashed walls. By the side of the door were several crates of stacked bananas, their long yellow fingers reaching out to him through the timber bands that made up every box. Each one was sealed with a brass wire that ran through the wooden spars, linking the lid firmly to the side so it could not be opened. All was as it should be for that early hour. The baker would arrive in a while to knead the dough that had been left in the small china pots to grow overnight. The breakfast chef would steal his way in, still drunk from the night before, and slowly and surely the gigantic whale would come to life. Five hundred slick waiters and two hundred housekeepers would soon rush to fulfil every desire of every patron, and Mariah would set and clean every magical trick for that night's performance.

From the delivery room he made his way quickly via the back stairs to the theatre. As he strode the passageways and dark corridors, he mused on the idea of doing his work before he went to sleep, hoping to please Sacha by having everything done. This would also give him time to understand what he had seen in the night. The thoughts of the Kraken crossed his mind again and again. It was an image of which he could not rid his wits. No matter how he tried to force his mind to think of other things, the wheedling thought came back, the image of the creature stronger and more recognisable.

As he turned into the last corridor and up the final flight of steps to the stage door, Mariah heard the clear crisp sound of scraping feet coming from far behind. He shuddered, stepping into a black shadow out of the glare of the lamp, and looked back. All was still. He dismissed the sound as a gesture of his imagination, coughing to clear his throat, half out of fear and half worrying that he might have to run at any moment. The echo went on and on. He gripped his hand into the shape of a fist, digging the nails into his palm as he clutched the gold coin tightly, never wanting to let go. 'Who's there?' he asked, hoping there would be no reply.

Mariah waited and waited for whoever was in the darkness. No one came, no sound, no scraping, just the gentle hum of the steam generator far below, rumbling on as it always did in its melancholy way.

In two steps he was through the door and into the theatre. He stood in the pitch black, knowing that to his right would be a small table with a brass candle-holder and stout candle, and by the side would be the Lucifer and striking plate. Mariah fumbled blindly, rubbing his hand across the table as he felt for the holder. Outside, the scraping footstep came again. He pushed his back against the door and felt for the bolt; taking it in his fingers he slid it home, then crouched in the blackness and listened. Again, all fell silent.

'Imagination,' he whispered to himself as he at last found the candle and the Lucifer. There was a bright spark, an all-engulfing light. Mariah gripped the lighting match in his fingers and pulled the wick ready for the flame. Gone was the darkness, banished from the room. He sighed loudly. It was as if the light cast out all his fear, as the dawn would kill the night terrors. With a shaking hand he lit the candle and allowed the match to burn out in the gutter of the holder until it had curled itself into a crinkled stalk of brittle charcoal.

Taking the candle he went to the stage. There he lit the gas lamp in the wings and pulled out the saw box, checking the mechanical feet and all of the latches. He wanted nothing to go wrong; after all, he was the one who would put his life into Bizmillah's hands. Mariah would sweep the stage, set the backdrops on their long twisted ropes and take twelve fat doves from their cages and press them into hats and boxes ready to be brought to life as if by magic.

He had almost forgotten the fear of the Kraken when the stage door rattled on its hinges. It was as if a sudden gust of cold wind had blasted against it for the briefest of moments. The curtains that hung from the high arch over the stage shook a little as a myriad of tiny specks of dust fell from the roof to the floor. They would have been invisible, had they not danced through the shaft of light that flooded the stage from the wings and cast out into the dense blackness of the auditorium. Mariah watched as one by one they slowly waltzed this way and that, sometimes touching each other like snowflakes.

The shudder came again, as if the whole of the Prince Regent had skipped the slightest grain of an inch. Mariah quickly pushed the box back to its place, stacking the other tricks in order of use upon it and covering them all with Bizmillah's purple silk cloth.

'Very late to be doing your work, young Mariah,' came the voice from the blackness of the vast auditorium.

Mariah stared out, unable to see anyone.

'Thought a Colonial boy would be tucked up in bed, in safety,' said the man sarcastically from the cover of darkness.

'Mister Bizmillah wants it to be perfect. Can't pack the pigeons in the daylight, they fly away.' As he spoke the slow realisation of who he was talking to came to mind.

'So you give away the secrets . . . Be bound by oath never to divulge the secret of the Order of Magicians. It would be on pain of death to give such vital knowledge to the uninitiated,' Isambard Black said loudly as he walked through the darkness towards the stage. 'Before you ask, like you I couldn't sleep. It is something that has avoided me recently. No matter what I do I just can't manage to let my mind go to the Land of Nod.' He coughed as he walked slowly down the dark aisle, clearing his throat as if he were about to make some majestic speech. 'I have even taken to walking the streets by the harbour. Interesting place, especially at night. You meet the most remarkable class of fellow – don't you think?'

'I wouldn't know, Mister Black. I am gainfully employed,' Mariah replied, trying to pick the shape of Isambard Black from the shadows.

'And so you are, so you are . . . I forget, you are a Colonial boy and as such would never venture away from where you are supposed to be.' Black grinned as he stepped into the shaft of dust-filled light and looked up at Mariah. 'But I'm intrigued. There is something about you that fascinates me. I was only saying to my good friend –' He stopped abruptly as if he had said too much. 'Pick a card,' he exclaimed loudly, and suddenly a deck of bright red-backed cards appeared in his hand as if from nowhere. 'Just one, that's all you have to do.'

Mariah walked slowly across the rake of the stage, bent down and picked a card from the offered deck. He looked at the card and held it close to his chest.

'King of Clubs,' Black shouted.

Mariah nodded in agreement.

'Pick another . . . '

Mariah picked yet another card and before he could even look Black shouted the suit, colour and crown of the King of Diamonds.

'One more for luck?' he asked excitedly, walking up the small wooden steps and on to the stage. 'Just take one more card and then we will end this frivolity.'

Mariah hesitated. He knew this was all a sleight of hand, that Isambard Black had memorised the cards or in some way had presented them to him so he could pick certain cards from the deck. He eyed the cards one by one, feeling his hand forced in some way by Isambard Black. Purposefully he plucked the card furthest from Isambard's fingers, at the outer edge of the fan. The sight of the Joker with its telltale cribbed edge and brightly coloured mantle flashed before him.

Mariah tried to hold in the gasp and not give away his churning heart. He had held the card before. It had looked at him with its cross-eyes and magical wand in the carriage from London. Now it stared at him again.

'The Joker,' Black said gustily. 'It keeps coming in your life, Mariah. Perhaps the cards are trying to speak to you.'

'I would prefer it spoke in the language of men. If you don't mind, Mister Black, I have to work and Bizmillah will be angry if things are not done for the morning.'

'Bizmillah, the friendly magician? He'll be well pleased, especially with *my* magic,' Black said. He twisted his hand and from inside his coat slipped a triple-bladed dagger, looking like that which had been carried by the Kraken. 'Now this is of interest, I am sure,' he said as he held it out towards the boy. 'Only three were ever made. They say they were forged in the burning volcanoes of Iceland from a piece of metal ore that has never been found again. It has the sheen of gold and the strength of steel. I am searching for them all and I will hopefully find them.'

Mariah closely scrutinised the triple blades with their jagged tiger-tooth points – gleaming, sharp metal, a whalebone handle and golden hilt. The blades matched perfectly the marks he had seen on the murdered body outside the Three Mariners.

'Do you think you'll find them?' he asked as he stepped away from Black, picking up the sweeping brush. He looked at the knife and then idly sauntered to the shelter of the wings.

'I search for many things – a pack of cards, a precious box and the daggers. I am a collector of trickery and mechanical conjuring,' Black said as the shudder came again, spilling more dust from the high ceiling and gently shimmering the stage.

Mariah turned to reply, but Isambard Black had vanished. He looked back and forth, feeling this was part of yet another trick and that Black would appear as quickly as he had vanished. 'Mister Black!' Mariah shouted as he walked across the stage and peered into the gloom of the auditorium. 'Mister Black!'

With great reluctance Mariah turned the gas tap to extinguish the lamp. The stage vanished in the gloom that covered the falling sparkles of silver dust. He held the candle-holder nervously in front of him as he slowly retraced his footsteps to the stage door. Slipping back the bolt, he looked into the passageway leading to the stairs that would take him to the tower. Far away he could hear the voice of the baker, singing as he stacked the oven with the first loaves of the morning. Mariah was cheered that he was not alone and that if he were to call out then at least there was the faint possibility that someone would hear him.

He leant into a shadow and listened warily, then snuffed out the candle and placed the holder upon the step before striding out to the stairway. Mariah couldn't look back. He grabbed the door to the stairs and rushed through, keeping his eyes to the dimly lit floor for fear of seeing anything other than carpet and stone. Taking the steps two at a time he ran as fast as he could until he reached the top landing and the door to his room. The steam elevator chugged higher, hissing and bibbing as it drew near. He pushed the door and quickly stepped into the moonlit room. The he took the chair and pressed it against the door handle so that it could not be opened from the outside.

Mariah sighed as the moon beat in at the window, having scattered the clouds and sea mist. The door to the steam elevator rattled open and then came the scraping steps that he had heard before. Slowly and stealthily they took the three laborious paces from the open lift to his room. He waited, expecting to hear a knock or tap at the door. Mariah could feel the presence of someone outside. *Isambard Black*, he thought to himself as he stepped to the bed and sat on the coarse blanket.

The door handle slowly turned. Someone pushed against the door. Mariah saw the wood move in the frame. He jumped back further on the bed, grabbing the rough pillow and clutching it to his chest. The door moved again. The handle turned faster. He looked to the window, thinking of a way to escape. A gentle tap, tap knocked against the wood. He couldn't speak, his voice frozen.

'Mariah,' came a whisper. 'Mariah, let me in . . .'

He didn't reply. Then there was a sudden kick against the door and the chair fell from its place, releasing the handle. Slowly and forcefully the door was pushed open and the chair brushed to one side, scraping across the boarded floor. Mariah clutched the privy pot that was by the bedside, holding it by its thin handle, ready to strike at whatever creature came upon him.

'Mariah,' came the voice again. 'I've been waiting for you to return . . .'

A cloud crossed the moon like a thin black blade as a figure stepped into the room. Mariah looked up as he drew back his arm ready to strike –

'Sacha?' he asked as he stared at the dark shape before him. 'Is it you?'

''Tis I,' she said as she struck the match and lit the lamp by the door. 'Where have you been? I got rid of my father and came straight here. Been waiting by the back door for ages and you never came. I met Isambard Black and he told me he'd seen you in the theatre so I came to your room. Surprised to see me?'

'Surprised?' he said quickly. 'Sight for sore eyes. When you went, I was chased by the Kraken – found by Captain Charity – met a crocodile – and then Isambard Black appeared and then vanished again. Not the most normal of evenings, I would say.'

'So you met Cuba. She's nothing but a big lap dog. He found her on the beach, you know,' Sacha said, hoping to fill in any gaps left by Charity. 'And the Kraken, you say?'

'It's real, Sacha. I've seen it with my own eyes.'

'So says many a man on a Friday night on the way from the Three Mariners,' she said curtly as she brushed the dark hair from her eyes.

Mariah told her every detail of the night. Fried fish, Mister Grimm and the meeting with Charity. He showed her the coin in his pocket with its worn face and clipped corners and how the Kraken had attacked.

'The trouble is . . . the trouble is,' he said slowly as he

reached under the bed, 'I felt more fearful of Isambard Black than the Kraken. It was as if it wanted to speak to me and do me no harm. Black wants something,' he said, looking nervously around the room. He reached for the box of Panjandrum cards that he had hidden. 'I think he knows I have *these*.' Mariah held out his hand. Resting on his palm and glowing in the moonlight was the pack of cards, still neatly enclosed in the box. The Joker stared out, his eyes glowing softly as from inside the box a hidden light glowed through them.

'A fine and fancy deck of poker cards,' Sacha replied as she stared at the pack of playing cards, the golden braid that encircled the box shining boldly with an incandescent light.

[16]

The Dancing Panjandrum

TWO dirt-black chairs were jammed against the door, their spindly legs pressed into the hard wood of the planked floor that ran seamlessly from wall to wall. Against them was wedged the small cupboard with its bowl and wash pot, full to the brim with cold water, all wrapped in a threadbare towel. The last part of the barricade was the bed, which now spanned the narrow room like the spar of a metal bridge, squashing everything tightly against itself. Sacha peered over Mariah's shoulder as he knelt in the firelight and unpacked the Panjandrum from the safety of the taut box. The cards were wrapped in a stiff piece of white paper, neatly folded at each corner like the pleats on a well-made bed. He slipped his finger beneath the flattened red wax seal and slowly folded back the wrapper. It burst open with a sudden crack, giving out a shower of tiny blue sparks and filling the room with the musty odour of old damp books. On the inside of the paper was a fine line drawing of a tower of cards, each one placed against the other until it formed a tall column. To one side was a list of instructions, giving the name of each card and how they were to be placed together.

Mariah looked up at Sacha. She nodded to tell him to go on, the flickering of the flames dancing across her face as she tried to read the dark etched words that glowed through the folded paper. She pressed one hand against the cold damp wall, her palm sinking into the pattern of the paper as she looked on.

'Is it a game?' she asked quietly, looking at the heavy drops of rain that fell from the clear sky like crystals of fine ice tapping gently upon the panes.

Mariah said nothing as one by one he placed the cards together, following the plan written out before him. Each piece of crisp card clicked firmly to another, as if they were waiting to be joined together and by some strange means became one solid piece. King followed Knave, wands linked with pentacles, as quickly each suit came together until the tower grew and grew in the firelight. Finally, Mariah held the last two cards in his hands and stared at the crossed-eyed Jokers. One smiled back, the other grimaced with one eye closed and a hand placed over his mouth as if he would never speak.

Sacha tapped Mariah on the shoulder to bring him from his dream and finish the tower that was now twelve cards in height. He placed the Jokers on each side of the final span, their faces staring to each wall as he sat back and looked at the tower that sat firmly upon the wooden floor.

It was then that a tremor shook the hotel. It rattled the whole of the Prince Regent, juddering the steam elevator, sending a shower of dust cascading from the ceiling. The window of the room rattled in the frame, then cracked across the glass pane as if twisted too far. The tower of cards didn't move. Mariah looked at Sacha and then to the scrawled commands etched in the paper. He read the words, which looked as if they had just appeared on the page. '*Once the tower is complete – then amaze your audience with its magical fortuities. Chi – Samekh –*

Digamma.' Mariah read the words aloud in one long breath with a voice that came from another place.

There came the faint sound of whispering. Sacha looked about her, sure that the voices came from outside the room and that the barricade would not hold against whoever was upon them. She looked to Mariah, hoping he could hear the shy murmurs that irked her soul and spoke gentle whispers from the high corners of the room.

'Can you hear . . .?' she said as the muttering grew louder in her mind.

'*Chi – Samekh – Digamma* . . .' Mariah said again as if he hadn't heard a single word. He sat spellbound by the miniature but spectacular event taking place before him.

'Where is it coming – ?' she shrieked as the clamour vibrated in her head.

'Don't say a word,' Mariah said, his face fixed in a deep stare as the Panjandrum burst into life and began to hover above the floorboards. 'Sacha . . . Take my hand,' he murmured as if he could see something in the cards. The tower spun faster and faster, each card blurring into the others as the manifestation whirled in the deep firelight, sparking with every turn. 'Can you see it?'

Sacha stared, unsure that she should believe her eyes. 'It's a trick,' she said quickly, not wanting to believe what she saw. 'Just like what Bizmillah would have done.'

'Not a trick,' Mariah said, his stare fixed upon the spinning cards. 'This is more like magic. Now I know why Perfidious Albion gave them to me. Look!' He gasped as the tower unfolded to form a living, framed depiction of jostling images. It glittered and sparked as each card melted and transformed into a single image. There, unfurled before them, was a London street made up of tiny fragments of the Panjandrum. They swirled and changed with every second to form a moving picture in which dark figures walked back and forth. Striding boldly along the pavement was Perfidious Albion, who pulled his collar up against the driving rain, his floppy hat tugged across his face. The bright sign of Claridges Hotel lit the scene, as close by two men followed on behind, trailed by a hansom cab, its horse decked in funeral black plumes and a rain-wet running coat.

The Panjandrum raised itself higher into the air as the scene began to change. Inside the frame of spinning cards, Perfidious Albion stepped upon the stone threshold of the entrance to the hotel. In his hand Mariah could see the postcard that he had sent, the painting of the Prince Regent twisted in his grip. Without warning, the dark-clad followers that lurked behind grabbed Perfidious roughly by the arms and lifted him from his feet. Turning him to the road, they bundled him quickly into the awaiting carriage. There in the corner of the picture, lurking as if not wanting to be seen, was a grey-faced figure who brushed the steps with what appeared to be a long black broom. When Sacha and Mariah stared even harder into the picture they saw the man begin to walk the pavement, and here and there as he went along he tapped a rain-soaked pedestrian gently upon their forehead with the tip of a long gnarled finger. With every unseen touch he left behind a blood-red mark that set them aside from those passers-by who went on their way unchosen.

'What is it?' Sacha asked, more intrigued at the spectacle than frightened by its miraculous appearance.

'Whatever it is, it's wrong – I can feel it. This shouldn't be happening,' Mariah replied, and he edged further away from the Panjandrum as they spun into another scene. 'We have to stop it.'

'Stop it?' Sacha replied. 'This is amazing. Look, Mariah – who would have thought, moving pictures.'

'But Perfidious Albion, what happened to him?'

'Doesn't mean it was true, could be a trick of the cards,' she argued.

'He had the postcard I sent to him, I saw it in his hand.'

It was then that three dark letters edged in bright gold appeared in the corner of the shimmering card frame. In the soft glow from the fire they spoke the letters together as a word appeared: '*A – S –K*'.

'It wants us to ask something, Mariah. What shall we say?' Sacha spoke quickly, her heart excited as she fumbled her words.

'Say nothing, I don't like it. It's not good,' Mariah cut back quickly, not knowing how to stop the cards from performing their trickery.

'You're just a stupid boy frightened of his own shadow. If it is a trick, it'll do us no harm. If it can see the future than we have something that'll make us rich . . .'

'Rather die poor than have this chasing me forever. It can't be good – it's not right.'

'Right or wrong, it's dancing before our eyes and it wants us to ask it a question.' Sacha thought for a moment and tried to edge Mariah out of the way of the cards that danced before them. 'Is Felix alive?' she blurted before Mariah could stop her.

The Panjandrum shuddered. One by one the cards fell from the air and landed in a neat and growing pile on the floor. A final card hovered above the floorboards as if suspended by an invisible piece of string or magician's charm. Mariah wafted his hand above the card, hoping it would snag against that which caused it to dance in the air. And then the deck burst into life – several cards leapt from the floor, chasing each other higher into the room like a flock of geese that circled the ceiling. More and more began to dance this way and that, like an army brought to life, before they too leapt high in the air and flew to become one large mass that blanketed the ceiling.

Mariah looked up: it was as if the night sky had crept inside the room and pinned itself to the coving of the lime-plastered roof above. Deep blue stars twinkled and winked brightly, and a glowing moon slowly crossed the firmament. Then, without any call or expectation, all grew dark again. The far side of the ceiling began to glow with a bright red light. Steam billowed crisp and white as far away a young boy took shape, one of many hunched and sweating in a long dark hole, the floor strewn with a covering of milky pearl-stones. From beneath a mantel of matted hair, two bleary, tired eyes stared out as blue, bloodless lips mouthed silent words.

'It's Felix!' Sacha shouted. She leapt to her feet and jumped towards the apparition above her. 'I can see you Felix – you're alive.' The boy didn't reply; his stare was fixed, lips mumbling, deaf to her words. 'Where are you?' she asked impatiently, her voice whining.

The words jarred with Mariah. He saw from her eyes that she thought the boy to be special, and that in some way he occupied a sincere place in her heart. 'He's a million miles away from here, can't you see?' he shouted back at her as he pushed her away. 'I want this to stop. Felix is dead and this is a lie. Look at him – sat on a bed of pearls and looking half starved. If that isn't a wicked trick of these cards then what is? Should never have taken them from Perfidious Albion. I want them to stop, NOW!'

'Tell me where he is,' Sacha said urgently, ignoring Mariah as she spoke to the cards. '*Please*,' she pleaded. 'TELL ME!'

'NO! Stop it now!' Mariah shouted above her as he pushed her out of the way. 'We don't want to know. Felix is gone. Never to be found.'

The cards twisted their shape, imploding with each second to the shape of a golden orb that pressed closer and closer.

'It'll crush us,' Sacha shouted as Mariah dived to the floor and scrambled to find the box of instructions.

'Stand back and say nothing more,' he shouted, and he rolled under the bed with one hand clutching the sheet of paper.

Sacha stood alone. The orb hovered in front of her, sparking blue and gold flecks of bright light that danced like the candles on a Christmas tree. Through the thin veneer of gold, she looked down upon the world as if she were a swirling corbie, brooding from its nest. Far below she could see the sunlit rooftops of the Prince Regent. As if cracked like a gigantic egg, the building was split open as floor by floor was revealed to her eyes. She was taken deeper and deeper. Spiralling down, she circled until the black rocks of the deep foundations opened up before her. There, nestling in the hollow earth, was a dark cavern, the floor littered with oyster shells and creamy droplets of pearl, and in a sunken corner was a gathering of children, huddled together as a dark beast flicked its scaled tail back and forth, swishing a rain of sparkling shingle.

From beneath the shielding of the bed, Mariah clung to the commands that were etched in black upon the sheet of paper he had plucked from the floor. It struggled and twisted to free itself from his grip as if it had a mind not to be read. The black etching now appeared to smear itself within the paper, each word slowly beginning to smudge beyond recognition. Quickly he came to the final three words that faded before his eyes: 'Za-yin – Za-yin – Za-yin!' He shouted them aloud as they melted out of sight.

A crack of lightning cut through the air to the heart of the orb. The vision exploded, throwing Sacha against the wall as she still stared deep into its heart. The Panjandrum fell from the air, the cards scattered like gale-blown leaves across the floor.

Mariah heard her muffled scream and looked up from his hiding place. Sacha struggled to gain her breath as the Joker smothered her nose and mouth, clinging to the contours of her face like a grasping hand. Several cards held her tight against the wall, piercing her clothes and pinning her to the plaster as if they were a conjuror's daggers. Her arms were tethered tightly, locked by a cluster of cards on each wrist that shackled them to her. He could see the life draining from her as she fought against the smothering, her lungs about to explode.

Like a springing cat he jumped to his feet and pulled at the Joker. It melted through his fingers, sticking to Sacha's face, squeezing her mouth firmly shut. Mariah saw a look of panic radiating from her eyes. She began to slump down the wall, held only by the embedded suit of Spades that stuck her like iron nails to the wall. He pulled at the Joker again. It stuck to his fingers, holding his hand fast against her skin.

'Za-yin – Za-yin – Za-yin!' he shouted again and again as he tugged at the card with his other hand. Sacha's eyes rolled to the back of her head and she slumped forward, unable to breath, her lungs crushing her heart as the veins in her soft white neck visibly pulsed with its penultimate beat. 'Za-yin – Za-yin – Za-yin!' he screamed the command, pulling frantically against the liquefying card.

With a sudden and ear-splitting squeal, Sacha gulped at the air. Mariah fell back towards the small fireplace, his hand clasping the now stiffened Joker. It grinned at him, teeth clenched and eyebrows raised. One after the other the suit of Spades fell from their holding places and tiny spirals of plaster dropped to the floor.

'Quickly!' Mariah shouted as he attempted to grab with his hands as many of the Panjandrum cards as he could. 'Catch them before they can do more harm – the box is the only safe place for them.' Sacha looked on as Mariah scurried about picking up the cards and pushing them into the stiffened case, then wrapping them in the sheet of commands. 'Help me!' Mariah snorted as he gathered the cards, got to his feet and placed the box beneath the bed.

Sacha didn't move. She gripped to the wall plaster with her fingernails. 'Old Scratty . . .' she said slowly, her eyes fixed to the wooden chair that lurked in the shadows in the far corner of the room. 'She's here . . .'

Mariah looked to the chair. There in the shadow, lit only by a small chink of light that seeped in through the circular porthole cut into the roof, was Old Scratty. She was sitting bolt upright, a slight smile etched on the lips of her white china face as if she had watched all that had taken place. The doll was leant slightly to one side, as if resting her wearied self against the back of the chair. Her hands were stuffed in the pockets of her smock, sleeves rolled back to expose the white sea-washed wood.

'How did *she* get here?' Mariah asked as Sacha began to pull the barricade away from the door.

'She wasn't there before. I looked at the chair and it was empty – no one was there, no one.'

'She must have been, Sacha. Dolls just don't appear,' Mariah said doubtfully as he looked at the manikin. It was then that he saw the silver bangle upon her wrist. The metal tarnished to almost black and the straw figures etched deeply into the silver looked as if they were veiled in dark smoke. A sudden thought flashed across his mind as an image of the Kraken appeared again in his memory. 'That bracelet – I saw one just the same on the wrist of the Kraken.'

'Take it from her, then we can see,' Sacha said, not wanting to move an inch nearer the smiling doll.

'You take it. I don't want to touch her.'

'We can't leave her here. Bizmillah will wonder where she's gone,' Sacha replied as she pushed Mariah towards Old Scratty.

'It's how she got here that bothers me. She wasn't in the room until the Panjandrum blasted everywhere. She just appeared, moved on her own, just like she did in the cellar,'

Mariah blurted angrily. 'That's the thing – dolls like her can't move on their own. She's got wooden arms and a painted china pee-pot for a head. Don't tell me she could have got here by herself.'

'And don't tell *me* that cards can dance in the air and pin me to the wall, smothering the life from me,' Sacha snapped back. 'We both saw it and it was me that Joker tried to kill.' She paused for a moment, drawing her breath, her voice calming. 'I know where Felix and the others are being kept. They're not dead . . . Just before the explosion I looked into the depths of the earth and Felix was in a cavern under the Prince Regent. That's what the cards showed me.'

'And that's why they tried to kill you, so you couldn't find him,' Mariah said as the thought crystallised in his mind. 'If the cards are right, then Perfidious Albion is in trouble . . .'

'And Felix is trapped.' Sacha looked hopelessly at Mariah. 'We have to help him.'

'They'll know that the Panjandrum cards are here,' Mariah went on, ignoring what she had said. 'He had the postcard of the hotel. They'll come looking here and find me. Isambard Black!' he said quickly. 'I should have known. He said on the train he had been waiting for someone. He was waiting for Perfidious Albion, he talked about tricks and magic and . . .'

Old Scratty interrupted. Her long wooden arm clothed in its black smock sleeve clattered against the wall, its hand hanging limply by her side. Mariah saw that Scratty's wooden fingers clasped a large metal key. He stepped to the manikin and carefully unravelled each of the stiff jointed fingers, thinking that at any moment she would spring to life. The silver bracelet slipped suddenly across her wrist, scraping against the wood.

'It is the same as the Kraken's,' Mariah said as he looked up at Old Scratty's face. For the briefest of moments he was sure that the smile had slipped from her face and that she gave the mildest look of anguish as he spoke the Kraken's name. Then a single tear fell from a blind eyes and rolled across the white china cheek, as if he had spoken the name of someone long missed.

'You here to help us, lass?' Sacha asked Old Scratty as Mariah plucked the key from her fingers and held it to the light. 'Is there a door for this key, Old Scratty?'

The doll's right hand suddenly fell from her lap, a finger pointing to the floors below.

'Let me see,' Sacha insisted as she grabbed the key from Mariah and looked at the thick shavings of rust flaking from its surface. She sniffed it intently and with the tip of her tongue tasted the metal. 'Seawater,' she said brightly. 'This has been tide-washed many times.'

'Deeper than the cellar?' Mariah asked.

'Deeper and more dangerous,' Sacha replied as she stroked the long locks that hung raggedly from Old Scratty's head.

[17]

Pagurus

MARIAH opened his eyes and stared at the empty chair. The call of sea hawks heralded daybreak and the sound of the crashing surf of the morning storm echoed around the towers of the Prince Regent as it washed against the steaming sands. Sacha huddled against him, wrapped in the coarse hair blanket, not wanting to leave his side, fearing the shadows and the power of the Panjandrum. She held the rusty iron key in both hands, cradling it as if it were some great prize snatched from another.

He looked to where Old Scratty had been and smiled to himself. The manikin had vanished, slipped from their lives as they slept. Old Scratty had gone as silently and surreptitiously as she had appeared. Her white face had been the last thing he had stared upon as he fought against the onset of sleep. As the oil lamp had faded and its light had thinned to a whisper, they had spoken of what to do next. Sacha had told him over and over what she had seen as the golden orb had exploded. She had described in the minutest detail how the earth had opened before her eyes and she had plummeted from the sky and into the depths of the cavern. Mariah had hoped that it was but a chimera, a fanciful dream. In the cold grey light of morning the events of the dark hours became a faded memory. It was only the sight of the Panjandrum on the hearth of the fireplace that reminded him of the reality of what had gone before. The Joker smiled a thin fretful smile, as with one eye it appeared to stare at the sliced plaster hanging from the wall where Sacha had been pinned like a rag doll.

'She's gone,' he said softly as he tried to wake the girl from her deep slumber. 'Old Scratty has vanished again, not a trace . . .'

The wind-blown chiming of the steeple-house clock warned of the seventh hour. Its clatters danced above the pounding surf and the calls of seabirds. Sacha lifted her head and peered out of tired eyes rimmed with the desire to sleep on until the late of day.

'Morning?' she asked as she pulled the blanket up around her head and snuggled against the pillow, hoping that the day-light would vanish once more and time would return to night. She looked at the empty chair. 'Gone?' she asked not waiting for an answer. 'Was any of it real?' Her thumbs rubbed the flaking metal of the old iron key.

'It happened – that's for sure,' Mariah said as he rubbed the sleep from his face and tousled his hair. 'But whether it was real . . .' There was something about his voice that echoed the thoughts of his mind. What he had seen in the glow of the fire and on the steps in the town had somehow remained on the edges of reality. It tapped gently on his consciousness like the lamplighter's staff rattling the wicks of the fireheads.

'Do you think she – ?' Sacha asked, unable to finish the question as her thoughts raced ahead of her words. ' Could she – ?'

'Better not ask. Old Scratty turns up whenever you think about her. I know we'll see her again. She wants us to find something.'

'Or someone,' Sacha said quickly, wanting it to be Felix.

'One thing,' he went on slowly. 'The bracelet was the one the Kraken had when he saw me and Charity fought him off. Trouble is . . . the trouble is, Charity didn't tell me where he had been and why he was skulking around in the dark. Just came out of nowhere – said he'd followed us.'

'Do you think he knows?' she asked.

'I'm afraid he does. I think he knows everything.' Mariah looked to the Panjandrum. 'I want to hide these so no one will find them. Soon they'll come looking. If they have Perfidious Albion then they'll come for me. He's bound to crack and tell them who he gave them to and all about the postcard. I'm going to have to move on. I can't stay here much longer.'

'Throw them in the sea and lie till your teeth fall out. That's what my father did. He burnt the secrets of the armoury when a Frenchman sailed into the harbour. Threw the ashes down the old well in the castle. He thought we were to be invaded. Oh, the look on his face when they sailed away after firing a couple of cannon. Red as a baboon's ar–'

'You need a good memory to be a liar. Better I just go back to London,' Mariah said sharply as he picked the Panjandrum from the fireplace and stuffed them into his pocket.

'You'll do what you have to do,' Sacha snapped as she got from the bed, pushing it away from the door. 'I'll be finding Felix myself, no problem in that. I have the key and somewhere there'll be a door to fit it. If Old Scratty is right then Felix won't be too far behind.'

'But you can't go on your own,' Mariah said as he reached out to stop her. 'You don't know what'll be waiting.'

'Then come and don't run away,' Sacha replied as she pulled her arm from his grip and opened the door. 'It's beyond us now, can't you see? It's as if there's a wheel turning and you and me are on it going around and around. You can't go now, whatever happens.' She held the key in front of his face. 'This is our future, Mariah. Yours and mine, and there's nothing we can do to change that. Old Scratty knew, that's why she found us. Whatever is going on in this place has to stop. We can't go to the police, they'll never believe us.'

'We could try – tell them about the murder last night and the Kraken.' Mariah sniffed.

'And they'd believe that?' Sacha asked mockingly. 'I'm a Fenian. I've been running from things for most of my life, and I'm not going to run from this. If I stand alone, then I stand alone.'

'What about Captain Charity?' Mariah asked impatiently.

'He's not here. It's just you, me and a cellar full of secrets. If you're in, Mariah, then we have to be gone.' Sacha didn't wait for his reply as she stepped through the door and into the small corridor. She pressed the button to summon the steam elevator and stood back against the wall listening to its groaning as it slowly pumped itself higher and higher. Mariah followed sheepishly, his hands pressed deeply into the pockets of his coat.

'What shall we do about Bizmillah?' he asked anxiously as the elevator steamed closer.

'You did everything last night. That gives us until eight o'clock tonight. Should be enough time to see what's going on down in the cellars.'

'What if we get caught?' he asked, his throat tighter than before.

'Then we end up like Felix.'

The steam elevator stopped suddenly. Sacha pulled the cage door open, stepped inside and waited for Mariah. He paused for the slightest of moments as he looked back to the door of his room, wondering how Old Scratty had found him. Within a second they were plummeting deeper and deeper into the depths of the Prince Regent. From far below, the smell of dank seaweed seeped from every stone and crevice as the steam elevator slowed to a juddering halt.

'As deep as we go,' Mariah said as he quietly slid the gate open and checked this way and that along the dark corridor. He peered from the elevator's blanket of amber light and listened to the swish of the waves by the faraway portal.

'A storm and the tide is in,' Sacha snorted to herself, sniffing the air as if it would tell her the secrets of the cellar. 'Perfume,' she whispered to Mariah. 'Monica has been this way.'

Mariah suddenly perked up his ears and listened even more intently than before. He sniffed the air, trying with all his might to capture the tiniest essence of her fragrance. 'How can you tell?' he asked as Sacha stepped from the elevator and sniffed again, following the scent as if she were a bloodhound. 'All I can smell is the stinking sea and the cess Luger pumps into the Galvanised Bathing Machine.'

'It's what you can't smell that's important,' Sacha replied just above a breath. 'They went this way – scent and cigars.'

Mariah lifted his nose higher as he stood tiptoed and gulped the sharp breeze that rushed back and forth through the cellar from the sea like the laboured breathing of a stranded whale. There was the faintest, mildest whiff of pungent tobacco that hung momentarily in the air and then vanished like an ancient spectre. 'Gone,' he said to himself as he followed Sacha, quite disappointed that he couldn't taste Monica's scent upon his lips. 'Are you sure it's her and not another?' he asked through clenched teeth.

'Cheap,' she whispered back, much to his annoyance. 'From a penny cart in the market but strong enough to cover the smell of her salty sweat.'

'What?' Mariah asked, pulling her into a small arched doorway.

'She drips with it, constantly powders her face to soak it from her skin. Lead paste and lime plaster. Why do you think she doesn't take off those gloves?' Sacha said as she nodded to herself in approval. 'If she sits she leaves granny dabs wherever she's been. Mister Murrybuck calls her *the slug*. Follow the trail and you'll find Monica, dressed in black, sweating in the corner. Told me that as he carried in some cases.'

'Murrybuck's a fat old farting porter who stinks himself. Shouldn't be talking about people in that way.' Mariah scowled.

'That he may be, but *she* still stinks. Snuggle up to her and it's as if you've stuck your head in a chamber pot,' Sacha said as she turned to follow the scent that only she could smell.

The corridor led several turns to the left and only one to the right. It spiralled lower and lower, passing open doors and empty rooms, each lit by a single oil lamp set high upon the wall. The air grew thick with salt mist that clung to their skin, drying upon the lashes of their eyes like crisp white icicles. With every step the heat grew more intense as the steam thickened and swirled in the fading light.

They turned a final corner and there in front of them was a short flight of steps that led quickly to a long, damp passageway. Far away in the darkness they could hear the sound of the sea crashing through the doors and rushing into the cellars. Mariah looked down to his feet as the sound of sharp scurrying rushed about him. The green-tiled cellar floor moved as one. Sharp shells clattered against each other. Grinding black-tipped pincers snapped at the air and red eyes on stalks stared back in the dim light.

'Look!' Mariah said as he stared at the thousands of tiny red eyes that reflected the dim lamplight. 'What are they?'

'Cancer Pagurus,' Sacha replied as she stepped down one step to take a closer look. 'Sea crabs, but twice the size of any I have seen before. We'll never get that way – claws like that would snap through your ankle.'

'How did Luger get through?' Mariah asked as a particularly

large red crab, the size of a dinner tray, crawled on another's back and pulled itself up the step towards him, snapping its pincers.

'They went in here,' Sacha replied, pointing to a door set into an alcove in the wall and covered by dangling throngs of damp sea grass.

Mariah continued to stare at the Pagurus that scraped its shell against the side of the step as it beat its two large claws against the green tiles. 'Where do they come from?' he asked quietly as he gazed at the creature. 'It's amazing – look at the size of the beast . . .'

'Never been in this place before. Not even Bizmillah would come down here. Nothing but the wine cellars and –' she stopped speaking and pointed to the corridor.

In the misted half-light, Sacha saw the crabs quickly scurry to the sides of the passageway as from below their sharp point-ed legs there slowly emerged an even larger, more gigantic back of an even greater creature. It shook the sand from its piecrust shell as it slowly and silently lifted itself to the very tips of its spiked legs. It hulked from side to side like a clawed grand piano set on six long pink legs.

The creature turned slowly, picking a smaller crab from the floor. Crushing it in its pincers, it gorged itself with the drip-ping red mucus that oozed from the broken shell like the filling of an overstuffed sandwich. The Pagurus squealed with excite-ment and its mandibles quivered over its mouth. Its black eyes set on stubby stalks scanned the passageway, flexing in and out with every sharp and sudden breeze that gusted towards it.

The Pagurus picked another crab the size of a small dog and again snapped it in two before pushing it ravenously into its mouth and crunching it with its mandibles. The creature shud-dered and bristled the hairs upon its legs as it turned, and with one stem-like eye stared at them.

Sacha and Mariah stood frozen with foreboding, hoping they would not be seen. All about them a host of small crabs scurried by, running into the open doors of the many rooms that lined the passageway. Mariah pushed her to one side, took hold of the large iron ring that formed the handle to the door in the alcove, and turned it as quickly as he could.

The large Pagurus took two long and slow steps towards them, tasting the air as he picked his way through the scurrying masses that snapped at his bony, spiked feet. It stopped and snapped its pincers three times and then stepped even closer.

'The door's stuck,' Mariah shouted as the creature came towards them through the steam-mist. 'There has to be a key somewhere.'

Sacha took Old Scratty's key from her pocket and tried it in the lock. It twisted part way and then stuck tight and would move no further. She pulled it back and forth as Mariah pulled upon the circular handle and strands of sea grass fell upon them like cold wet hands.

The Pagurus ambled slowly along the tiled corridor, too big to turn, its size forcing it to squeeze itself along the narrowing passageway. The chafing of its shell squealed into the distance like chalk on board as it snapped out its pincers with every step.

Sacha pulled on the rusted key, which finally gave way and cracked from the lock. She looked crestfallen as she panted her breath and glanced back towards the creature that edged its way closer.

'Just run!' Mariah said, pulling sea grass from his face as the horror of what his eyes fell upon dawned in his mind. 'We can go back.'

'What about Felix?' Sacha asked quickly as she held the key like a knife in her hand.

'There must be another way . . . Quickly, run!' Mariah

pulled Sacha by the arm as the Pagurus quickened its gait towards them. 'This way!'

Together they set off at a fearful pace, running back the way they had come, up two flights of the spiralling corridor and then on to a long landing. The tiled green stone reflected the gas lamps like old moons rising from the sea. Far behind they could hear the clattering of the Pagurus as it chased on, its mandibles echoing like jagged, chattering teeth.

'Which way now?' Mariah screamed in a panic as he spun from his feet, slipping sideways and cascading across the steam-damp tiles.

'Straight on, I think,' Sacha said, knowing in her heart that she was lost in the labyrinth of passageways that honeycombed the cellars of the Prince Regent. 'It all looks the same. Have we been here before?'

Growing closer was the scraping of the Pagurus as it dragged its immense carapace towards them upon its spiked feet.

In the distance, lit by the last lamp, was a small doorway. It was set two feet from the floor, as if it were a hatch into the roof of a lower room. The door had been cut from a single piece of oak that now twisted from the shape of the entrance and was held tightly shut by a rusted metal latch. As they drew near, Mariah could see that the corridor opened up to the right and then suddenly stopped. They could go no further.

From a thick black ceiling vent there billowed a vast cloud of white steam smelling of the sea. It curdled along the dripping tiles as hissing drops of boiling water splattered to the floor. The sound of the steam generator juddered the corridor, shaking the walls. By accident, they had discovered the heart of the Prince Regent.

Mariah waded through the cloud of steam that hung at waist height until he found the latch to the door. It held fast, corroded by a thick salt crust that gripped to every contour. Sacha stood by the far wall, looking to the ceiling as a thin film of condensation bowed from the ceiling and fell to the floor with a dull splat.

'No way out,' she said. She looked back and saw the first gigantic claw of the Pagurus edge its way slowly around the corner of the passageway, snipping at the steam.

'Give me the key,' Mariah insisted. 'It might be of use.' His voice was twisted with fear.

He snatched the key from her and began to hammer at the door catch. The salt crust cracked open, following the line of the rusted metal. Mariah turned as the Pagurus scuttled closer, stopping every few feet to wipe the swirling mist from its stalk eyes with its mandibles. It spied them, chattering its teeth and clashing it claws as if they were cavalry sabres. It suddenly darted forward, lashing out with a long claw that caught Sacha by the hair, pulling her from her feet. She vanished beneath the pall of steam that blew from the vent above them.

'Mariah!' she screamed as she was dragged backwards across the dank tiles closer to the creature's mouth. 'Mariah!'

Without hesitation Mariah hit the lock for a final time and saw the door spring open. He turned to the Pagurus as it snapped at him with its other claw. The great crustacean lurched again and again, unable to turn the bulk of its carapace in the narrow width of the passageway. Sacha screamed as it beat her against the wall, holding her tightly by a thick lock of hair.

Seeing his chance, Mariah stepped towards the Pagurus and smashed the key against its eyes, with one blow cutting the iris from the top of the stem. It flinched back as a thick goo seeped from the wound. All around was filled with scalding steam.

'Now!' Mariah screamed in terror as he hit the half blind creature again and again. It instinctively flicked Sacha from its grasp, spinning her across the floor towards the open doorway.

She got to her feet, rising from the mist, and quickly jumped inside.

'Come on, Mariah!' she shouted as the crab twisted itself to one side and then suddenly freed both claws, pulling the boy towards its mouth.

'Shut the door!' he shouted as he vanished in the churning steam and the crab squeezed him to itself.

The Pagurus looked at her through the thick salt fog filling the passageway.

'Mariah!' she shouted again, not knowing where he had gone.

The crab staggered towards her, its legs dancing and slipping this way and that. It slammed against the hot tiles as it lunged repeatedly.

'Mariah!' she screamed, desperate to see the briefest glimpse of him in the furling mist and know all was well.

There came a sudden thud that pounded again and again on the back of the creature. A shadow veiled in steam like a phantasm leapt from its back and to the floor.

'The door!' he shouted as the crab attempted to see its attacker. Mariah leapt towards the entrance that was cut in the tiled wall and was now filling with steam.

Sacha fell backwards as he landed upon her, the Pagurus thrashing at the entrance as it tried to pluck them like small periwinkles from the shell. Mariah got to his feet as the heavy claw pushed its way deeper into the room snapping wildly in the air. With all his might he pushed against the oak door as the crab picked and poked, seeking to gouge them from the hiding place. He pushed with every ounce of strength and fibre from his failing and bruised body.

In the darkened room Sacha struck a Lucifer. As it burst into life the Pagurus suddenly recoiled in the dazzling brightness. Mariah, seizing the advantage, slammed the oak door against the creature and slid the bolt. He looked at Sacha and smiled, holding out his hand to hers.

'Many left?' he asked as the match began to fade.

'Enough to light this,' she said as she brought a thick stubby candle from her pocket and with the dying flame of the Lucifer gave it new life. 'Don't really like the dark,' she said softly. 'Father would lock me in a cupboard and leave me there. He said the Boggat would come for me if I got out. Always carry matches and a candle. Never feared the Boggat or anything since.'

'Does that include vanishing dolls, Krakens and giant crabs?' Mariah said breathlessly as he leant against the oak door, smiling at her in the soft light of the candle flame as the steam generator hummed and hissed somewhere close by.

'*And* a London boy who brings pandemonium with him . . .'

[18]

Moon Sand

THEY sat for several minutes in the shimmering candlelight and listened to the Pagurus. It coughed and chirped
in the dark steaming passageway outside the room. The crab
tried to force its claw into the warp of the door and prise it
open, but soon gave up its search and reluctantly clambered
and clumsily clattered its way along the passageway. Stopping
momentarily, it squatted in the mist, its one stalk-eye peering
from the gloom like a black mushroom.

Mariah peered through a crack in the door, watching the
creature's every move. It slowly crawled out of sight, but he
knew it would be waiting – that in the darkness the Pagurus
would be ready to pounce and snap them in two with its black-
tipped claws, then lusciously feast upon their flesh. Sacha sat
quietly, playing with the candle wax as it dribbled down her fingers and into the palm of her hand. From all around them came
the hissing of the steam generator that gulped and yawned as it
pumped the boiling water to the farthest corners of the Prince
Regent.

'How long can we stay here?' Sacha asked Mariah as he sat
down once more and looked about him.

'The Pagurus is still there,' he said, motioning to the passageway outside the room. 'Doubtless it'll just wait. There must be another way of getting by.'

Sacha raised the candle above her head, lighting the high ceiling and a far stone wall. 'Do you think that these are the foundations?' she asked as she stared at the large thick stones cut neatly into blocks the size of a carriage that made up the wall. 'They say there used to be a hot spring here and people would come to swim in the water. There's still a tap in the refectory. A golden tap that the guests can drink from at a *shilling* a time. I tried it once – tasted like horse pee.'

'That's why Isambard Black said he was coming here – to taste the waters. Hope it is horse pee and that it chokes him,' Mariah said as he got to his feet and ran his hand along the rough blocks. 'These are old stones,' he said. 'Look at the marks – cut by hand. Do you think we're below the sea?'

'Far below,' Sacha replied thoughtfully. 'The store to the theatre is on a level with the beach. How much further down we are I don't know.'

'And the steam generator – who looks after it?' Mariah asked.

Sacha paused and thought. It was the one thing she had never considered. She had seen the waiters in their fine coats and neat trousers, an army of maids, chefs, cooks and bottle-washers, but she had never seen anyone come from below the ground.

'Takes care of itself,' she said after a while. 'It must do, I don't know anyone who works down here.'

'Then it'll be the first steam engine that runs on its own,' Mariah exclaimed as he walk further into the shadows, following the contours of the wall as if he were looking for something. 'Here!' he shouted from the blackness. 'Bring the candle and see what I've found.'

Sacha followed his voice, bringing light to the darkness. The tiled floor soon became broken stone and then turned to small boulders of brittle rubble that littered the floor. It was as if she had walked into the ruins of an old castle, overcast by the darkest of night skies with no moon to guide her feet. In her mind she thought the hissing of the steam generator sounded like the panting of a sleeping dragon. Sacha could not believe that she was still deep inside the Prince Regent, far below the level of the sea. All around were remnants of the building of the hotel. Discarded shovels, picks, broken bottles and empty pot mugs were strewn by the wall in a makeshift rubbish dump.

'Look at this,' Mariah said excitedly as he stood in a sealed-up doorway. 'It looks like the entrance to whatever stood here before the hotel.'

Sacha went over to him and held up the candle. It cast long shadows across the room. She could clearly see the old doorway that had been cut into the thick stones and then sealed with the same fine red bricks that clad the Prince Regent from sea to sky. Looking up she could see that the lintel above the door was made of stone and that running through the centre was a fine crack the size of a finger's width. It hung with salt webs that glistened in the light like a fall of fresh snow clinging to the mistletoe.

'And look here,' Mariah said pointing to some missing mortar where the new met the old. 'I can smell the sea and feel the breeze.' Sacha stepped forward, the candle suddenly blustering in the whistling draught that seethed through the narrow slit. 'A way out,' he boasted. 'Should be easy to knock our way through and see what is on the other side.'

'There could be nothing,' Sacha moaned. 'Could be full of rubble or sand.'

'It could be a way out. It's either this way or fighting old Pagurus,' Mariah said earnestly as he flicked out several pieces of damp mortar with his fingertip. 'If I just get one brick free then the rest should follow.'

'And the whole place fall upon our head,' she moaned again.

'Pagurus?' Mariah asked. He held out his hands to mimic two large claws as if this would give steel to her decision.

Sacha handed him the candle and took the broken pick from the rubble-covered floor. 'I'm Irish, born with a pick in my little fingers and English persecution on my back. Never give a boy a man's work.' Sacha smiled as she swung the short handle of the rusted iron claw and with a sudden sharp blow smashed it into the bricks. 'There,' she said in a satisfied voice as rubble and mortar fell to the floor. 'That'll be your first one out of the way.'

Mariah looked through the small hole that had appeared at waist height in the brick wall. In the light of the candle he could see several stone columns, each one supporting the floor above. He could hear the sound of the steam generator close by as it huffed and pumped faster and faster.

Sacha pulled him clear and in two swift strokes had forged a hole big enough for them to enter in. She dropped the pickaxe and wiped the dust from her hands on Mariah's sleeve, then she struck another Lucifer.

Mariah walked ahead on the hot dry sand that covered the floor. From the meagre light he could only see a few feet ahead and it looked as if the ruins went on into the distance. Following some inner feeling, he instinctively allowed himself to be drawn in the way of the steam generator. Every other pace he looked to see if Sacha followed. There she was, an arm's length behind, key in hand.

They threaded their way through the stone columns, the hiss of the steam calling them on and the heat reddening their faces and wetting their brows. Mariah held the melting candle above his head, hoping that the light would claw its way further into the distance and that he would see some other light. After a short while he looked behind like he had done so many times and realised that he was alone. Sacha had gone. A sense of panic rushed through his body, setting his senses on fire and stealing his breath. He turned suddenly as a shadow chilled him, like a hand about to strike. The sound of the generator quickly turned into the breath of a beast as his wits twisted, each wheeze and exhalation becoming its grunting.

Shadows danced from the flickering candle as his eyes invented strange creatures from benign gloom. In two paces he could feel the blood drain from his heart and his lip began to quiver. In the half-light of the flickering wax candle he tried to call out Sacha's name but all that came was a sullen murmur.

'Sacha . . .' he said again as he clawed the spittle back into his mouth and coughed to free the icy grip that had seized his throat. 'Sacha . . .'

In the ruins there was complete silence. Mariah pressed himself to the wall, fearfully looking this way and that to catch some glimpse of his friend. It was then that he saw a glow many yards away. By the base of a stone column was a small fire. Hunched over the glow was a dark figure.

'Sacha?' he asked, hoping she would turn and smile at him and he would no longer be alone.

She turned and waved him to her with one hand. Mariah ran quickly from column to column, stopping at each before he took another pace. He saw that what at first he had thought to be a fire was an old glass lamp, full to its brim with blue-whale oil. It gave a warm light and lit her face. Sacha sat quietly looking into the gloom.

'Why did you go?' he asked.

'When I struck the match I saw something. It glinted. You had gone ahead and I just had to come and see.' In her hand she held a black leather wallet encrusted in salt. It was stuffed with crisp five-pound notes all neatly folded. 'I found this,' she said as if the value mattered not. 'And something else.'

Sacha pointed to the wall that stood four paces behind. In the deep dusk, Mariah saw the outline of a man lying in the sand, a salted top hat placed next to him. He raised the candle and cast its light upon the body. It shone against the crisp white bone skull and glistened upon the skeletal fingers.

'He's dead,' Mariah said with a degree of certainty.

'He's certainly not well,' Sacha mocked. 'And more than that, he's supposed to be running this hotel.'

Mariah didn't ask what she meant. Sacha was already holding out a calling card in its neat silver case and a folded envelope.

'Otto Luger,' she said as she gave the card to Mariah. 'I glanced at the letter – it's to him. I think he was murdered.'

Mariah looked again at the corpse. It was picked perfectly clean. Every ounce of skin and tissue had been gnawed from the bone. The suit of fine clothes lay in a tattered pile upon the thick bones. The jaw of the skull had fallen open and the once proud head had tilted to the side. There to see were three small round holes neatly placed in the temple.

'The knife again?' Mariah asked, not afraid of the pile of bones. 'Who could have done something like this?' he asked, unable to take his eyes from the corpse, lured by its deep fascination. It was as if the skeleton had never walked, talked or had life. Lying there in the hot sand it was as hard as the stones that lay about it and as lifeless. It held no threat, only allurement. The gore had been dried or eaten or had soaked away. There was no trace of the stench of death and those bones that were visible shone as if they had been washed in egg glaze.

'How can it be Otto Luger?' Mariah asked.

'I found the hat. It's inscribed with his name and the letter too. It has to be him.' Sacha sounded certain as she looked at the crisp piece of white paper in her hand. 'It's to Luger and it's not signed. Listen.' Sacha began to read the missive. It was scrawled in an unsteady hand in shaky black ink. The paper was embossed with a crown and two lions, and in the murk she could make out the words *Claridges Hotel*. She coughed before she spoke. '*Dear Otto, something has brought dissatisfaction to my door. I need to see you urgently. If we are to continue in our venture then you must meet me tonight* . . .' Sacha held out the note for him to see. 'It has to be Otto Luger, and whoever is running the hotel is . . .' She didn't say another word. Mariah had gone to Otto's carcass and lifted the hand. He carefully slipped a gold ring from its third finger and held it to the oil lamp.

'It's the same as Luger's, a ring with a swan crest. A gold sovereign, wedged on his fat finger. Two the same – one on a dead man, the other on the living,' Mariah said as he put the ring in his pocket.

'Leave it Mariah, you can't take from the dead.'

'I'm sure he wanted us to find out who did this to him. When all this is over we can do what is right and give him a proper send-off. Captain Charity would see to that, I'm sure he would.' Mariah spoke quietly as he looked at the glistening bones and wondered what he would have looked like. From the cut of the fine suit he could see that the corpse would have been the same size as Otto Luger and dressed in the same elegant style. Even the shoes bore a remarkable similarity to those that had squeaked along the corridor when Mariah had hidden away behind the aspidistra. Whoever was the owner of the Prince Regent, they had a strong resemblance in height and frame to the skeleton that now rested against its foundations. 'We better search him for anything else,' Mariah said as he got to his knees and rifled the pockets of the empty suit.

'Done that,' Sacha gasped as if she wanted to hide something from him.

'And?' he asked in expectation.

'It's this.' She opened the palm of her hand and there, glowing like a bright full moon in a dark sky was a large cream pearl the size of a chestnut. 'It's a sea pearl. I found it in his pocket.'

'You can't take from the dead, Sacha,' Mariah scoffed.

'It must be worth a hundred pounds. With that and the money in the wallet it's more than I would earn in a lifetime'

'Enough for a man to die for at least,' he said as he picked the pearl from her palm and held it to the light. 'But it wouldn't be come by honestly. Better to starve than steal your bread.'

Her face shone like the bright pearl as together they gazed upon it. In her heart she said goodbye to all that she dreamed it would have brought her. As Mariah held it in his fingers, the desire slowly left her. She felt as if she had held the answer to her meagre life in her hand, that the shackles of poverty had fallen from her. Now in her honesty she felt as if she had picked up the manacles and placed them back upon her wrists, double-bolting them to remain for life.

'If I had sold the pearl,' Sacha mumbled, 'I could have left this place and never worked again.'

'And forever had the image of that corpse dancing in your dreams to remind you of where it came from,' Mariah said as he gave the pearl back to her. 'Take it, change your life and see what good it would do you.'

Sacha held the pearl in her palm and felt its warmth. Holding her hand to her mouth, she squeezed it deeply into her skin.

'A pearl of great price,' Mariah said as he searched the floor where the body lay. 'There must be something to tell us what happened here.'

'He was murdered,' Sacha gasped out.

'Well, but not for his money, all that and a pearl.'

'For the Prince Regent?' she asked.

'And whatever secret this place keeps locked within its walls,' Mariah said as the candle finally melted away in his hand. 'If this really is Otto Luger, then the man who masquerades in his identity is the one who did this to him. Do you think you could find this place again?' he asked as he bent to examine the body once more.

'I could try. But for what reason?'

'So we can show Jack Charity. He'll know what to do. He'll tell someone who can sort the whole thing out,' Mariah replied as he opened the coat and looked at the crisp white shirt that lay beneath covering the boned ribs. Just above the heart were three small puncture wounds cut into the fabric; around each was the slightest smear of faded blood. 'He died quickly. Not much blood.' He pulled the shirt to one side. There, tucked into the trouser belt was a pearl-handled pistol. 'Otto Luger carried a gun,' Mariah said as he carefully picked the pistol from the belt, blew from it a thick covering of salt and checked the chamber. 'And he never used it. So he was either surprised by or knew who would kill him. Brought down here and then killed for what he had.'

'So why did they leave him?' Sacha asked.

'Bricked him into here and thought he would never be found. If it hadn't had been for the Pagurus we would never have come this way. There must be another way out . . .' Mariah lifted the oil lamp and watched the lamp flame flickering in the unseen draught. 'We can't go back.'

He turned and walked on with the lamp, this time checking that Sacha was still near by. Sacha quickly stuffed the wallet into her deepest pocket. She patted her frock coat and gripped the pearl in her hand. In the distance she could see the light picking its way through the stone columns into the darkness. She followed on, every now and then putting the pearl to her lips as Mariah traced the breeze.

Soon they had reached the far wall of the ruin. It was made of the same hand-cut stone that had been Otto Luger's tomb for so long. Here there were just two granite columns holding up the roof. A thick covering of hot sand swathed the floor. In the amber glow of the oil lamp, it was just how Mariah had imagined the surface of the moon when he had stared up in his saturnine melancholy so many times from the garden of the Colonial School.

As he looked at the shadowed sand beneath his feet, the long-forgotten September nights came back to him. In his mind he was taken back to standing on the grass banks of the Thames and looking out as the full moon rose up from the spindly fingers of the trees on the distant shore. Its light turned the sky to black and the world to shivering silver. Like a giant face it would stare upon him, pock-marked and frowning a sombre smile as it thinned in its rising. Mariah would look back and hope, knowing that it shone on others whose fate he could not guess. He would stand out the hour, his toes chilling as the deep dew crystallised the grass beneath his feet. Then he would turn his dazzled and moon-burnt face to the earth. There about him, standing like so many gravestones, markers of their own bereavements, would be many children. All would be in silence, as if the luminary had commanded them to join him in veneration. Mariah would say nothing; he knew their thoughts for their hearts burnt like his own. In the gloom, walking as if from the passing of a friend, he would tramp his way mournfully through the damp grass. Thoughts of a far-away place, a sanded desert that lit the sky, were etched in his mind. But as soon as his feet crunched the coarse grit that covered the drive of the Colonial School, all such considerations would be gone and he would set his mind on what was to come.

'There should be another way,' he muttered to himself as the world came back to him. 'Check by the wall, I can feel a breeze but can't tell which way it comes from.'

Sacha searched the shadows by the wall and moved her

hands across the stone along each line of mortar. Somewhere nearby she could feel the quick movement of the sea-tainted breeze.

'Here!' Mariah fell to his knees and held the lamp above a small pile of sand that bubbled and hissed as a strong draught fermented through each particle to form a small volcano-like mound. 'Come and dig!'

Sacha began to scrabble in the dirt as Mariah scooped handfuls of hot sand away from the geyser of hot air that blew through the floor. Quickly they found a lattice of small stones that gurgled like a narrow stream as the air gushed through each one.

'It must be a way to the floor below,' Mariah said as he now picked larger rocks from the ever-widening hole.

'Could be nothing there,' Sacha replied. The rocks grew hotter and began to char her fingertips.

'Listen,' Mariah said, gesturing for her to be silent. 'I can hear the steam generator.'

Coming from the hole was the sound of the generator. It was louder and more urgent than they had heard it before. It was as if they sat within the boiling tank of a large steamship that pushed its way against a high sea. The churning of the engine was timed by sharp jets of air that bubbled through the rocks. Mariah dug even quicker, picking the hot rocks with his reddening fingertips.

Then his hand struck against a strip of hot black metal. He perched himself upon a lintel of thick stone as he picked away the rocks from each side of a thick grate. 'Must be an air vent to the generator,' Mariah said to Sacha as she piled the stones from the hole behind her. 'If I can get my finger around the bar and pull then we shall be able to . . .'

Mariah had no time to finish his words. Suddenly and without warning, the vent gave way and the hole quickly began to deepen. He scrabbled for a footing as Sacha was sucked by the cascading stones deeper into the hole, slipping by him and into the darkness without a chance to scream. She vanished from his sight into the chasm that opened up beneath and swallowed her without a trace. With both hands he grabbed at the rocks, hoping to pull himself from the avalanche. It plucked at him as he teetered on the lintel, a torrent of shingle and sand dragging him deeper. Mariah could hear stones falling and clattering far below as they pelted through the opened vent. With every second he slipped deeper. The lamp that had lighted their progress spilt its blue-whale oil upon the rocks and this burst into bright flame all around him, catching his sleeve in a ghostly fire as his feet slipped from their perch.

Mariah reached out, away from the flames, his footing lost in the streaming rock. Falling, he grabbed the stone lintel that was buried deep in the sand. He dangled from his fingers as stone upon stone pounded his head. The rock burnt against his palm as he clawed and dangled in the blackness. One by one the tips of his fingers broke their grasp. Mariah hung like an old puppet.

From above his head he heard the sound of shifting stone as if the whole floor was beginning to move. The lintel juddered as it slowly tilted towards him. He gripped it tighter, finding a firm hold against a piece of jagged rock that fitted his hand. Mariah looked below. The darkness went on forever, clouded by billowing spouts of hot dust. Nearby, the throb of the steam generator hissed out its heartbeat.

'Mariah!' came a shout from below. 'I'm trapped . . .'

He could hold on no longer. The heat loosened his grip, his sweated fingers slipped from the rock as hot blisters burst on each tip. In one breath he tried to scream, then fell silently into the bottomless pitch of the black hole.

[19]

Camarilla

THE wheezing of the steam generator appeared to come from somewhere nearby. Mariah sat in complete blackness, unable to see a hand in front of his face. He rubbed his palm over his eyes, hoping he could push away the dark veil and see the world again. It was no use; all was covered in smothering gloom.

The chamber into which Mariah had tumbled was much cooler and the subterranean breeze stronger. He sat on a pile of sand and shingle, breathing slowly and listening to the echoing sound as he wondered what he could do. The trickle of slipping shingle finally stopped as the hole above his head filled itself, the lintel holding back yet another fall of rock. A slow dribble of sticky blood seeped across his forehead. Instinctively he touched the wound with his raw-fleshed fingertips. He coughed loudly, the dust from the rockfall filling his nostrils and swirling about him.

'Sacha!' he shouted, the walls whispering back to him. 'Are you here?' There was no reply.

Wiping his mouth with the sleeve of his coat, Mariah slid from the pile of stones, knowing he would have to fumble blindly to find an escape. His hands felt their way in the darkness, painfully touching each stone as he slithered sideways across the scree. He felt the gun in his pocket and clicked the hammer gently back and forth as he listened to the wind seething through the darkness. As he lay against the pile of stones, unaware of what was about him, not even which way was up or down, his mind whirred and tumbled and spun dizzily as he stared wide-eyed into sightlessness.

Something touched his chin. At first it brushed against him like a wind-blown web that fleeted by. Then it came again, bolder, firm, grasping his face as it scraped against his skin.

Mariah didn't dare move. Whatever touched him was warm and soft. Like a lightning bolt he suddenly realised that this was Sacha's hand buried in the mound of rock. He pulled at the stone and shingle, the sharp jags ripping at raw fingers. The rocks spilled ever downward as Mariah dug to set her free. In the sand and grit he could feel the contour of her face as he kicked away the tumuli of small boulders piled against her like an ancient tomb.

'Sacha!' he shouted as he lifted her from the grave with bleeding fingers. 'Can you hear me?'

She coughed, spitting sand and pulling him close as she gasped for breath. 'I was drowning in the shingle,' she said, squeezing him as if she would never feel anyone alive again. 'I could hear you shouting, but couldn't speak.' Sacha coughed in the darkness as they sat holding each other. 'How far did we fall?'

'Too dark to tell,' Mariah said as he looked up, and then laughed to himself for his folly. 'Do you have a Lucifer?'

Sacha tapped her pocket and, sitting back, opened the thin box and struck the match. In the sudden glare, Mariah could see the far wall of the room and glimpsed a rusted grate hanging by a broken hinge from the roof. To their right was a large stone vaulted entrance and a short flight of steps that ran down and turned sharply to the left. In the brief moment of illumination it looked as if it were the entrance to an old church, etched in carved ivy leaves and with a gargoyle's head looking down from the high arch.

'Again,' Mariah insisted as the match failed. 'Light another.'

Sacha lit a Lucifer and held it tightly in her fingertips. 'I haven't many left,' she said quickly. 'We'll have to find something more or we'll be walking blind.'

'At least we're alive,' Mariah replied. 'I was beginning to think that this place was trying to kill us both.'

He pulled a long white handkersniff from his pocket, then wrapped and knotted it against itself to form a long wick. He lit the end aligned with the match and watched as it slowly started to smoulder and then burn. 'Should last the hour,' he said as he saw the surprised look on Sacha's face. 'We learn many things at the Colonial School.' He smiled.

'Me, I didn't get the chance,' she said curtly as the shadows criss-crossed her face. 'Taught myself to read and write. Cleaned for the cleric and pinched his paper and quill pens. Easy, when you really have to. Didn't feel bad about it either. Silly man, with spectacles that perched on the end of his nose. Squandered all his time swigging port wine, mumbling curses and scrawling in his book. Spent more time writing than he did on his knees. The Reverend H. F. Cataxian . . . He wrote *The Incredible Adventures of Doblin the Goblin.*' Sacha mimicked a squeaking voice. 'Nearest he'll get to Paradise was having his manse built next to it. You must have heard of him?' Sacha seemed thankful to talk of something other than their plight. 'My house is across the road from his. We lived clattered together in the rooms above the inn. He lived all alone in a house so big you could lose yourself for a week. So far to the privy that he would up the sash and do it out of the window.'

Mariah laughed, the sight of Cataxian gushing from the

window of his house etched in his mind. 'I have the book, brought it with me from London. I've read it several times.'

'Then when we get from this place . . .' she said slowly as she looked to the ground. 'Then, perhaps we could visit him.'

'That we'll do, and sooner rather than later,' Mariah replied uneasily as he pulled her from the stone pile and walked towards the stairway. 'I have this,' he said as he showed her the gun that glistened in the flames. 'Never thought there would come a day when I would think of this. If they were prepared to murder Otto Luger, then the same could come to us.'

'Then it's a chance I'll take. Rather die for something than live for nothing. Felix knew there was treachery in this place. On the night before he disappeared he wanted to tell me a secret. He said he wasn't safe, that Otto Luger had a box and it would change everything in the world. Felix said the answer was all in the stones and they would speak for themselves. Then he was gone.'

'And we will find him, Sacha. He must be here somewhere. Him and all the secrets that this place contains.' Mariah spoke quietly as they took the first steps down and then turned quickly as they spiralled the sand-covered treads.

Soon they reached the floor below. It looked as if it had been cut from the solid rock on which the Prince Regent had grown. The sound of the steam generator grew louder with each step they took along the narrow passageway just wide enough for them to walk arm in arm, linked against the darkness.

Mariah held the pistol in his hand as Sacha clutched the light above them, its smouldering wick illuminating the damp sandstone walls that oozed with tendrils of hot salted water. Coming from a hand-chiselled entrance was a shaft of bright amber light that sliced through the darkness ahead of them. Sacha moved quickly on, then waited for Mariah as she peered around the rough-cut edge of the small stone doorway.

Inside the large vaulted room was the steam generator. It was unlike anything Mariah had ever seen. A large green, polished pipe was screwed into the rock face with thick brass bolts. To one side was the steel piston that juddered back and forth along a bright rod fixed to the far wall. Behind this was an engine the size of a small house that chugged away like a slowly beating heart. Every so often it would spurt soft jets of steam from its ventilating valve and a rush of burning air would be sucked through a labyrinth of pipes around the room and then into the high ceiling. All was lit by a stand of blue lamps fixed to the high ceiling.

'A steam engine,' Sacha exclaimed.

'Not one that I have ever seen. There's no stoker, no firebox and no water. It's as if it sucks the steam from the earth itself.'

'Listen,' Sacha said as though she had been spoken to by a voice beyond hearing. 'Can you hear the crying?'

Mariah listened. All he could hear was the chugging of the generator and the whistling of the steam through the miles of piping that circled above him like the coils of some vast snake. The clanging pipes echoed through the cavernous chamber. He shrugged his shoulders and screwed up his face.

'It's there again . . . Can't you hear it?' she asked as a faint cry came yet again.

Mariah holstered the pistol in his pocket and bent forward. He cupped a hand against his ear and tried to listen. The noise of the generator and the garbled chuntering of his own thoughts filled his head. 'Nothing,' he said.

Sacha moaned to herself in deep frustration. 'I'm sure I could –' she said as the faint cry came yet again. 'There – you *must* have heard that.'

Mariah shook his head as Sacha walked towards a carved doorway half hidden behind the generator.

'This way,' she said as she walked quickly, her hand grasping the key.

Mariah followed on, taking in the last sight of the steam generator that grew up from the solid rock floor into the high vaulted roof. The glistening of the arc lamps shone from the bright green and glimmering paint and polished brass bolts. 'Amazing,' he whispered to himself as he walked backwards. 'Perfectly amazing.'

Sacha followed the sound of the whimpering that had called her into the long and brightly lit passage. Running far into the distance were a thousand tiny lamps with neither wick nor flame. She looked at the clear glass spheres that covered a thin burning wire. They glowed brightly without flame, dazzling the eyes. Mariah followed on, pistol in hand; every second pace he would stop, turn and aim at some imaginary creature.

Soon they passed into yet another vast chamber. They crossed a steaming pool of fermenting blue water on a high metal gantry suspended from the roof by thick linked chains. They swung gently back and forth with every step until they reached another stone-cut archway. It howled with a stiff gale that pushed them back with its ferocity. The wind shimmered the waters and spiralled mist into the heights.

The sound of crying seemed to be as far away from Sacha as ever. It was as if she chased a rainbow and no sooner had she stepped nearer than it had moved another pace away. But still the faint murmuring came again and again. Sacha turned to Mariah and he would just shrug his shoulders in reply, as if she were the only one who could hear the ghostly whisperings.

Mariah pulled the collar of his coat over his face to protect it from the wind. He pushed Sacha on as she struggled to keep upright in the air stream that hurricaned through the narrow tunnel.

'It cools the steam generator,' Mariah shouted, his voice carrying just above the howl of the gale. 'Sucked from above – find where it comes from and we'll be able to get out again.'

Sacha got to her hands and knees and crawled the last few feet of the corridor. As she pressed herself to the ground the wind beat against her head and peppered her with blistering specks of golden sand. Mariah staggered on behind, unable to look ahead as he cupped the pistol in his hand, holding it close to him.

There was a sudden tremor as the whole passageway juddered with the sound of sliding, grating metal that rasped against the stone. The gale squealed its final breath and then all was silent. From far behind, the shuddering came again as a strong metal door clamped firmly shut.

'VENTS!' shouted a voice from ahead. 'CLOSE THE VENTS!'

There was another slithering of metal far away. The grinding and crunching of rock trilled through the passage. Sacha looked up to Mariah. She was covered in a thin layer of golden powder that lined every feature of her face and encrusted strands of hair against her skin. They crept forward, not knowing who was ahead of them.

From just beyond yet another stone archway they could see the light of a glistening crystal chandelier. It hung majestically from the hand-cut, vaulted roof of the chamber, at the same height as the gantry on which they now crouched, just out of sight of the people below.

Mariah peeked carefully over the metal rim of the elevated pathway that linked the two halves of the vaulted room. There below was Otto Luger, smartly dressed and very much alive. He wore the same crisp white shirt and neatly pressed jacket. His monocle was crunched against his nose; his hair was slickly greased back from his face. Monica fussed about a stone table, wiping piles of golden sand from its surface with a horsehair brush as she stood on a long stone bench that looked as if it was hewn from the floor.

Standing together by the large wooden doors were two men. Mariah recognised the ruddy-red face of Mister Grimm. He waited impatiently with his companion, his hand rubbing the top of a golden lion's-head mahogany cane. The other man was tall and thin, with a white face, pinched cheeks, thin lips and a small black beard that tipped the end of a long and very pointed chin.

'*Grendel!*' whispered Mariah to himself.

Mister Grendel fiddled with his blue-lens spectacles. He took a fat silver timepiece from his pocket and checked it several times with agitated fingers. Grendel visibly twitched every sinew in his body, the muscles in his face shivering beneath his thin white skin.

'Mystery, mystery, so much mystery. Why we can't meet in an upper room and not far below the sea I'll never know,' Mister Grimm said quickly.

'Is he ready to perform for us?' Otto Luger asked as he sat at the head of the stone table and nodded for them to join him. Monica brushed the last of the sand to the floor. 'This dreaming he does better find out who was in my room last night. I've a feeling they will be back and I have far too much riding on this caper.'

'Have we ever let you down?' Mister Grimm asked passionately as he took Grendel by the hand and led him to the seat opposite Luger. 'Best he sits here and then he can see you face to face, Mister Luger.'

'All I ask is he sees the one who is messing up my head.'

'You are an impatient man, Mister Luger,' Grendel said as he sat on the cold stone. 'Projection is something that has to be learnt. It isn't stumbled upon or bought, it is a gift.'

'Thought it came in a little green bottle and smelt of laudanum,' Luger mumbled as he looked at his fob watch.

Mister Grendel laughed to himself as he scratched the hairs

on his chin and adjusted his spectacles upon the elfishly thin bridge of his nose. 'That substance just takes me from this world and allows me to wander where I please. And it is *not* laudanum, nothing so crude or so vile and corrupting. Just three drops of this linctus and I am free of worldly passions and desires. There is nothing greater than to escape the twitching of this carcass of tremulous timidity. Just three drops, Mister Luger, and you could come with me. Could this be what is more powerful than *the sigh of the hard pressed creature – the heart of the heartless world – a soul of soulless circumstances*? If Mister Hegel's philosophy is to be believed . . .'

'Drink and have done with it,' Luger barked as Monica sat down at table, the words echoing around the vault. 'Have your dream and be paid well. Tell him, Mister Grimm. I *have* to find the one who was in the penthouse.'

'Then I shall, I shall. Nothing would give me greater pleasure than to leave this present company. But first, tell me, is there anything that you don't want me to see – for once I am projected there is no door that is closed to me and no wall that can keep me out. Secrets will be a thing of the past. Do you understand?'

Luger looked to Monica, hoping she would say something. She smiled at him and shrugged her shoulders, tilting her head to one side like a cooing dove.

'There . . . there are many things that I would not like the world to know and hope you would keep secret. I am sure we can come to some sort of *agreement*?' Luger spoke as if aware he had unleashed a creature that would cost him more than he ever knew.

'Shall I see what I can find and then discuss a price?' Grendel asked as he unscrewed the top of a small glass bottle that he had quietly removed from his hip pocket. 'I assure you that we can keep many secrets and our prices are very reasonable.'

'It's insurance, Mister Luger,' Grimm chipped in nervously as he wiped sweat from his brow and cast a sly look to Mister Grendel to say no more. 'Consider it an investment. We would become *guardians* of whatever we found, with the promise that the secrets would die on our lips.'

'I would prefer if you kept your nocturnal wanderings to the rooms above the ground,' Luger replied as he again looked to the silent Monica for help. 'I have a business venture in which I am cultivating certain *things* . . .'

'Of value?' Grendel asked as he sniffed the neck of the bottle.

'Of significant value, and beautiful,' Monica interrupted. 'Tell 'em, Otto. If he's gonna see through the walls then he'll see the kids and the pearls – so have done with it.'

'*Monica!*' Luger bristled as her words zimmered upwards.

'We'll cut you in on the deal,' she said briskly, avoiding Luger's staring gaze. 'Otto is cultivating pearls. Far below this room is a cavern stuffed with oysters. He feeds them on . . .' She paused and looked to Otto Luger, whose face was reddened in a deep blush and whose neck swelled in the confines of his tight white collar.

'Steam and ordure,' Luger chirped.

'Or-*what?*' Grimm asked, his face so screwed up that his spectacles dropped from his shrinking nose.

'Excrement – poop – jobbies. Whatever else you would like to call them,' he moaned.

'And you feed it to the pearls?' Grimm asked, amazed that the creatures would survive such a diet. 'Now I know why my mother told me never to eat shellfish.'

'They adore the ordure,' Monica chortled to herself.

'It's steam-heated, taken from the town sewer, filtered and then fed into the cavern. Twice the heat they would be in the sea, and tended by kind loving hands. Just think – super size,' Luger said, as if offended by the tone of Grimm's voice.

'You get people to work down there?' Grimm said as he loosened the tie around his neck.

'They have no choice. How can I say this in the kindest way?' he asked Monica.

'Slaves,' she said cutting to the chase. 'Mister Luger gets a particular type of brood to work in the hotel. Ones where the family has no care or concern for them. They have been well paid for and they come here. The strongest are selected and disappear from upstairs to go and work . . . downstairs.' She giggled and pointed below with her long glove-clad finger, and gave a little shiver of delight.

'And the pearls?' Grimm asked, his voice falling to a whisper as he slavered over the words. 'They are disposed of . . . locally?'

'Let us just say that the ladies of Paris are adorned with the finest molluscs that hot, steaming sewage can grow,' Luger said as he smiled at Monica, raising a thick black-dyed eyebrow.

'Smuggled?' said Grimm cautiously as Mister Grendel put the green bottle to his lips and sipped the linctus.

'In a way that you would never expect.' Monica chuckled.

Grendel quietly convulsed in his chair as the linctus seared through every vein in his body like hot lead. He coughed gently, an issue of deep red blood dripping from his lip and trickling through the fibres of his beard. With that he closed his reddened eyes and slept.

There was a sudden swirl of sand that spiralled up from the floor beneath the table as if disturbed by someone's passing. Monica shivered, pulling her feather boa high around her milky-white neck as her eyes searched the room.

'How does he dream?' Luger asked sarcastically. 'This is the most expensive sleep I've ever paid for.'

'But it'll be worth it, Mister Luger. We will find your tormentor, *and* I have had news from London. Associates of mine have found the man you were looking for and are bringing him here right now. He was located on the steps of the Claridges Hotel and is now enclosed in a carriage that tramps the roads to this very place.'

'What of the Panjandrum?' Luger enquired cautiously, pulling nervously on his moustache. 'The telegram was obviously vague. We cannot have our secrets displayed for the world,' Grimm said. He pulled a crumpled piece of paper from his pocket. 'It says . . . *all is well* . . . *bringing our friend from Claridges – surprised to find a postcard of the Prince Regent in his pocket.*'

'Someone *is* here. It all begins to fit into place. Sleep on, Mister Grendel, and find the thief and the Panjandrum,' Luger commanded wistfully. 'There is every chance he will be found and my suspicions confirmed.'

'I tell you, Otto, it's Bizmillah. He's the one Grendel should be scoping out,' Monica insisted.

'Leave it to the master and he will soon have the answer. Mister Grendel is not dreaming, he has left his body and walks in another realm. He can see that which we cannot with our veiled eyes and there are those who also walk in that world who can show him the way to tread to find your answer,' Grimm murmured, as if he did not want to be overheard by souls unseen to their eyes.

Monica blushed and shuddered at the same time. She looked uncomfortable and stared around the room.

'You say he can see things from the other side, things that ain't human?' she asked nervously.

'Indubitably, Miss Monica. If there were a single ghost, ghoul or spectre then he would see it, and not only that but tell us where it had been. You see, all creatures leave behind them a trail,' Grimm said as he took out a long case from his pocket and withdrew a pair of spectacles from within. 'With humans it takes the form of heat. See, I have these spectacles that when tuned correctly can see the footsteps of someone long gone. All I need is to have the merest piece of the suspect, a hair or fragment of clothing, and I can stalk their track days after they have walked that way. These are said to have once belonged to an angel that tramped the streets of London, but that is just an improbable fiction.'

'And when will he wake from his sleep?' Monica asked feebly as she stood from the table and walked to the doorway.

'Not long, he never takes long. Time is not time where he walks. It is compressed, shortened and of a spiral nature. Today and tomorrow are of the same place, linked sideways and not in a continuum. Moments here can be a lifetime elsewhere. Wherever elsewhere is, of course . . .' Grimm spoke quickly, hoping his words would cover his own confusion.

'CHILDREN!' screamed Grendel viciously as he lurched from his dreaming. 'What are you doing to the children?' he sat bolt upright, staring at Luger. 'All is not as it appears, Mister Luger. Bizmillah argued with one of your guests as your room was invaded by *children*.'

'What?' asked Luger urgently.

'Two of them, a boy and a girl. They know more of this place than you would think. They are near, Mister Luger, very near. That is not all, is it, Miss Monica?' Grendel said shakily as he stared at her.

'Where are they now?' Luger asked.

'There!' Grendel said calmly as he took his lion's-head cane and pointed the tip to the gantry above their heads. 'They are hiding and have listened to everything you have said.'

Luger spun around and looked up, not noticing Monica slowly slipping from the room. 'I can't see them – are they ghosts?'

'For the moment they are alive, Mister Luger, very much alive.'

Mariah had heard enough. He pulled Sacha and ran across the gantry to the stone doorway on the other side.

'Quickly!' shouted Luger, bolting from his seat. He waddled as fast as he could, urging Grimm and Grendel to follow. Monica had vanished, slipping from the room and into the dark corridor. 'There are stairs to the left. We must stop the children.'

'They will not go far, Mister Luger. Not from London's finest detectives.'

[20]

The Pearl of Great Price

MARIAH didn't wait for Sacha to run. He scuttled swiftly along the gantry like a chased rat, moving on all fours and keeping his face to the wall. From below he heard the sound of the slamming of the chamber door as Luger and the detectives rushed into the darkened corridor in an attempt to cut off their escape.

'They have Felix – it's true,' Sacha said, holding the key she had been given by Old Scratty. 'We have to get them out.'

'They have Perfidious Albion as well. Did you hear them? That's what we saw in the Panjandrum,' he said as they stopped at a junction of four narrow tunnels just wide enough for one person to pass at a time.

'It's true what was in the cards about Felix and the oysters,' Sacha said as she rested against the wall to regain her breath. 'Which way shall we go?'

Mariah looked this way and that. Far away he could hear clanging metal doors and footsteps beating against the stone. The sounds shuddered against the cold air as if coming from three directions at once.

'That way,' he said pointing to the narrowest tunnel that

dropped steeply away and pushing Sacha ahead. 'Grimm's so fat he'll never get down this way.'

They ran on, flickering past the glistening lights that hung from the ceiling. The walls pressed in against them, narrowing to the width of their shoulders.

'I don't think this goes anywhere,' Sacha said as she felt the rocks pressing in and stealing her breath. 'If we go much further we'll be trapped.'

'Look at the floor, Sacha – footprints, all going the same way. Something has to be ahead of us.'

Sacha felt the iron key twitch in her hand as if it wanted to be free. It seemed to pull her onwards as it searched for the lock that it knew was close by.

'The key,' Sacha said as it began to twist free from her fingers. 'It has come to life.'

Mariah looked on as the salt-rusted metal twitched and snagged back and forth, trying to break her grip. 'Every key must find its lock,' he said as the words appeared in his mouth. 'Follow on. Let it go.'

Sacha hooked her finger into the large rusted ring and let her grip loosen. It pulled quickly against her hand like a divining rod, as it dragging her on towards its lock. They followed on, the sound of Luger and the detectives coming nearer. The lights of the passage began to flicker and dim as they went deeper. The key pulled her forward like a wild horse in full flight, lifting her to the tips of her toes.

Mariah followed, turning back to see if they were being pursued. The noise of the chase had fallen away. The chuntering of Grimm and Grendel had subsided into a far whisper. The slope on which they now ran steepened, the rocks breaking up under their feet into loose gravel. They were far away from the steam generator, and yet the throbbing of the machine reverberated through the solid rock. Every few paces, chunks of falling grit and stone crashed to the floor, smashing into tiny splinters like exploding shells about them.

Sacha ran on, the key taking her deeper and darker into the tunnel. It juddered frantically, vibrating in her fingers and singing like a tuning fork. Piece by piece the fragments of crispy salt rust fell from the key as the pitch grew louder and louder. Far ahead they heard the note reply an octave lower, rumbling like a double bass.

'We're there,' Mariah said as he chased behind her, clutching the pistol in his hand and wondering if he could ever use it against Grimm and Grendel. 'Look ahead . . .'

Forty feet away was a turn in the narrow passage that opened out into a hallway cut from the stone. It was as if a fault in the rock had split in two, opening into a small cave that had been hewn by hammer and chisel into a vaulted room. In front of them was a metal door with a large iron lock set in a wooden frame. In the centre of the door was a glass bull's eye.

The key knew it was home. It sung merrily to itself, altering its pitch to that of an excited song-thrush. In return, the mortise housing the lock hummed and buzzed loudly, awaiting what was to come. Sacha was dragged across the vault as the key slipped itself into the lock. It clunked home and shivered, turning itself several times in delight.

The door slowly opened, creaking on two rusted hinges as if pushed by an unseen hand. A smell of sewage billowed into the cave as a sea-green mist leached across the floor.

'Do you think there is another way out of here?' Sacha asked as she tried to pull the key from the lock to no avail.

'It's a chance we'll have to take, but I can't see Luger being able to get in here through that tunnel. It looks as if the walls of rock were being pushed closer together.'

Sacha went inside the narrow stone entrance as Mariah carefully examined the lock. He twisted the key back and forth, and with one taut shift it sheared in half, giving out a feeble twitter that melted away to nothing. He held the metal in his hand as he looked at the lock. The keyhole moulded into the metal plate as if it had never been. To his surprise, the key grew another head, the iron glittering with a blossom of sparks as if fresh from the foundry.

'Look,' he said as he held out the key to Sacha. 'It's just snapped off in the lock and now look at it.'

The key looked fresh and newly made, the scaling rust all gone. It chirped in a higher note, warbling like a wagtail. Sacha took the key from him and pressed it into her pocket.

'Changed to another lock?' she asked as she felt the shape. 'It's different than before, just one solid piece.' The key warbled as if in agreement, then, as quickly as it had sprung into life, fell silent again.

'Whatever it's doing, once we close this door it will never be opened from the outside,' Mariah said as he slammed the thick metal plate against the rough stone. The door sealed them into the tunnel. Gone was the lanyard of bright lights and now they were in shadows of gloom, dimly lit by the blustering tallows that smouldered on bone plates stuck into the wall like a hundred teeth. Each was smeared in thick wax from the remnants of a thousand candles. All were at a height just above the floor, so as Mariah and Sacha walked by their flickering shadows were cast against the roof of the tunnel.

Here there was no breeze. The heat was intense and a soft glowing mist threaded between their feet. They stumbled on; Mariah took off his jacket and slung it over his shoulder. In one hand he held the pistol, the metal cool and smooth against his ruddy-blistered fingertips.

'So we go to find Felix?' Sacha asked as she led the way. 'He's been a prisoner all this time.'

'Chosen by Luger because he found out what was going on,' Mariah replied.

'Then it'll be the same for us,' Sacha said quickly. 'Wouldn't be surprised if there are two wax manikins already, one for me and one for you. We'll end up as slaves. Shovelling poop and up to our knees in oysters.'

'Then at least you'll be with your Felix,' Mariah said cuttingly.

'So why the manikins?' Sacha asked, ignoring his remark. 'What do you think Luger could be doing with wax dolls?'

Mariah didn't reply. He thought for several paces as he mulled the image of the wax doll over in his mind. The sarcophagus was filled with black sharp sand, and the manikin fashioned to look like a boy. He looked down and saw a pool of tallow melting on the hard white bone of a candle-holder, seeping across its surface in long thin dribbles.

'Luger's smuggling the pearls out of England inside the manikins,' he said, as if he had suddenly discovered some wonderful secret. 'It has to be that. Just think, here we are in a seaport. Ships come in and out every day. Luger sends the pearls to France by boat disguised in the waxworks and hidden in the coffins. Who'd want to look in one of those to check if something had been hidden inside?'

'My father...' Sacha said softly. 'It's his job to check the cargo of everything that comes and goes from the harbour.'

'But I thought he was a coastguard?' Mariah asked.

'That and a customs officer. It's all part of the same job. Defending the coast and stopping the smugglers,' she said. 'Sometimes he's been known to turn a . . . blind eye.'

'To the smugglers?' Mariah asked.

'To everyone. It's a small place and we have ways of doing things you wouldn't understand. Doesn't make him a crook, letting the odd gallon of brandy come from the sea and over the pier wall,' she said indignantly. 'How do you think I really got the job here? It wasn't because of my hard work. Luger knows my father; they drank together and played cards. Ever since he came they've been pally. Only stopped drinking away the night when Miss Monica turned up. An American and an Irishman – Luger said they had something in common.'

'It looks like it was more than a sniff of the barmaid's apron,' Mariah snivelled as he pushed past and went on ahead.

The narrow tallow-lit passage soon opened out into a large cavern, criss-crossed by metal gantries that ran across the high vaulted roof. It looked like the inside of an idle factory built into the side of an immense cliff. Sacha and Mariah stood on a high metal platform overlooking a brown lagoon of steaming water. All was quiet except for the gentle lapping of small waves that spilled from a faucet in the rock wall. They looked about them; there was no sign of Luger or the detectives.

On the far side of the cavern was a small wooden door with an even smaller metal grate cut into its centre. Mariah could make out a shadowy face pressed against the bars as if to suck at the stagnant air that filled the chamber. Two white hands gripped on to the thin metal lattice as the face peered out.

'Felix,' he whispered to Sacha. 'Over there, behind the door.'

'FELIX!' Sacha shouted, her words vibrating around the cavern. 'We can get you out.'

'No,' came the muttered reply. 'Not safe . . .'

Sacha looked frantically for a way from the gantry. To her right was a narrow flight of metal stairs that fell steeply to a shingle path leading to the door. She ran quickly and scurried down the steps, clattering against each tread.

'NO!' shouted Felix as he rattled the grate, pulling against the door. 'Go back, go back!'

Sacha pressed on, ignoring his shouts, taking the metal steps two at a time as Mariah raced on behind her. In the hot muddy water a single eye, woken from its sleep, peered up at her. It squinted just above the surface of the water and with a swish of its long tail moved silently closer.

'Stay back!' Felix shouted again in desperation, knowing what was to come. 'Ixion will find you – a crocodile, in the water.' His words echoed around the vault.

Mariah stopped and stared into the thick brown pool looking for a sign of the beast. The water was still but for two insignificant ripples that shimmered for a moment and then were gone.

'Sacha, stop!' Mariah shouted, knowing that below the dark surface lay the waiting beast. 'Come back.'

There was a sudden sharp blow that knocked Sacha from her feet, pushing her to the waters edge.

'Ixion!' shouted Felix as he rattled helplessly on the door.

The beast fell back into the water in a swirl of mud, turning to strike again. Sacha got to her feet, unaware that the creature was about to assail again. High above, Mariah aimed the pistol at the churning water. Ixion launched itself again from the pool, pushing higher, teeth-filled mouth gaping wide and hopeful. There was a dull thud as the pistol let its shot. It cracked around the cave like a bolt of thunder. It stilled the moment and the beast fell across the shingle path, staring at Sacha. It panted, unperturbed by the blood that trickled from the cut across the side of its cheek. Then it raised itself to the tips of its dragon's legs and stood as if it were a racing hound ready to give chase.

'Stay still,' Felix said softly. 'It can only see with one eye. Luger cut out the other with a sword when it attacked him.'

Mariah turned the chamber of the pistol and pulled the hammer to fire again. There was a dull click as the hammer struck the spent cap. He aimed the gun and pulled the trigger four more times. Each one clicked the sound of its emptiness, its shell spent and fire gone. 'No more bullets, Sacha. I can't help you . . .'

She stood motionless, staring eye to eye with the crocodile. It grinned its crocodile smile and shed a single tear from its eye. Then, with dragon steps, it paced slowly towards her as it sniffed the air.

Sacha stepped back towards the staircase of the gantry, holding out her hand to grasp for the rail. The crocodile paced faster, sensing she was there, somewhere very near. Grunting to itself, barking like a dog and dribbling mucus and spit from its multitude of razor teeth, it crunched closer along the path.

Mariah crept along the gantry and down the steps as silently as he could, crouching as he stalked towards Sacha.

Ixion drew even closer, giving a final sniff to the air and hunching his long scaled back as he prepared to strike. He twitched and shivered, bristling his sharp scales and stiffening his tail. Sacha screamed and stumbled backwards, knowing what was to come, sensing the anger as the creature stared at her and flared its nostrils.

There was a scrabble of shingle as Ixion leapt at Sacha. Its skull twisted as the two long jaws quickly opened, ready to snap at her neck. The crocodile leapt its own length in a single stride as it pushed forward. Sacha fell backwards and the creature soared towards her.

With one hand, Mariah suddenly pulled her back and on to the staircase. Ixion fell short and his jaws clamped shut. He landed upon the shingle and then slipped into the mud, scrabbling against the side of the oyster lagoon with his claws. Sacha got to her feet and turned to run as the creature snapped at the air and pulled itself from the water. She panicked as it gripped the bottom rung of the metal staircase, twisting and shaking it and writhing back and forth.

Mariah dragged her higher, shouting and screaming for her to run. She was stiffened with fear, every part of her refusing to obey her mind as her heart raced faster. The crocodile pulled itself from the lagoon and on to the staircase. It gurgled and spat muddy water from its thickset jaws, appearing to smile at the fleeing girl.

'Go back!' Felix shouted. 'Come again tonight. Ixion's always tethered at night, Monica sees to that. Find the pearl of great price, 'tis all you need to live.'

Sacha got to the gantry and looked back at the pitiful face that stared at her. Felix pushed his starved wrist through the metal door grate as if to wave farewell and then it slipped away back into the darkness like the hand of a drowning man.

'Go, find the pearl!'

'We can't leave him,' she said as Mariah dragged her away.

'Nor can we stay. The creature would kill us if we tried to help Felix escape,' he said as they ran along the platform, jumping from gantry to gantry as they quickly made their way to an entrance high up in the cavern roof. Far below, a metal door clunked open. The sound of voices flooded the lagoon. Ixion slithered from his perch on the stairway and grunted hungrily across the cave floor.

'Come to Daddy,' Luger shouted, holding out a mutton joint in one hand whilst wafting a sabre in the other. 'Can't be too careful,' he said to Grimm and Grendel, who cowered behind him. 'I didn't buy this beast for its timidity.'

Mariah looked down through the lattice of rusting metal braced thickly with cables that criss-crossed at every angle. He could see Luger feeding Ixion with the meat as the two detectives huddled against the wall. The sound of the crunching of bone skimmed like a bouncing stone from the water and rose up on high to where he was hiding in the dim light of the vaulted roof.

'Doesn't look like they are here,' Grimm said as the crocodile snapped greedily at yet another piece of meat.

'Doesn't mean they didn't try,' Luger retorted cynically, his voice tense and dry. 'Only way they could have come was this way. We checked every other entrance and they had to be here.'

'But they're not here now,' Grendel snapped in his caustic voice, not sure that he liked being in the presence of so fierce a beast as the crocodile.

'Then we should wait and see if they arrive. I can always allow you to feed Ixion,' Luger said, quite pleased by a thought that fleeted momentarily and then evaporated like a mist.

'I am not fond of crocodiles, Mister Luger, not fond at all,' Grendel chattered as the spectacles on the end of his nose vibrated from side to side.

'Crocodile?' Luger asked, as if Grendel had made some tedious mistake. 'This is no crocodile but a crocogon, a changeling of two strange creatures. *Varanus komodoensis* from a small island in the Ocean of Sumbawa. A real dragon and a crocodile brought together by selective breeding.'

'It is like a creature I once saw in one of my convulsions and not something I would like to pass the time of day feeding,' Grendel said, stepping back.

'From that fragment of cloth it would appear that it has already eaten,' Grimm said slyly as he pointed to a ripped piece of black calico on the shingle path by the side of the lagoon.

Luger threw the meat into the pool and watched as Ixion slithered away. He took several steps, then picked the ripped cloth from the ground and looked intently, searching each neat weave for the identity of the wearer. Mariah listened from high above as the words echoed up to the great rock ceiling. Sacha looked to the hem of her torn garment, where a single crocogon tooth had torn through the cloth.

'Could I help you?' Grimm asked as he took the spectacles from his pocket and slipped the frames over his fat ears.

Luger handed him the torn cloth and said nothing. He looked about him and listened. Sabre in hand, he walked to the door of the cell and peered in through the grating. 'All is well,' he muttered to himself. 'None of you been seeing things? Not even you, Felix?'

No one among the huddled group of small bodies in the dark corner of the cell answered.

'It's very straightforward, Mister Luger. For a price, Grendel and I could follow them and have them done away with. Obviously whoever left this behind had a close call with your *pet* . . . I would think they have not gone far and with these spectacles they should be easily found. Now that we have this piece of their garment I can track them for days and they will never escape.'

Luger thought earnestly as he rummaged in his pockets for a trinket to bargain with. 'I would give you seven of my finest pearls.'

'It should be twenty at least, Mister Luger. I can see eleven at least in the shingle about my feet. And that is twenty each.' Grimm couldn't hold the chortle that came into his voice. 'Payment strictly on completion of the task?'

'Done,' said Luger, as the chiming clock rang in his pocket. 'I have to sleep and sleep here. It is something I must do and must do now . . .' He climbed the steps of the gantry and, propping himself on the corner of the rusted metal bridge, fell into a deep yet fitful sleep.

'Come, Mister Grendel, we have feet to follow and pearls to collect,' Grimm said through his billowing jowls that hung like the flaps of a bloodhound. Taking the spectacles from his nose, he pushed the cloth into a small phylactery that hung from a short strap. He then twisted a tuning knob by the side of the blue lens, placed the spectacles back on his face and stared about him. 'There!' he said quickly. 'And there, and there!' He pointed to different places along the path. 'Quick, Grendel, they are not long gone and I think they are just ahead of us.'

'What shall we do with Mister Luger?' Grendel enquired as he strutted over the comatose body blocking the gantry.

'Feed him to Ixion?' Grimm replied.

[21]

Aria Ceroplastica

MARIAH placed his hand over Sacha's mouth as she sobbed to herself, trying to dry the trickle of blood that ran down her leg and into her ankle boot. She picked the small crocogon tooth from her flesh. The realisation that she had been bitten by the creature slowly came to her mind and overwhelmed her with grief.

'Grimm has a device that can track our footsteps,' Mariah whispered. 'We have to be ahead of them.'

Far below, Mister Grimm sauntered along a narrow gantry, his head bowed low as he looked at the footprints that only he could see. Grendel followed, looking back to the snoring Otto Luger, who lay against the metal bars, his heaving chest labouring under its great weight.

Mariah sneakily peered over the balustrade as his pursuers followed their every step from platform to platform. He looked into the long dark tunnel that lay ahead of them, pulled Sacha to her feet and dragged her into the darkness.

'What of Felix?' she asked as they were engulfed in the muffling black of the passage.

'If we can escape the Prince Regent we will get help and

come back for him,' Mariah replied, convinced they shouldn't stay a moment longer.

'But who can we ask?' Sacha said quietly as they stumbled up a stone stairway in pitch darkness.

'Captain Charity, anyone,' he said reluctantly and feeling quite alone. 'I wish my father was here, he'd know what to do.'

'The one who left you at the Colonial School to pursue his own ends?' She said without thinking, the words tripping from wits to tongue so easily.

'They had to go,' he blurted back. 'It's not that easy. Choices have to be made all the time. They would have come back . . . They would.' Mariah hit the wall with his fist.

'At least my father brought us with him.'

'At least my father wouldn't have been a drunk and a thief,' he parried.

They went on in a seething silence, unable to shake off each other's company. Mariah hoped she would fall from some hidden precipice and be eaten by the crocogon that stood below and watched.

'Who would do all these things?' he muttered to himself not wanting a reply. 'I'll go for Jack Charity and you can stay here.'

'On your own life – I'm coming with you,' Sacha snorted as she tugged on to his coat-tail. 'Leave me with Old Scratty and Monica?'

'You'd be in good company,' he said as they turned a corner in the passageway. It led on to a landing that was dimly lit by a wickless light encased within a glass orb.

Below was a narrow door with a lattice of metal that formed a flexible iron grid. To one side was an illuminated red button glowing brightly against the black painted rock in which it was set. Instinctively, Sacha pressed the button. From far above came the rumbling of a steam elevator.

'I thought there was only one in the building?' Mariah asked.

'This is no ordinary one,' she said. 'Listen to the sound it's making.'

The steam elevator gushed hot mist as it approached at high speed. It forced the air down the tunnel like wind from a whistle. It then suddenly stopped and the metal cage opened by itself as a green light lit their feet.

Mariah stepped inside, followed by Sacha. There were two buttons set in a brass plate. The first was etched with the word *Laboratory*, the lower one with *Office* inscribed in bold black lettering.

Sacha reached out her finger to press the lower button. Mariah stubbornly pushed her hand to one side and with a satisfied look upon his face pressed for the laboratory. The door slammed shut as two steel bolts shot from a hidden enclosure like sharp bayonets and held it fast. The elevator trembled and then with a hiss of steam shot upwards at such a speed that they both fell to the floor. Within the second they had arrived at the laboratory. The door opened and they rolled out.

Inside the laboratory was a large wooden desk and a vast copper kettle covered in cold wax. The room appeared to be on two levels, with a split wooden floor that looked like the stage of some amateur theatre. A thick velvet curtain divided the room, and leading up to it was a small flight of wooden steps. They were held in place next to the wall by a handrail of rough-cut wood that looked as if it had been smoothed by centuries of floating in the rolling sea.

Mariah got to his knees and sniffed the pungent smell of cooling wax. Around the walls were splatters and drips that hung like oversized bogies. Hanging from drying rails were various outfits: trousers with patches to cover torn knees, dresses and smocks. In the corner, draped over a manikin, was a long black dress covered in sequins and a pair of the finest opera gloves that glinted as if studded with diamonds.

234

Sacha had seen these before. They were the same as those worn by Miss Monica. They covered her long thin arms to the fingertips. Sacha walked across the room and slid a glove upon her hand. It was soft and warm, glinting in the glow from the light-holders that adorned the ceiling.

'Do you think he's made a waxwork of Monica and will have her in the cavern for knowing too much?' she joked with Mariah, who still sulked as he walked about, head downcast and miserable.

'And one of you for being so cheerful?' he replied as he walked up the wooden steps and peeped behind the curtain. 'That's if there's not one already,' he said in his muffled voice. He pulled his head quickly from behind the blood-red drape and called her over. 'You're in for a surprise, Sacha – look!'

Sacha disappeared behind the curtain and all was quiet. Mariah could hear her muffled footsteps walking on the wooden boards. Suddenly she appeared again, clutching a wax head in her arms.

'Does this really look like me?' she said as she clutched the wax image of herself, her hair tied back in a horsehair bun.

'Ceroplastica,' Mariah said as he gently touched the waxen nose. 'The art of taking a human image and creating it in wax. Once read a penny dreadful that told all about it. Never thought I would see one of you.' He laughed.

'That's not all,' she said as she pulled back the draped curtain. 'You're there as well and it looks as if you've been hung for your troubles.'

Mariah pushed his way beyond the drapes. There above him, filling the entire roof of the wooden platform, were several wax manikins hanging from long steel hooks. In the corner was a boy of his age with deep brown curls that spiralled this way and that. Beneath was its thin face and wide bright eyes. Hanging from the sleeve of the black jacket in which it was clad was a vellum label. He walked to the manikin and read the words: *Mariah Mundi – next week*.

'He planned to have me gone by next week?' Mariah squealed in anger. 'We'll see who'll be gone by then.'

Sacha laughed to herself as she turned the label and showed him the date. 'It was done on the day you arrived. *This* is now next week.'

'Then he'll have all on to catch me. I'll not work for him in his oyster lagoon – and what happens when you get to be old? Does he feed you to that old crocodile?' He angrily snapped a hand from his waxwork. 'He shan't have the joy of packing me off to France, that's the last place I'd want to go.'

Mariah pulled at the legs of the dangling wax corpse, heaving it from the hook and letting it smash to the floor. He took two paces back, then ran and kicked the head as hard as he could, sending it through the air and smashing against the wall. 'That's for Nelson – king of the sea,' he shouted triumphantly as his wax head splinted into tiny pieces and scattered about the floor.

'Look, Mariah! Pearls!' Sacha shouted as a cascade of pearls burst from the skull and spilt across the floor. 'You were right.'

'And this hand is all we need to prove his guilt,' he said as he pressed the hand into his coat and looked for the door.

The elevator that had brought them to the laboratory burst into life as the door jangled shut. The compartment was sucked far below with a single breath of steam.

'Luger?' Sacha asked as she threw her wax head to the floor than stamped on it several times to reveal a cache of fine wild pearls. 'Then these are for my sisters,' she said as she grasped at the pearls, pushing them into her pockets as they rolled about the floor. 'If he's in the business of killin', then I'm in the business of takin'.'

'And not a moment too soon,' Mariah said as the sound of

the approaching steam elevator came again with a whistle of hot air that sang like a phantom aria. 'We have to get back to the Prince Regent.'

It was Sacha who found the door hidden behind a small drape at the side of the room. She twisted the key and pulled back the wooden gate that opened into the tunnel by the entrance to the beach. She knew this place well. To the right would be the theatrical store where Old Scratty lived, and further along would be the staircase that led to the first steam elevator and the Prince Regent.

In the laboratory the elevator ground to a sudden halt, the sound of its sliding gate echoing about the room. The voice of Grimm shouting to Grendel and Luger was the last thing they heard as they slammed the door. They turned the key to lock the door from the outside, then Mariah threw it down the steps and on to the tide-washed beach below.

In two minutes they had sneaked through the corridors and summoned the elevator. Now they stood holding the brass rail, feet fixed into the safety rings as they hurtled, double-speed, towards the dining room of the hotel.

The gate slid open and they were bathed in sunlight. Mariah held a hand to his face as a waiter pushed quickly by with a silver tray stacked with dirty pots from the tables. Sacha pointed to the kitchen door that swung back and forth. The service for the morning was completed and the staff had gathered for second breakfasts.

'Not eating?' shouted the steward as he pulled a cloth from a window table, scattering crumbs into the air. A seagull crashed into the plate glass and slid, stunned, down the window. 'We serve theatre staff,' he said joyfully. 'Bizmillah has left the building with a guest so he won't be here to chide you for being lazy.'

Sacha smiled and turned away, pulling Mariah by the sleeve.

'Come on,' he said as the steward swept the table with a

small bristled brush. 'Rhamses has eggs and salt beef, just go and ask.'

Mariah pulled against her and smiled at the steward as the man disappeared into the kitchen. His stomach twisted with the words and he remembered how hungry he had become. The smell of salt beef, eggs and smoked haddock filled the room. The bustle of waiters clad in their tight jackets and bow ties swirled the air in a mixture of intoxicated confusion.

'Just one sandwich at least . . .' Mariah pleaded as Sacha pulled away from him.

'One, and then we go. Luger won't be locked in the laboratory forever. They could take the elevator to his office and then come and find us,' she whispered.

'But Grimm would have to go all the way into the cellar and retrace our steps. Just enough time to eat – please?'

Sacha had no time to speak. The door to the kitchen swung open and out stepped the chef, robed in white, a kitchen blade pushed into the belt of his trousers. He searched about the room with steely blue eyes, the wrinkles on his forehead creasing with anticipation as he looked for a straggling guest to harangue to tears before he threw them from the restaurant.

'You!' he shouted at Mariah, pointing a finger of one hand as the other grasped the blade in his belt. 'They tell me you don't want to eat my food. Not good enough?' He screamed, the spikes of his blond hair bouncing sweatily like a freshly preened parrot. 'No one dare refuse my food. I am the chef – Rhamses. Understand?' The man's voice blistered around the room, hot enough to strip the paper from the wall and turn his face crimson red.

Mariah didn't move, frozen like a startled hare by the ferocity and venom of the man's northern accent. He began to sidle closer to Sacha as together they edged nearer to the doors that would take them through the Great Hall and into the street.

'Don't think of walking out of here without tasting even the merest morsel of my food! That is not allowed . . .' he sang angrily as he took the kitchen blade from his belt and waved it back and forth. He pointed the tip to a small table in a dark corner of the restaurant, commanding them to sit there. 'You *will* eat my food, both of you, and then you can go about your business.' Rhamses pulled an enormous gurgling frog from his pocket and, with one quick slice through the air, removed the legs from the rest of its juddering body. 'And I'll decide what you'll eat – none of this picking from a menu. Breakfasts are of my choosing.'

They had no choice. Rhamses pointed again to the table with the sharp-tipped knife and crinkled his forehead into deep furrows of expectation. The table was in the far corner of the restaurant, surrounded by tall silk screens covered in flying dragons and large parlour palms in red earthen pots.

Rhamses curled his lip in mock disappointment as the long blond spikes of hair bounced from side to side. 'Sit!' he said loudly. 'It will be sent to you, and don't move.' He waved the knife from side to side as he held the twitching frogs legs in his hand. 'It is amazing how sharp these become with use.'

He vanished through the doors as Sacha took her seat and faced the windows that overlooked the sea. Far below, two bathing boxes had been pulled into the water and already she could distinguish the bobbing of a red bathing cap in the cold Oceanus Germanicus. 'Sit here,' she instructed Mariah as she patted the leather of the mahogany chair. 'Keep lookout, and if they come we will at least see their reflection in the window.'

Mariah looked behind him to the doors of the steam elevator. All was quiet. At several tables the waiters sat and waited for their breakfast. They all looked the same: tall, thin with a wisp of a moustache etched across their lips. One looked towards Mariah, disgruntled, as he twisted his fork in the quiff of greased hair that hung loosely over his face. He stared at them through deep murky eyes, set beneath the darkest brow Mariah had ever seen. The waiter stared and stared as he scooped spoonfuls of thick grey porridge from a porcelain bowl, sucking it from the spoon with disgusting dribbles. Mariah looked away and then moments later looked again. The waiter still had his stare fixed upon them.

Then the kitchen door suddenly sprang open and Rhamses strutted into the room carrying a large silver tray stacked high with gleaming white plates all trimmed with shining bands of silver warmers. He balanced the stack upon his fingers as with one hand he laid out the food before them. He gave a gracious smile that wrinkled his chin and twisted a small white scar on his top lip into the shape of a rising moon. Rhamses's bark ebbed to a soft voice as he saw their eyes light up with fervent anticipation.

'Food, good food, and I know you'll like it,' he said eagerly. 'Eat and then work.' Rhamses looked at Mariah. 'You're new? Work for Bizmillah? Can tell by the clothes. Always dresses them in black.' The chef wrinkled his nose. 'You'll stay around longer than Felix. He was my best customer and liked my food. Then he vanished. Some say he was washed from the pier, taken by the Kraken.'

'I heard it was food poisoning,' Sacha mocked as she picked what looked to be a small roasted chicken wing from a china bowl and crunched upon it.

'And I heard you didn't like frog's legs,' Rhamses replied. As he strolled from the table through the kitchen door and out of sight Sacha realised what she'd just eaten.

Mariah turned again as he peeled a boiled egg and sprinkled it with salt. The waiter still stared at them through the gap between two silk-screens. Then he wiped his chin with the edge of the tablecloth and got up and walked away. He glanced over his shoulder as he slipped through the mahogany doors that swung back and forth on stiff springs, rattling the glass panes.

They ate well, Mariah constantly checking the ivory-faced clock that hung above the door, its skeleton-hand pendulum swinging with each second. 'Time to go,' he said as the steam elevator began to churn. 'Could be them.'

The elevator whooshed past the restaurant in a jet of steam, destined for a higher place. Mariah breathed a sigh of relief as he realised it couldn't be Grimm and Grendel that had called it.

The door to the restaurant opened and the sultry waiter came into the room wiping his moustache with long, greasy fingers. He had a smug smile etched on his face, and an eyelid twitched nervously as he grinned at Mariah. The waiter took his seat, staring at them constantly. Mariah said nothing as he pushed the wax hand deeper into his coat. He nodded to Sacha to finish the banquet and, when she continued, kicked her under the table. She looked up startled and caught the waiter's eye for the first time.

Sacha chewed the last of the food and raised her eyebrows, nodding to Mariah as she placed her knife and fork across the plate and creased the napkin to one side in seven deliberate folds.

'He was a friend to Felix,' she whispered. 'He was with him on the night he disappeared. Says he's French. Spends a lot of time talking to Luger.'

The waiter smiled and then gave a genteel wave to Sacha as he cleared the table and disappeared into the kitchen.

'Now,' said Mariah as he pushed back the mahogany chair and got to his feet.

'Going?' said a voice from the other side of the silk screen. 'And so soon. We've been waiting for you to finish your break-fast.' Grimm pushed his fat jowled face around the dragon prints and smiled like a bloodhound. 'I was just saying to Mister Grendel that it would be far better to wait for them to finish before we asked them to come with us, wasn't I, Mister Grendel?'

'Indeed, Grimm, indeed.' Grendel quivered as he peered down at them from above the screen, his hands gripping the wooden frame to stop them shaking.

'So . . . Now that you have finished, I would like you to come with us,' Grimm said as if was inviting them for tea.

'GUESTS!' screamed a voice from behind the kitchen door. 'In the restaurant?' the voice screamed again. 'NEVER!'

Rhamses burst through the door, knife in hand, a scowl like sour milk across his face. 'YOU!' he screamed as Grimm turned to look at him. 'Yes, you. The fat dwarf with the face like a bulldog sucking a thistle.' Grimm opened his mouth in protest but could not say a word as Rhamses grabbed him by the throat and dragged him across the room to the door, followed meekly by Grendel. 'Out of my restaurant, now.'

'But we're here on Mister Luger's business – we have to take the boy to him,' Grimm replied as the chef's large hand squeezed the breath from his throat, his voice pitched to that of a choking cockerel.

'They are my guests,' Rhamses replied as he lifted Grimm from the floor with one hand and summoned Grendel to leave with the other. 'They will stay as long as there is food on the table.' He looked to Mariah and signalled with his eyes for them to run.

Mariah grabbed Sacha and pushed her through the kitchen door. They tumbled to the floor at the feet of the sultry waiter. He grabbed Sacha by the arm, dragging her to her feet.

'This way,' he said as he pulled them both through the kitchen. 'It'll take you through the cellar and into the street. 'Go – Felix was my friend.' He smiled as he pushed them down a short flight of steps and into a basement packed with fruit and stacked cases of wine. Ahead they could see the two open doors that led into the square. They clattered through the darkened room and into the bright light of morning, the sound of Rhamses haranguing Grimm and Grendel fading into the distance.

[22]

The Emporium Vaults

MARIAH ran from the building, chased by his shadow. The streets were full of people milling around the large market that took place outside the Prince Regent. He ran in and out amongst the brightly coloured stalls, with Sacha chasing on behind. A small black dog with a head like a snarled lorica snapped his heels as he ran, biting and gnashing. Mariah kicked out, sending the creature spinning headlong through the dank mud that covered the square.

There was a sudden shout from the crowd for him to stop, as if he had been recognised for some crime. A large man of burly frame and bristling moustache lashed out, seeking to grab him by his coat as he ran. Mariah ducked, managing to fall beneath the blow as he rolled in the mud, then got to his feet and started to run again. Sacha hid amongst the stalls, trying to avoid the gazing eye of Isambard Black as he looked on from the balcony of the Prince Regent.

'Here!' she shouted in a panic, as Mariah ran further away, cutting close to a man hacking at a joint of cow's leg that splattered fragments of bloodied meat into the air and on to Mariah as he stormed by. 'This way!' Sacha shouted even louder, above the cackle and babble of the market, vainly attempting to gain his attention. Mariah turned and caught a glimpse of her some way off. 'If we get through here, we'll get away,' she said quickly as she danced in agitation, hoping to draw him to her. Mariah stumbled as he ran, picking himself up and falling again in the deep mud.

Outside the Prince Regent a carriage stopped abruptly. Mariah looked back and saw Perfidious Albion dragged from the coach and into the mudded square. Two men dressed in black suits and long coats held him by the arms. Both wore red hats shaped to the form of a flattened pork pie and braided in gold. He could see they were unshaven and bleary-eyed from the journey. For some unknown reason, Perfidious Albion turned and, glaring through the market stalls, saw Mariah. He tried to smile at him, then quickly looked away, nodding his head as he was hauled up the marble steps and into the hotel.

From the revolving door of the Prince Regent stepped Grimm and Grendel. They greeted Perfidious Albion with a glove slapped about his face then looked up and down the marketplace. Each was holding his black walking cane, tipped with a lion's head. Grimm rubbed his throat; his ruby-red cheeks and shining skin glistened in the first rays of the morning sun. Grendel adjusted his spectacles as he squinted in the bright morning light. They looked to each other, then stepped into the dirt, sullying their crisp black shoes with the mud that now engulfed the tips of their feet.

Together they wobbled across the market, Grendel sniffing the air as if he could trace where Mariah had run. Grimm looked at the soil, examining each footprint. From his pocket he pulled the large round spectacles and placed them on his stubby nose. He gazed intensely at the ground, pointing to the mud with a stubby squat finger.

'This way,' he said, his irritating voice echoing against the brick wall of the Prince Regent Hotel. 'I can see their foot-marks. The spectacles work well, even in daylight,' he said as he adjusted the gold frames and turned a small dial on the side of the lens. 'Even better,' he said as he walked quickly. 'With one more turn, I'll be able to see every footstep that they take. Stupid cooker,' he muttered to himself. 'Thought he could stop me finding them, did he? His goose will surely be burnt to a crisp when I return.'

Grimm hobbled on like a large fat penguin, his coat-tails billowing in the breeze. Grendel tried to pick his way through the mud, tiptoeing with each step.

'I can smell them!' Grendel said as he sniffed a bellyful of air and made a pouting expression with his thin lips. 'Fear, dripping from their bodies like dew. There's nothing better than a chase, especially on the day of the Christmas market.' He plunged his cane firmly into the mud, squelching it deep down beneath his weight as he strutted behind his fat friend.

Grimm bumbled on. He pushed his way through the revellers, knocking a stand of fine ale to the ground and ignoring the comments and swearing of the man who stood close by.

'Leave him be. This isn't your matter,' Grendel said to the man, who glared at Grimm, hoping for compensation. 'We are *detecting*, and nothing can stand in the way of that!' He pushed the man, who fell on his backside, squelching in the mud with deep indignation.

'This way!' said Grimm happily, as he strutted through the market. 'Their footsteps are still hot. I can see them through the spectacles. They are not long ahead of us. They are running, running, but they will never escape.'

'A good investment, good investment,' Grendel replied as he scurried on behind.

'There is a man in Utah who will not be able to read the writing on a plate. I took them from him,' Grimm said. 'Told me he was a prophet, said he could speak Greek but couldn't utter a word.'

Far ahead, Mariah and Sacha beat their way through the market. Sacha turned and caught the glimpse of a fine black silver-topped hat far behind. She realised that Grimm and Grendel followed in their wake.

'They're behind us, Mariah. We'll have to go this way,' she said as she pointed to a narrow side street that led as an escape from the market. Mariah looked up, his gaze reaching from the dirt to the heavens. He saw before him the tall castle bar and, taking several steps across the street, they went through the archway and into the narrow lane that led into the centre of the town.

To each side were arcades of the strangest shops that Mariah had ever seen. In the window of a fishmonger's was a large black skate hanging from a hook by its tail. It wallowed like a hanged man, its mouth open, seawater dripping from its face and doleful glazed eyes that stared at Mariah.

'We can't stay!' Sacha said, pulling at his coat sleeves, trying to get him to walk faster to get away from the marketplace.

'I know someone who we can go and see. There's a man. He's a collector. He works at the Emporium. If we go there, I *know* we'll get away. I know he can help us.' There was desperation in her voice, as if she spoke to convince herself. As they clattered into the crowded street across the bright stone cobbles, she turned back. Far behind, two silk hats followed, one squat, the other tall and thin, to match their wearers.

Together they ran along Bar Street, its narrow buildings reaching high above them and clawing at the dark sky, protecting them from the large raindrops that now beat down on the grey slates and thatched roofs high above them.

Sacha stopped suddenly and dragged Mariah into the doorway of an old snuff shop, its windows clad in sticky brown slime and displaying the words: *Ebenezer Bartholomew's. Magical Snuff. Guaranteed to blow the cobwebs from even the most stifled of brains.*

Mariah read the fading gold and bronze words and wondered what Ebenezer's goods could do for him. Sacha turned to the door but didn't go in. She pressed her face upon the glass, as if to see who was inside. She grabbed Mariah and turned him towards her.

'Look inside!' she said. 'Look inside!' They hid their faces against the glass. In the reflection of the window Mariah saw a Peeler in his long black cape and helmet amble by. He looked in and out of every window up and down Bar Street as if he searched for someone or something. Sacha waited.

'It's safe,' she said. 'He's gone.'

'Why were you hiding from him?' Mariah asked as he turned and looked into the street. The constable was walking away, hands firmly clasped behind his back as he swaggered.

'It's Jack Teal. He's a friend of my father. If he sees me out, he'll know I'm up to something. You don't understand, Mariah. This place has got eyes and ears and whatever we do, someone or something's going to see us.'

Sacha looked back along the street and saw Jack Teal talking to Grimm and Grendel. They engaged him in polite conversation, bowing and nodding as they passed the time of day. Grimm took the spectacles from his nose and folded them neatly, placing them in a black silk bag and slipping them quickly into his inside jacket pocket. He gave them a reassuring pat as he slithered a pair of fine black gloves with silver-trimmed fingers on to his hand.

'He knows them!' Mariah said, as he saw the discourse taking place. 'What are we going to do?'

Sacha thought and then grabbed his hand. 'This way,' she said. 'If we keep on going, we can outrun them.'

They left the narrow lane of shops and turned when they heard a clattering of carriages. The whole street was squashed and filled with horses, neighing and braying as they tried to push past each other. Sacha pulled Mariah as they ran down the hill towards the harbour, the fresh smell of the sea blowing in the breeze. In front of them they could see the pinnacle of the Emporium decked with a large Jack that flew in the wind.

'Not far,' Sacha gasped as she smiled at Mariah, the confidence coming back to her face.

In five minutes they stood beneath the tower of the Emporium. By the doorway to the market vault there was a pillar of bright yellow sandstone that reached up above their heads to a now bright blue sky. By the side were blackened windows etched with news of the latest sale of remnant goods and all that had survived the most recent wreck upon the rocks.

The door to the market vault was firmly shut. A gargoyle of a coiled lizard looked down upon them as they stared at each other, not knowing what to do. Sacha pushed at the brightly painted blue wooden slats and the large metal handle that ran across the door. It opened suddenly. They fell inwards with a jolt, down the four worn slabs and on to the stone floor beneath.

There before them the vaults opened up like a large ornate bazaar, candle-lit and yet still dark. The only shadows were created by a soft light in the distance. Cautiously they went further inside, Sacha leading the way.

At the end of the corridor of shops, all with their windows tightly shuttered, Mariah could see a faint light reflected through the thick glass of a window. To each side of him were arched doorways covered with beaded blinds and symbols of their trade hanging above.

The palm of a large hand etched in golden lines swung silently above them. Mariah read the words above the shop door: *The Great Plagiarus – Palmist and Phrenologist – May the bumps on your head speak great voices of the future – No Credit.* Beneath the sign and stuck to the window glass was a small note, quickly etched in a child's crayon: *Closed – Due to unforeseen circumstances.*

Mariah felt he himself was a lad of unforeseen circumstances, a child of constant sorrow. His feet suddenly drudged, the life ebbing from them, turning his toes to lead and his knees to rigid iron. Within his heart he had an overwhelming desire to give himself to Grimm and Grendel and do whatever they wished. It was as if a dark cloud had blown from horizon to horizon, blotting out the sun and turning day to night. All hope had suddenly gone as he fretted mournfully about the voices of his future and wished Plagiarus had not been so called away.

'Would be good if we could consult the future,' he said to Sacha as they gazed in each shop window they passed by. 'Should have asked the Panjandrum what would happen . . . All we did was watch it like a circus – a waste, really.' He sounded downcast, his words fading.

Sacha tried to smile, but in her heart she knew that, somewhere not too far behind, Grimm and Grendel would follow them. Grimm would be wearing his spectacles and would see their hidden footsteps, following like a faithful hound to a home's hearthrug.

On the far corner of the covered arcade was the brightly painted front of Quadlibett's Fine Vendorium. It appeared to glow in the dark shadows with its ornate provisions. Every tin, bottle and bag that filled the window begged to be purchased. Mariah found himself mesmerised by the sight of jar upon jar of luscious delights. His mouth welled with anticipation and stirred his stomach. He had never in all of his life seen so much that would provoke such desire.

In front of him stood a man, a small tasselled hat upon his head, a pair of cobalt spectacles stuck firmly upon his nose. He was dressed in a neat black suit and a cravat of the finest gold thread etched with purple dragons. A white shirt with a stiff collar was wrapped around his neck and his cuffs fluffed and flustered from under his sleeves. What caught Mariah's eye the most was the bright shining of a beautiful emerald ring. He gave a polite cough. Startled, Sacha turned, not realising he stood there. The man laughed.

'What took you so long, Sacha?' he said as he twiddled the ring on his finger. 'I thought you'd have been here a long time ago.' He held out his hand in a gesture of friendship. 'And who is this?'

Sacha turned to Mariah, unsure as to what to say. She saw the look in Mariah's eyes.

'Oh, this is Mariah. From London. The Colonial School. Works with me at the Prince Regent.'

'Like young Mister Felix,' Quadlibett said as he spun the emerald ring on his finger. 'I am Quadlibett, owner and patron of this arcade. Sadly not all my tenants have lived up to expec-tation, but you can buy things here from around the known world. Headbands from the native Indians of the Americas, the finest herbs from Tibet and any article of clothing you would ever wish to wear. And in my very own Vendorium, the best chocolate known to man.'

'We're in trouble, Mister Quadlibett,' Sacha blurted out.

'Sacha, you're always in trouble!' Mister Quadlibett said, as if to brush her comment to one side to digest it later. He led them to the doorway of the shop, took out a bright brass key from his pocket, put it in the lock and quickly turned it. He opened the door and Mariah gasped. What he hadn't seen through the full windows was the most amazing tabernacle of delight the eye could perceive. There before him were shelves and shelves of tinned biscuits, boxes of sweets and packets of the finest delicacies that he'd ever seen. His stomach twisted with hunger, prompted by his eyes. He gave a gentle laugh, as if he had fallen into paradise. Mister Quadlibett tapped the side of his nose and gave him a knowing wink.

'I take it, Mariah, you're like everybody else that comes into this shop. You can see in their eyes that they devour everything, desiring to devour it in their stomachs!'

The lad gasped. 'It's true. Sorry, Mister Quadlibett, my eyes gave me away but I've never seen anything like this before!'

'Then you will be my guest,' the man said. 'Pick anything you want. Just point to the box. Pick and sample what's inside and let it be a magnificent surprise.'

In the bright light of the lamp, Mariah's eyes searched every tin. They shone in a myriad of colours: greens, blues, blacks, turquoise, the deepest of reds and a scarlet that almost burnt the eye to gaze upon it. He read the labels. Mariah had never heard of such wondrous names. *Gallacto's Bubble Mints*, *Caruso's Chocolate* – they were all there, all the favourites, waiting for him to eat. He thought long and hard as his hand wafted backwards and forwards along the line of tins and then he decided.

'I'll have one of those. Just one!'

He pointed to a box made of tin, neatly crafted into the shape of a row of books. He read the label: *Madison's Magical Wonders*.

Mariah had only ever seen one such tin before in his life, sent by a grieving parent to the Colonial School, a price paid, a guilt offering for the abandonment of her son. So expensive a gift that the boy had held the tin in his hands, marvelled upon it, watched it for days, before he even dared to open the lid.

There, inside, he knew would be the most marvellous, the most wonderful and the most colourful thing that a young eye could ever gaze upon. Even to hold one of Madison's Magical Wonders was a pleasure beyond pleasures. Mariah remembered that day well. He had stood with several of his friends, waiting for that moment, desiring the boy just to open the golden wrapper and give him a glimpse of what was inside. The boy had taken the gold edges between his fingers and gently pulled each side of the tin lid. It was then, for the first time in his life, that Mariah saw a Madison's Magical Wonder – there, in gleaming gold, coated in sugar, twisted in pearl barley and with several drops of the finest, darkest chocolate. The boy had held it in his hand, closed his eyes as if to pray, and then with one swift movement pushed the whole of the chocolate slab into his mouth, never to be seen by the light of day again.

A deep sigh had gone from boy to boy, their vain hope of sharing in this dream finally quashed as he chomped away, his mouth full, a dribble of black and red spit crossing his cheek and dropping to the floor at his feet the only sign of what had taken place.

For Mariah, this had been a sacrament, a holy moment like one that is shared between priests and people, yet Mariah and his friends were not part of that covenant. The boy had giggled to himself, clumsily chewing, chomp after chomp, as he devoured the marvellous thing within his mouth. His *once* friends turned away in their deep disappointment, never to speak to him again.

Now Mariah stood in the vaults beneath the high tower of the Emporium and suddenly it was his chance. There was the tin, the open hand of Mister Quadlibett reaching out to the shelf, looking to where Mariah was pointing.

'You choose well, lad. You choose very well. The most expensive thing that I have. Yet let this be a free gift from me to you.' He took the box from the shelf. He opened the tin lid and held it towards Mariah.

Mariah's hand darted inside, clutching the chocolate between his fingers. Then quickly he ripped it from its golden skin, shedding the foil like the dead membrane of a lizard. He looked upon it and, like the boy from the Colonial School, didn't wait to be asked. He pushed the chocolate deep within his mouth and chomped and sighed and chomped again. He sat at the small table in the corner of the shop and ate to his content. He tried to smile in thanks to Quadlibett, but all he could do was dribble chocolate down his chin.

As Mariah gazed about the Vendorium, Quadlibett took Sacha to one side and whispered to her. 'Trouble?' the man asked. 'You said you were in trouble, Sacha? Real trouble that you cannot fix yourself?'

Sacha looked at him, then looked back along the dark arcade, into the alleyway and out to the street.

'Being followed,' she said nervously. 'Something has happened at the Prince Regent.'

'And where does young Mariah fit into this trouble?' Mister Quadlibett asked, as he watched him chewing away upon the fine chocolate.

'There's something else. It's at the Prince Regent. It's to do with Felix.'

'Felix? I remember him well! Did he not choose exactly the same as Mariah?'

'Exactly,' Sacha said. She was quite anxious. Her hand scratched the side of her face, then curled itself upon the wisp of hair. 'There's something wrong. Something not right. Felix disappeared, he vanished. We thought he was dead or had run away but we found him, he's still in the hotel.'

'Could well be,' Mister Quadlibett said, as he looked out to the street. 'I think conversations such as this should be catered for behind closed doors.'

He reached and pulled the door shut. Taking the key from

his pocket, he locked the thick brass lock then slid the two bolts. He turned to the oil lamp behind him and lowered the wick.

'Now,' he said. 'Let us sit down. Let's talk about what you have seen, and maybe Mister Quadlibett will be able to pour some oil on your troubled water.'

Mariah didn't speak. He continued to eat the fine chocolate, his eyes trying to tell Quadlibett all that he had seen. Sacha spoke for him. Quickly, impatiently, she told of all that had gone before.

[23]

The Shovel Hat

MISTER Quadlibett opened his coat and pulled on his braces. He looked at Mariah, searching out all that was going on within him. Then he gave a half-smile and picked his teeth with his finely trimmed fingernails. 'I can tell you're a lad of secrets,' the vendor said as he offered him another chocolate.

Mariah picked one from the box and placed it quickly in his pocket.

'For later!' he replied, hoping it would not be snatched back and taken away.

'Later is always worth preparing for,' Quadlibett said with a smile of satisfaction, knowing that his delights enticed the meanest of hearts. 'I am suspicious when a man does not prepare for what is to come. I *always* carry a satchel of food whenever I leave the house. But never that which I would eat straight away. It is best to pack that which you only marginally like. For if you took your favourite it would be gone before you were not much than a yard from your door.' He looked at Mariah and handed him another candy. 'You never know how long it will be before you will eat again. And, come to think of it, I should take a change of clothes, a spare hat, galoshes and my last will and testament – should I die in the street, I would not want them scouring my house to find what I haven't left to them.' He finally sucked in a breath that whistled through his teeth. 'To think of it again. If we were to be always prepared then we should carry a sack – nay – have carried for us by a donkey all that we should need for every eventuality of life. Yet we set off on the daily grind with nothing more than a hankersniff and a tub of snuff. That is the human condition, young Mariah. No preparation and much ado when all goes wrong and we are not prepared.' Quadlibett grabbed yet another candy and pressed it into the lad's hand. 'Best you don't go the way of the world. Take plenty and always have a candy in your pocket.'

'How much do I owe you for these?' Mariah asked, suspiciously.

'For you, lad? Nothing. Treat it as being a pleasure, my pleasure. Now tell me, your eyes speak of secrets. There's no room for those between the three of us, so tell me what troubles you.'

Mariah glanced up and down at the man, looking for some flaw, some petulance or deceit. There was none. He smiled at Quadlibett.

'Since I arrived from London, things have been happening. There was a man on the train, said he was called Isambard Black. Said he'd been booked into the hotel for three months, but yesterday, yesterday just after breakfast, I found out that he arrived with no reservation, nothing. He lied, and yet he seemed to know so much about me.'

Mister Quadlibett looked at him. 'Maybe a coincidence. People come to the hotel all the time. What makes him so different?'

'But it was what he did. He was in the same compartment of the train. He shared with me secrets, told me things. There was a man I met at Kings Cross, said he was called Perfidious

Albion. He gave me a pack of cards, told me I had to keep them safe, then send him a postcard to the Claridges Hotel. I sent him a card from the Prince Regent. This morning, some men turned up at the hotel, dragging Perfidious Albion from a carriage.' Mariah stared at Quadlibett as if he were part of some game that had spun out of control. 'There are also two others who say they're detectives. They followed us through the streets. Is this just some other coincidence?' Mariah asked.

'One tall, the other short and fat?' Quadlibett asked as if he knew them well. Sacha nodded her reply. 'Grimm and Grendel.'

'You know them?' Sacha asked.

'Know of them. They have reputation in the town already. Things are not kept a secret for too long. Like the body that was discovered outside the Three Mariners. Strange how it was found again this morning under the new bridge – people said there had been a fall – a lost vagrant. I have never known dead men to throw themselves from bridges.' Quadlibett spoke quietly as if to himself. 'Kraken's back . . . or so they say, and the beach steams.' He thought for a moment. 'Best we see Mister Charity. He will know what to do with this. A strange adventure for you both.'

There was a sharp rattle upon the door of the shop, agitating the glass.

'Best go in the back,' Quadlibett said to Sacha. 'You know the way out, should our guest be unwelcome. Barrels and stairs . . . barrels and stairs,' he muttered.

The door was rattled again, this time more urgently than before. There followed a frantic banging.

'Grimm and Grendel?' Mariah asked as he stepped from the brightly lit shop and into the dark storeroom hidden behind a blue veil.

'Whoever it is wants to see us,' Quadlibett said lightly as if it mattered not that the detectives could be at the door. 'Go and hide. Keep listening. If it should be them there is a way of escape that may intrigue you.'

Sacha pulled Mariah into the darkness and slid the veil across the doorway, blocking it further with a wooden stand decked in jars that when closed made the entrance look like nothing more than another display of finest sweets.

There came another rattle at the door, this time followed by a raucous voice that sounded as if a gull had taken human form.

'Quadlipet . . . Mister Quadlipet.' A woman's voice cackled and gurgled as if her lungs were effervescent. 'I need *string*, Mister Quadlipet, string, and you are the only man I know with a large enough ball.'

'Mrs Sachavell, with all this shouting and ranting I thought the world had caught fire and all you require is *string*?' he said as he took the key and turned the lock.

'String, Mister Quadlidot, and without a good length I shall be undone and unable to work.' She shouted and banged at the same time. 'There are customers afoot and money to be made and how can I wrap my cod ends without a decent yard of string?' She spat out her words and pulled her shovel hat over her ears.

Quadlibett opened the door slowly and looked carefully out-side.

'Quickly!' she ranted, pushing the door from his hand and stepping into the shop. 'It's getting late in the day and all's not well.' Her eyes devoured the shop and scoured each surface for a hint of gossip to pass on as she wrapped the dead heads and slithers of fish she called a fillet. 'Taken to eating your own stock, eh, Mister Quadlipet? Leaving the golden wrapper behind is a sign of tardiness.'

'It's Quad-lee-bett, Mrs Sachavell, Quad-lee-bett. A *dot* is a mark on paper and a *pet* is an animal kept that women stroke and men detest,' he said, addressing a large woman in a once fine dress that had been expanded several times to cope with her increasing size. Mrs Sachavell shimmied into the shop as if she were an egg-bound hen, pushing Quadlibett to one side as she ogled the shelves.

'And *string* is something that keeps me in business,' she retorted quickly as the Vendorium began to smell of stale fish. 'How much can I have?'

'As much as your conscience allows you to take without payment, my dear Mrs Sachavell,' Quadlibett said patiently. He went behind the counter and then handed her a ball of rough sisal as big as an ostrich egg.

'Without payment, Mister Kudlipet? Such a gent and I know I can return the favour. My fish is so fresh and dainty that it will please a man's heart. I'll bring some delight when I close up and see you taken care of,' she said fondly as she plucked a hair from her nose, eyed it for size and then threw it to the floor.

The thought of sampling any delight of Mrs Sachavell's chilled him to the bone as the smell of her *fresh* fish permeated the shop. Impatiently, Mrs Sachavell took the yardstick and began to measure what her conscience would allow her to take free of charge, the indulgence of Mister Quadlibett's charity.

Sacha watched on, her eye pressed to the gap between the wall and the stand as Mariah searched the storeroom for a way of escape. As he looked around in the dim light he noticed that the shelves were not stacked with sweets but with cases of wine, tobacco and jeroboams of gin. Everything was covered in a layer of what seemed to be dust, but when inspected, Mariah could see that it was in fact the skeletons of tiny creatures. Some of these beasts were crushed to a fine powder, others were in their shells or in varying stages of dried decay. He crept back to Sacha and whispered in her ear.

'Smuggler – gallons of gin hidden,' he said, loud enough for his whisper to be heard in the Vendorium.

'Did you hear that?' Mrs Sachavell asked anxiously as her eyes twitched uncontrollably from side to side and she scratched the wart that hung from the end of her nose.

'What?' replied Quadlibett with a straight face as he bit the smile from his lips. 'I heard only the sound of your conscience stripping the ball of string.'

'Voices,' she said earnestly. 'Someone called me a smuggler. I heard it well enough as if they stood behind me. And they know about my —' Mrs Sachavell held back the words in case whoever had spoken could hear what she would say and make much capital of it.

'She'll hear us,' Sacha said, unaware that the partition could not withhold even the slightest murmur.

'What would they know of? *If* it was a voice speaking to you,' Quadlibett asked.

'Nothing Mister . . .' She paused unable to remember his name as the accusation of her smuggling gin simmered like a pot on the fire. 'I've heard many voices of late, often when I'm alone. That's the first one when I've been in company, and makes things worse if only *I* heard it.'

'Do they say much, these voices?' he asked.

'Often wake me, tell me to do things, often quite unsavoury and not for a woman of my age.'

'Nor any age, I should imagine,' Quadlibett replied as he watched her empty the ball almost completely of string.

'They tell me to dance, to go into the street and dance in the rain. But I can't. Carbuncles, Mister . . . They crush my feet, I have all on getting a shoe to fit,' she said as she pulled up her skirt and showed Mister Quadlibett her sea boots, cut off at the ankle to form a cumbersome pair of oilskin shoe-ettes. 'And they pinch,' she said as she took yet another yard of string and wincing her face, puckering her lips into the shape of dried prune.

'Has your conscience taken enough?' he asked.

Without warning the door was pushed brutally open and in stepped Mister Grimm.

'What shop is this?' he asked petulantly.

'Quadlibott's Fine Vendorium,' Mrs Sachavell grunted, thankful that the voice that had spoken was possessed of a body.

'Are you Quadlibott?' Grimm asked the woman as he took the divining spectacles from his face and put them into his pocket. 'And what do you do?' he asked Quadlibett without giving Mrs Sachavell a chance to answer.

'I am measuring the length of a woman's conscience,' he said as he took the yardstick from Mrs Sachavell and held it like a school cane in front of Mister Grimm's face. 'And at the moment it measures twenty-five yards.'

'Thankfully, a conscience is not something I have to suffer. Tell me, you both, have you seen a lad and lass nearby? Could be said to be in a hurry?'

Before they could answer, Grendel stepped into the shop, lowering his head to ease himself through the door. He sniffed as he squeezed by Mrs Sachavell, doffing his hat and smiling to reveal a row of perfectly formed gold teeth..

'Can't smell them here, Mister Grimm. Are you sure they came this way?'

'To the door,' Grimm snorted. 'To this very door and no mistaking.'

'Then they must be here somewhere,' he said nonchalantly as he lifted Mrs Sachavell's many skirts and peered at her voluptuous undergarments hidden beneath. 'Not there either,' Grendel sniggered as he continued to stare at her pink-laced bloomers.

'Nor will they be,' said Sachavell as she bolstered herself and shook like a broody hen. 'What kind of a gentleman are you?' she asked.

'One who will not be put off the scent by the frills of a hag's petticoat,' Grimm butted in, wanting the conversation to end and his work to continue. 'They *are* here, Mister Grendel, I know it to be true. Don't be deceived . . . *sine die, sine die* . . .'

'Be assured we will not delay your search, but this is not the place for it to continue. There *were* two children here but they've now gone. Mentioned a train to London and a hotel, if I heard them correctly,' Quadlibett said as he looked at Mrs Sachavell. 'Now you have exceeded the limits of your conscience, Mrs Sachavell, I am sure there will be a queue at your stall awaiting a ready supply of fresh fish.'

Mrs Sachavell awakened from the entertainment of watching Grendel twitching her petticoats and trying to peer deep within. She was not sure if he still searched for his lost child or whether he just intrigued himself in some strange pleasure.

'Best be off,' she said, even more earnestly than before and thankful that the voices had ceased. 'But will be back with some nice cod ends, can't beat a bit of cod, fish gone scarce since the Kraken came back,' she twittered as she rolled the string around her hand and left the shop with it trailing far behind. 'Hag?' she shouted. 'Far too pretty for a hag,' she scoffed.

Grendel closed the door and turned the key as Grimm took the divining spectacles and placed them on his nose, looking about the shop.

'You don't tease and play with us, do you, Mister Quadlibett?' Grimm said as he looked up at him.

'I tell you what I have heard many times. Many a lad will come in here and talk of things that they believe to be true, and today was no exception.'

Grimm looked at the shop floor and studied each plank. 'Certainly been here at some point. I can see the footprints. Still very warm, think they're close – too close.'

'Then you have eyes better than a man of your age should

possess. I can see no footprints of anything but the mouse that lives within my old chair,' Quadlibett grumbled.

'But not everyone has what my eyes have,' Grimm said as he pushed the divining spectacles closer to his face. 'And not everyone can see what I can see.'

Quadlibett turned briskly, stepped on a small set of running ladders and took a large tin of sherbet from the highest shelf. 'I have something for your journey, gentlemen.' He pretended to gasp as he turned and slipped from his footing, opening the lid as he fell to the floor.

The shopkeeper showered a cascade of the whitest of powders across the room. It dowsed Grimm and Grendel in a fine sticky dust and billowed in bright clouds in the lamplight. Grimm spat with dissatisfaction as the sherbet covered the glowing footprints he had followed with his spectacles. Quadlibett got quickly to his feet and purposefully tipped even more of the sherbet tin across the floor and down the front of Grimm's stained trousers.

'Fool – nincompoop – miscreant – imbecile – Sisyphus!' screamed Grimm. He was steeped in sherbet crusted like snow upon a winter roof. 'How can I see where they have gone if this is what happens?' he moaned as Grendel wiped his sleeve with his finger and licked the sherbet from it.

'I've always loved sherbet,' Grendel said piggishly as he scooped a handful of the powder from the floor, attempting to fill his pockets.

'Gentlemen, what an unfortunate travesty of my complete inebriation. How can I apologise?' Quadlibett said remorsefully as he turned the key, opened the door and in one movement managed to usher them both from his bazaar without them noticing what had been done.

'Which train?' Grendel asked as the door was shut and locked in his face.

'We are deceived. There is no train and he knows more than he will tell,' Grimm scoffed.

'And we are on the wrong side of the door.' Grendel shook the dust from his coat and wiped the powder from his long thin nose.

'Then we will wait – there has to be no other way from this place. It is built like a castle with a portcullis for a door and a high tower for us to keep our watch,' Grimm said as he brushed the sherbet from his silk hat.

Quadlibett smiled to himself as he double bolted the door and dimmed the light. As he pulled the blind on the windows he watched Grimm and Grendel waddle into the darkness of the arcade.

Turning about, he crossed the shop, his feet pattering the spilt sherbet. He smiled as he rubbed his hands together. 'A job well done, well done,' he said out loud. 'You can come out – the way is clear. Mrs Sachavell has stolen all of my string and Grimm and Grendel are showered in sherbet.'

All was quiet. From the far corner of the shop, beneath the counter, came the scurrying of a rat. Lifting the door veil to one side, Mister Quadlibett pushed the false shelves back into place and looked into the storeroom. He walked three paces and slid the cases of gin across the hatch. Then he took an old silver condiment and sprinkled the floor with a thick grey dust. With one breath he blew the dust into the corner of the room.

'There . . . Dust is dust, nothing more, nothing less, all that we are – and all we will become. Then we'll be worn on the bottom of a man's shoe,' he said to himself with great satisfaction. 'It's as if they have never been.'

[24]

Caladrius

THE sewer smelt like a charnel house on a hot summer's day. It twisted and turned as it steeply descended to the harbour. Sacha carried a small lamp she had taken from the shelf in Mister Quadlibett's storeroom. It lit her feet so that she could see the large brown rats that scattered this way and that as she squelched through the drain. Mariah trailed behind, holding his nose and trying not to bring back the half-digested frog's legs that now jumped in his stomach as the fragrance of the pit turned his guts. He vainly attempted not to touch the walls of the culvert. They dripped with green slime that formed itself into sparkling mercurial stalactites hanging from the roof in small clusters. Every few yards he could see a shadowy opening cut into the side of the culvert and packed with boxes and barrels. Every casket was char-branded in black and carried the shape of a small bird, its head turned against the full moon. Some were covered in thick horse blankets, others tipped end on end and left to bob in the pools of cess that formed against the brick dams.

Sacha walked on, ignoring all that lay about her as if she had no business to look. She was bold with every step, sure-footed, keeping to the high ground and leaving Mariah to wade through the dirt. At one point the roof above had given way, washed by some heavy storm that had cleansed the sewer of every rat and barnacle, spewing them into the sea. Now, several months later, the rats and smugglers had returned, the collapsed roof and the contents of the Saint Sepulchre crypt lying scattered before them.

Hanging like a high seat in the Royal Opera, an open black coffin dangled from the roof. It was snagged by a single piece of wood that pierced the soil. Sacha said nothing. Briefly she lighted it with the lantern and then walked by, not turning.

Mariah stared at the cadaver as he passed by. It shivered him coldly, standing the hairs on his neck and giving further life to the frog's legs that swirled inside him. He tasted each one again as they leapt in his throat, burning like caustic bile.

'Happy to see you,' he said to the corpse, as if to allay his own fear of death and make light of his circumstances. The corpse stared back, covered in thick webs, bone separated from bone and teeth dropping from its jaw.

Sacha bid him be silent, signing with her finger to tighten his lips and say no more. She pointed above to a string of metal grates that allowed the fleeting daylight to shadow momentarily upon his face.

'Princess Street, corner of Tuthill,' she whispered, her words running the length of the sewer and back again. 'Soon be at the harbour.'

'And then?' Mariah asked as they walked on.

'Then we can find Charity and get Felix,' she said.

'You say his name as if he were a beau,' Mariah replied as he looked at the dirt on his shoes.

'*Friend*,' she scorned. 'More to life than a beau, rather throw stones in the sea than hold hands and canoodle.' Sacha smiled for the first time in many hours. In the lamplight it added an extra radiance, showing her face abundant in joy and hope. She looked at Mariah. 'Do you believe in yourself?'

'If I knew what you meant I could tell you,' he replied.

'Do you believe we'll get out of this?' she pressed him again.

Mariah couldn't reply. His mind raced. In an instant he had thought of Otto Luger, the waxworks, Grimm and Grendel, the corpse that stared at him through empty sockets. Everything brought his wits to wretchedness. His mind took him uncontrollably from mayhem to misery.

Sacha butted into his thoughts. 'You have to believe. It's a state of heart. Think we're done for and we are. Drop your head to the ground and we'll end up in the dirt.'

'If life were so simple,' he muttered to himself as he looked to a shaft of bright sunlight streaming through the drain overhead, 'then I would have done with this sack of despair that I carry all these days.'

'Then we go on?' Sacha asked, prodding him in the arm. 'Take this to the end and find Felix and the others?'

'It is all I have to do – there is nothing else,' Mariah replied.

'My grandfather said that if a people don't have a vision then they will perish. He said it was the same in life. If we don't have a dream then we fritter away our lives with nothing. Our days are like grass, one day green and fresh, the next dry and ready to be burnt in the fire. I don't want to live a life like that.' Sacha stood in front of him, her faced flushed with indignation. 'We can make a difference – set them free – put an end to Luger . . .'

'Get caught by Grendel and Grimm and end up in the oyster prison, or have Isambard Black catch us?' Mariah replied as he bathed his face in the sunlight.

'You can change the way you think, Mariah. It's here and now – no future, no past. This is where we live.'

'In a sewer, running from two madmen and into the arms of another?' he asked.

There was a heavy thud that resounded through the tunnel from far away. It was as if the earth had shivered and trembled. The coffin fell from its hanging place, splashing in the pool of stagnant cess and floating slowly towards them. The thud came again as another iron drain cover was picked up and then dropped to its place. One by one the loud thuds sent billows of dust and soot-filled webs into the sewer.

'Here, Grendel, here!' came Grimm's voice, half-heard and far away. 'It comes as a vapour. I can see it clearly. This way – they must be in the sewer.'

Two streets away, Grendel pulled on another cold black-iron sewer flap. Grimm adjusted his spectacles, turning the dial until the lenses glowed bright blue. He stared at something only he could see. Rising from the drain was a red mist telling him of their presence far below. He looked into the distance, beyond the steeple-house of Saint Sepulchre, to the small square of houses that lined the cobbles. Like the crimson breath of a sleeping beast, the vapour rose from the ground. 'Leave it, Grendel,' he shouted, his words echoing far below. 'They are ahead, far ahead, down beyond the square.'

Grendel looked up, hoping to see what Grimm perceived. 'Where?' he asked.

'I can see them and that is all that matters. By the beer house – quickly . . .'

His words carried far below as a feeble echo spoken from another world.

'They're tracking us – they can see us,' Mariah said.

Sacha stepped from the light of the drain back into the shadows. 'They have to use the street. We can get to the harbour before them and across the beach to the Golden Kipper. They won't take on Captain Jack, not if we tell him what they've done.' She made off along the thin ledge of bricks that flanked the pools of dirt-filled water and then down a flight of narrow steps that stank of stale beer.

'I'll show him the hand,' Mariah said, dragging behind in the blackness as Sacha strode on ahead with the lamp. He looked at the outlines of the brick above him and pictured so many feet clambering through life, and there came to him a memory of the boy wrapped in a thin blanket and pushed away from the fire. The feebleness of life, the fleeting of each breath . . . 'What does it matter?' he thought out loud as he pushed the waxen hand deeper into his coat. 'I cannot change what life has done to me.'

'Not far,' Sacha said as the sound of lapping water filled the sewer. 'One more flight and –' All she could see was the sewer tunnel disappearing into the black water. 'High tide. We won't get out for hours,' she said as she held the lamp above her head to light as far as she could.

'There's another way,' Mariah said as he saw a tunnel at the far side of the sewer vault, a thin plank of wood crossing the bubbling mire of sludge backed up against the swirling tide.

'It's from the castle – we never go up there – nothing's ever hidden in that tunnel.'

'We have to get out of here before Grimm comes and gets us,' Mariah snapped.

'But not that way, not now.'

'Don't tell me you get scared?' he asked.

'I'd go anywhere but up there . . . Please.'

'A ghost-demon, or just another story to keep the nosey away from your smuggling?' Mariah asked. 'Don't want me to see what's hidden so I can't tell?'

'Let's just wait for the tide and then we'll be out.'

'And don't you think they'll be waiting for us with some story of how we've robbed Otto Luger? And me with a pistol in my pocket – they'll have us in irons and clinked before you can call your father.'

'Not much of a pistol without any bullets, is it?'

'And you with a roll of notes bigger than a gypsy wad.'

'We could go back,' she said. 'Sneak back to the Emporium.'

'You know what, Sacha? I had a vision . . . back there in the dark with Grimm shouting above my head. A thousand feet busying themselves in life and running back and forth for bread and fish. All these years I have worried about life and know now it could be snapped away in an instant. In a stinking sewer amongst the filth and the rats I found out that it doesn't matter. Life . . . Life . . . more than bread and running after a ball of string. My parents are dead and I'll find out why before I leave this earth.' Mariah took her face in the palms of his hands and felt her soft skin. He smiled at her. 'I'm going to the castle and I'll take whatever comes my way.'

'Then I'll come too,' Sacha said, and together they precariously walked the plank.

As they climbed the steps that ran beside the dry sewer floor, Mariah could hear the distant chiming of a musical box. He picked out its shrill notes against the sloshing of the water far behind. They sounded like the plucking of metal fingernails dancing on thick wire. The sound came again and again, and as they drew closer a sung whisper followed each note with a faint, wailing voice.

'It's coming from in there,' Mariah said cautiously as they saw a gap in the wall where the bricks had been pulled away. 'Smugglers?' he asked warily.

'Not here, not now,' she whispered back as she dimmed the lamp with the cover of her hand. 'Hasn't been a boat in this last week – not one until tomorrow.'

'Then who?' he asked in a murmur as he crept slowly to the side of the entrance and tried to look beyond the shadows.

Sitting by a small fire of broken fish boxes and holding his head in the cups of his hands was the Kraken. He wailed as he wound the handle of the music box time and again. Pressing his eyes into his palms, the Kraken sang a tedious refrain over and over in words they couldn't understand.

Mariah edged closer, Sacha pulling against his coat-tails and wanting to run. He knew he had to see the creature again, that it wasn't to be feared. He stepped into the dark shadow and climbed the rubble.

It was then that the midden on which he walked collapsed beneath his feet. Mariah fell into the room and the Kraken leapt up and thrust a three-blade knife towards him.

'No!' Mariah shouted as he held out his hand. 'We won't do you harm.'

The Kraken lowered the knife and looked at Mariah, understanding not his words but only the look in the lad's eyes. He stepped back and sniffed the air, pointing to the light in the sewer beyond.

'He knows you're there,' Mariah said as Sacha hid. 'It's safe . . . Come in.'

Sacha stepped into the chamber. It was warm and dry and lined with Persian carpets and swathes of fine cloth. Hanging from the roof was a silver cage which imprisoned a pure white bird the size of a sea hawk. A flickering silver candelabrum rested upon a walnut table by the figurehead of a ship. The figurehead was cut from a single piece of oak into the shape of a smiling sea maiden, her parlour pink hands outstretched in welcome.

'Elvira . . . The figurehead is Elvira . . . She went missing from the Three Mariners. Been there for years and then disappeared.' Sacha stepped towards it. 'He had it all along and he's nothing but a sad old man.'

She looked scornfully at the Kraken with his bent neck and

frail old bones. He tried a half-smile as he coughed and held his chest.

'He's sick, dying most like,' Mariah said.

'And that's what we were fritten of?' Sacha said as she looked at the Kraken, his old eyes bulging in his head, his hair hanging in loose patches between pockmarked lumps of flesh. 'Just a legend . . . When you see the real thing it couldn't harm you.'

The Kraken slumped to the small leather chair on which he had sat. He rubbed his face with his blistered hands and flakes of salt-dried skin fell to the floor. He pulled his coat together, snuggling in the folds to keep warm.

'He needs a doctor,' Mariah said as he went to the creature. He picked a stretch of sailcloth from the floor and wrapped it across the Kraken's bony back.

'They say he slaughtered people,' Sacha said.

'I don't think it was him. Thief, yes. But no murderer.'

The Kraken looked at him and tried to speak. 'Scratty . . .' he said in a voice choked of all moisture. 'Scratty?'

'He's talks of Old Scratty, he wants the doll,' Mariah said.

'From the look of this place he wants everything,' Sacha replied. 'Kraken's been a-stealing. These are from a ship that set sail to France a month ago,' she said as she pointed to the Persian rugs strewn across the floor. 'So is the music box – saw 'em go on myself. It sunk on Brigg Rocks, not a soul saved.'

'Caladrius . . .' The Kraken spoke again in a feeble burnt voice as he showed Mariah his parched hands, then held them to his blue and blistered lips. He stood up and fumbled with the minute lock of the silver cage, his fingers too swollen to turn the key. The white bird sat perfectly still, its head folded under its wing. 'Caladrius,' the Kraken said again as he slumped to his chair and held his head in his hands. Fading in heart and mind, he looked to the bird, pointing with a long leprous finger. 'Caladrius . . .'

'He wants to free the bird,' Sacha said. 'He can't turn the key.'

Mariah reached to the cage and turned the key. The door opened by itself as the Kraken wound the musical box, bringing the notes to life and letting the tune dance. He slumped back against the worn leather, resting his head against the high-winged chair back. He swayed his hand back and forth with the chimes of the music, hoping that the bird would fly from the cage. But it sat motionless and then, in time to the music, as if it too were part of the machine, slowly unfurled its long neck.

The bird looked like a pure white swan with an eagle's wings and the claws of some great auk. It shimmered in the firelight as it cropped and gawked, then opened its golden eyes. Staring at Mariah it slowly edged to the door of the cage and stuck out its long neck. The feathers shimmered bright white and in an instant turned to silver as if they were liquid mercury. It looked at the Kraken, then turned its face away and glared at the roof of the vault. With one wingbeat it took flight, flying round and round above their heads, cawing and hooping. It then landed between the Kraken and the fire, shuddering every feather. It stared at the creature as it shook its great silver wings. The Kraken looked back, the skin peeling from his face, his hands blistering and breaking open as his fingernails fell to the floor.

'Caladrius,' the Kraken said as new skin covered his old bones and hair sprouted upon his head.

'He's healed,' Mariah said quietly. He watched the silver wings of the Caladrius begin to tarnish and age as feather after feather dropped from the bird, piling about its feet. 'The bird's dying.'

'It's dead,' Sacha said as the Caladrius dropped to the floor by the fire.

'Not death . . .' the Kraken mumbled. 'It brings life.'

'You can speak,' Mariah said as he stood back from the beast.

274

'And laugh and eat and do many things now that new life has come to me.' The Kraken smiled at them. 'Am I sad and old?' he asked Sacha.

She looked to the floor shame-faced and then turned to Mariah.

'Sacha never meant it,' he said as he stepped to the Kraken. 'They say you're a murderer, that you steal children and leave money behind.'

'I look for Scratty. I killed no one. I have seen who does these things, always at night, always with a three-bladed knife. I am a Kraken and the one you seek is like you. He carries a cane with a silver tip.' The Kraken got to his feet, opening his webbed hands and gazing on the covering of fresh skin. 'The Caladrius was on a ship. I saved it from the sea and kept it for her, to bring Scratty to life. Now I can't find her.' The Kraken picked the bird from the floor and placed it in the bottom of the silver cage.

'We've seen her, we know where she is. She's in the Prince Regent,' Sacha said, trying to smile at him. 'Bizmillah uses her in his act – he's a magician.'

'And a woman with him?' the Kraken asked. 'Tall, thin, elegant, with a painted face?'

'Monica!' Mariah blurted out.

'Monecka Carpova. More than a magician – a sorcerer – a temple master – a witch of the ocean. It was she who took Scratty from me, turned her from flesh to wood and gave her the face of a puppet.'

'Then we will find her for you and bring her back,' Sacha said as she held out her hand. Then she hesitated. 'We've a slight problem . . . We can't go back yet as we are being pursued by a man who can see through the ground and follow us even though we are in the sewer.'

'We need to find a man called Captain Charity. The night

you followed us I saw you in the mirror of his restaurant by the quayside. We have to find that man,' Mariah insisted.

'I am from the sea. I cannot go in the light of day. Look how I was before – the sun melted my flesh as if it were wax. I looked for Scratty at sunrise and it took my skin from me.' The Kraken thought for a moment, his eyes looking around the room. 'I remember the place. There is another way, a dark way.'

[25]

Lex Non Scripta

THEY waited out the hour. The Caladrius lay in the cage, its long limp neck wrapped around its body. The Kraken had left the pile of discarded feathers by the fire. As they talked of his life, he picked them one by one and dropped them into the flames that were surrounded by a neat frame of rocks. Each time a silver feather touched the blaze, it sparkled and glowed. The deep black that had sullied it upon the healing of the Kraken was banished and it burnt pure and white.

Mariah was eager to hear the stories of where the creature had come from. The Kraken spoke with tears and laughter; then he looked at his hands, got to his feet, crossed the vault and stared at himself in a looking-glass that hung lopsided from the wall.

'Am I not beautiful?' he asked, half laughing. 'If I was born this way then it could be understood. Strange what life does to you.'

'You speak as if you have not always been like that?' Sacha asked.

'If you but knew of what I have endured,' the Kraken said as he brushed his long coat with his hand. 'If you but knew . . .'

'And this place,' she said as she looked at the finery that decked the room. 'Do you wreck the ships from which you steal?'

'I salvage what I can, but the wrecking I leave to wind and storm and the deceitful hearts of men with their false lamps strung from cliff tops.'

'Who would wreck a ship?' Mariah asked.

'You'd be surprised what man would do if there was a shekel to be made. Isn't that so, Sacha?' the Kraken asked.

She shrugged her shoulders and looked to the ground, not wanting to make reply.

'What does he mean?' Mariah asked her.

'Expect he's been skulking and listening to conversations he shouldn't,' Sacha replied.

'I came here to search for someone,' the Kraken said. 'Listening to drunkards plotting was not of my making. I am glad my life is in the sea – there is too much death in this harbour.'

'How many people have been murdered, Sacha?' Mariah asked

'Eleven, could be twelve . . . they said it was the Kraken. Started when he turned up. He was seen running away and into the sea.'

'I saw the one who did it. I would recognise him again,' he protested. 'But would you stay, looking like me, as twenty men with burning torches and swords come a-chasing you?' he asked. Sacha was silent. 'Very well . . . I have lived in this place to find her and then we will go back.'

'So why do they think you're the murderer?' Mariah asked again.

'Blame that which is different – the outsider, the ghoul. It is easier for them to look for me than believe it could be one of their own,' he replied quietly.

'And *what* are you?' Sacha asked as she looked him up and down through narrow, screwed-up eyes.

'I am whatever you want me to be. A phantom, a vampire, a ghost seen with the corner of your eye, a sea monster. Take your choice and make stories of it. Isn't that what they all do? I am a Kraken and that is all I know.' The creature stopped and looked at the flames. Sacha saw the reflection of the fire burn in his eyes. 'There was something far away, a thought, a dream that often comes to me and then it's gone. It is as if I should remember but cannot. Perhaps if I could recall what it was I would know more.' The Kraken looked at Mariah. 'When did you find Scratty?' he asked.

'She found us. Turned up in my room at the top of the hotel. It was as if she just appeared from nowhere – she left a key.'

'Then there is still life left in her,' he said as he stood up and paced the room. Then he looked up to the ceiling of the vault and bid them all to be silent. 'This is the time, they are nearby,' he said. He took the Caladrius from the cage and folded it under his arm, its dangling head hanging by his side, and without saying another word he set off from the vault.

Sacha picked up the lamp and followed. Mariah plucked a tall candle from the stand and shielded it from the draught as they snaked through the tunnel back to the entrance and across the plank. The Kraken went on ahead in the pitch blackness; each time he turned his eyes blazed as if they were fire. He turned sideways and slipped through a small entrance that they had not noticed as they fled the Emporium. He waited for them on the other side, pulling Mariah through the narrow brick-built slit.

'Your *friends* wait for you at the harbour mouth. They make enough noise to wake the dead. Soon there will be just a foot of water and they will come looking for you. This way they will never find you.'

'They can see where we've been,' Mariah said. 'It's as if we leave our footprints in bold ink across the land.'

'Even if they can see you, they will never come this way, not unless they cut off their stomachs and fat rumps. When I have seen you to the one you seek I will come back and wait for them.' The Kraken grinned, his long green tongue falling from his mouth as it rolled over his sharp fish-like teeth.

For a quarter of an hour they walked through a maze of passages, each one growing narrower. Finally they reached a long metal ladder that was loosely cemented into the intricate brickwork that spiralled to the surface. The Kraken carried the Caladrius, pushing it into his jacket. He climbed quickly. Sacha left the lamp behind and followed on. Soon they sat beneath a grating in the surface of the street, the sound of seagulls cawing above.

'This will take you to your friend. It is near where I first met you,' the Kraken said to Mariah, and he took a golden coin from his pocket and gave it to him. 'Take this, give it to the man. I have been stealing his fish and this should cover all that I have taken. Now go. Push upon the plate and it will give way.'

'What about Old Scratty?' Sacha asked as the Kraken slipped down the ladder.

'I will go for her tonight and then we shall be gone. When the Caladrius sees the moon it will live and Scratty will be well.'

'Then will we see you again?' Mariah asked.

'You would want to be in the presence of a sea monster again?'

'Only if they were like you,' he said as he smiled at the creature that slipped away into the darkness of the tunnels.

They sat together in the narrow shaft of light that slipped through the grate above their heads. 'You stink,' Mariah said to Sacha as he pretended to retch at the smell.

'And you're no rose. Bizmillah will want to know where you've been in those shoes,' Sacha replied as she looked at his muddied feet.

'I'm not going back to work for him. It's over for me, Sacha. When we've set Felix free I'm going back to London.'

'And leave me here?' she asked.

'You'll not be alone for long. There'll be some fool to take over this friendship.'

'That's what Felix said and look what happened to me . . . You turned up on a stormy night and stood the world on its head.'

Mariah pushed on the metal grate above him. It slipped easily from its mounting and he peered out into the alleyway. All he could see was the white-painted wall of the Golden Kipper and the shiny black door with its brass knocking plate. To the right was a small ice-house cut into the stone with two bent hooks hanging from a piece of flax.

'Come,' he said as he pushed himself from the sewer flap, stood on his feet and then pulled Sacha from the hole. He looked about him, stepped a pace back and knocked briskly against the door.

Sacha slid the metal grate back into place and jumped towards him as the door was opened a slat and a large eye peered out at them.

'Yes?' came the weary voice.

'Come to see Captain Charity,' Mariah said, as the eye looked him up and down.

'Not here,' the voice replied, irritated that it should be disturbed at such a time in the day.

'But he must be,' Mariah insisted, feeling a growing sense of unease.

'Gone away – business – left me in charge and even though I have only one leg I still know what to do. You're not the physic, are you?' the voice asked, the tension growing in its throat and rasping like an old branch. 'I may be eighty but I know today is Wednesday and Napoleon is the King of France.'

'It's not Wednesday and Napoleon's dead,' Sacha interrupted as a clatter of feet came from far away down the alley.

'Died? Napoleon? What will the Duke do now?' he asked as if his world had come to and end. 'You *are* the physic, aren't you? Come to take me to Saint Mary's workhouse? Well, I'll tell thee this for now't – I'm not going.' The door was slammed, leaving Mariah to listen to several bolts being slid quickly across the entrance.

Mariah stood with Sacha at the front of the alley that led to the quayside. Far away he could see Grimm and Grendel standing by the mouth of the sewer and waiting for the tide to subside. Grimm fiddled impatiently with his divining spectacles as Grendel looked about him, nervous of the cawing gulls that swooped above his head.

'This way,' Mariah said, and he turned to the half-glass door of the salon. It opened to his turn of the handle. 'He has to be here, he said he'd be in.'

The Golden Kipper was empty. All the tables were neatly dressed in white covers and silver cutlery. The wooden floor had been freshly swept and the steps to the upper tables and kitchen had been freshly waxed. Mariah could hear a fumbling of the lock at the back door. Taking Sacha by the hand he sneaked through the long corridor and watched as a small man with one leg, a bushy white beard and curly hair slid a bolt back and forth.

'Open or closed, open or closed?' he asked himself as he tried to understand what he was doing and where he was. 'Can never remember how new-fangled things work out . . .'

'Captain Charity, where is he?' Mariah asked as he startled the man from his dreaming.

The old man jumped back, his wooden leg slipping on the waxed boards as he fell to the floor in a crumpled heap. 'Who wants him?' he asked as he gurgled in his own spit.

'Mariah Mundi – an old friend,' Mariah replied, holding out his hand to pick the man from the floor.

'Old friend? Codswallop, never heard such rubbish in all my life. Captain's friends are all young – he doesn't have any old friends – except me and I'm not that old . . .' The man appeared to mutter his words into his beard as his deep blue eyes, set in the finest whites ever seen, glared about him. They flickered quickly from one side to the other, spying the room as if he looked upon the place for the first time. 'Monday, did you say?'

'Mariah Mundi,' Sacha chipped in.

'He mentioned something was happening on Monday – but never said what it was.' The old man went back to sliding the brass bolt in and out of its keeper as if they weren't there. His wooden stump scraped against the floor. It was carved with several small mice that appeared to run back and forth, their long tails entwined in sprigs of holly etched in the stump.

'We'll be going,' Mariah said as he left the old man in his slobbering. 'But first, you don't mind if we take a seat for some food?'

'Take what you want. I've counted the cutlery so no pinching the spoons . . . It's always the spoons, they never take anything else.'

'Cuba about?' Mariah asked.

'That's it, that's it – he's taken that beast for a walk. Bit my leg clean off it did. Couldn't walk for a week, had to sit and carve a new one. Fancy keeping such a thing as a pet, and it's me who gets to look after it when he goes jaunting about the world fighting for Queen and country.' He spoke as if he was almost in his right mind, his eyes fixed on Mariah. 'Go on then, up you go, better get seated before the rush.'

The old man ushered them to the ornate staircase that ran from the bow-windowed salon that overlooked the harbour to the dining room above. Sacha rushed ahead and darted to the window seat, pulling the curtain so that she was hidden from the crowds of out-walkers below.

It was low tide and the street on the quayside was packed with people in their finest coats taking the air. They watched the fishermen scraping upturned boats and mending torn nets. Grimm and Grendel could be seen looking into the emptying harbour, waiting for the water to go before they finally took it upon themselves to dance nervously through the mud and search the sewer.

Mariah pulled up a chair next to Sacha and sat in the window as they waited for Captain Charity to return. There was a simmering smell of cooking fish and the slosh of buckets of fresh batter being hand-mixed in the back kitchen. Looking along the narrow promenade that led to the Prince Regent, Mariah could make out the form of Captain Charity walking in the roadway, leash in hand. Cuba strutted proudly at his side, snapping at the passers-by as if they were titbits to be chewed upon. Charity paid no attention to this; his eyes were fixed upon the sea and the shimmering mist that filtered from the wet sand. By the harbour wall, a small brig was beached and a caravan of donkey-carts hauled coal up to the road.

Grimm and Grendel waited ever more impatiently. A whelk-woman in a long and tattered frock pestered them with a tray of whelks and vinegar, thrusting the stinking lumps of gristle into Grimm's face and laughing as he baulked. Grendel was far fiercer of heart. He quickly pulled a shilling from his pocket and forced it into her hand, snatching from her a cone-bag and small fork and dowsing the contents in a sea of vinegar. Without hesitation he fed the whelks one by one into his mouth and chewed.

Even from such a distance, Sacha and Mariah could see the muscles flexing in Grendel's long antelopian neck. He swallowed each mucus-like creature with a perceptible gulp, to which Grimm visibly recoiled further and further; when all had been eaten he tipped the cone and supped the liquor, crushing the paper in his hand and throwing it into the ebbing tide.

Grimm slapped him in the chest, chastising him with a short waggy finger and much gesticulation. Then he turned from him and looked at the slowly disappearing water and the long pole that waited for Saint Stephens's day.

The door to the Golden Kipper slammed briskly, and heavy boots and scampering claws were heard upon the stairs. There was a boisterous shouting from the old man, who screamed that it was Monday who waited for him and that never before had he been visited by a mad man who thought he was a day of the week. Charity laughed as he held on to Cuba, who tried to race ahead, sniffing each step as if she could smell the sewage upon their feet.

'Aha!' Charity laughed, a broad smile spreading across his wind-reddened face. 'Both of you villains stinking out my restaurant, eh?' He gave another laugh as he loosened Cuba and let her run free.

The crocogon leapt towards them, fussing around their feet and biting the leather soles.

'Thinks you're supper,' Charity said. 'And so you could be – about the size of a good meal, the pair of you put together.' Charity stopped and looked at Sacha. 'My dear girl, haven't seen you in ages. My, how you have grown. Father still up to his usual tricks?'

Sacha nodded and gave a shy grunt.

'He'll learn. One day they'll all get caught – can't go on for too long. So what's new in the land of misadventure?'

'I have this and we're being followed and –' Mariah blurted.

'One thing at a time,' Charity said as he looked at the gold coin, which Mariah held towards him.

'The Kraken gave *this* for you – he stole fish and said you should take the money to cover the cost.'

'Kraken? Fish? Where did you learn such a tale?' Charity took off his large overcoat and threw it to the horned stand that captured it upon a curled prong.

'He lives in –' Mariah said before Charity finished his words.

'He lives in the sewer and has done for a while. His room is decked like a fine lodging house and he has the Caladrius,' the Captain said as if it were known to the whole world.

'You knew?' Sacha asked.

'I have visited the room on several occasions – took him some bread and left it for him. I thought it was the Kraken that was taking the fish. The heat of the water has moved all the cod away. The beast would starve in an empty sea.'

'And this causes you no concern?' Mariah asked.

'Far from it. I am concerned the creature is sick and that the Caladrius was not used for the task it was born into the world for. Had I found the Kraken upon his lounge then I would have set the bird free and seen him healed.'

Mariah handed Charity the golden coin and quickly garbled all that had occurred since he last ate at the Golden Kipper. The Captain strutted up and down, and Cuba curled herself tightly in the corner of the room and went to sleep, leaving one large eye open.

'At last you have done something of great worth,' Charity said as he pulled back the curtain and peered down to the har-bour. 'What I would have given to see that bird in flight. I have heard so much of its power, followed its creator for so long and dreamt to stand in its presence – and *you* two wretches get there before me.' Charity shrugged, then stared out to see Grimm and Grendel as they cautiously climbed down the old ladder to the sewer mouth. 'Your two friends are about to come searching for you,' he said.

Mariah looked on as Grimm disappeared over the harbour wall, his powder-splattered silk hat slowly bobbing from view.

'What if they find the Kraken?' Mariah asked Charity.

'I have a good mind to take Cuba for a walk – into the sewer. She hasn't had sport for such a long time.' Charity laughed again, his mind musing on the sight of Grimm and Grendel scurrying like frightened rats from the chomping jaws of the crocogon. 'There is one thing,' he said. 'What of Otto Luger and all you have found?'

Mariah looked at Sacha, wanting her to speak for him. She remained deathly silent, her eyes cast down to the table. He realised he would have to speak for himself and that something had struck her dumb.

'I also found this,' he said, and pulled the wax hand from his jacket. 'It was on a manikin, it was made to look like me in every way. There was one of Felix. Luger has them hanging from the roof.'

Charity took the hand and held it to the light. 'French wax,' he said as he sniffed the fingers. 'Looks like there is something inside.'

With that he put the wax hand on the table and went to the kitchen. Moments later he returned, a metal bowl of bubbling water in his hands and a soup ladle wedged in his pocket. Charity placed the bowl on the floor and then dropped the hand into the water. They all stared into the water as if looking into an old leaky cauldron.

'What's it doing?' asked Sacha as she tapped her fingers nervously on the table.

'Melting,' replied Charity as the wax began to liquefy before them. 'Look,' he said as the fingers began to break from the hand and float to the surface.

Within the hand they could see small pea-sized droplets. As the wax melted they all began to fall to the bottom of the pan.

'I thought as much,' Charity said with a smile on his face. 'Pearls!'

[26]

Smutch

THE day's light had faded as the lamplighter made his way along the empty seafront, pulling his coat against the wind and rattling the gas tap of every light. As he tipped his flame to the lanterns they slowly burst into life. Mariah stood by the large brass telescope and watched from the window of the Golden Kipper as the man walked by. The lamplighter looked up at the boy and smiled, touching the tip of his grubby oilskin hat, and then walked on.

Sacha sat with Captain Charity, engrossed in conversation. She had chattered through the afternoon hours until dusk had begun to fall and Charity had lit the table candles. He had pulled the red velvet rope across the stairs, keeping away the customers that had trickled in from the cold wind. There had been a constant gabble from the chef as the fish had sizzled and crisped, filling the room with the most luscious odours that Mariah knew would hang upon their clothes for days.

In all that time, Sacha had told of what she knew. She had no reason to doubt the Captain; his eyes told her that there would be no betrayal. He was a man who listened deeply and intently to all that she had to say. Sacha enjoyed talking, but she enjoyed his listening even more. Through the hours, Mariah had chipped in here and there, filling in the missing details so as not to leave anything out. He told of finding the stripped bones of Otto Luger and his thoughts of who had murdered him, but Sacha dismissed him with a wave of the hand as if this were her story and one in which only she took part. Like the wind she would change course and opinion, her mind fleeting like a dancing butterfly.

Mariah had finished his fourth mug of chocolate and had left them to talk as he stared from the window towards the darkening mass of the Prince Regent.

'How far will this look out to sea?' he asked as he stared through the eyepiece of the telescope to the distant summit of a grey, mountainous wave.

'To the very limits,' Charity replied, turned towards him. 'You can see a ship on the horizon as if it were sat in the harbour.'

Mariah scanned the murky water for the starboard light of a ship. The ocean looked cold and empty, the white crests of the swell glowing in the moonlight. He thought of the Kraken scavenging from the wrecks on the far Brig. He searched the distant cliffs for lamplighters hanging lanterns to lure ships upon Cornelian Rocks. Mariah followed the line of the coast, peeking through the windows of the large select houses of the Esplanade overlooking the bay until he finally spied the very top of the Prince Regent. It was as if he could reach out and touch each pane of glass with his hand. He felt a shudder of excitement run through his bones as he gawped into a gas-lit room and spied a man plucking the hairs from his nostrils with a fine pair of silver tweezers, then adjusting a ginger rug of curls upon his head to cover a bald pate.

Mariah giggled to himself and a knot in his stomach coiled with deep exhilaration as he went from window to window, peeping inside and looking at the guests. He tried to make out what the guests spoke of as he viewed them from afar, the telescope transporting him to within an arm's length of each room. It was like standing and peeping from the outside balcony, watching the inhabitant of the room without being seen.

Everything was exposed to the view of the telescope. From his vantage point he could see Rhamses barking orders as the service began for early supper. His tall white hat flashed by the open window of the fourth-floor restaurant as he ran through the parlour palms and into the kitchen. A floor below Mariah could see the windows of the water-spa and, swinging the telescope higher, he tried to pick out the casement of his tower room. He searched the slate roof of the first tower looking for the white porthole that overlooked the town.

It was as he alighted on the high tower that he saw the face of Perfidious Albion. He was pale and drawn, pinched at the cheeks, with dark bruising around one eye. The man stared down upon the harbour from a high window lit by a single candle that flickered against his face. He was speaking, as if there was someone in the room with him, listening from the shadows. Albion closed his eyes and continued to speak; he lifted his manacled hands and touched his forehead, then lowered them and touched his heart and each shoulder. He mouthed one final word, as if he had said the name of someone he loved.

'Captain, Captain!' Mariah shouted. 'I've seen Albion! He's in the east tower and his hands are chained.'

Within the second, Captain Charity had pushed him from the telescope and stared through the lens. 'You're right, my lad, I can see the man and another behind him. Looks like . . . looks like *Bizmillah*, the old scoundrel,' Charity exclaimed as if he was the first to see a new planet. 'Then we have a chase. Not only will we rescue Felix, but we'll have Albion as well.'

'We'll go alone,' Sacha said as she stood from the table, her sharp voice stirring Cuba from her dreams.

'You'll not go at all if you speak to me like that, will they, Cuba?' Charity said quickly, his voice sabre-sharp as the crocogon got to its feet and snapped the air.

'But this is our business,' she replied angrily. 'We got into this and we'll get out of it.'

'Not since my foot stepped from the train the night Mariah arrived,' Charity said. 'Do you think I have idled my time frying fish and listening to old wives' tales since I was back? I was called home, a letter sent from the Prince Regent a year ago begging me to return. It was signed by Otto Luger.' Charity pulled a crumpled note from the pocket of his trousers and laid it on the table in front of them. 'On my very first morning I went to the hotel and saw Otto Luger. The man denied ever writing it to me or knowing who I was. I showed Luger the note and he nearly choked on his fat cigar. He had me thrown from the building and told never to return.' Charity banged the table with his fist. 'You, my friends, have done work for me and now together it will be completed. Luger is dead and an impostor is in his place. As an officer of the Crown I will have the murderer and you shall have your friend, and Mariah – Mariah will have that which is rightfully his.'

Sacha chuntered to herself, knowing there could be no other way. It would be futile to argue with Jack Charity.

'What do you mean?' Mariah asked, but his question was ignored completely by Charity.

'Smutch!' Charity shouted as loud as his lungs would bellow. 'Smutch, come hither – I have a plan of merit of which you will play your part.'

There was a stomping against the wooden boards as from below came the hobbling sound of the old man. His peg leg tapped against the floor like a stick on tight drumskin as he slowly climbed the stairs. The man sang to himself in a voice that sounded like a groaning pig. With one hand he clutched the thick leather strap around his waist as if it held his innards together, and with the other he pulled on his wiry beard.

'Captain?' he asked as he turned the landing and looked about the gallery in search of Charity.

'Going hunting, Smutch. You and this young Sacha have the task of keeping watch.'

'Keeping watch?' Sacha remonstrated in the voice of a fish-wife. 'You'll take Mariah and leave me behind? Why do I have to keep watch with some old codger?'

'Only for this part of the game, my dear,' Charity said quietly as he leant towards her as if to take her into his confidence. 'Come tonight and we all shall have our tasks as we storm the Prince Regent.'

'Storm? Prince Regent?' muttered Smutch, unaware of the world around him. In his head the cannon of Napoleon rattled his distant thoughts, clouding his eyes to the night. 'Sea looks fair to me, just a few white tops and nothing more,' he muttered as he sat down at the long table and looked at Charity.

'I want you to keep watch on the sewer. Mariah and I will take Cuba and see what we can find. Should be less than an hour. Stay here until we return and then we shall take on Otto Luger – or whoever he may be.'

Sacha attempted a faint smile as Smutch snuggled into the window seat and stared out to the quayside. He twitched with every breath he took, the long hairs of his brow trembling like a wind-blown hedge. 'Keeping watch,' he said to Sacha as Charity and Mariah slipped from the room, taking the croco-gon on its long leash.

Within the minute they heard the door slam behind them. Mariah looked up to the bay window and smiled at Sacha. Smutch waved a white handkerchief and then mopped his brow as he nodded his head back and forth in time to the marching music that danced his wits.

'Frightened?' Charity asked as they walked down the slipway and along a wet causeway clogged with bladderwrack.

'Should I be?' Mariah replied as Cuba dived from her leash and into the slowly filling harbour.

Charity looked each way then stepped closer to him. 'There was once a drummer boy like you. The master of the castle found a hidden tunnel. On the inside of a door that had not been opened for two hundred years was a writ. It told of a curse that would be on anyone who entered in. Not wanting to suffer the curse for themselves, they sent in the drummer boy. The master told him to bang the beat every yard he walked until he discovered where the passage led. A whole brigade waited above ground. They listened to the bang, bang, bang coming from far below. Suddenly there was a brief cry and the drumming stopped. The boy was never seen again. When they summoned the courage to follow on, they discovered the tunnel from the castle went under the Three Mariners and came out in the sewer. They never found the boy. He was a brave lad, just like you. Ever thought this may end the same way?'

'I've nothing to lose, Captain. Anyway, we've got Cuba, surely nothing will harm her?' Mariah said, gleaning a sense of threat from Charity's voice.

'And I have this,' he replied as he brushed his cape to one side and pulled a three-bladed knife from his belt. 'Cuts with every side and slices through any meat.'

A sudden chill blew through Mariah's coat. It slithered down his back and stood the hairs on his neck. This was the third knife he had seen with a triple blade.

'Why does it have three blades?' he asked. 'I have seen the likes of that before, the Kraken has one just the same and –'

'So he should, so he should,' Charity said as he walked along the causeway that was slowly being overwhelmed by a rising tide. 'A triple blade for a triple death. Not only kills the body but the soul and spirit, a blade for each, and will keep even the most fearful ghoul in its tomb for eternity.'

'That's how they killed the *real* Otto Luger. The body in the foundations had the mark of that knife upon it.'

'Not *this* knife,' the Captain said, half smiling, the moon shadowing his face. 'Surely not *this* knife? That would implicate me in a murder.'

'The Kraken said –' Mariah gasped.

'Krakens tell tales. They are storytellers of the sea. Krakens sink ships, eat whales and turn into giant squid when the sea covers their heads. It's only when they appear on land that they look like *he* does now. If you saw him in the midst of the ocean you'd never listen to any of his tales again.' Charity paused and looked Mariah in the eye. 'And if he saw you, he would pick the flesh from your bones and think nothing of it.'

'So he's not a man after all?' Mariah asked as they reached the entrance to the sewer.

'Not in the slightest, not now. The Kraken is the curse of a sea witch, a changeling.'

Mariah said nothing. He thought of what the Kraken had said of Monica. Suddenly everything was beginning to make sense. He stopped for a moment and looked at the moon that appeared to float on a veil of steam-mist that came up from the far away beach. By the entrance to the sewer he remembered the Colonial School. Gone was the rising at seven and eating hot toast by the fire; gone was the jipperdyke who had polished his shoes and cleaned his room. No longer could he sit and be waited on by the junior boy. Now Mariah was alone in a world that had changed beyond all recognition. It was as if the town at the end of the line was of another dimension, that somehow the laws of nature had been suspended and the track of the Great North Eastern Steam Railway had travelled across the boundaries of the mundane and into an earth filled with Kraken and murder.

The crocogon slithered from the harbour and into the sewer. Charity climbed along a rusted iron gantry that led under the long pier and into the darkness. He was followed by Mariah, the lad's trust of him fading with each step. He felt like a child of Abraham being led up a mountain to a burning pyre.

They listened as they waited in the tunnel entrance. Far away they could hear the fumbling of short footsteps that slipped and fell, and voices moaning in the faraway darkness as a dim echo.

'Lost,' the Captain whispered. 'I had kept an eye to see if they would come from the tunnel. If you don't know the sewer then you could stay in here forever.'

'We found our way to the harbour easily,' Mariah said.

'But you had Sacha to show the way. She grew up here, scurrying like a rat and hiding contraband.' Charity brought out a long silver tube from his coat. It was tipped with a glass lens the size and shape of a whale-eye. He opened a small rivet on the top and unscrewed the cap. With a pair of tweezers he dropped in three pieces of what looked to be lumps of white bread from a silver tin. The Captain then stooped to the water and submerged the tube and quickly screwed on the cap. There was a loud hissing sound as the chemical and the water mixed together, then slowly the lens began to glow with a bright phosphorescent light so powerful that Mariah turned away his eyes. An explosion of brilliant white lit the entrance to the sewer as the whale-eyed lens cast its blinding light from wall to wall.

'Lasts for a half of the hour,' Charity explained as he took a leather hood from his pocket and cupped it over the lens. 'Can't be having them see if we're about. In battle you always have to have the edge. Now we'll find Grimm and Grendel and have some sport.'

Mariah hesitated, a bone-numbing dread creeping through his body and stopping him from following. Soon Charity had disappeared ahead and all the lad could see was a faint outline lit by the escaping glow from the torch. He listened to the gulping water of the return of the tide and the drip, drip, drip from the crumbling bricks of the sewer roof.

Swimming below was Cuba, her eyes visible as if they were charged with an internal fire. They glowed like two red jewels floating upon the black velvet that filled the tunnel from wall to wall. The creature moved effortlessly in the thick watery soup that spilled from the town sewer, a rising mist of stench dancing in wisps upon the water. Mariah slowly walked on, the crocogon keeping pace as if it were luring him to the coda of his life. Mariah bit his lip nervously as he left the night behind and entered fully into the dripping, festering world of the tunnel. The crocogon swam on and mimicked his discontent as it churned in the turbid wastes.

Ahead, Captain Jack Charity had hidden in a small alcove, cut like a stone coffin in the sewer wall. He shone the metal torch back to the entrance. A pinpoint of light burst through a minute hole cut in the leather hood, shining like a white lance on Mariah's coat pocket. He walked on as if dragged closer by the beam. The light began to smoulder the fibres of his coat, and tendrils of smoke spiralled from the stands of fabric. Without thinking he put his hand to his chest, where the light warmed his skin until it began to singe the hair. It was as if the torch had stolen the rays of the sun and funnelled them through a glass. Mariah wanted to shout for him to stop but knew Grimm and Grendel would hear him. He stepped to the wall and quickened his pace. Charity shone the torch to the water, looking for Cuba; all he could see was a trace of bubbles that slowly burst through the tension of the surface.

Ahead they could hear the muttering of Grimm as he barked at Grendel. Their words were distorted by the many echoes that rushed back and forth as the sound billowed from the north tunnel that led to the castle and the Kraken's lair. Charity stood deathly still as he holstered the torch in the bottom of his coat pocket and with the other hand pulled Mariah towards him. There was a glint from the three-bladed dagger as if it sparkled from within, and a churning of the water by their feet spoke of the nearness of the crocogon.

A dim light came from the lair in the tunnel ahead of them. Grimm's voice was brash and clear. It was easy to hear that they were neither lost nor afraid. Grimm scolded Grendel for being so stupid in not having the foresight to bring a lamp, and now all they had would be the candlestick from the table to show them the way through the tide.

'Do you think he'll speak?' Grendel said. They could hear a rope being dragged across the floor.

'He'd better tell us where he took them or he'll never put to sea again,' Grimm replied.

'We could sell him to the *London Chronicle*,' Grendel chuntered. 'I once saw a picture of a man covered in hair who had been brought up by wolves. Surely a living Kraken is worth more than that?'

'If we find the lad, Luger will pay us more than any photograph. Anyhow, I have been thinking that it would be more profitable for us to take over Mister Luger's enterprises and have him done away with.'

'Again? But I thought you'd already murdered –' He stopped as the Kraken moaned loudly, the bonds cutting into his wrists. 'Lucky we fell on him when he slept – he's been out killing swans. I've a good mind to have that one plucked and roasted before the night is out.'

'It's not a swan, Mister Grendel, not with the feet of an eagle,' Grimm said as he kicked the body of the Caladrius out of the way.

'Once had a swan myself, when I was a lad,' Grendel said, his words murmuring through the tunnels. 'Didn't have a bird for Christmas and wasn't going to be without one. I took a rope and a wad of bread and walked the Thames at Rotherhithe.' He paused momentarily as he thought of what he spoke about. 'You know, Mister Grimm, they were so tame they would take the food from your hand. So it did, Mister Grimm, so it did . . . And as it plucked the last crumbs from my fingers I slid the rope over its neck and with one pull had myself the finest Christmas bird my father had ever seen. Plucked, dressed and halved for the baker's oven, legs so big that it took you two hands to eat them.' Grendel gurgled with delight and sighed. 'Shame to leave this dead thing just to rot. Once we've finished with Mister Kraken we could take it with us.'

'For once so thin, Mister Grendel, your mind is uncommonly annoyed with the passions of food,' Grimm barked as Charity and Mariah listened from the passageway.

'Always been the same – thinking of food and eating food all the day long and never fatter than a lath. And look at you, Mister Grimm, never eating more than a mouse and growing wider by the day. What justice is that?' Grendel snorted in false concern. 'Well, he's trussed and ready to be transported back to Luger's dungeons. The tide should be topping out and we need to be away. Don't want to spend the night staring into this creature's eyes.'

Grendel tied the last knot around the Kraken's wrist and lifted him to his feet. He dragged him to the doorway and across the midden and into the dark tunnel. Grimm followed on, candle in hand to light the way.

'Slowly, Mister Grendel, slowly . . . My stride is not the length of yours and we may need to be together.'

Grendel didn't reply. He clutched the Kraken with one hand and stood motionless, staring down the long chamber to the lapping water far below. In the distance he could see the red glow of two large eyes coming towards him. In the dark, the crocogon took on a larger, wilder frame. Grendel sunk back, pulling the Kraken with him as he chirped and gurgled in surprise at seeing such a creature.

'Fiend – ogre – beast!' Grendel screeched loudly as the crocogon pulled itself from the water and began to walk towards him.

'Beast? Mister Grendel, we have the beast and we will take it to the Prince Regent for *interrogation* –'

'Beast, Mister Grimm, a sewer beast, there before us, a red-eyed sewer beast!'

'Nonsense,' Grimm said as he lifted the candlestick into the air to light all that was ahead.

Cuba scurried by Charity and Mariah as they pressed themselves against the wall, covered by the shadows. The crocogon flicked its tail back and forth as it almost danced with excitement, breaking into a trot as it lumbered its black shimmering mass towards them.

'Use your cane, Mister Grendel, USE YOUR CANE!' Grimm shouted at the top of his voice. He turned and ran up the steep incline of the tunnel.

Calando

T HE last they saw of Grimm and Grendel was the turning shadows that dodged in and out of the shaft of pure white light that exploded from Captain Charity's phosphorescent torch. Cuba had been called to heel as her master laughed and grunted to near choking at the sight of the two detectives scurrying into the darkness, chased by the crocogon.

Upon the return of the beast, Charity pulled out several slices of malodorous sausage from his pocket and fed the creature one piece at a time. Cuba sat upon her hind legs with her tail wrapped about itself and snapped each piece.

'Job well done,' Charity said as he untied the tight bindings that cut into the Kraken's wrist. 'At least we know where they will be in the hour, *if* they can pick their way through the passageways.'

The Kraken attempted to smile, unsure as to what Charity would do next. Mariah saw the look upon his face and gently took him by the arm.

'I fell asleep,' the Kraken said. 'It had been so long since I last rested. Every night I have searched the streets for Scratty.'

'Then you will search no more, for tonight she shall be

found and all will be well,' Charity said as he finished pulling the bindings from his wrists.

'This is Captain Jack Charity,' Mariah said as he stroked the Kraken's arm. 'It was his fish that you stole – but don't fret, I gave him the money.'

'I know,' the Kraken said earnestly as he pulled the sleeves of his frock shirt to cover the iron manacles that enclosed each wrist. 'I saw you bring the bread. I was hiding from you. No one was supposed to come into this place. It is –'

'Haunted?' Charity asked finishing his words. 'Never been one to be afraid of ghosts. It's only the living that can do you harm.'

'Believe me, Captain Charity, I have met others who can work in realms that you would not believe existed.'

'And turn you from a man into a Kraken?' he asked boldly as the torchlight penetrated though the lining of his coat, casting a net of shadows at their feet.

'Even that,' the Kraken replied. 'If you had not come back, then I know not what they would have done.'

'Cooked you alive and served you like a Christmas swan.' Charity laughed. 'Where they hide, they shall find neither comfort nor food, and they will have to pass this way again. What do you do this night?'

'I think we are united in the same task and our fate lies entangled in the Prince Regent,' the Kraken replied as Cuba brushed her tail back and forth, sensing a nearby run of rats being chased by the high water.

'Whatever, we will not pass through the entrance to the harbour. And we have but a quarter of the hour within this lamp, so we will depart your company. Do you remember the way?' Charity said to Mariah, who watched as the crocogon snapped a large rat in its mouth and, tossing it into the air, opened its jaws and swallowed it whole.

The Kraken led them to a small dam crossed by a long plank that would lead them to the tunnel and the chimney. Below them, the water bubbled. Charity clicked his fingers, and Cuba leapt obediently into the dark waste and in an instant had vanished from sight.

'Do you walk the way of men or Kraken?' Charity asked as they stood beside the deep pool.

'I go the only way I know,' the Kraken replied as he stepped into the water.

'Then bid us safe passage?' Charity asked.

'I may be a monster but will never eat my friends,' the creature replied as he sank further into the depths.

Captain Charity took the torch from his pocket. The brilliance had begun to fade and yet still was bright enough to light the whole chamber as if it were day. The Kraken slipped down into the water, and as it was overwhelmed it began to be transformed.

Mariah stared as the long tentacles of a gigantic sea beast slowly replaced the shape of the man. It was as if he were being absorbed inch by inch by an enormous squid-like creature, as if he were being turned inside out and something hideous born from within. The water began to bubble and boil as the Kraken grew in size and shape. Long spiked tentacles thrashed about in the black foam as the Kraken opened its horrendous beak and sucked a draught of stagnant air from the sewer.

The pool swirled and twisted as the Kraken was finally transformed. Suddenly it lashed out towards them. Charity jumped from the grasp of a long thin spiked limb. Mariah was grabbed around his neck by a thousand minute cups that sucked at his skin and gripped him tightly. Another and another tentacle took hold of him by the arms and legs, raising him to the height of the roof. The creature dragged itself from the water, filling the entrance of the sewer as it rose up on what seemed to be a hundred thick, blood-red tentacles strong enough to pull any ship to the depths. Through two gigantic eyes the creature stared into Mariah's as it held him from the ground. With a gust of stinking wind it opened the two claws of its blue beak, hissing and panting – and then, as if to answer some faraway call, placed him down with the gentleness of a father's hand, sank into the water and disappeared.

'Thought you'd met your end, did you?' Charity said unhurriedly as he brushed some mire from his coat. 'Knew it wouldn't keep its word. Never trust a changeling – what they say to you in the flesh is not the word they will keep when transmuted to another form. Once heard of a werewolf who would always lose at cards and then promise never to steal back his money. In a strange way he kept his promise – he would just eat the throats of those who beat him at blackjack.'

'You have the manner of someone not too concerned by his circumstances,' Mariah said as he pulled a small claw from the skin of his neck and held it before the torchlight. 'The Kraken only kills in the minds of men and those frightened of the tales you tell.'

'I have seen many things and nothing will ever surprise me again.'

'In the restaurant you said I would have what is rightfully mine. What did you mean?' Mariah asked.

Charity turned away and walked along the narrow path to the tunnels that led onward to the brick shaft and the street above. 'My words ran away with me,' he said. 'Often say what I shouldn't and if I was asked to remember what I meant I would have to say I had forgotten,' he mumbled as he scanned the sewer with the fading light. 'Best be making haste – like life, the brightness fades and all we will be left with are the memories of this place.'

'But you said I would have what is mine. I remember clearly,

Captain Charity. *As an officer of the Crown I will have the murderer and you shall have your friend, and Mariah – Mariah will
have that which is rightfully his –* that's what you said. Word for
word. What belongs to me that I don't know of?'

'If you could have something, anything in the world, what
would it be? A new life, a certain future, an inheritance? What
would you choose?' Charity spoke quickly, giving him no time
to answer. 'See – you don't know. So why should I tell you now?
It's all about patience, Mariah . . . Mulciber . . . Mundi.'

'Who told you? I have never said my full name to anyone and
yet you just said it. How did you know?'

'A guess, a stab in the dark, a wild chance, an insight into
that which goes on in the subconscious?' Charity replied as he
weaved through the passageway towards the rusted iron ladder
and the alleyway. 'Mulciber? Doesn't that mean someone who
can bend metal?'

'It was my grandfather's name,' Mariah snapped, knowing
that Charity amused himself at his expense. 'You know me well,
Captain. So what of my future?'

'It'll come to pass, *Colonial boy* . . . Now we must keep to the
task in hand.' Charity slipped through yet another opening and
the light of his torch faded to an amber glow. Soon they were
near the rusted iron ladder that led up to the street. They
walked on in silence. Mariah felt as if he were about to climb a
high mountain. His mouth had dried with fear; his eyes stung
with the stench of the sewer. The thump of his heart beat loudly in his ears. He turned his thoughts again and again, wondering what would become of them all. He realised that Charity
was more a part of his life than a stranger met by chance in a
railway carriage. It was as if he were an actor given only his own
lines and were waiting for some unknown voice to speak the
other part. Mariah knew too that the journey to his future
would start with the first foot he placed on the metal ladder, a

step that would take him not only to the street above, but also to the unknown.

'Climb quickly,' Charity said as he forged ahead. 'Now that Grimm and Grendel are out of the way we are free to attack the Prince Regent. You up to it lad?' he asked as he pushed slowly on the metal grate that covered the entrance to the sewer.

'If the Kraken isn't killing the people, who is?' Mariah asked as Charity peered through a narrow slit between the cobbles and the grate.

'That remains to be found out,' Charity whispered. 'The streets will never be safe until they are stopped.'

'The Kraken said that he saw a man with a cane with a silver tip, that every time someone was killed the man would appear.'

'Krakens say many things. Once saw a Kraken pull a four-mast ship to the bottom of the Indian Ocean. Came at her like a mad dog and dragged her into the depths.' Charity stopped and looked at Mariah, who clung to the blistering metal with white, bloodless fingers. 'Look beyond that which you can see, understand that there is a veil cast upon your eyes, find the pearl of great price and you'll have all you need to live.'

'That's what Felix said,' Mariah blurted out as Charity pushed against the grate and let in the cool of the night. It brought with it the smell of the sea, tainted with the sweet flavour of fried fish.

'Good to be home,' Charity said, licking his lips, and he pushed the grate from its collar and pulled himself into the narrow passageway of the Bolts.

They slipped quietly along the narrow passage and through the front door of the Golden Kipper. The streets were empty; the steam-mist from the beach hugged the sand and the cobbled road that led along the quayside. Mariah stayed a pace behind the Captain; he was concerned as to how Charity knew so much about his life. He had seen the Captain look sideways at him on several occasions during the afternoon's conversation. It was as if he weighed him up, checked him out. The Captain must have heard much about him from someone before, and he was looking to see if it were true – that was the thought that Mariah couldn't get out of his head as they climbed the stairs. But the only other person who knew Mariah's name was Professor Bilton, and how could he have ever told Captain Charity? Mariah wrangled with his thoughts as he slowly climbed the stairs.

'Smutch,' Charity called as he turned the landing.

Smutch was still in the window seat overlooking the harbour but his hands were tied with several knotted cotton napkins stolen from the table places. Around his head was a tight gag that forced his teeth to stick out like an old horse.

'Who did this? Where's Sacha?' Charity insisted.

Mariah covered his face with his hand. The sight of the old man trussed up and gagged made him look even more ludicrous. Hanging against the wall from the antler of an elk was Smutch's wooden stump. Mariah instantly knew this was Sacha's doing.

'Only playing a game . . .' Smutch muttered as he sucked in his teeth and pulled his lips back from their mordant grin. 'She'll be back soon. Tied me up, took off me leg and gagged me gob. Said she would go away and then come back and I had to guess who she was . . .' In a momentary flash of lucidity he realised he had been fooled. 'Knew I shouldn't Captain, but she had such a smile and the voice of an angel and –'

'Enough, Smutch. How long has she been gone?' Charity asked as he fished the wooden stump from the horned beast and helped the old man strap it to his leg.

'Just after you'd gone, saw you disappear under the quay and she joshed the game. Did you see where I've put me powder?' the old man asked as his brain slipped from the world of others and back into his own.

'Prince Regent?' Mariah asked as he looked through the telescope and scanned the beach.

'She'd be a fool to go alone. And yet that lad, Felix, has a power over the girl.'

Mariah continued to search the promenade and the beach through the thick lens. It was only a few minutes' walk from the Golden Kipper to the Prince Regent, but somehow he hoped that Sacha had dawdled in her loneliness. He swept the brass arm back and forth as he systematically scanned each foot of sand.

Funnels of steam broke through the beach, pressed down by the cold night air. They billowed out like the jets from a fissure in a gigantic volcano about to erupt. By the edges of the sand the water bubbled and spat as the gases from below percolated and simmered to the surface.

Then Mariah caught sight of the Kraken striding through the mist, his long hair trailing over his shoulders. He stepped boldly from the sea towards the Prince Regent, stepping in and out of the long shadows cast by the thousands of tiny lamps that lit the whole building. And Mariah could hear, whispering on the wind, the first notes of Bizmillah's orchestra as they picked the notes on their violas. They came like the sound of distant summer birds calling from far away. He followed the Kraken as he stepped across the beach, returned to the form of a man.

'What do you see, lad?' Charity asked as he put an arm around his shoulder.

'The Kraken – going to the Regent.'

'Sacha'll be there already, up to some trick or other. This has taken so long to put together and for it to be spoiled when we were so close –' He stopped, knowing he had thought too much out loud.

'I suddenly feel as if I am a pawn in your game,' Mariah said openly. 'I feel like a greater hand has played my life and that all is not as it first seemed to be.'

Charity gently lifted Mariah's head from the eyepiece of the telescope and pointed to a small picture above his head. 'It's surprising how we never see the obvious, lad. Do you recognise the place?'

Mariah scanned the faded painting. The yellows and greens had oozed at the edges and blurred together. It was obvious that this was a house, set at the end of a long drive lined with trees. In the distance he could see the banks of a river and beyond that the far hills of the south. In the foreground was the portrait of a young boy with fine blond hair. The child smiled out from ages past, but in an instant Mariah had recognised the eyes.

'It's you!' he said as his mind raced to recognise what lay behind. 'And the Colonial School?' he asked slowly, unsure that the faded eaves and slate roof in the picture were those of his home for the last years.

Charity said nothing. He crossed the room and went into the kitchen. A short time later he appeared through the scullery door clutching a folded piece of parchment. Religiously he cleared the table by the window and with great ceremony unfolded each flap until it was laid out before Mariah.

'Recognise this?' he asked as he smoothed the paper with the back of his hand.

'A writ of worthiness,' Mariah said as he read the lettering at the top of the page. '*I, Professor Jecomiah Bilton, in this, the first year of my incumbency as head of the Colonial School, do hereby discharge from duty John Mariah Charity into the company of Her Majesty's Army for Colonial Service – Student First Class – 23rd December 1866.*' He read the lines again and again. 'It was twenty years ago today. You're a Colonial boy. You have my name. You . . . you . . .' He gulped his words; his head was full of tears that burnt his lips and tore at his throat. 'It can't be true – that means you would have known my father.'

'Why do you think you carry my name? How did you ever not know who I was? I was your father's best friend. We shared everything, closer than brothers. When you were born he gave you *my* name. I was in India at the time and never saw the young lad that he wrote so much about.' Charity pulled a wad of finely wrapped letters from his pocket and placed them on the table. 'You can see for yourself – they're all in your father's hand.'

Mariah untied the wide band and slipped the letters from their clasp. He carefully opened the first one. It was written in purple ink on white vellum. His eyes scanned each line and followed each curl and scrawl. In the bottom corner of the note, folded back to stop the ageing, was a pen drawing of a small boy wrapped in a swaddling band, his head full of wiry hair. A line underneath read: *Mariah – the only time he's quiet is when he sleeps . . .*

'See,' Charity said as he smiled at the boy, 'all I have said is true.'

'Why didn't you say?' the lad asked.

'Bilton wrote to me and told me of your discharge. I had been in the Sudan searching for your father and mother. The professor was concerned that so many boys had left the Prince Regent, and having had the letter from Otto Luger I took the fastest ship I could find. The train was a coincidence. I never expected a Colonial boy to travel First Class. I would have waited my time and kept watch. Then, when the moment was right, I would have made my presence known.' Charity looked to Smutch who had fallen asleep in the window seat. 'There is more to tell, but tonight we must end what has gone on. I know you have it in you. Just like your father. I can see a lot of him in your eyes.'

'What was he like?' Mariah asked. 'He was away so often my memory fails me.'

'Fine people, Mariah, fine people, kept from you by *circumstances*,' Charity said, stifling the words.

'Are they dead?' Mariah said, rubbing his hands together nervously.

'That I do not know, but I will return as I cannot rest until I have found proof.'

'And what of tonight?' Mariah asked as he stacked the letters on top of each other and tied them again into a tight bundle.

'We will find Sacha, Felix and Perfidious Albion, and who knows what will become of us?'

[28]

The Sea Witch

ABOVE the steaming beach, in the darkness of the entrance
to the Prince Regent, Sacha felt she was being watched.
She had slipped quietly from the moonlit sand and into the
cover of the brick portico. Looking back, she saw long moon
shadows reaching in like dark fingers. To her right was a large
storeroom filled with bathing carriages with their candy-
striped covers and large wheels. The wooden lattice door that
led into the labyrinth of underground tunnels was unlocked; its
chain hung limply as she slipped the bolt and sneaked within.

The sound of the steam generator chugged over and over,
the faraway hiss, hiss, hiss echoing though the passageways like
a whisper inviting her further inside. The sound came as a reas-
surance to her, though her journey was blunt and harsh like
entering a madhouse against her will.

She was gladdened to see the oil lamp by the door of Luger's
workshop was still lit. Its feeble light shone towards the
entrance, clipped by a corner of shadow from the tunnel wall.
The ceiling dripped with hot dew that slithered along the stalactites and then fell to the floor, forming large steaming pud-
dles. Sacha knew she would have to find Felix alone. She

couldn't wait for Captain Charity to decide how it would all be done – it had to be her, *she* had to be the one who set Felix free. As she walked on she tried to justify tying up Smutch and leaving him turkey-trussed and gabbling to himself.

Within a minute she had reached the door at the end of the passageway. It was wedged slightly open by a small dune of sand that had been washed into place by the last high tide. She pulled against the thick iron handle, and the door opened with a low moan like a growling dog. Sacha shuddered as the urge to look behind overwhelmed her. For a moment she thought she could hear faraway footsteps. Quickly she pulled the door shut and slid the bolt on the inside, breathing heavily as she caught her breath. She fought against the urge to run. She began to regret leaving Mariah behind and coming alone. The thoughts of what could be following her multiplied with each step.

In ten paces she had turned the corner and was now spiralling deeper beneath the Prince Regent. To her left was the long dark tunnel that would lead her back to the oyster lagoon; ahead was the passage that would guide her to the Pagurus. She stopped and looked about, sure that the sound of footsteps echoed somewhere beyond – it was the tap, tap, tap of metal tips clattering against the sharp stone floor. Occasionally the sound would come through the tunnel as a muffled thud, then back to the crisp click of metal on stone.

Sacha found the noise would vanish and mix with the sound of the steam generator, and then suddenly it would be there again, echoing closer to where she stood. For a moment she looked at each tunnel, unsure as to where the echoing came from. Far away a door slammed shut, sending a chilled draught towards her. Sacha set off into the narrow chasm towards the oyster lagoon. Her footsteps danced rapidly over each stone as she ran from whoever was behind her.

Drawing nearer and nearer was the sharp sound of clicking

heels. Just ahead was another wooden door, strapped with iron braces. She pulled the metal ring and the door edged slowly open, grinding against the hot stone floor. Her hands sweated upon the metal and she could feel panic slowly rising from the pit of her stomach. She rushed through and pulled the wood against the frame, then slammed the bolt and turned the key.

Sacha looked along the tunnel. To one side was a cutting in the rock as if a burrow had been commenced and then abandoned. It was warm and dark and deep enough for her to hide in without being seen. Quietly she went inside, pressing herself against the wall, holding her breath to stop the panic from breaking out. From beyond the door she could hear the clatter of footsteps coming along the corridor; then they stopped, and the door was suddenly rattled against the lock. Sacha stepped one pace closer and saw the iron ring of the door handle move again.

The rumbling of the steam generator seemed far away. In her heart she knew that someone stood on the other side of the wood and metal slats firmly bolted into their stone casement. She tried to listen even more intently, but all she could hear was the thump of her own heart. The door handle rattled again as someone pressed against the wood. Sacha instinctively slipped a little further into the darkness, just far enough that she could still see the door, and pressed her face against the warm stone. It was soft and dusty against her skin and smelt of the sea.

It was then that she saw a black-gloved hand, the tips of its fingers breaking though the fabric like red talons. It slipped through the wood of the door as if it wasn't there. The hands grasped for the bolts, attempting to slide them back from the frame.

Sacha cowered down, trying to make herself as small as she could, hunching into the darkness and covering her face with her hands. She felt a twist in her gut as it rumbled and groaned.

Sacha looked again, hoping the hands had vanished back to the far side of the door, but to her terror they had grasped the lock. There was a sudden painful groan like the sound of a dying animal. A shoulder was pushed through the solid wood, then a foot, a long white ankle and finally half of the body.

It was clad in a long black dress that clung like a second skin to its wearer. Sacha had seen this person before. It was Monica.

From her hiding place Sacha could see the woman convulsing every fibre of her body, attempting to penetrate the solid wood. It was as if the door fought against her, making a trial of her effort to pass through it. Where Monica's body had been squeezed through, the wooden slats were dripping with a glistening blue liquid that sparkled in the faint light as it slithered slowly down. By her incredibly neat right foot, sheathed in a shining black shoe, was a pool of the viscous liquid. It was as if it oozed from each molecule of her constricted flesh.

Sacha watched as the first layer of the woman's forehead was forced through the door. A long, white and very powdered nose slowly appeared and then a bright red-painted lip pushed against a perfect set of American dentures. They sparkled white and twinkling in the soft light of the tunnel as a thin chin then appeared, unmoulding itself from the dark wood and leaving yet more liquid to trickle to the floor. It was a smile Sacha knew well. From inside the cutting in the rock she quickly got to her feet and began to hug the wall as she made her way along the passageway, hoping that she could sneak out of sight before Monica realised she was there.

In a matter of moments, the whole of Monica's head had been forced through. She peered suspiciously into the tunnel, her sharp eyes looking around her. In a long glance she saw Sacha's shadow as it crept further away.

'Don't think this door will keep me for long,' Monica said as she pushed with her gloved hands against the stone, trying to pull her struggling flesh to freedom. 'If a door can't keep me then running away won't do you any good.'

Sacha stopped like a rabbit trapped in Monica's stare. She felt a sharp tremble of her fingertips as fear took hold of her.

'That's a girl,' Monica growled. 'Look at me . . .'

Sacha huddled against the wall, hoping the stones would speak and tell her what to do or that they would suddenly open and swallow her up. 'I won't,' she said as she tried to walk on, suddenly realising that her feet were as heavy as lead.

'You're charmed, girl. You won't get far. Feeling weaker?' Monica said as she struggled to free herself from the door.

Sacha turned and sheepishly looked towards her. 'I'll still get away, I've got to –'

'Get the boy? Felix?' Monica said as Sacha stared at what looked like a disembodied head stuck to a wooden door. 'Is that what you want?'

'You can't keep him!' Sacha shouted, pulling against the walls in an attempt to free herself from whatever power now held her fast.

'And you can't move,' Monica grumbled. 'Caught like a spider in a web and never to escape.' She mused for a moment and rolled her tongue around her mouth and then moistened her ruby-red lips. 'Now, what shall were turn you into?'

'Nothing!' she shouted, the words echoing down the long tunnel to the oyster lagoon. 'I'll be turned into nothing. You won't call me Scratty and have me china-faced.'

'So you know? Very clever . . . Who've you been speaking to?' Monica asked in her Yankee drawl, her neck appearing to be stuck in the door. 'You'd make a better waxwork than a china doll, or perhaps . . . perhaps a *stuffed* child would look nice in my room. Covered in paper mashie and painted in bright pink. I could hang an umbrella from your arm and a coat over your head. You could be a hat stand or a lampshade.' Monica giggled.

'And you'll be dead if the Kraken finds you,' Sacha said, her feet rooted to the ground as if they had penetrated the rock and taken root.

'The Kraken? So, you've found a new friend? How charming. Is he still pining for his companion? Still weeping for his loved one? How romantic. I know many a man who would pay a golden guinea to have his lovers turned into ageless china dolls that sat in the corner and never complained or spent their money.'

'He said you were a sea witch,' Sacha said as her feet began to brittle in a fine white powder. A growing stench of brine and old cod oil filled the tunnel, billowing from Monica with every breath.

'And that I am, gloriously powerful and here for a purpose – to capture you.' Monica pushed against the stone doorway and managed to pull her dripping flesh halfway through the wood. She stood one-legged, her left foot stuck on the other side. Sacha was frozen to the spot. She glanced to her feet and saw what looked like a rising frost slowly climbing up her legs and crisping her clothes inch by inch.

'Salting.' Monica laughed as she tugged on her leg to release it from the grip of the door. 'It'll hold you until I am free of this door and can get you myself.'

With a final pull she freed herself from the wood and shook like a wet dog. Drips of bright blue liquid showered the tunnel and mixed with the dank smell of sea salt. Monica looked at Sacha as she stepped towards her. The salting had crawled up to her waist, holding her fast.

'Now let me see who you are,' Monica said as she peered at Sacha through eyes that were milky white and misted with a fine skin. She reached out with a long gloved hand, the red fingernails piercing through the black silk.

Sacha panicked as the hand came towards her face, the thick

claws reaching to touch her skin. 'Leave me!' she screamed as she pulled away, wanting the sea witch to stop. 'Leave me now!'

'Or what will you do?' Monica said looking even closer to make out her complexion and the shape of her face. 'Nothing, you'll do nothing. Just like all you creatures.'

Sacha cowered as the first finger stroked her skin and Monica slid her thin hand around her neck. It was then that she noticed Monica's face began to dry and crinkle. The pool of brine grew about her feet and the stench of the sea became even more intense – it was the smell of dead fish, fish left in the sun and covered in flies, eaten by maggots and festering until the guts retched. She tried not to breathe, gasping quickly through clenched teeth as Monica's face was pressed closer to hers. The sea witch peered at her through an ever-milkier eye, the membrane thickening as the fluid seeped from her body.

'It's Sacha, isn't it?' Monica asked quietly as she scanned the girl's features for a single point of recognition. 'Worked for Bizmillah – he'll be sad you're gone.'

'What'll you do?' Sacha asked, unable to get away from the stench.

'Otto's been looking for you. Who did you come with? There were two of you,' Monica whispered closely, almost like a kiss. 'Don't tell me you came back on your own. Grimm and Grendel chased you from here this morning. I wasn't foggy-eyed then and even I caught a glimpse of your friend.' Monica let go of her grip and she counted her fingers like an eagle's talons. 'Imagine, Sacha, what these could do to your pretty face. Was it Mariah Mundi who was with you?'

Sacha cast her glance to the floor, her downcast eyes speaking all truth.

'I knew there was something troublesome about that boy. Otto should never have taken him on. Told him he was one too many but he never listens to any of my thoughts, never listens to any of his own.' Monica curled her long nails in front of Sacha's face like a cat. 'Still, come midnight, Otto will have enough trouble of his own.'

'He's gonna turn you into a waxwork,' Sacha blurted as she grabbed Monica's hand and pulled the glove.

'Never,' she replied.

'Saw it myself, hidden in his laboratory. There you were, as bold as brass and made of wax. You're done for – he doesn't want you any more.' Sacha spoke fearfully as slowly the salting that now encased her legs began to crumble. Monica pulled against her, the glove slipping from her arm, then hand and finally from her reddened fingertips.

Clutching the sequined black silk in her hand, all Sacha could see were fleshless bones tipped by painted fingernails. She stared wide-eyed and open-mouthed, her voice stuck in her throat. Monica smiled dryly as the moisture seeped from her painted face.

'So you finally know. First one to see that in a long time. Can't have you tell anyone about this, my little girl. The secret has to stay in here. I was gonna take you to see your friend, let you spend your time with Felix and all the others Otto has got stuck in that hell-hole of an oyster farm. Now . . . now it's a different end to the story.' Monica reached into the small purse that she carried around her shoulder. From within she brought out a pair of silver handcuffs. 'Had other plans for these but I guess you'll have to be the lucky lady.'

'I won't tell, I never saw anything, nothing,' Sacha said as she closed her eyes, not wanting to see any more.

Monica snapped one cuff upon Sacha's wrist and squeezed the metal against the flesh. 'Too late, my girl, far too late. I wouldn't want Otto to see his hot date was rotting from the inside out.' Monica sniffed as if about to cry. 'But if what you say's true then maybe he won't be around for much longer either,' she said as she slipped the handcuff on Sacha's other wrist and squeezed tightly. 'There, my baby. I'll rest you with your friend and see what Otto has to say for himself before I deal with you.'

In the far tunnel the sound of a slamming door echoed through the dusty passage. Monica muttered some strange words that Sacha couldn't hear. The salting crumbled from her feet as the sea witch pulled her by the arms and dragged her towards the oyster lagoon. Monica seemed distracted, as if her thoughts kept her mind from knowing where she was and the presence of Sacha was a small diversion in all her affairs. Her misted eyes twitched and squirmed as they crusted even more, parching with each step. Flakes of powdered skin fell to the floor as Monica led Sacha on and on.

'Soon be there,' the sea witch said as she turned the corner of the tunnel that led down a flight of steps and on to a gantry across the oyster lagoon.

'What about the beast?' Sacha asked.

'My little friend is locked away, ready for later – and to make sure you don't escape. One word to Otto, one squawk, and you die on the spot – *before* you see your friend.'

Sacha looked down at the steaming brown water, lit by a crescent of lamps that hung from the ceiling of the chamber. Far across the lagoon was the cell where she had seen Felix. The water was still, its surface broken only by the gentle simmering of a million oysters bubbling below. By the side of the pool was a discarded pile of opened shells that shimmered in the light.

'Get you tucked up and then I'll see the fat freak himself,' Monica muttered as she opened the door of the small cell and pushed Sacha inside. 'He's in there somewhere, him and the others.'

The door slammed behind her. Sacha grabbed the small

barred opening and looked out. She watched as Monica walked towards the lagoon, her skirt-tails trailing behind her. The sea witch strutted into the lake and slowly submerged herself in the pool, vanishing below the surface.

'Does it every day, has to bathe in the seawater or she'll dry up and die,' a voice said behind her. 'Never thought I'd see you again – thought they had you,' Felix said as he pulled a rag blanket from himself and got to his feet.

'She's gonna kill me, Felix. I saw what she is, she's gonna kill me . . .'

[29]

Imprimatur

THE steam elevator was completely dark. It shrugged reluctantly up the floors from the lowest basement of the Prince Regent to the very top without stopping. Mariah Mundi had left Captain Jack on the beach. He had been told to find the fortune cards and meet him in the Trisagion within the hour. Now he stood in the darkness with his thoughts and fears, wondering where Sacha had gone. He thought of her in the hotel, somewhere alone, knowing she had come to set Felix free. He considered what bound them together in their friendship, that she could leave himself behind and seek the quest alone. Their own alliance had grown over the past days: he had seen her changeable heart that reminded him of his own. She could be both brave and fearful in the passing of a single breath; she was torn between duty and desire, never caring for the gravity of what they would endure.

Everything began to make sense for him. Charity made it all the better. At last there was someone for whom he could care – a man he could get to know, and with whom he might share all that he would experience. No longer would he need to look to the sky and talk to the moon and tell it his secrets. Charity was as good as family, a nearly father, but one fraught with trouble.

The thoughts comforted Mariah as the elevator chugged on. They were tinged with a glimmer of excitement and hope for the future. Knowing that the Captain was there made all of what he had agreed to do somewhat easier: he was no longer alone in the adventure.

By the time the elevator had stopped on the very top floor of the hotel and the doors had been slid open, Mariah was convinced he would succeed. He knew that all he had to do was go to his room, find the Panjandrum cards, put them in his deep pocket and return via the stairs to the ground floor and await Captain Charity, who by then would be in the theatre bar with Cuba at his feet.

'Simple,' he said to himself as he stepped from the lift and opened the door to his room. Everything was as it had been left. The lamp was dimly wicked and cast a gentle and welcoming light about him. The bed was neatly made and looked undisturbed. The window that overlooked the bay was half open, the curtains gently blustering in the night breeze. Yet as he stepped in through the door he was aware of something that was not how it should be.

Hanging in the room was a subtle smell, a fragrance that he had known before. On the mantel of the fire, propped like a plump sausage against the cold brown tiles, was the smoking butt of a fat cigar – an Otto Luger cigar, wrapped in a thick gold band and chewed at the end. As he closed the door behind him Mariah suddenly became aware that he was not alone. For a second he froze; then the silence gave way to a gentle cough and a cloud of smoke was breathed over him.

'Wondered how long I could hold it in for,' said a voice as it grunted the words between coughing. 'Been looking for you, Mariah, thought you'd left for good.'

Mariah turned as he stepped back towards the window.

'Mister Black! What could you want of me?' he asked. 'Guests shouldn't visit the staff.'

'Nothing of you, but that which you were given at Kings Cross. Some playing cards?' Black said as he stroked his chin.

'Never heard of anything like that,' Mariah replied, taking a step further back and putting his hand upon the window ledge.

'Surely they were given to you by Perfidious Albion, a man you met before you boarded the train.'

Mariah's eyes darted to the bed and gave away his thoughts.

'Hidden somewhere near, are they?' Black asked grimly as he stepped to the mantel and picked up the cigar, taking a long gasp and inhaling the noxious fumes.

'I have nothing for you in this place, it would be best if you were to go and I to get on with my business,' Mariah said. He was sitting on the narrow ledge, placing one foot upon it as he tried to lean casually against the frame.

'According to my friend and magical partner, Mister Bizmillah, you are no longer employed by the hotel. *Apparently* two youths were chased by a certain Grimm and Grendel from the establishment this morning and are to be charged with theft.' Black grinned and for the first time Mariah saw that his front teeth had been tipped with gold. '*Apparently* they have stolen something of value from Otto Luger and made off into the town with the two detectives in hot pursuit.'

'Never heard of such a thing. I've been in the company of a family friend. This is my day off and if Bizmillah chooses to sack me for that then well and good. I'll take my leave and fry fish.' Mariah now sat fully on the windowsill, looking to the small ledge and the sea far below.

'So the cards are here?' Black insisted, holding out his fob watch that appeared to glow and vibrate in his hand. 'In fact they are nearer than you think, young Mister Mundi. I need to have them back; they were given to you for safe-keeping. Now tell me, what have you done with them?' He shouted at the lad and kicked the bed with his booted foot.

The Panjandrum cards fell to the floor from their hiding place, spilling from the pack across the fireside rug. The Joker slithered across the floor to Mariah and looked up through his crooked eye.

'Panjandrum,' Black grunted, wide-eyed and short of breath. He dived upon them as if to stop them from running from the room. 'At last I will have them back.'

Mariah saw his chance. He scooped the Joker from the floor and placed it in his pocket, and as Black clumsily attempted to gather up the cards he jumped from the window and fell to the narrow ledge below.

'No!' came the shout from inside the room as Isambard Black realised what was happening. 'It's not as you think.'

Mariah didn't want to listen; all he sought was his escape from Black. He held fast to the small ledge that ran just above his head, his feet gripping the row of narrow bricks beneath them. Around him he could hear the calling of the gulls as they swooped upon him, pecking at the long strands of his hair that billowed in the breeze. Mariah didn't dare look below. He knew that he stood above the sea and the waves that beat upon the shore, and that if he fell from his precarious footing he would fall and crash against the surf.

Hand over hand he made his way along the ledge to the slope of the roof. The gulls swooped and dived like dark angels, one flying so close that it bit sharply at his right ear. Blood seeped from the wound and across his face. He held tightly to the ledge, the pain intense, the gull mocking him as it dived again and again to pull him from his grip.

Isambard Black looked from the window of the room and called to him. 'Come back, Mariah, it's not as you think – I'm

here to help you.' The man smiled at him and offered his outstretched hand.

Mariah pressed on, turning his face away and looking to the
moon. In two paces he jumped from the ledge to the lead-
covered roof and the long balustrade that ran at waist height
the full side of the hotel.

'Come back, Mariah,' Black shouted. 'I need to talk. It really is not as you think.'

Mariah cast him a glance as he felt the blood trickling down
his neck. With one hand he touched his ear and felt the wound,
then set of across the roof.

He knew that to escape he would have to break into the
Prince Regent. The birds chased him as he ran, swooping and
diving, claws outstretched, beaks pecking at his hands as he
tried to fend them off. Soon he was at the far tower and six feet
above him was the porthole of Albion's room.

Mariah could see faint candlelight and a shadow cast upon
the ceiling. He crawled up the grey slates and peered in. There
was Albion. He was standing alone, chained to the bed by one
hand. Mariah watched as the man reached out to the mantelpiece where a silver key was tantalisingly lying.

Wedging himself against the roof, Mariah took off his jacket
and wrapped it around his hand and then smashed it against
the glass. The fragments shattered, falling into the room as
Mariah picked the pieces from the frame, put his jacket over
the edge and then proudly slipped through window.

'Perfidious Albion!' he exclaimed as he quickly took the key
from the mantel and undid the lock upon the man's wrist. 'I
have lost the cards, a man has taken them, he's a magician.'

Perfidious looked to the door. 'I was kidnapped and brought
here. There is a box of fortune in this place that has to be
destroyed. That is all I can tell you and it is all you need to
know.'

'The Midas Box?' Mariah asked as he twisted the pearl door handle.

'How did you know?'

'Otto Luger has it – it would seem everyone knows what the man is up to . . .' Mariah smiled, looking Perfidious in the eye. 'I have to meet someone in the bar to the theatre within the hour. He'll help us to get the cards. Now let' s get out of this place.'

Together they climbed through the window, slid down the grey slates and ran across the roof. By the high chimney that puffed grey steam from the generator was a small black door surrounded by iron railings and approached by a small flight of steps. Mariah led the way, his white shirt covered in the blood from his wound. Perfidious Albion hesitated as he walked, looking down across the roof to the crashing waves. Black clouds sped across the sky as to the east a storm gathered in the depths of the sea.

Soon they were down the steps and through the door that led into a long passageway flanked by guest rooms. At the far end a flight of stairs led to another lamp-lit corridor and eventually to the steam elevator. Mariah ran, followed by Albion, unaware of the steam elevator coming towards them.

With a sudden clunk the door slid open and Isambard Black stepped from the carriage. In his hand he carried a short cane. At the sound of approaching footsteps he twisted the handle, pulled the sword from its holder and stepped into the shadow of a doorway. He waited, unsure as to who approached but intent on defending himself.

Mariah and Albion ran on, not knowing he was there, lying in wait. Black listened as the pounding feet echoed closer.

With a sudden yell, Isambard Black leapt upon them, holding out the cane and in the half-light lashing out above their heads. 'Away with you!' he shouted, not knowing who or what he was shouting at.

'Black?' screamed Perfidious Albion as he stared up at the man. 'Isambard Black?'

'It can't be – surely not – Perfidious?' There was a surprise in his voice as if he had discovered someone long lost and was glad to remake the acquaintance. 'Perfidious Albion? Peradventure –'

'There is nothing of chance in this, Isambard,' Perfidious said as he got to his feet and held out a hand to the man. 'I have been saved by this young rascal. A simple introduction should suffice – Mariah Mundi, meet Isambard Black.'

Mariah's eyes flickered from one man to the other. He looked for a place to run to but knew he would be cornered upon the roof. Black stood within a sword strike of him and could cut him down easily with one blow should he desire.

'I've met him before . . . He's the man who has stolen the Panjandrum from me,' Mariah said as he stepped behind Albion.

'And you never told him, Isambard?' Albion asked lightly.

'He never asked. I tried as he ran off, jumped from the window and across the roof like a frightened rat.' Black laughed. It was the first time Mariah had seen the slightest hint of mirth in the man's life. Gone was the crusted grimace of the train as he smiled warmly and was changed in an instant.

'And you have the cards?' Perfidious Albion asked.

Isambard Black held out a gloved hand and showed him the case of the Panjandrum. 'All except one that Mariah has in his pocket. The Joker. Quite fitting for such a lad.'

'Are you in on this, Perfidious?' Mariah asked as he tried to step away.

'In on it?' Black laughed. 'He *is* it!'

'Mariah, meet my brother, Isambard Black, and like you, me and Captain Charity a former pupil of the Colonial School. In short, you have been followed from the day you left. Sadly, so

327

was I. That is why I handed you the cards, knowing you would be in good company and that my brother would keep you safe.'

'But he doesn't have your name?' Mariah questioned him.

'No, a slight perchance of different mothers but the same father. Shall we say that Colonel Albion liked to stroll below stairs . . . We were born in the same year and the old Colonel took us as his own.'

'He took *you* as the heir and *me* as the spare,' Black said roughly under his breath.

'And you knew of Charity when you sat in the carriage?' Mariah asked angrily.

'Who ever could forget old Charity? Four years older and still as stern now as he was then.'

'So I am a pawn outplayed by a powerful Queen with hands that work both black and white?' Mariah asked indignantly as he looked at them both.

'It is our job to track down items of interest. Things that are *unusual* and whose presence in the world would cause . . . *alarm* to those who –' Perfidious flustered.

'Those who are not used to the supernatural. Cards that can foretell the future, boxes that change objects to gold,' Black finished his brother's words in a matter-of-fact way.

'The Midas Box?' Mariah asked.

'Precisely, the Midas Box. We are here to take charge of these items and revert any damage that may have been done,' Isambard Black went on.

'So you're the police?' Mariah enquired as his mind raced to discover who they were.

'Not exactly, more the Bureau of Antiquities,' Black replied as he straightened his collar with one hand and sheathed the sword-cane.

'Spook hunters,' Perfidious Albion said with a smile. 'We have to find the Midas Box and destroy it before Otto Luger can turn everything into gold. But . . . we don't think he is who he would like us to believe he really is.'

'Otto is dead,' Mariah said, adopting of their matter-of-fact way of speaking of such weighty things. 'Found him in the foundations with a knife wound in him.'

'Then it is as you thought, Isambard,' Perfidious said. 'It *is* Gormenberg . . .'

The two men looked at each other and then to the boy. Isambard Black nodded to Albion, saying much in the raising of his brow and a stare of his eye.

'But he looks just like the paintings of Luger that are around the hotel,' Mariah said.

'He is an artist of a different kind, a sculptor and maker of the finest waxworks in Europe. What you see is a reconstruction of Luger's face and not even his closest friends could tell the difference. We have been tracking him for many years. Suddenly all went quiet and no one knew where he had gone. Then we heard that a man had found the Midas Box. Gormenberg had changed identities, stolen someone's life and become them. Easy, really, if you know how. Quite a business he's got going on.' Black fumbled with his fob watch.

'How did you know I had the Panjandrum?' Mariah asked Black as the two men huddled together.

'You were traced by your own intrigue. Remember in the carriage when I fell to the floor? I left the small skull, knowing you would find it. Inside the skull was a fragment of stone chipped from a larger block. When another piece from the same block comes into its presence and is mounted in gold it vibrates. How it works I don't even dream to know, but with my fob watch I can find it every time. Look.' Black showed Mariah his watch, the thick second hand glowing in the dark and pointing to his room. 'I knew that if you were involved you would have kept the Panjandrum and the skull together. Perfidious sent a telegram to say he had given the cards to you and the rest was, shall we say, down to modern science.'

'But I saw you talking to Bizmillah and he works for Luger,' Mariah argued.

'Shall we say, that after my conversation he is now of a different persuasion?' Black laughed again, the smile suiting his face.

'Not enough to free me from my room when he came a-visiting with my supper,' Albion moaned.

'He knew not of our relationship and before the performance he told me quite clearly where you were lodged. But this is enough of talk. It is vital that our work is done at midnight.' Black stopped and looked to Mariah. 'One thing,' he said slowly. 'The Joker – slide it into the deck.'

Black held out the cards towards him. Mariah took the Joker from his pocket and slid it into the middle of the pack. They shuddered in his hand as if they all were alive and had suddenly hiccupped.

'I take it that your inclination *was* to see what they could do?' Black asked Mariah.

'Never again,' said the lad

'Good. It is always best to leave such things until you know what to do with them. The only way these can be destroyed is by being turned to gold – we need the Midas Box for that, and then it too will meet a similar fate.'

'Why destroy the cards?' Mariah asked.

'We can't have people looking into the future. Knowing what is to come does us no good. Yet it is man's fascination. We cannot be content with here and now. The Panjandrum knows that and tells us half-truths. The cards mix our imagination with what will happen and then spin it before our eyes.' Albion tapped the deck of cards in Black's outstretched hand. 'They have a life of their own, but soon they will be solid gold.'

'How will you find the Midas Box?' Mariah asked as the

steam elevator chugged away from the floor, summoned from below. 'It could be hidden anywhere.'

'At midnight Gormenberg will try to use it again and we will be there to free him from his misery.'

'You'll steal the Midas Box?' Mariah asked.

Both Black and Albion hesitated and looked at each other, neither wanting to speak.

'We'll kill Gormenberg first,' Albion said quietly. 'It's the policy of the Bureau of Antiquities – leave no one to tell of what has gone on.'

'So what of me?' Mariah asked slowly.

'Your future was decided on the day you left the Colonial School,' Black said softly.

[30]

Trisagion

THE brass-studded leather door to the Trisagion was locked from the inside. When Mariah knocked gently, a small silver letterbox was opened and a pair of dark eyes glared through.

'Yes?' asked a deep voice the colour of the stare.

'I have to meet Captain Charity,' Mariah said as he looked up. 'He's expecting me.'

The man scowled at him. Mariah heard the lock quickly turn and the door slowly opened.

'Quickly!' said the voice. 'Visitors are not welcome, residents and members only.'

Mariah was hurried through. He stood in a large smoke-filled room that looked like the saloon of a gigantic ocean-going vessel. In the far wall were row upon row of portholes surrounded by circles of brass. High above them was the mast of a sailing ship festooned with flags of merchant vessels and men-o'-war. A hand-carved ebony drinks bar ran along the side wall. It was guarded by a tall thin man with poky eyes and a thin moustache that clung to his lip like a spider's leg.

The doorman pushed Mariah in the back to move him along. Mariah searched the room with his eyes, looking for the

Captain. A sea of high-backed leather chairs rested on the polished wooden floor like so many coracles upon the water. From each came a plume of bright blue smoke. All was silent except for the rasping of an occasional cough and the folding of the pages of a large sail-like newspaper.

The doorman pushed Mariah again, grunting for him to move and pointing to a chair by the log fire that burnt in the hearth of a high marble fireplace. On the mantelpiece was an ornate clock that chimed the hour, merrily keeping time with his steps. He walked among the chairs and quickly glimpsed the occupants of each. Many were hid behind columns of thick black letters, their piggy fingers gripping the pages. Each chair was equipped with its own candelabra, attached to its wings. The candles burnt brightly, shining through the translucent pages and casting a shadow of the reader across the paper. By every reader was a small table, every one the same, leather-topped and ebony-based. Some had crystal decanters at various stages of emptiness. All had a large tumbler of whisky, a metal ashtray and a cigar scissor.

At the four corners of the room were waiters dressed in dark suits. Each stood silently, tray in hand, waiting for a hidden signal of some requirement. They eyed Mariah as he crossed the room. It was as if they knew whom he was to visit, their glare going from him to the chair by the fire and then back again.

By the fireplace he found Captain Charity sat in a dark shadow, the candelabra on his leather chair extinguished. The Captain sat back, a blanket covering his legs and white gloves upon his hands.

'Mariah,' he whispered expectantly, his voice gruffed so as not to be overheard. 'Did you find the cards?'

Mariah hesitated as he glanced to the fire and then to the Captain.

'Did you find them?' he asked again just above a moan.

'Yes . . . No . . .' Mariah said.

'The cards, Mariah – have you got them?' the voice whispered insistently.

'I was found out. I was told to give you this.' The lad held out his hand and pressed a small visiting card into Charity's grip.

Charity read the embossed gold letters: *'Isambard Black . . . Bureau of Antiquities.'*

'They told me to tell you that they would see you outside Luger's room just before midnight.'

'*They?*' asked Charity.

'Yes. They have the Panjandrum for safekeeping. They said you would know who they were. Black and Albion – they told me they knew you all along, that –' Mariah stopped short. In his heart he knew there was something wrong.

'Indeed,' said Charity as he sat further back in the chair. 'They are here . . . Good,' he went on, thinking as he spoke. 'Now I want you to do something. Take this key and go to the cellar. The man at the door will go with you – don't worry, he can be trusted. Wait for me by the door to the sea and when I have finished my business I will join you. Find Albion and Black and tell them to come with you.' Charity coughed, his voice somehow different. 'Now go on, this is members only.'

Mariah stared at the shadowy face, unsure what to do. Charity attempted a half-smile and nodded slightly. For the briefest of moments, Mariah thought he had seen the skin on Charity's face move, as if it suddenly melted in the heat of the fire.

'Go on,' Charity said as he put his hand to his chin and wafted his face with a folded copy of the *London Times*. 'My man will see you to the cellar – go with him quickly.'

Mariah nodded and stepped away, unsure if he had witnessed an aberration of nature or if his eyes deceived him.

'This way,' said the doorman with the black piercing eyes. 'I know where you have to go – do you have the key?' His voice sounded like it had come from far away, from another continent, a land torn with enmity and revolution. 'We will take the steam elevator, it will save time.'

They were out of the door and along the corridor before Mariah could think of what was happening. Mariah turned and saw Albion and Black in the lobby of the hotel as he was pushed on by the doorman. They were sat on a long couch with red tassels, Albion clutching a leather bag as Black rolled his walking stick from hand to hand.

Mariah looked at his escort, staring at the scar on the side of the man's face. It was fresh and looked like a strip of salted meat standing proud of his skin. 'Must've hurt,' he said, pointing to the scar.

'An accident. My own fault, I should have been quicker,' the man replied proudly.

'Known Captain Charity for long?' Mariah asked.

'Charity?' The man asked as he rubbed his chin. 'Ah! Captain Charity!' He sniggered as he slid the door to the steam elevator and was about to step inside.

'ALBION! BLACK!' screamed Mariah suddenly as he set off to run, suddenly realising the doorman didn't know whom he was talking about.

'NO!' screamed the man, and he jumped for Mariah, grabbing him by the arm and pulling him to the elevator. 'You come with me.' The man pulled on his sleeve, tearing the material from the shoulder.

'ALBION!' Mariah screamed and waved his hands, trying to attract their attention. 'HELP!' The words dropped from his lips as he fell to the floor. Albion looked up and saw him being dragged from the corridor and into the elevator. He sprang to his feet and ran towards him.

'Quickly, Isambard,' he said as he ran towards the elevator. 'They have Mariah.'

The two men ran along the corridor as the door to the Trisagion opened quickly and out stepped a stunted Captain Charity.

'Jack!' shouted Black as he twisted his cane and slipped the sword hidden in the case a hand's breadth from the hilt. 'They have the lad.'

Charity didn't move. He stood in the marbled passageway holding the side of his face, whose flesh appeared to drool through his fingers.

'What's the matter, man?' asked Black. 'They're getting away.'

Charity reached into his waistcoat pocket and pulled out a silver pistol, pointing at the men. 'No further!' he said, slowly stepping towards the elevator. 'One more step and I'll shoot you dead.'

'Don't be a fool, Charity,' said Albion as he got closer. 'They'll hang you.'

Charity aimed the pistol. 'Gustav!' came the voice of Otto Luger from behind the wax mask of Captain Charity's face. 'Hold the elevator, we have unwelcome guests.' With one hand he pulled the melting wax from his face. 'Not my best creation, but one which worked well. Stay back, Mister Bureau of Antiquities, or you will be dead.'

'Gormenberg!' Said Albion as he stood back from the man. 'After all these years and halfway across the world we finally meet. Every city a different name, and we find you keeping a boarding house at the end of the line.'

'Not a boarding house but the finest hotel in the world, a pearl in a sea of periwinkles. You will have to search again, for I am about to disappear. The sea air was so good for me that I think I will return to the city.' Gormenberg pulled the shreds of waxed skin from his face. 'The Bureau of Antiquities will never find me.'

'We want the Midas Box, Gormenberg. It should have been destroyed years ago.'

'Gentlemen, gentlemen. If it were mine to give then I would oblige, but only those with the highest ideals should keep such a thing. Is the Bureau so short of money that it would want to make its own gold?'

'If that were the case, Gormenberg, then we would use the Philosopher's Stone – that we have had for many years,' Black said as he slipped the sword from the hilt of his walking cane. 'We never leave empty-handed.'

'How about empty-headed?' Gormenberg asked as he aimed the pistol at Black.

Black and Albion walked towards him, steely-faced.

'Then not for your own safety but for his?' Gormenberg asked as he turned the pistol to Mariah. 'One more step and I will shoot the boy between the eyes – simple . . .'

'Do it, Gormenberg! Right here and now,' Mariah shouted as he kicked out at the doorman, smashing his feet into his shins.

'Do it, Mister Luger, kill the little brat right now,' shouted the doorman as he tried to dance away from Mariah's sharp feet.

'Later,' Gormenberg said, quickly slipping into the lift with Mariah and the doorman and sliding the metal door firmly across. 'Don't wait for us, gentlemen of the Bureau. All the doors to the cellars are now secure and the steam elevator will be turned off. In fact stay right where you are for when I close the valve on the steam things should become quite . . . *explosive.*'

The steam elevator dropped suddenly from sight. It flashed past many floors until the air brakes suddenly began to drag the carriage and slow it to a halt.

Gormenberg took Mariah by the ear and twisted it in his fingers. 'So glad you can come. You'll have a ringside seat for the end of your world.'

337

'Where's Charity?' Mariah asked, not caring what would be done to him.

'Detained, indisposed and tied up. Not really an adversary of any worth. All I desire in life is to be challenged by a foe who is truly worthy.' Gormenberg picked the last pieces of wax from his face and stared at Mariah eye to eye. 'You had possibilities, boy. I didn't want to have you in the oyster farm – thought you could have worked for me in the real world.'

'My father told me –'

'From what I've heard, your father is in no place to tell you anything,' Gormenberg snapped as he twisted Mariah's ear even harder, dragging him from the elevator and through a narrow tunnel until he came to his laboratory. He shouted to the doorman, who pushed Mariah into the room.

The room was filled with Bizmillah's discarded magic tricks and scientific devices, and sitting by a long table, each in cuff chains that were bolted to the floor, were Felix and Sacha. In front of them were bowls of brown porridge mixed with an abundance of bright white pearls. The two sat staring at the wall but turned slightly as Gormenberg entered.

'Eat, I told you to eat!' he bawled as he banged the table with his fist. 'If I can't use the waxworks then I will have to use you.' Gormenberg crossed the room and lifted the lid of a metal vat that oozed cold steam over its sharp lip and across the floor. 'Once you've eaten, then –' He stopped and laughed to himself before turning to his companion. 'Stick him in the sarcophagus and make sure it's well locked, can't have him escaping. Might have to use Mariah as well. Now come on, eat.'

Gustav pushed Mariah across the room before he could say anything to Sacha. The man slammed him face-forward into a large painted coffin that was leant against the wall, then crashed the two parts of the lid tightly shut and turned the key.

From where he was imprisoned, Mariah could hear the

sound of footsteps leaving the room and the door shutting behind them.

'Mariah,' whispered Sacha as she gulped the pearls. 'They have us all. Captain Charity is locked next door. Luger wants me to eat the pearls and then he's gonna freeze us both and ship us to France. He showed us what's in the vat. It's a chemical that'll freeze anything faster than winter. There'll be no chance.'

'You should have stayed, Sacha. We had a plan.'

'Whatever plan you had didn't work. He got everyone of you,' Felix said as he crunched upon the pearls a spoonful at a time.

Mariah ignored what he said as he felt the inside of the sarcophagus with his hand. 'Have you seen the Kraken, Sacha? He followed you here.'

'Just Monica. She *is* a sea witch, she can walk through doors and do magic.'

'And so can I,' Mariah said – and suddenly, to their huge astonishment, he appeared behind them in the room. 'They took the coffin that belonged to Bizmillah. It's a magic trick, all you need to know is how to undo the back and hey presto . . . I saw it the first day I was here.'

'Still haven't got us from the room, have you, Mundi? Still as wet as ever,' Felix said, bringing the dark edge of reality back into place.

'Never expected to ever see you again, Felix Schlemihl. Once you'd left the Colonial School I thought you'd be making your millions. That's what you always said, wasn't it?'

'You know each other?' Sacha asked.

'I know the dreamer,' Felix said quietly, not liking his fate to be in Mariah's hands. 'Spent all his time looking at clouds or the moon and the stars, never a thought for life – eh, Mundi?'

'Never a bully, dowsing boys in water as they slept, filling their bed with cockroaches, putting a rat in a cooking pot or making a fresher drink mushroom water, eh, Schlemihl?' Mariah spat back through his teeth.

'There's no time for this,' Sacha shouted angrily as Mariah stepped towards Felix with his fist clenched. 'Luger will soon be back.'

'That's what I have to tell you – he's not Otto Luger but a man called Gormenberg. He's a crook and Black's from the Bureau of Antiquities and so is Perfidious Albion. And more than all that, Captain Charity is really –' Mariah stopped in mid sentence and looked at them as they stared incredulously towards him. 'There is so much I need to tell you, Sacha, so much. Look what Charity has given to me – there are only three in the whole world.'

Mariah held out the three-bladed knife proudly. It glinted in the candlelight.

'Why did he give you that?' asked Sacha as she rattled the chains that held her to the floor.

'Said it would be for my own good. That one day it would come in useful, and I think I know why.' Mariah took hold of the chain and stabbed the fine point of one blade into the lock, twisting it back and forth. Soon Felix was free. He rubbed his wrist and ran to the door and peered through the lock.

'No use,' he said desperately as he looked about the room. 'There's a key in the other side.'

Mariah didn't hesitate. First he quickly undid Sacha's shackles and then, pulling a piece of discarded newspaper from the shelf, he slipped it under the door and pushed at the lock with the blade of the knife. Within seconds the key fell from the other side. Mariah pulled the stiff sheet of paper back into the room, and the key was there before them. Felix smiled.

'Clever lad, this Mariah Mundi. I'll soon be out of a job.' He tried to laugh.

'Learnt it at the Colonial School. I was the one who trashed your room and burnt your money. Got the key from the caretaker's house just like this, and no one knew. Bilton thought you'd done it to yourself. Teach you for all you did. I laughed when I saw you in that cage, wanted to leave you there forever. Hoped that crocogon would eat you alive.' Mariah spat in his face and he clenched his teeth, ready to fight.

'Then why did you come back?' Felix argued, his face flushing with rage.

'I came back for her, not you. You made my life hell. When you left the school it was the best day of my life. Just 'cos you're a year older, thought you were the big man, and who had to save your skin? Me!' Mariah held the knife to his face. 'You're a joke, I know that now. Always the joker, poking fun, but that stuff hurts, hurts deep. Never told her I knew you, never wanted to. A bad memory best forgotten.'

'Stop it!' Sacha shouted. 'Luger will be back and you two will still be fighting.'

'Was him,' they said together, pushing their fingers into each other's face as if they had done it a thousand times before.

'She's right,' Mariah said reluctantly. 'Save this until another day. It's waited this long, it can wait another hour.'

'Likewise,' Felix grunted.

'Gonna get us out of here then, Mariah?' Sacha asked.

She had spoken too late. The door shimmered as the outline of a body broke through the fibres of wood. First a face and then the shoulders, until a whole body appeared in the room.

'My dear little friends,' said Monica as she materialized before them, dripping blue liquid to the floor in a large pool at her feet. 'You weren't thinking of leaving?' She looked at Mariah. 'All together at last,' she said, her eyes jumping from one to another.

Mariah hid the knife behind his back and stepped across the

341

room as Sacha looked at Monica. A growing stench of salt water and dead fish emanated from the sea witch, filling the room like a rising tide. Monica appeared to steam, a haze of fog falling from her shoulders like a white cowl. Yet her face looked young and fresh and was neatly powdered, her lips etched in bright red paint.

'I see you've eaten the pearls . . . Good, now I can have you dipped in liquid nitrogen and frozen for your journey. Who shall go first?' she said as she looked at Felix and Sacha in turn. 'I think . . . Felix.'

Before anyone could say a word she grabbed the boy by his throat, her hands strong and powerful. She lifted him from his feet and dragged him towards the steaming vat of freezing steam.

Felix screamed and looked at Mariah with eyes that called for help. Sacha tried to move but found her feet salted to the floor, encrusted in a thick layer of brine that held her like cement. Mariah too was held fast, the salting running up his leg and encrusting his body to the waist. Monica laughed as she dragged Felix closer and closer to the metal vat.

'Soon we'll have a boy who looks better than any of Otto's waxworks,' Monica said.

'He's not Ottto – he's Gormenberg,' Mariah said quickly.

'What?' she asked.

'You heard. He killed Otto Luger. I can show you his bones in the foundations. Otto's dead, has been for a long time. He lied to you and he's gonna kill you.' Mariah spoke quickly as she took Felix closer to the vat.

'I would have known, he tells me everything,' Monica replied, intent on killing Felix. Her grip tightened around his neck and he began to stop struggling.

The salting gripped them to the floor as her unspoken spell worked quickly about them. Mariah could feel the brine cutting into his flesh as the crystals multiplied upon him. Monica lifted Felix up the first of the three steps that led up to the top of the vat of freezing liquid. He had become limp in her hands as the life was strangled from him. She laughed to herself as she went up the next steps, and the sound of Sacha's frightened screaming filled the laboratory.

'I promise I'll be quick,' Monica shouted above the noise. 'Death comes easily – so many people have done it before, it can't be that bad.' She laughed again as Sacha ripped at the salt that now enfolded her up to her waist; her legs were like those of a giant snowman.

'Don't do it to him, please!' Sacha shouted, sobbing.

Mariah looked at the sea witch and the words of Captain Charity came back to his mind as if freshly spoken in his ear. *'A triple blade for a triple death. Not only kills the body but the soul and spirit, a blade for each, and will keep even the most fearful ghoul in its tomb for eternity.'*

'Take me!' Mariah shouted as the sea witch dropped Felix to the steps before she lifted him over the lip and into the liquid nitrogen.

Monica stopped and glared at him, holding her hands against her waist and tipping back her head in mocking laughter. 'Your turn will come,' she scolded.

Mariah seized the moment. His hand flashed from behind his back, then quickly stretched to full length and fired the triple blade through the air. It flew like a hawk swooping to the ground, taking on a life of its own. It shuddered the air, whistling and groaning as it sped towards the sea witch. It knew its purpose, as in the second it pierced her tight black dress, sending sequins exploding across the room. There was a flash of bright green light as the knife was absorbed into her body and then burst through her back, embedding itself in the far wall.

343

Monica laughed as she put a hand to her chest and felt the dribbling fluid running over her skin. 'I'm not flesh and blood . . . I'm a sea witch – you can't kill me.'

She crooked herself to slide Felix into the vat of liquid nitrogen. He moaned as she gripped him by the chest and began to lift him higher to roll him into the vapours.

'It didn't work – she lives!' Sacha shouted as Monica charmed the salting higher and higher up her waist.

It was then that the sea witch stopped and looked at Mariah. She smiled, but a look of concern flashed upon her face and fluid began to pour from her chest. As she looked to the triple blade embedded in the wall, minute orbs of green light burst from her and she began to glow. She gasped for breath, holding her hand across the rupture in her skin as she sought to quench the escape of life.

Felix began to breath again. The salt melted from Sacha and she broke free of its bindings. The sea witch gasped harder as if the air she gulped was of no worth and empty of life. A multitude of sparkles gushed from her wound like fireflies. She looked around the laboratory, her eyes searching for something familiar and her hand stretched out as if to reach for someone she knew.

Mariah walked towards her, knowing she was dying. His face was lifeless; there was not a single trace of emotion in his eyes. All he knew was that she had to die and that he could bring her life to its end.

In a few paces he had crossed the room. Felix stared at him, not knowing what he would do. Sacha grabbed his arm to hold him back, only to be shaken free as he pushed her to one side and made for the sea witch.

'There had to be the first one and it'll have to be you,' he said as he contemplated what he was about to do, pressed on by a growing force that welled up inside him. 'There will be no witnesses.'

Mariah stepped up to the vat of frosted liquid and took hold of Monica's shoe, which looked as though it were sprayed upon her translucent foot. He twisted it to one side, pulled her leg towards him, then stepped towards her, pushing her backwards. Without a word, he tipped her into the tank. Then he grabbed hold of Felix and dragged him away.

Like a graceful and silent swan, Monica the sea witch fell into the icy pool. In her final seconds of life she looked towards Mariah and smiled. It was as if she could see his future and knew all that life would bring to him. As she was consumed by the chilling fluid the sound of cracking bones echoed through the laboratory. In an instant she had disappeared, only to float to the surface holding out a frozen hand as if she reached for mercy.

Mariah picked Felix from the floor and looked harshly into his face. 'Don't get any ideas, Felix. I did it for Sacha.'

[31]

Iqtar

IN the faint light of the passageway, Mariah peered through a narrow slat that was cut into the cell door. In the corner of the room he could see Captain Charity leaning against the wall, his head held in his hands.

'I can't open the door,' Mariah said as he peered inside. 'I met with Albion and Black – they told me everything. I know who you are – and what's more, Luger is *Gormenberg*.'

Charity smiled as he stepped to the door. 'Gormenberg? I realised that when I was captured. If I cannot escape, then you'll have to go alone. Did you find Felix and Sacha? I heard their voices.'

'They're safe, still in the laboratory. Felix is hurt. I . . . I . . .' Mariah stuttered the words as he pushed his hand through the slat to take hold of Charity. 'I killed Monica – she was a sea witch.'

'Did you use the knife?' Charity asked. 'And it worked?'

'She's dead,' Mariah said as he held his hand.

'I'm not surprised, never known the knife to fail in its task. Do you have it now?'

'In my belt,' Mariah said softly, wanting more than this,

346

wondering if everyone in the Bureau of Antiquities talked like this in times of great consequence.

'Good . . . Find Albion and the Midas Box and Gormenberg will not be far behind. Sacha will help me from this place. Go – go now.'

'Gormenberg has closed the steam valve and said the whole building will explode. You have to get out of here.'

'Fear not, Mariah. I have no plans on leaving this life. The land of the table-rapper will not take me yet. Find Gormenberg, and swiftly – he must not get away from the Prince Regent.' Charity spoke quickly as the cell filled with a sudden gust of steam from a bursting pipe.

'But how will you get out?' Mariah asked as the sound of the steam generator suddenly stopped.

'That's not your concern, Mariah. Do as I say. Find Albion and Black. They will need you in what is to come.' There was the sound of grating rock above their heads. The foundations seemed to jump as they were showered in a pall of thick dust that fell from the roof.

'I can't leave you here, not like this,' Mariah argued as he rattled the door to the cell.

'I'll find a way to escape. You have to go and go quickly,' Charity insisted as more dust fell upon him.

Mariah turned to set off at a pace but stopped dead in his tracks. He cast a glance through the door to the laboratory: Sacha was lifting Felix to his feet.

From inside the darkened laboratory Felix looked at Mariah and smiled. 'I judged you wrong. There's more of a Colonial boy in you than I thought,' Felix said as he hobbled to the door still holding his neck, his hands covering the bright blue fingermarks around his throat.

Mariah nodded and smiled at him. Somehow all that had gone before mattered not, it seemed so trivial and commonplace. The mountains of hurt had crumbled around him in his present circumstances.

'Take Felix to the beach,' he heard himself saying to Sacha. 'Charity needs you to help him escape. I have a task I must complete alone.'

Sacha vainly tried to call him back, her words echoing along the empty tunnels as his footsteps sped off into the distance.

Mariah ran and ran until he came to the steam elevator. He pressed the bell as the sound of the emptying steam generator gurgled and gulped all around him. He waited, in his heart knowing that the machine would not come.

Wet sand covered the floor. Upon the wall the gas lamp burnt dimly, casting shadows through its broken glass shield out and along the tunnel that led to the sea. Mariah pressed the button for the lift and again waited. There was a long moan as the steam escaped from the ramrod far below, and he now knew for certain that the elevator had died. Looking around him, he walked on, keeping to the tunnels that went upwards and towards the Prince Regent. It was lighter and drier here. The sea was left far behind, the corridors covered in a fine sand that didn't show his footsteps.

The foundations tremored yet again as the earth shivered and twisted, the pressure mounting in the geyser deep within the rocks. In a few minutes Mariah had walked the length of the longest passageway and stood before a double door with salt-rusted handles. It was blocked with a pile of sand. Nearby was a discarded shovel with a broken blade that had split in two; it was half buried in the dry sand that was stacked all around him.

Mariah pulled upon the doors. They were jammed fast. He thought of going back, finding some other way through the labyrinth of tunnels that he knew would lead him to the surface. But when he peered through a cracked pane of glass in the doors he could see on the other side the steps that led to the spiral staircase and eventually the lobby of the Prince Regent.

Taking the shovel, he smashed at the glass, only to find that it had been barred in place long ago with iron braces stronger than any prison. He kicked the sand and then began to dig. In a short time he had pushed the fine white sand back into the tunnel, piling it as high as himself. Still there was more to be moved. He dug the spade in deep until it cracked against something hard. He burrowed with his hands, moving away as much of the fine debris as he could, until he came to something that felt as hard as iron yet as smooth as a silken handkerchief.

Mariah tapped upon it three times. It rang out with a dull thud and sounded strangely hollow. It was then that he felt the earth move slowly beneath him. There was no sound of a tremor or fall of sand from the roof, but he was sure he had moved. It stopped as suddenly as it had begun and he knelt there, waiting. He again tapped upon it as he smoothed away the sand, and there he saw the thick red shell of the Pagurus.

It was as if he were in an earthquake. He was violently tilted back and forth as the sleeping creature got to its feet and shook the sand from its body. Mariah was pressed against the ceiling. The Pagurus snapped its claws as it tasted the air and its one large red eye swivelled in its socket and stared at him.

As the Pagurus pressed him higher against the stone roof, hoping to scrape him from its shell and then pick him limb from limb and suck upon the juice, Mariah suddenly dived and flattened himself upon its back, keeping one hand upon the shovel as the other grasped for the beast's eye. It snarled like a simmering pot as he held the eye in his hand, wanting to pull it from its socket. The Pagurus leant back, raising its claws high into the air as it snapped at him. It lurched from left to right, confined by the sand and the door as its sharp toes danced upon the stones below.

The beast showed no fear as Mariah hung on to its back, his hand upon the shovel. He had run from the creature before but now he felt compelled by powerful voices within him to stand and fight. The Pagurus stopped and looked at him as he cupped its eye in his hand. It seemed to taste the air and shimmer the long spiny hairs that covered its mouth.

'I won't run this time,' Mariah said.

The crab rattled its claws like a jangling sabres, as if it had understood his words.

'You or me?' he asked as he flashed the shovel back and forth.

Another shudder of the rock exploded a shower of fine sand all around them like a swirling mist. The Pagurus trembled, and the clatter of snapping claws echoed through the tunnel. Mariah stared at the beast and the beast stared back. For a moment the Pagurus hesitated. Mariah took the broken blade and sliced it across his hand, shattering the creature's eye.

It hissed and moaned as it then spun this way and that, grabbing blindly with its claws at everything and nothing. In one movement it threw Mariah to the floor and blindly took hold of the door, instinctively holding upon it with its large right claw.

Mariah smashed at the creature as its powerful legs stabbed at him time and again. He thrashed it across its back, the shovel bouncing from its carapace as if from the hardest steel. It backed against Mariah, pressing him against the wall with the cusp of its shell. He slid to the floor as it tried to dance upon him and impale his body to the sand, and as he grovelled beneath the beast he saw a multitude of fine red berries that clung to its underside. He brushed against the thick spines that covered each speared leg, while the Pagurus darted its fat claw towards him, trying to pluck him from his hiding place. Mariah stabbed the nest of eggs that clung to the queen's shell. They burst upon him like a fall of fresh cranberries as he scrambled into the light. Taking the shovel, he rammed the blade into the creature's mouth.

Like a madman he twisted the shaft back and forth, each time pressing it deeper and deeper. The Pagurus snapped with its mandibles and held its claws before it like praying hands. It froze upon its feet and then backed away, shuddering with every step.

Mariah pushed the shovel even deeper until the full handle was plunged within the beast. It groaned and spat as its claws were held in rigid spasm. Taking the triple blade from his belt, Mariah stabbed the crab again and again until his hands ran pink and green with the mucus that spewed from within. It juddered once more then fell to the floor – dead.

With the sand cleared, Mariah wasted little time in opening the doors and walking through the musty dank tunnels until he found his way to the landing that led into the hotel. The sound of moaning and creaking pipes vibrated the air around him, and he felt thoroughly alone. In the distance he could hear the crocogon wailing in the depths, barking and roaring like an old caged lion wanting to be fed.

Mariah pressed on, climbing the spiral staircase until his mind swirled. He jumped the stairs two at a time, clattering his footsteps against the stone. The brass pipe banister that coiled upwards was cooling to his touch; the whole of the Prince Regent began to groan and creak as it contracted with the growing cold.

Soon he had come to the door that would lead beyond the theatre to the lobby and eventually to Gormenberg's office. It had been bolted from the inside with a sweeping brush wedged between its handles so that no one could come through, but Mariah managed to jolt the brush free and pulled the door open. He peered down the long corridor beyond the Trisagion and onwards towards the brightly lit foyer. The gold clock above him chimed the quarter hour and was echoed by the landing clocks throughout the hotel.

The lobby was empty, except for the old janitor who doddered back and forth with his brush and pail, sweeping the remnants of ashed cigars from the floor and turning down the lamps one by one.

Mariah walked as calmly as he could. He felt taller, almost a man. A painting of Luger – or was it Gormenberg? – stared at him, its eyes following his every step, an outstretched finger pointing accusingly. He smiled and nodded at the janitor as he walked past, turned the corner and stood before the oak-lined door of Luger's office. His black suit was now tattered and torn, his shirt ripped and covered in the slime of the Pagurus.

For the first time he looked at the wall above the entrance to the hotel. It was a perspective he had not seen before. The revolving door had been folded shut and locked for the night. As he stared through the glass, Mariah could see a night porter stood on the steps outside in his thick padded coat with gold cuffs, beating his arms against himself to bang away the chill.

To one side a grand staircase swept upwards, its gold handrail shining in the dim light like the back of a coiled serpent rising from the deep green carpet that stretched from wall to wall. Pinned to the ceiling like an ornate plaster rose was yet another clock face. Its second hand swished anticlockwise as the minutes clicked onwards. A moon appeared and then set across the face, growing from new to full in a matter of seconds, as small stars like jewels and a golden sun went back and forth from behind silver clouds. Mariah was mesmerised by the whirring golden hand that appeared to spin faster and faster.

There was no sign of Albion or Black. Apart from the janitor there was no one at all. Mariah waited impatiently, strutting up and down outside the office door. He looked up to the clock several times and watched the minutes pass by slowly. There was still no sign of the agents from the Bureau as the janitor finished brushing the floor, gave Mariah a sorrowful glance and then walked away.

From above he finally heard footsteps. They thumped slowly down the steps from the high landing. He tried to follow them with his eye but in the dimmed lights could see no one. Mariah stepped back away from the door and into the shadows of a small alcove. He pressed himself against the dark oak panel and held his breath.

Gormenberg turned the corner and walked towards the office door. He seemed unconcerned, as if this was a night like any other night. Mariah could at last see his true face without the cover of the waxen mask that he had moulded to convince the world he really was Otto Luger. He looked younger than Mariah had expected, with a thick brow and razor-like jaw. His cheek was slashed with an old duelling scar that had been treated with salt to make it stand proud. It was longer and finer than the one Gustav had so arrogantly carried. The mark ran from Gormenberg's right ear to just below the eye and looked like a crescent moon carved into his skin.

Mariah watched from his hiding place as Gormenberg fumbled in the deep pockets of his coat for a set of keys. He farted, then glanced to the clock that spun above him, opened the office door and stepped inside. There was still no sign of Albion and Black. Mariah looked up at the swirling clock: nine minutes to midnight. As he felt the shape of the dagger in his belt, he knew he had to go alone. He tapped on the door and waited nervously for a reply. The door to the office was slowly opened and Mariah stepped inside.

'Mariah Mundi . . . How well you have escaped,' Gormenberg said as he welcomed the lad into his office. 'Of course you now know Albion and Black.' He pointed to the two men tied

353

together and strapped around a large marble pillar that appeared to hold up the roof. 'I thought I had taken care of everyone and like a bad penny you keep appearing. Whatever shall be done with you? I gave instructions to Monica to have you frozen and yet you are here before me alive and well.'

'She's dead,' Mariah said calmly as he held the knife behind his back. 'Fell into the vat and was frozen. Careless, really . . .'

'And of course you had nothing to do with it?' Gormenberg asked.

'Everything,' Mariah replied as he looked at Black.

'Did you enjoy it, Mister Mundi? Did it give you a feeling of power?' Gormenberg asked.

'I felt nothing, my heart was cold, it had to be done,' he said as he sidled across the room to the marble pillar and leant against it. Gormenberg sat in his leather chair, leaning against his wide desk.

There was no sight of the Midas Box. Mariah looked about the room, hoping to see a trace of the artefact.

'So . . . What now?' Gormenberg asked.

'Why did you kill Luger? I found his bones in the cellar. It was you, wasn't it?'

'What does it matter?' Gormenberg said to himself. He picked a handkerchief from his top pocket and folded it into his shirt neck as a napkin. 'You'll all be dead within the hour and I will be far away.' He yawned and then farted again as he licked his fingers and then rubbed them against a bloodstain on his gold waistcoat. He glanced to the clock and then to the drawer of his desk. With a shaky right hand he slowly slid the drawer open and brought out a large golden plate. It was filled with cold fat sausages, gherkins, pickled onions, strips of bacon and stale fried bread. With his stubby fingers he began to pick a piece at a time and slip it into his mouth. 'Always like to eat when I'm thinking – the more I think the more I eat. Especially animals. Once met a man who'd never eaten meat in his life – he was scrawny and thin with a pallor of death. Sort of man who'd die of measles or whooping cough. I've often wondered what it would be like to eat the ultimate meat – you know what I mean?'

Mariah knew exactly what he meant. He looked at Albion and Black, who struggled against the ties of the rope that bound them to the pillar. 'How did you catch them?' Mariah asked as he nodded towards the two men. 'They'd come to get *you*.'

'Our own fault,' Albion said as he jabbed Black in the ribs with a sharp elbow.

'Was your idea to check his office before midnight,' Black squalled.

'He was supposed to have been in the cellars,' Albion protested.

'Grimm and Grendel saw to that. My two friends had chased you through the sewers and got themselves lost – they eventually came out at the castle and with a shilling cab ride they were back at the Prince Regent just in time to catch your companions rummaging for the Midas Box where their greasy little fingers shouldn't be . . .'

'Grimm and Grendel caught you?' Mariah asked them as he edged closer.

'Not so much them but the pistols they carried,' Black sniggered. 'Albion insisted that this affair would not require the use of firearms – didn't you, Perfidious?'

'Soon be midnight,' Gormenberg said, and to Mariah's surprise he pulled the Panjandrum cards from his pocket and began to take them from the box one by one with his greasy fingers. He chomped and spoke at the same time, rolling the food around his mouth and dribbling constantly. 'You see, Mariah, I now have everything I desire. A device to make gold

355

and another to make the future. It would be tragic to allow these two buffoons to take them from me.' He took the last fat sausage and slid it between his teeth like a succulent cigar. 'Now I go in search of an alabaster box filled with mercury that can take me from one world to another. You, my friends, will await the largest explosion this country has ever seen. After, they will say I was lost in a natural disaster of Icelandic proportions, a Pompeii beyond Pompeii. When the steam from below the ground is not vented through the hotel it will blow a hole in the side of the earth that will engulf the hotel and half the town, and I will watch it all from the safety of the sea. Listen . . . Isn't it wonderful? Silence . . .'

'You'd kill us all for that?' Mariah asked.

'I'd kill you for less and would never get caught,' Gormenberg replied as he rang a dainty bell that he kept on the top of his desk. 'Grimm, Grendel,' he called. 'All our guests are now assembled and I am to leave. Five minutes to midnight and I have one last task before I say goodbye the Prince Regent.' Gormenberg put the Panjandrum cards back into the box and then into his pocket.

The door opened and the two detectives stepped into the room. Their fine suits were covered in mud and torn at the knees. Each held a small pistol uncomfortably in his hand.

Grimm smirked his usual smirk and ruffled himself like a cock hen. 'Nice to see you face to face. Chased your dust for so long I wondered what you would look like,' he said to Mariah.

'Suppose I'll be tied here to await my fate whilst you all escape?' Mariah asked as he stepped against the column.

'Suppose you're right, lad. Take your place and I'll see to you,' Grimm said as Grendel hovered nervously behind him, a twitch taking hold of his left eye and jerking his head.

Mariah quickly stepped against the column and with the knife began to secretly cut the bonds that held Albion to Black.

'I will see you on the steamship *Tersias*,' Gormenberg said as he stood from his desk. 'Do not be longer than the hour or you will share their fate. I have to get the Midas Box. Don't be late.' He placed his folded handkerchief upon the plate, picked a pickled gherkin, stuffed it into his mouth and then left the room.

The door slammed behind him and he was gone. Mariah could hear the strands of rope being cut through as he pressed the knife against them.

'Careful, lad,' Black whispered. 'Nearly through.'

'Do you think you could show me the glasses just one more time – the ones you followed me with in the sewer?' Mariah asked boldly as he played to Grimm's pride. 'Show them to my friends, it would be most interesting.'

The detective cast a glance at his companion and shrugged his shoulders. 'Suppose it'll do no harm – always best to end a life on a curiosity.' Grimm pulled the spectacles from his pocket and placed them on his nose, slipping the wire frames around his cauliflower ears.

'So you can see where anyone has been?' Mariah asked.

'Like a vapour trail of red mist that goes behind us all, unseen by everyone,' Grimm chortled like a proud professor.

'Even where Gormenberg has gone?' he asked.

'Even Gormenberg,' Grimm said bluntly. 'All I would have to do is take his handkerchief and hold it here.' He held the stained white cloth to his face. 'And then I turn this dial and once the frequency is registered I could follow him forever.'

'I must see,' Mariah pleaded as whimsically as he could rouse himself to be. 'Please?'

Grimm looked at his sad and pleading eyes and lopsided smile. He took the spectacles from his face and placed them carefully upon Mariah's nose. 'There,' he said kindly. 'The lad can go from this world knowing what they're like.'

Grendel nodded, his hand shaking and his twitch growing stronger as it lurched his head from side to side.

Mariah suddenly could see a swirling red mist that formed a trail of vapour from the seat behind the desk and through the door. Upon the wooden floor were thick red blotches like the footprints of a monster that trailed across the room.

'And you got these from the Americas?' he asked.

'From a prophet, a man who said he could read etchings on plates he found on a mountain. Never a stranger tale have I ever heard,' Grimm said. He looked at Grendel, who was having trouble keeping his feet upon the ground.

'So, Mister Grimm. You are finally the victor and we the defeated,' Albion interrupted.

'Quite so, quite so. A strange accident of fate,' Grimm replied, quite distracted.

'There are no such thing as accidents, Mister Grimm, no such thing,' Albion said, and he twisted his wrists and snapped the severed ropes. As if he were some mountain beast, Albion threw himself at Grimm, knocking him to the floor. Grendel, stunned by what he saw, raised the pistol to shoot, but it danced around on the end of his fingers as if it had a life of its own.

'No!' shouted Grimm, in fear of his life as Grendel aimed the pistol at his head.

Black leapt towards Grendel, kicking out as he jumped over Mariah's head and landing on the twitching detective like a leopard on a jackass. 'Run, Mariah!' he screamed. 'Find Gormenberg before he escapes the town,' he shouted as he punched the detective in the face and grappled with the gun in his hand.

Mariah hesitated. Albion held Grimm to the floor and looked momentarily towards him, his brow sweated as he wrestled with the detective. 'Go, lad! Find him and we'll follow.'

The Prince Regent lurched suddenly as a fresh tremor

arched the building and shuddered it violently. Debris fell from the ceiling, and the sound of cracking wood on the panelled oak walls ripped the air like splintering bone. The deep silence of the dormant hotel was broken as the screams of guests in faraway rooms filled the night like the cry of a thousand ghosts lamenting their own death.

As Black and Albion fought on, Mariah ran to the door and into the lobby. The staircase and the hallway were filled with panicking people escaping to the street clad in only their nightclothes. A trail of red footsteps led to the stairway. Mariah scoped the scene, the divining spectacles casting a glow around everyone at whom he looked.

The fleeing bodies left a trail of dark light like a living shadow; it was as if Mariah stared upon a field of ghosts that ran down the stairs. Many were screaming, the shuddering of the hotel having frightened them from their warm beds and chased them into the cold street. He pursued the footsteps as fast as he could, the red vapour billowing about his feet. Far behind he heard four gunshots, and then complete silence.

The SS *Tersias*

THE clocks struck midnight with a chilling sound. It was as if their call was different than on any other night. The Prince Regent shuddered in time with each beat, the sound of the chimes almost deafening Mariah as he ran. He could hear the echoing carillon coming from all around him as he chased the red glow of Gormenberg's footsteps. As the clocks struck the third chime of midnight, he turned a corner of the stairs and into a long corridor. He had never been this way before. It was cold and damp and had the smell of cordite and pepper. It reminded him of the odour an old aunt who would carry her wheezing and toothless dog everywhere she went.

In front of Mariah a door stood a fraction open, the light from inside shafting into the dark corridor. The footsteps led through it; they were bright and fresh and shimmered with red vapour. He knew Gormenberg was near. From inside the room he could hear the man fumbling with the lock of a safe and the clitter-clatter of a dial ratcheting loudly as he turned it back and forth to find the combination. Mariah heard the safe door creak open on squeaky hinges, followed by the slithering of metal across a shelf.

He waited outside the room, not daring to venture in. The chimes of a gentle clock picked out the hour again, as if time had stood still. Mariah counted the twelve strokes of midnight, repeated over and over like the call of a faraway bird.

He listened as Gormenberg slammed something heavy against the slats of a wooden table. There was the click of another lock. The man mumbled to himself, half cursing, half laughing. It was as if he recited a charm under his breath, not wanting the world to hear the secret words he recounted.

'Guardian of Gold, open the door to riches and grace . . .' he said again and again, his words seeping out through the open door as Mariah listened, wondering what to do next.

It was circumstances and not bravery that forced his hand. Mariah was leaning against the door to hear more of what Gormenberg was chanting when suddenly he fell into the room and to the floor at the man's feet.

Gormenberg didn't look at him. Mariah could see that he held the outstretched wings of a plain lacquered box, the Panjandrum lying by its side.

'Stay, boy, and don't move,' Gormenberg said as he placed a piece of black coal into the box. 'I must do this before I deal with you.'

'I've come for the Midas Box,' Mariah said, his voice trembling.

'Brave or stupid? I haven't decided which you are but will soon find out,' Gormenberg nagged through chattering gold teeth, as he was about to close the lid of the box upon the lump of coal.

'Neither!' shouted Mariah as he jumped to his feet and stepped towards the man, grabbing him by the hand and thrusting it into the Midas Box as he slammed the lid upon it.

Gormenberg screamed in agony, his face turning blue and then deep crimson as throngs of white spittle blew from his mouth like foaming wave tops. The box juddered against the wooden table, vibrating and alive, as shards of golden crystal light beamed across the room, the light so intense that it dazzled. Mariah struggled to hold Gormenberg's hand fast as they both became absorbed within the blazing light that escaped from the Midas Box.

'You don't know what you do!' screamed Gormenberg as he struggled to be free. 'I had altered time and at last would have succeeded. It will kill us both if you don't set me free.'

His voice sounded feeble. Mariah could smell the noxious odour of stale cigars and old cologne that clung to Gormenberg's jacket. Tiny ribbons of wax began to melt from his face as his nose began to drip and liquefy. His eyes bulged as if they were being pushed from his head. As he screamed, darts of golden light shot from his mouth.

There was a sudden and terrifying explosion. The room was darkened as the lights flickered. Mariah was blown from his feet and landed against the wall. Gormenberg was nowhere to be seen. A thick layer of black smoke hung like a pall of winter smog across the stone floor. As Mariah got to his feet he saw Gormenberg's arched back rising from the mist. The man stood up, clutching his left hand. It glowed in the gaslight. It was completely golden, every finger frozen in bright precious metal.

'My hand . . .' Gormenberg stuttered as he stared disbelievingly at what had been done to him. 'Look what you've done!' His voice sounding like that of a child who had discovered a broken toy.

Mariah looked towards Gormenberg, who had been showered in golden rays. Upon his coat were globules of shining metal; his skin shimmered in a fine gold powder. Droplets of gold hung from the ceiling of the room, sparkling in the light. It was as if everything had been bathed in gold and outlined like a finely painted icon. He looked again at Gormenberg's hand – it was solid gold.

The Midas Box lay on the table, the cards close by. They appeared to have been undisturbed by the explosion of light that had knocked Mariah from his feet. The lad saw Gormenberg's eyes flash from box to cards and then to his golden hand. 'Want to take them both?' he asked as he felt for the dagger in his belt. 'Your move, Gormenberg. Go for which one you want, but go for both and I'll pin you to the table with this dagger.' Mariah couldn't believe he had spoken the words – his fear had gone, and his heart pounded as if with each beat it changed a boy to a man. He clutched the dagger and heard the disturbing sound of soft metal touching against the hilt.

Mariah held out the dagger before him and looked at his own hand. It was then he saw that the tip of his little finger to the second knuckle had been transformed to pure gold. It was perfect in every way and joined seamlessly to the flesh, as if the gold had grown from his skin. He stared at it intently, mesmerised by what he saw.

Gormenberg saw the look of panic on the boy's face and laughed.

'Slightly less than mine,' he said jovially as he grasped his hand. 'If we had fought for longer then we would both be turned to solid gold.' With that he reached out, grabbed the Midas Box and ran from the room.

Mariah picked the Panjandrum cards from the table and followed. The mist swirled red before his eyes as the divining spectacles followed Gormenberg's every step. They ran on, down and down, Gormenberg's stride lengthening as he left Mariah trailing behind. Through door after door and around dark landings they ran. All Mariah could see was the plod, plod, plod of red footprints in the sands that covered the stone steps. They clattered into a long tiled corridor that Mariah knew led to the beach.

Gormenberg darted quickly into a side passage far ahead as

Mariah ran on behind. In the distance, Mariah saw three figures coming towards him, their bodies outlined by a fine blue aura.

'Mariah!' shouted Sacha. She held Felix by his arm as Charity carried the boy along.

'He's running for the harbour. Gormenberg is going to catch the *Tersias* before she sets sail,' Mariah screamed as he ran on, in his heart knowing he couldn't stop.

'I'm with you, lad,' Charity shouted as he laid Felix to the ground. 'Take him to the beach. Can you make it, Felix?'

The boy nodded as he leant towards Sacha, and Charity joined the chase.

Mariah snatched the eyeglasses from his face and plunged them into his pocket. At last he could see without stumbling, free from the blinding of the divining spectacles. He ran even faster, trying to make a yard on Gormenberg, but the man ran like the wind, faster than Mariah had ever seen a man run before – it was as if his feet didn't touch the ground as with every step he bolted a further yard. Soon they were upon the beach, where a growing storm was mounting in the bay. The waves washed across the top of the North Pier, the dolphin buoys dancing in the water.

Mariah watched Gormenberg leaping across the sands and stretching the distance between them with every step. The man danced across the strand like a gazelle, soaring over the dispersing mist.

'CU-BAA!' shouted the distant voice of Charity, who ran far behind Mariah. 'Get the man!'

Several yards from Mariah the soft white sand burst open, and out sprang the crocogon who had been basking in the warmth. The beast looked about it, hearing the call of its master, and then, sighting Gormenberg, set off to run.

'Go, Cuba, go!' shouted Charity as he ran on behind Mariah

and together they watched the beast chase Gormenberg through the mist and towards the pier.

Gormenberg turned and cast a glance behind, slowing his steps as if he taunted the crocogon to run faster. He stopped and held out his golden hand to tempt Cuba, and looked across the sands to Mariah and Charity as they raced on.

'Do you think a dragon can catch me, Captain Charity? Is that the best you can do?' he screamed, his voice shrill and angry. 'You have no idea who I am, do you, Captain?' he shouted mockingly as Cuba rushed towards him, about to strike.

Cuba leapt the last six feet, launching herself through the air with all the strength of her dragon legs. Her long tail twisted as she dived towards him, and at the final moment she snapped her mouth.

Gormenberg sprang to one side. The crocogon fell into the surging water of the surf, perplexed as to how it had missed the man.

'Better luck next time!' Gormenberg laughed as he ran towards the fish pier lined with gutting sheds that were silhouetted against the moonlight.

'Run for the ship, Mariah!' Charity shouted as Mariah raced on, his lungs fit to burst and his throat burning.

The blackened and sooted funnel of the steam-tramp *Tersias* poked above the chimneys of the houses that lined the pier. A thick column of black smoke rolled upwards like the blade of a knife cutting the sky as its engine chugged and clanged, ready to set sail.

Gormenberg ran on, leaping from the beach to the top of the pier like Spring-Heel Jack as the crocogon followed up a flight of stone steps. Mariah came behind, with every pace losing his breath. He stumbled up the steps, slipping on the jagged winkles and seaweed that clung grimly to each tread. Long swags

365

of draped nets pulled at his face as he ran past the scaling huts to the harbour side.

In the faint gas light of the pier end Mariah could see Gormenberg leap from a stack of fish boxes and on to the ship. At once the *Tersias* put to sea, crashing the boats that were moored to its side to matchwood. Mariah ran along the pier, knife in hand, as he caught up to the ship. Gormenberg stood aft, the Midas Box held proudly in his right hand as he waved to Mariah with his five golden fingers and shimmering palm.

'Next time, Mariah. I am sure there will be a next time. Out of them all it was you who came the closest to capturing me. Imagine – a boy, a Colonial boy! Keep the hotel, whatever is left of it . . .' Gormenberg laughed as the ship slipped through the mouth of the harbour. Its portholes glimmered with a meagre yellow light that seeped through the dirty windows.

'I expected your escape on something finer than this,' Mariah shouted back to him as he stood on the end of the pier.

'I have a bilge full of pearls and the Midas Box, what more could I ask for?' Gormenberg swaggered as he turned to walk away. 'One more thing,' he shouted. 'The man who was killed outside the Three Mariners – I didn't do it. It was another.'

'We'll find you, Gormenberg,' Charity shouted as he found Mariah and stood watching the vessel put to sea.

Gormenberg waved his golden hand and laughed as the *Tersias* sailed clear of the stillness of the harbour and into the turbulent open water of the Oceanus Germanicus.

'Lost to us . . .' Mariah said as he turned to Charity. 'He got away.'

'But you fought well, you proved yourself. The struggle changed you . . . And you and Sacha did it together.'

'But Gormenberg got away with everything.'

'Sometimes things are never the way we wish. Often it looks as if evil has triumphed and light is weaker than darkness. That is life, my lad. Loose ends and misery.' As Charity spoke, the panting crocogon came and wrapped itself around their feet like an attentive lapdog.

'The Prince Regent!' Mariah blurted. 'I must go, the steam was switched by Gormenberg . . .'

'And the faucet released by Captain Charity. Sacha helped me escape – she did well, no one could have done better. Together we found the valve and the Prince Regent will shudder no more.'

Mariah shooed the crocogon from his feet and together they turned to walk away. In his heart he felt saddened, as if the burden of the world had been thrust too early upon his young shoulders. The cold night clung to his face and dewed his eyes. Nothing of what he had done or seen made any sense to him. It was as if life had become an opera and he a player against foul fiends.

As they stepped away, Mariah smiled at Charity and then turned to cast a final glance to the sea.

'LOOK!' Mariah screamed and pointed to the sea just beyond the harbour mouth. The tentacles of the Kraken wrapped themselves around the bow of the *Tersias*, tearing the wooden slats from the steel hulk. The sea boiled as the creature took hold of the ship and pulled at its smokestack, ripping it from the ship and hurling it to the water. 'The Kraken – it did come back!'

'What did I tell you?' Charity said as he looked on. 'Never trust a creature like a Kraken, you never know what they will do.'

They stood as onlookers, watching the waves break over the ship. From below another beast gripped itself upon the craft's stern, and a gigantic tentacle broke open the bridge door and searched inside. Three crewmen leapt to the foaming sea, to be lost in the waves. Gormenberg stood proudly on the top of the ship, waving to the shore in defiance, his screams drifting upon the wind with none to hear them.

In seconds the vessel was no more. The Krakens together pulled it from the surface to the depths below. Gone was Gormenberg, gone was the Midas Box.

'What's to be done?' Mariah asked of Charity.

'Nothing. All has been done for us,' he replied calmly as Albion and Black ran towards them.

'He escaped . . .' Mariah said before they could ask.

'Only to be caught again,' Charity continued.

'We saw it well but couldn't believe our eyes. In all these years at the Bureau we have never seen the likes before,' Perfidious Albion snorted enthusiastically.

'And the Midas Box?' Mariah asked.

'The sea will keep it safe . . . for the time being,' Black said seriously. 'Until it calls to be found again to ensnare some other madman.'

'I have the Panjandrum,' Mariah added.

'Then all is not lost,' Albion replied as he held out his hand.

In the Golden Kipper, Smutch polished with vinegar the head of a stuffed elephant that was fixed to the wall above the door. He stood precariously on a rickety old ladder, his foot propped against a covered parrot's cage. The smell of fish blistered from the kitchen as the gathering sat waiting in anticipation. Sacha held her head in her hands, trying to keep herself from sleeping as Mariah and Felix chattered constantly.

'So you'll be staying longer?' Black asked Mariah as Charity entered the restaurant with a platter of steaming fried fish.

'At least a year,' he said, smiling at Felix. 'And Felix is staying too. He needs the time to get over the drubbing he got from the sea witch.'

'And to keep an eye on you and Sacha. Here less than a week

and the whole town nearly explodes. Heaven help us if he stays for longer,' Felix said as he jostled him with his shoulder.

'Then you'll take this?' Albion asked Mariah. He slipped a felt-covered case across the table.

Mariah opened the case as they all looked on. It felt warm and soft in his palm. He pulled the lid and looked inside. There in a silk sheath was a silver badge. It was imprinted with the shape of a Caladrius rising from the sea, and around its edge were seven stars cut through the metal. Along the outside were the words: *Bureau of Antiquities*.

'This is for me?' Mariah asked, wide-eyed, a look of surprise across his face.

'If you're up for the task,' Charity replied as he placed the fish upon the table and handed everyone a silver fork.

'Then I will take it,' he said, and they all laughed.

Under the cover of its cage, snug and warm, the Caladrius warbled and chirped quietly to itself. It had rested in death, its life spent, and in the light of the moon had been revived. Opening one eye, it gazed at the shapes that were outlined beyond the swathe of calico. By the fire Cuba flicked her tail back and forth as she dreamt of an ocean far away.

Beyond the harbour, further than the headland and away from the shadow of the castle, the two Krakens swam contentedly together, the spell of the sea witch broken. Upon the beach the bodies washed from the *Tersias* lay like waxworks in the bright lights cast by the Prince Regent.

There in the steaming sands the sea had taken the sacrifice it was due. Gormenberg laid in the ebbing surf by Long Rocks, his golden hand shining in the sinking moonlight, his face looking to the stars. Slowly, as the sound of the last steam train hooted its departure from the end of the line, he turned his head, smiled and stared out to sea.